IN FOR A
POUND

Tim Waterstone read English at Cambridge before moving to Calcutta to work for a broking firm. On returning to England, he worked at W.H. Smith for eight years, and went on to establish the bookselling chain Waterstone's in 1982, which he left in 2001. He is currently the chancellor of Edinburgh Napier University and a board member of Yale University Press, as well as being a novelist and business speaker.

Tim Waterstone

'Novelists often struggle to depict high finance, but Waterstone's background guarantees easy authority... The book is very good on a world in which people who don't really have the money can buy companies from people who don't really want to sell them... [Waterstone's] psychological insight – especially into the emotional lives of his characters – is far superior to much of the market that he is trying to take over.' *Guardian*

'Waterstone is rather a skilled thriller writer... his own experience of publishing and business give the thriller a convincing feel.' *Spectator*

'High finance, based on deception, fast-dealing, greed and struggle for control in the world of newspaper and book publishing is the subject... The author's personal experiences have obviously given him an insight into that world... Extremely readable, sometimes shocking... *In for a Penny* depicts the present as perhaps historians may one day see it.' *Islington Tribune*

'The financial acrobatics are breathtaking... the drama comes from the dynamics between characters. And it is no surprise, given Waterstone's capacity for reinvention, that his principal interest is in how people survive. He is indulgent of our tendency to self-delusion, and painfully good at describing emotional shock and its aftermath... as a portrait of a world driven by narcissism, the novel is, dare one say it, first among equals.' *New Statesman*

'An exciting Boardroom Struggle tale... very good and very gripping... it rings true... there are wonderful scenes of the clash of wills, the jostling for position, the desperate machinations and dirty deals in the offices, boardrooms, quiet restaurants and hotel rooms of London and New York.' *The Lady*

'A searing treatment of the world of books that contains recognisable caricatures of several figures in publishing, newspapers and high finance... the saga tells of double-dealing, infidelity, deceit and hypocrisy.' *Observer*

Tim Waterstone

IN FOR A PENNY, IN FOR A POUND

CORVUS

First published in Great Britain in 2010 by Corvus.

This paperback edition first published in Great Britain in 2011
by Corvus, an imprint of Atlantic Books Ltd.

1 3 5 7 9 10 8 6 4 2

A CIP catalogue record for this book is available from the British Library.

ISBN: 978 1 84887 426 8 (Paperback)
ISBN: 978 0 85789 137 2 (Ebook)

Printed in Great Britain.

Corvus
An imprint of Atlantic Books Ltd
Ormond House
26–27 Boswell Street
London WC1N 3JZ

www.corvus-books.co.uk

For Rosie

Part One

1997

1

The Huber Publishers offices were tucked away in a dark, litter-strewn corner of Holborn, at the furthest end of what in its time had been a fashionable arcade. These days it was a desert of boarded-up shop fronts, among which were scattered two or three little newsagents, a charity shop, a bookmaker, and a Chinese restaurant, filthy, tiny, in its window the suspended carcasses of ducks, orange, naked, obscene. Then, beside a chiropodist, was the Huber office.

In Huber's window, propped up on plastic supports, were faded, dusty copies of their books. These were backed on either side by curled posters of Lenin and photographs of the Jarrow March and a gaudy, vast oil painting of gallant, shiny-booted, rigid-backed Russian soldiers striding out in step, their heroic women, shawled, babies on hips, seeing them off to war. More formally, displayed behind glass, were some Gustav Klucis lithographs of the 1920s, with titles like *The Strength of Millions of Workers Drawn into the Building of Socialism*.

Hugh Emerson stood for a moment admiring the Klucis lithographs, and wished they were better lit. He hesitated, then pushed the door open and walked in. He'd explained to Huber why he was coming, so it was too late to back down. The door had set off a chime, and after a moment Huber himself, a bearded, tall, bulky figure, emerged from the back office. He came across the corridor to Hugh, arms outstretched, the cuffs of his poorly laundered shirt grey and threadbare.

Looking at him, Hugh wondered, not for the first time since he had called him earlier that day, whether Huber actually had any money. If he hadn't, then this visit was pointless. But four or five years before, when Huber had offered to help finance the fledgling Emerson Publishers list, Huber had showed him his accounts. The books Huber published sold barely a few hundred copies each year, and many of them fewer than that. But he had possessed a goldmine: a contract with the Soviet licensing agency, giving him exclusive translation rights to a great number of Soviet technical and academic journals, all of which had an automatic advance sale to every major library. Perhaps, post the Soviet collapse, he had managed to sustain this with the new Russia.

'Hugh, dear,' Huber said, holding Hugh's proffered hand in both of his, and squeezing it. 'Hugh, the great white hope of the book world. Come in, and tell me all about it. Tea, please, Phyllis dear,' he called out to his assistant, by publishing lore his mistress of many years, full bosomed and flushed in her purple jersey and faux pearls. 'Earl Grey – and our very best biscuits for our distinguished visitor. The fatted calf for Hugh Emerson, Phyllis, if you please.'

His hand on Hugh's sleeve, Huber guided him into a small office at the very back of the building, plunged into gloom by the rear of the dilapidated Edwardian hotel that abutted it. Books, manuscripts, a fax machine, proofs of technical drawings – there was a clutter about it all that reminded Hugh of his own office in a Camden Town cul de sac. But the Huber version of it was much more feminine. On the windowsill stood a prim little miniature rose in a pink vase, a tiny watering can beside it. The curtains, suburban chintz, were tied at their centre by a neat bow. Huber's pencils and pens were tidied away into a pewter tankard on the battered, antique walnut desk, and beside this two or three of his pipes stood in their rack; anachronistic to the fashion of mid-1990s Britain, but, Hugh thought, in their Middle European style, somehow part of the Huber persona. Laid carefully parallel to the pipes was a leather pocket case containing his spectacles.

Huber sat Hugh down in what he appeared to consider the best chair, first sweeping off it an Abyssinian cat, white and fluffy, its hairs left embedded in the worn purple velvet of the seat.

'Well, Hugh, tell me again what's on your mind,' Huber said. 'I feel rather like your headmaster. You've spent all your money, and you want some more, and if you don't get it there's going to be a nasty scene with your bank manager. You told me, or rather you muttered something I could hardly catch, so I rang that finance man of yours – Joe? – while you were on the way, and he . . . he gave me the gen.'

He speaks in quotes, Hugh thought. 'Gave me the gen.' There was an arch, pedantic manner about it, a foreigner in his third or fourth language attempting what he imagined to be the very latest in modish street argot.

Huber sipped his tea, which Phyllis had served in pretty pink porcelain cups and saucers. Chipped, Hugh noticed, as was the walnut desk, but hinting at refined gentility.

5

'Well – yes,' Hugh replied, 'that's pretty well what's happened. Publishing is not easy in the early years, as you well know, when one is building the list. We were going very well, then we made two or three mistakes. And, rather quickly, we found ourselves very illiquid, and with a new bank manager who didn't like the look of the business.'

Huber kept his cup to his lips, peering at Hugh over the rim. His benign expression had disappeared. 'How much is your monthly overhead?'

'We run Emerson on about £90,000 a month. Then we have our production costs to pay as we print the list. Plus authors' advances, and because we are trying so hard to grow, we need to carry an increasing investment in stock. So we have quite a requirement for cash – all the time.' He tried to smile in cheery self-confidence, hating the camp pantomime he was obliged to act out. Phyllis came into the room to clear away the tea, Huber gazing pleasantly at her great bottom as she bent to gather the cups on to the tray.

'Do you have any more money to put in, Hugh? Or a rich aunt, or an adoring godfather, or anybody? Or an adoring wife, if it comes to that? I seem to remember she's a great star around your firmament, am I right? She's a barrister? Your age, thirty and a bit, and already earning millions?'

'Hardly that. She's a barrister – yes – but of course she's not earning millions. No, Nicola and I can't afford to put in more than we already have. We've already gone too far, probably.'

'Your parents?'

'No, not my parents.'

'So I'm the end of the line.'

'Yes – you're the end of the line.' Hugh replied too quickly, then flushed at his rudeness.

'Well, here you are with me, you poor child, at the end of the line. But tell me, Hugh – why should I help you? I offered you a hand when you were first starting out, but you turned me away. Tough titty – wouldn't you say? Tough titty,' he repeated, chuckling, delighted with the phrase. 'Why shouldn't I just let you go under? One less competitor and all that sort of thing? What's it to me?'

He shrugged, but then half smiled, and leant across to pat Hugh on the knee. 'That's not fair. I'm playing with you, you must think. Perhaps I am. These things happen, and you don't have to tell me that the early days of a publishing venture are very tough. I found my way through, I'm glad to say, but only just, and that almost entirely due to my connections in the then Soviet Union. But most don't survive, at least not in independence. You will, perhaps, because you have that sort of cut about you, but it will be touch and go.'

He smiled, reached into his drawer and drew out a cheque book and a receipt pad. He took a pen, then hesitated. 'The bank has given you just seven days, your Joe told me. So we've got a little bit of breathing space with them, if not very much. You owe them £240,000. And this collection agency want their cash tomorrow, I gather from Joe. Insisting on it: £13,000 cash.'

Hugh was appalled that Joe had told Huber so much, humiliated. But left to himself, Hugh would have prevaricated. Joe had simply told the truth, no doubt having in his mind already abandoned Emerson and started interviewing for his next job. 'Yes,' he said, grimacing in his embarrassment.

'They want £13,000, in cash,' Huber repeated and pretended to wince, 'by tomorrow morning. You're not cheap, dear, are you?'

He went to the door, opened it, and called up the passage. 'Phyllis – how much cash have we got in our secret money-box we don't worry the tax man about?'

There was a muffled reply.

'It can't be. As much as that? Oh yes, of course. There was that little receipt of ours last week. Well, get the key out, poppet, and open it up. This is a stick-up. We are about to be robbed.'

Huber returned to his chair, motioning Hugh to remain where he was. 'Give the beastly people their money tomorrow, get the proper paperwork and a receipt for it, and keep it all safe. During the early part of next week we'll transfer into your bank the funds needed to pay off your overdraft – when Joe told me the amount I nearly fell off my chair, I have to tell you – and we'll help to negotiate another arrangement with my bank, covered by my guarantee. Give Phyllis your account details, and sign a little note for her, agreeing we'll settle terms between us later next week. And then, Hugh, we'll need to make our plans for the future. Or otherwise I'm afraid you'll have to give me back what I'm now advancing to you, and I will leave you to your own devices with your bank.'

Hugh looked like stone, then Huber laughed. 'But of course it won't come to that!' he said, and reached out to shake Hugh's hand. Hugh rose to his feet, and Huber fussed over him and his raincoat and whether it was still wet and if Hugh should borrow a hat and scarf, then saw him out into the arcade and on his way. He had pushed into Hugh's inner breast pocket the two thick envelopes of fifty-pound notes. Given the seediness of the Huber offices, the notes were surprisingly crisp and clean.

Two days later they were again in Huber's office, once more with Phyllis's chipped porcelain tea cups in their hands. This time the Abyssinian cat was asleep on Huber's lap, its long white hairs moulting into his crumpled grey flannel trousers.

'Claus – look, it was very good of you to have done what you did,' Hugh said, smiling brightly, quick to get to the point. 'The reason I'm here today is that I'm conscious that we've left some ends untied, and we need to clarify where we are.'

Huber nodded, and pulled at his earlobe. 'That's right, my dear, we do. Putting it baldly, you've got six months' debt cover at the bank on my guarantee. And you owe me £13,000 cash, on a twenty-day note, that sum not to be taken from the account I'm now guaranteeing. You're right – we need to discuss how I'm going to get my little cash loan back and how you're going to deal with all that debt once my guarantee lapses. And what the future holds for Emerson.'

He reached forward and patted Hugh on the knee, patronisingly, too physically familiar. Hugh shifted his position. 'What do you have in mind?'

Hugh nodded. 'As far as the cash is concerned, I'm going to have to ask you to extend the note for a further seven days. I'll ask Nic if we can sell a couple of pictures, and repay the money that way, but I need another week to have the money in my hands.'

Huber shrugged, cocked his head, and smiled pleasantly. 'Of course,' he said. 'And then?'

'The company's debt, you mean? That's my main concern, but I'm planning to come up with a solution within three or four weeks, and then let you off the hook.' Hugh smiled, he hoped with a convincing show of warmth. 'Together with an appropriate fee, of course, that goes without saying. Perhaps we should both take professional advice as to what that might be.'

Huber nodded, and watched him, his hooded eyes disquieting. Hugh was sure that Huber was going to push for the guarantee to be converted into an investment into Emerson, at a level that would make the company effectively a joint venture between the pair of them. He was not going to allow that. Emerson Publishers was Hugh's alone, founded with a great ambition to create one of the foremost literary publishing houses in the country. And he had no intention of sharing that with Huber. He shouldn't have come to him in the first place. It was momentary panic that had done it, prompted by the call from the collection agency.

Huber suddenly switched his features into a smile, and made a dumb show of offering Hugh some more tea. 'A fee? I'm not sure I'd know what level of fee to demand of you, Hugh. Besides, we have the arrangement covered, don't you remember? You signed the little piece of paper Phyllis drafted up for us.'

'Of course I remember signing the paper. But it said nothing very much — just an acknowledgement of the cash

advance and a simple acceptance of the terms of your guarantee.'

'And those terms were?'

Hugh shrugged. 'Nothing. Terms to be agreed between
the two parties.'

'Well, that's splendid. Perhaps I should tell you what those
will be. Number one – I shall immediately withdraw that guarantee if we are unable to agree the terms of it; and, number
two, in the event of the bank debt not being cleared at the
end of two months – eight weeks – I will assume that debt
and apply it to the purchase of Emerson shares at one penny
each.'

Hugh forced himself to smile. 'I can't agree to that, I'm
afraid, Claus. I don't want another investor in Emerson. I want
it to stay entirely under my control.'

Huber leant over and patted his knee again, and Hugh let
him. He fought to remain calm.

'Then you shouldn't have run out of money, you silly boy,
should you?' Huber said. 'And who knows – perhaps you can
stay independent! All you have to do is pay off the debt within
two months, and there we are. Plus of course the £13,000
cash, and the interest, and if I do decide on a little fee, that
too. And then, thanks to me, this nasty little crisis of yours
will be over, and you'll go on to all the great things you've
dreamed of, without a backwards glance!'

'But Claus, there's no way I can pay the bank off in two
months. I'm so grateful to you for what you've done, but those
terms, by which you buy cheap shares – the shares have a par
value of one pound, not one penny – if I had realized that
was what you wanted, I would have . . .'

'Today's Thursday. Let's say you have until next Tuesday evening, would that be fair? Let me know by Tuesday evening whether you agree my terms, and then we can both initial one of Phyllis's little bits of paper and on we go. And if you don't – and I would quite understand it, Hugh, believe me, I really would – we can forget the whole thing and you can repay me the cash. And – you're right – my fee. Immediately. There and then on Tuesday evening. And at that moment I'll tell the bank that the guarantee has lapsed and that they should look to you for the money. Fair's fair?'

He got to his feet, fussed over whether cat hairs had stuck to Hugh's trousers, brushed down his coat and, holding his arm as affectionately as before, saw him out into the arcade.

'I'll hear from you on Tuesday then!' Huber called, and Hugh, returning his wave and his smile with an attempt at insouciance, set off on his way, trying to make his stride as jaunty and confident as he could. But inside he was numb.

Hugh looked across at his brother James, and wished that he had not come to see him.

Six years older than Hugh, James was a partner at the grandee advisory investment bank of Waring's. As far as Hugh could deduce he was these days not only very wealthy, but also, judging by Hugh's occasional sightings of his name in the financial press, considered to be something of a corporate finance star. Desperate on leaving his unhappy meeting with Claus Huber, Hugh could think of no one else to go to, uncomfortable with his brother as he had always been, so he had telephoned, been snapped at, but had been fitted into James's diary that very evening. And there he was now, ill prepared and ill at ease, seated before his brother in a quite impossibly grand office for a man of less than forty. It occurred to Hugh that the room might not actually be his, and that he had borrowed it for the occasion in order to overawe him.

'I always knew that rotten little company of yours would run out of cash,' James was saying, with satisfaction. 'Of course it was going to. Hopelessly undercapitalized, poorly structured on the debt side, I've seldom seen anything so amateurish in my life. And here we are, and you *have* run out of cash. Lock, stock and barrel. Even quicker than I thought you would.'

He barked out a laugh, contemptuous and insulting and, with a flick of the hand, pushed the Emerson Publishers accounts back across the table. 'You *publish* well, I suppose, or so people tell me, and in that sense you may be surviving, even thriving, how do I know? But as a financial entity, as an investment prospect . . .'

He shook his head, theatrically, and laughed again. 'You should have come to me for advice in the first place, three or four years ago, when you were setting the thing up. I would have made sure the firm was solidly financed, properly constituted, something that had a future. But now, as you are, in this state of collapse . . .' He shrugged, and looked at his watch. 'I'd like to help, regard it as my duty, you're my brother and all that sort of thing, but you've left it too late. In my view you're a very lucky man that this Claus Huber fellow has put his proposition to you, tough as it may be. You should take his arm off to close it. Get the best you can get from him – anything at all will be entirely out of the goodness of his heart – and be grateful for it.'

'Let's see what happens. I don't think you quite understand the potential . . .'

James snorted with laughter, got to his feet, and shepherded Hugh out of his office. 'This is the real world here, I'm afraid,' he said, as the lift doors opened, and he waved Hugh inside. 'Potential!! We don't talk about potential here, we talk about what is real and measurable. We don't deal in fantasies. We deal with facts.'

He nodded a curt farewell to his younger brother and, as the lift doors closed, Hugh could see him already striding off down the corridor, barking an instruction to a woman who jogged in his wake.

Nicola was in Brussels for a day or two, a delegate from her Inner Temple chambers to an international conference on human rights. Hugh was missing her painfully. Suddenly, shock at his situation had begun to overwhelm him again. Not just shock now, but near panic as well, and a sensation that his life had spun out of control. There had been a raw, street indignity to that threatening call, delivered in a thick Glasgow accent, from the man at the collection agency. It had shaken Hugh. He was a courteous, ordered man by temperament, and the anarchy of oral as much as physical aggression rattled him.

His visit to his brother had amused him rather than upset him, for James's tone was hardly a surprise. But it had increased his sense of loneliness. He had hated coming into an empty house when he arrived home. He and Nicola had both been barely twenty-two when they had converted an increasingly frenzied student relationship at Oxford into the conventional safe haven of the marriage bed. They were childless, but their emotional bond was central to their lives. He missed her so much at that moment that the longing for her was a physical, actual thing.

He went into the sitting room, poured himself a drink at the tray, and gazed at the chess board. He was in the middle of a postal game with his friend, Ned Macaulay. They had been playing chess by postcard and telephone for the best part of a decade. He had received Ned's new move that morning, and slumped down in an armchair to consider it. He studied the board, then saw his move. He reached in his pocket for his mobile phone, pushing his piece across the board with his other hand. 'Bishop to h8,' he said, the moment that Ned came on the line. 'Check. Get out of that, you prick.'

He heard the phone being banged down and then there was silence for several minutes. Hugh found himself humming some bars from Gershwin's *American in Paris*, and felt, for the moment, very much better.

Of all his friends Ned Macaulay was the most reliably congenial. Hugh and Ned had met when they were both seven years old, a pair of terrified first-term boarders at a freezing school in a deserted fold of the South Downs. In their long school shorts and blue blazers and cherry red caps, they had stood together on the gravel, watching their parents' cars disappearing off down the drive. The two little boys had gazed around them at sodden playing fields, still, thirty or so years on, enclosed by wartime barbed wire. A machine gunner's concrete pillbox, weather-stained, threatening, part covered in dank ivy, stood in the shrubbery. An unsmiling clergyman headmaster was waiting to take them into the gaunt school buildings. They were both homesick and close to tears, but too reticent and frightened in these surroundings to release them.

Five or six years of that, and then they were parted for a period when Hugh went to an undistinguished private school in Kent, and Ned to Eton. They stayed in touch, and then, went on together to Oxford. These days, both married, they still saw each other at least once a month, and spoke at least once or twice a week. They imagined, both of them, that they would never now lose contact. They quarrelled occasionally, but formulaically, and without malice, and they were integral to each other's lives.

'Knight to h3,' came the reply eventually. 'And you too.'

'Hold on,' Hugh said, went to the board to register Ned's move, and immediately saw what Ned was trying to lure him into. 'Fuck,' he muttered, and went back to his phone. 'I'll brood on that one, I think,' he said.

Ned laughed. 'Is that it?'

'Yes. No – can I come round?'

'Of course you can come round. Now? Tomorrow?'

'Now, if you don't mind. I'm on my own. Nic's in Brussels.'

'Daisy?' Hugh could hear him shout, his hand only partially covering the receiver. 'Hugh's coming round for supper. Christ – Hugh! For supper. Well – do some more. No – alone. Nicola's in Brussels. God above,' he muttered. 'Seriously dumb. Yes – see you in a moment, Hugh. It's pork chops and mash and supermarket red.'

For all Ned's private wealth as a member of the Macaulay newspaper dynasty, and his large Gilston Road house in Chelsea was a mark of that, Hugh found that pork chops and mash, out of the saucepan, was indeed what they were eating. Thank God it's Daisy cooking tonight, Hugh thought. On more formal evenings Ned greeted his guests in an apron, skillet in hand, and the food he cooked was a fussy production of over-ambitious recipes, for which he required continual and extravagant compliments.

Their baby, Ned and Daisy's fourth in barely more than six years of marriage, was suckling at Daisy's breast as she ate with one hand, her arm curled around the baby's back. A pang of paternal longing went through Hugh as he watched them, but then he realized the indelicacy of what he was doing. He looked away, and reached across for the wine, which was very far from supermarket red, as Hugh had known that it would be.

'Great kids you've got, Ned,' he said. 'You should be grateful. You're very lucky.'

'Thanks. Yes,' and he held out his arms wide for another of his daughters – Annabel was it? – to run into as she came into the kitchen sucking her thumb. He leant forward and hugged her, his cheek pressed to her head. Then, letting her go, he got up to clear the plates, with much loud banging and scraping and badinage about this and that with Daisy. He came back to the table with a bowl of fruit, a big pot of coffee, and three cups.

'Hugh, look, Daisy and I are going to leave the children with the nanny in a moment and walk down to Katie's. She asked us to look in after supper to meet up with our cousin Caroline, who's staying the night with her. Come too. You'll love Caroline, and Katie will be delighted to see you.'

Katie, Ned's younger sister and an aspiring artist, lived barely five minutes from Ned, in a little attic flat in Park Walk. She and Ned had always been close. She was surprised when Hugh arrived with Ned and Daisy, and kissed him warmly. Then she turned to Ned and goaded him with some New Labour story that had been much in the press that day, with the general election drawing nearer. Peter Mandelson had expressed his deep affection for new-money entrepreneurs. Ned, as was traditional in the Macaulay family, was a soft-centre, one-nation supporter of the Labour Party. Katie, emphatically to the left of that, the family took to be a Marxist. Enjoying that role, she had in her time joined the Socialist Workers' Party to underline the point.

Hugh talked for a moment or two with Caroline, and then they sat at the kitchen table, laden with the remnants of Katie's dinner.

Eventually Ned got up from his seat, and squatted beside Hugh, and spoke to him very quietly. 'Look, let's go into the other room for a moment. I think I know why you came tonight. Come on through.'

Hugh followed him, miserably embarrassed at his plight. But as they sat down together in Katie's tiny, wildly untidy study, Ned was so quick to come to the point that Hugh lost his discomfort.

'What I know about Emerson amounts to this: that in its short life you have done incredibly well on practically no funding. That you were fortunate enough to entice Anna Lavey to come across and join you as an author for your very first list, before she was famous and successful, and that off her you've built a really good stable of people and have the reputation of publishing them extremely well. And in time you

18

look set to build something really good. But that you have some quite severe financial problems. My source for that information, as you might suspect, is Christine, who is a great supporter of yours.' He hesitated. 'Christine talked to me last night. She told me about your troubles because she wants me to help you.'

Hugh appreciated Ned's tact, but also his directness. Christine Hoare, an established, elderly literary agent, was Ned's neighbour, and Hugh was very fond of her. There was an element of mother/protégé son in their friendship. Christine, a heavy socializer and drinker, had gathered Hugh to her like a mother hen.

'Christine told me that last year the market was tough, you made a publishing mistake or two, or three, or four – everybody does – and you lost control of the cash, which you never had much of in the first place, and that the next thing you knew was that you were nastily over-extended with the bank, and had some short-term debts that you simply couldn't pay. She also said that the bank had effectively foreclosed on you – right?'

Hugh realized that Ned was rushing the story to save him the humiliation of having to explain it himself. But he was appalled his affairs seemed to be so well known. He thought he had kept them secret. He certainly had from Nicola.

'So that's where we are, as far as I understand it,' Ned was saying. 'Your first instinct was to turn to that man Claus Huber, who wanted to get a stake in Emerson right from the start. Apparently he has been wildly indiscreet about your meetings with him. He gets you off the immediate hook. You're so relieved about that that you sign a bit of paper without thinking about it. And now you find that unless you do something pretty quick, not only does he get part possession of Emerson Publishers, but he gets it on the cheap.'

Hugh shrugged. He had intended to describe the situation in much less stark terms. 'Yes,' he said. 'But I feel just about as uncomfortable as I could do coming round here and speaking of . . .'

Ned held up his hand. 'How much money is actually involved? Give it me straight.'

Hugh was tempted to soften the numbers, but he found himself telling the truth, and in exact detail. Ned listened, and Hugh was aware that he was trying not to wince or do anything that might humiliate him. Ned looked in one of Katie's drawers, found a pencil and paper and wrote the sums down. He studied them for a couple of minutes, then asked for the details of Hugh's bank.

There was the sound of the others emerging now from Katie's kitchen, and Ned glanced over to the door. He got to his feet to join them, but as he did so he stuffed the piece of paper into his pocket and said quietly, 'I'll have to talk to my lawyers tomorrow morning. Can it wait until then?'

He paused, gazing at Hugh. 'Oh, to hell with it – I know I'm not going to change my mind. What I have to suggest is that I take the entire debt off the bank by investing £270,000 into Emerson, immediately, next week. I'll buy the debt and convert it into equity, for let's say 20 per cent of the owner-ship. With the extra £20,000 you can get rid of that cash debt to Huber and also his fee. We'll make that £7,000, and tell him to get stuffed if he asks for more. OK? And I'll get my lawyers to square the bank away themselves, so that they're happy and will do what they're told. Let's leave it like that until the morning. I'm sure it will be all right. The investment vehicle will be my Banville Trust, which I wholly own. I might even structure it so that you end up with a reverse holding in Banville. Yes – that's what I'll do. I'll get you 5 per cent or so.'

The other three walked in, and Ned turned to them, smiling. Hugh couldn't thank him at that point, or later. Ned, bustling away into the night with Daisy, seemed absolutely set to deny him the opportunity of doing so. And he was equally determined when he rang the next morning, to confirm that he had briefed his lawyers, and the deal was on.

Hugh put the telephone down and, for the first time since he was a child, he had to press his hands into his eyes to suppress his tears.

Joe, the finance director, stuck his head around Hugh Emerson's door. 'Can you deal with Anna Lavey for me? She's arriving in a couple of minutes, in a rage because her royalty cheque is six weeks late. And I mean rage. She swore at me on the phone in terms as I haven't heard since I was in the navy.'

It was only very occasionally that Hugh wondered why he had left a vast publishing empire for the arty uncertainties of owning an under-capitalized literary publishing house located in a dingy Camden cul de sac. This, fleetingly, was one of them.

'Christ, she's here,' Joe said, for Anna had appeared in the tiny cleared space in front of the reception desk. Hugh and she made their usual business, performed to be observed, of hugging and embracing each other. He then led her back to his office, and seated her on the best chair, a bright orange upholstered piece, vaguely Bauhaus in design and conception, which Hugh had bought for £15 the previous weekend in Petticoat Lane market.

He sat on the edge of his desk, smiled at her, and shrugged. 'Sorry, Anna,' he said, before she could get her own word in first. 'I know why you're here. We've been totally out of cash. But I've done a very good deal for us, and the problem's over and, very soon, maybe one more week, at most two, and you'll have your money. Sorry, sweetheart, but there we are.'

'Sorry, sweetheart,' she mimicked, in a painfully accurate imitation of him, but although the smile that followed was anything but warm, there was, to Hugh's practised ear, a lack of any real savagery in her response. He had got to know her very well over the last three or four years, and knew her moods. 'You're a fuck artist, darling,' she was saying now, 'you really are, and I've no idea why I put up with it. I'm not sure I am going to put up with it. Maybe this is the moment to . . .'

'Anna. Tell me this. When have I ever let you down before? How many times have I been late with the royalty accounts and payments?'

She waved a hand in dismissal, then brushed down her long peasant-style skirt, as if the squalor of his office had dirtied it.

'How many times, Anna?' he pressed, teasingly now, knowing that the crisis had passed.

'God knows how many times. I'll ask my agent. Frequently, probably. All I do know is that if you concentrated on me and my books a little more, and the rest of the pretentious twaddle you publish for your intellectual vanity considerably less, then

I'd get my money on time, and there'd be more of it – for you as well as me.'

Hugh laughed, and told her of the deal he'd just struck with Ned Macaulay. Anna pretended not to recognize Ned's name as a member of the famous family of newspaper publishers. Hugh then recounted some colourful and unkindly gossip about a common acquaintance, and they parted on decent enough terms, Anna insisting, however, that she took a post-dated cheque with her, including an interest payment for the delay. This gave Hugh only ten days to complete Ned's subscription into the company and have the money safely in the firm's account, which would be very tight indeed.

They kissed at the door, and Hugh watched her set off down the street, seizing possession of a taxi from under the nose of an elderly lady bent over a walking stick. Anna was a striking woman, Hugh thought, Jewish to the point of caricature, dark and tall. She radiated intelligence, and flaunted a strong sexual allure, but there was a gauntness about her, an aggression in her carriage and bearing, a rawness in her voice. All that repelled him a little, although there were moments when she could look very beautiful indeed, when her clothes were right, and the light was right, and her face was in repose. With her weekly newspaper column, and her books, and her appearances on radio and television, she was becoming a familiar name and face, but she would have turned heads without her fame simply because she was a physically compelling, proud, charismatic woman.

He turned back into the office, then chatted for a few minutes with an editor he had just, triumphantly, enticed away from Faber & Faber. There was a list of calls he had to return, and he put them into some sort of order, with Anna's agent last of all. Top of the list was Nicola, who had rung from the airport to say that she was going to work for the rest of the afternoon at home. It suddenly occurred to him, and graphically, that in his elation at the rescue of his company by Ned Macaulay, he wanted nothing more than to join her there, take her clothes off and make love. He grabbed his coat, made some sort of garbled excuse to his assistant, and did just that.

Hugh and Nicola lay in bed, naked under the blanket, their hands left affectionately on each other's groins. Each gazed up at the paint-clogged cornices of the high ceiling above. Nicola had for months been meaning to summon up the energy to replace the faded rose pink wallpaper, but looking at it now as the early evening light slanted across it she thought how pretty it looked.

Their Notting Hill house, one of dozens in the single unbroken line of a long Victorian terrace, was too big for them, but they'd grown attached to it. They had bought it at the time of their marriage, soon after university, and the size of the place was in anticipation of an immediate clutch of children. But the babies had not arrived. So three bedrooms were left spare, now full of their books and files, the overspill of their individual professional lives. They never talked of moving to somewhere smaller, since to do so would have been an admission of their barrenness, and that was not to be contemplated. Nicola had tested fertile on the single occasion when they had decided to subject themselves to scrutiny, and Hugh too, and they were advised to keep trying and all would in time be well. But nothing had happened. There was now an unspoken agreement that they should not discuss it. So they didn't. And this was the first of what turned out in their marriage to be a disastrous pattern of issues that they decided not to make more painful by discussing.

Nicola squeezed his hand, and turned on her side to look at him. In a moment they would get up and dress and go down for their supper in the kitchen. But first, both of them relaxed by love, there was her very good news. She told him that she had been selected as the Labour Party candidate for the Henlow constituency in the Thames Valley, barely twenty miles outside London. She hadn't told him that she was trying for it, let alone that she had reached the shortlist, and he was dumb-founded.

'I can't *believe* it!' he said, sitting up. 'Can't believe it. What absolutely *incredible* news! Why didn't you tell me you were standing for it? Why the secret? But I'm delighted for you, sweetheart, absolutely delighted, and very proud too. Henlow!'

'Yes, I know, Henlow. The Tories have got an enormous majority there of course, but it's a start, isn't it? I'm going to give it a really good shot, and see how close I can get, and – who knows – give them a bit of a fright. At least that's the idea. I'm so excited about it.'

'But why so late, Nic? With a general election so soon? I'm surprised that the constituency party there hasn't got itself organized before, aren't you? Still, I'm not complaining. I'm so proud of you, Nic, I really am.'

She was out of bed now, searching for her clothes, and Hugh got up and stood there with her clasped against him, rejoicing in the comfortable, female fullness of her body. She brushed back her dark hair, looked him in the eyes, kissed him, and laughed. Hugh had a small boy's enthusiasm, sometimes oddly disproportionate to the situation, but she knew she had done well, and she was proud of her achievement, and Hugh's reaction was certainly gratifying. She kissed him again, this time loudly on the cheek, and turned to pull on her tights.

'Why is it so late? Because old Barker, you know, Andy Barker, the LSE lecturer, only decided very recently that he'd had enough, having stood at Henlow with what must have been dispiriting lack of progress in each of the last three general elections. Plus his wife's ill, I think. And you know why I haven't told you before. Because I hate to tell you anything before I've actually got it resolved. Just like you do, Hugh,' she added, laughing.

'I'm surprised you could, actually. What happened at the selection interview? Aren't you supposed to produce your spouse for vetting?'

'Wives only, sweetheart, and only in the Conservative Party. To make sure they hold their knives nicely. The British class system, in one of its last manifestations.'

Hugh smiled, and again reached across to hold her hands in his. 'Well done, Nic. You won't actually win, I suppose, but I have an odd feeling that it will be the beginning of something very special in your life. That from this . . . other things, great things will spring. God knows what. But that's how it feels to me.'

He meant nothing much in what he said – perhaps he was only trying to extend the scope of her feat through his appreciation of it. But he remembered his words frequently in later years, and winced at their grotesque accuracy. For it was at her Henlow campaign in the general election, barely two months after her selection as a candidate, that Nicola met Henry Jackson. And this meeting led to more unhappiness and devastation than anyone could possibly have imagined. Until that point, Nicola had been the most loyal and instinctively monogamous of women.

2

Henry Jackson's assistant had arranged for him to speak at
Henlow because he had told her that he would accept engagements in no more than six constituencies during the campaign
in addition to his own, and Henlow was both high profile and
easy for him to get to. Jackson's own constituency was one of
the most rock solid Labour seats in London, but this time
around the Conservatives had put up an excellent young candidate to run against him, and he was privately just a touch
uneasy about that. So he was already grumbling that the
speaking engagements she was booking for him, at the request
of the party campaign organizers, were so far flung that he
would be stretched from pillar to post. But Janie Jones lived
at Henlow herself, knew the agent there and, to the man's
delight, had booked Jackson for a speech just two days before
polling day.

He arrived in his black Rover only a few minutes before
he was due to speak, and the agent, fretting, was waiting for
him outside the church hall, which was packed out for the
occasion. Nicola stood by the stage, greeting people, smiling,
working the audience with a shy charm. She surprised and

delighted Hugh by the response she was getting. He had been seated beside the agent's wife at the end of the front row, and was talking with her as pleasantly as he could, but his mind rested entirely on Nicola, and how she was going to cope. Her public speaking skills were, he felt, only just adequate, which was surprising, given her growing experience as a barrister. The intellectual content of her material in these political speeches was always strong and doggedly researched, but she was tight-voiced and monotone in her delivery, and humour was quite outside her range. As it was, Hugh's stomach tightened in fear each time that Nicola got to her feet. But she was improving as the campaign wore on. She had even dealt sharply and effectively with a heckler who had plagued her from the bar of a working men's club.

Hugh glanced around, and saw that the hall by this time was past the point of capacity, with some flustered officials trying now to turn back into the street a crush of people pressed up against the rear wall. Henry Jackson was a considerable star. In the previous Labour administration, as a much younger man, he had at one stage been only narrowly manoeuvred out of succeeding Harold Wilson as Prime Minister. He had become since then an iconic figure, probably one of the three or four of the best-known politicians in the country.

Now he was making his way into the hall, and the audience was rising to its feet to greet him. Smiling, reaching out with both arms to press the hands stretched out to him, laughing, charming, he struck Hugh, who had never seen him before in the flesh, as a man of pleasant appearance for his age: tall, scholarly, unfussy as to his attire, effortlessly warm in manner, even-featured and with a great mane of grey hair. Hugh noticed that his teeth were good too, unusual in that generation.

Perhaps, watching Jackson in public performance, so practised in it, one ascribed to him too much, Hugh thought. Some of it was no doubt simply the mesmeric effect of raw male power. It was possible that one was seeing him that night at his absolute peak. But it was an extraordinary performance, and Hugh observed it with fascination. He realized that he was not clapping, and he did so now, as he watched the man, sixty-three or four now, he imagined, step up on to the platform, self-assured, with a pleasing lack of attempt at a vulgar impersonation of youthful athleticism. He first shook hands with Nicola, then kissed her. She had never met Jackson before, Hugh knew, and he saw her first flush, then, as if to cover it, put her hands to her face. It was an uncomfortable, childish gesture, and Hugh stared at her as she drew her hands down, made an awkward smile, then stood aside, as if anxious she should not draw too close to him. Hugh thought she was acting too gauchely with Jackson, too awestruck. He didn't much like it.

Jackson was sitting now at the table, sipping water, smiling around the room. A colossal Labour Party rosette was pinned to his lapel. He was every inch the professional party politician on the campaign hustings, and Hugh, having read Jackson's last book, an erudite and critically admired work on the Holy Roman Empire, was surprised to see that he could pull the populist trick off. Now Nicola was on her feet to introduce Jackson, but inaudibly, as the microphone, installed there by the vicar, howled and whistled as soon as she spoke into it. Instead of making a joke of it, as a practised performer would, she blushed again, and ploughed straight on. It was Jackson who saved the moment, getting to his feet and, smiling, tiptoeing up to the microphone while Nicola was struggling to be heard.

This was a home audience for him, Hugh thought, and in a way all this business was wasted on them as they were diehard Labour Party supporters anyway. But Nicola did need a 100 per cent turnout of her Labour vote, and Jackson's performance that night would certainly assist in that.

Now Jackson made a great business of unplugging the microphone in front of the embarrassed vicar, who had rushed up on to the stage to help, and handing it over to him. It was performed with just sufficient ironic point that he would earn a surge of laughter, yet stopped short of making a fool of the man. It was nicely done, and so now was the way in which, standing at the very front of the stage, without a note in his hand, he wound his audience down through amusement to a gradual, quiet, rapt attention. He began by insulting the sitting member's record in the House of Commons since his arrival there after the 1970 general election, when he succeeded the previous Conservative member, who had sat since 1935. In Jackson's version, neither had done anything whatsoever either as parliamentarians or for Henlow itself. As a *coup de théâtre* he pulled out a scrap of paper from his inside pocket, and read out the dates of the sitting MP's oral contributions in the House in his twenty-seven years of 'residence', as Jackson put it. They amounted to eight, of which seven were grovelling feed questions to his party leader. Jackson read out verbatim the most recent of these, three years before: *'Would the Prime Minister agree with me and my constituents that the country has never been*

31

*happier and more optimistic than it is now, and for that it is the Prime
Minister's leadership and vision that we have to thank?'* The entire
hall once more shouted out its laughter, Hugh amongst them,
and on the stage Nicola too, who seemed to have settled.

Then Jackson turned, faced Nicola, spread his hands towards
her and turned back to face the hall. 'I haven't had the pleasure
of meeting Nicola Haile before,' he said, 'but I know of her
achievements, and I have heard of her quality from members
of the bar of my acquaintance. She is barely more than thirty
years old, and yet I can tell you that her professional reputation is extraordinary amongst her peers. She is exactly the sort
of candidate that we seek to attract to the Party and, if she
wins at Henlow, she will go on to launch a political career
that I am convinced will be one of great brilliance. Nicola
Haile is going to go very far indeed, and it is my privilege to
come down here to you tonight to urge you to do all you can
to help her succeed in two days' time. I urge you – *will* you
– to achieve what has never once been achieved before. To
achieve the dream – two dreams in fact, for that's how it seems
to me tonight: to gain a Labour member for Henlow, for the
very first time; and, for absolutely the first time, to gain a
Member of Parliament for Henlow worthy, truly worthy, of
the wonderful people here to be served.'

He smiled, playing self-disparagement now, and raised his
hand to the wildly applauding audience, then to Nicola, on
her feet now, flushed once more. She came to the front of the
stage and thanked Jackson, and thanked the audience, and
thanked her agent, and thanked everyone that in the rapture
of the moment appeared to come to her mind, with the exception, to Hugh's relief, of him. She was overdoing it in her

excitement, but it didn't matter. Her reticence was gone, and she was feminine, and vulnerable and appealing. At her most taut she could carry an air of daunting intellectualism, bullying almost in the quiet tenacity of her conversation. Now she was alive, and alight, and at last, for the first time that evening, she looked down to find him, and smiled.

Nicola lost, but only by a little, and it was a very good result for her. She had reduced a Conservative majority of about 15,000 votes in the 1992 election to barely more than 3,000, and that on a very high overall turnout. She made a most gracious and modest speech at the town hall, where the result was announced, and the Conservative victor a bombastic and arrogant one. That was noticed, and many people came up to press her hand and congratulate her, and encourage her to hold her candidacy and stand for the seat again. She handled all this so well, Hugh thought, and although she cried momentarily on the way home to London in the car, they were tears of exhaustion as much as of any real disappointment, and she soon drifted off to sleep.

When they got back to Notting Hill it was almost seven o'clock in the morning, and people were already setting off to work. The Labour Party had won, massively, and they were in power for the first time for eighteen years. Henry Jackson, re-elected in his own constituency by his usual colossal majority, had a heavy day of work ahead of him, in consultation with the new Prime Minister and his cabinet colleagues. But for all that, his thoughts had clearly been with Nicola too, for as she and Hugh stood at their front door, bags at their feet, struggling to find their keys, a messenger arrived. The message was from Jackson, and it congratulated Nicola on her achievement in running the Tories so close, and wished her well.

Nicola hesitated for a moment, as if guiltily, and then showed it to Hugh. 'Henry' it was signed, simply that, and a tiny knot of sexual anxiety hit him. But smiling warmly, he handed it back to her.

A few weeks later an invitation arrived for Nicola to attend one of Jackson's drinks parties at the Home Office, where he had been appointed Home Secretary, as he had served before, in Callaghan's administration. She and Hugh didn't discuss the invitation or make any reference to it, both of them anxious for their own reasons not to do so, and she went.

Nicola timed herself to arrive half an hour after the party had started at 6.30, but in her nervousness at the prospect of seeing Jackson again, found herself outside the Home Office exactly on time. She spent fifteen minutes walking up and down some side streets, then counted slowly to 500 before taking her invitation out of her handbag to show the security people, and climbing the staircase to the great reception room on the first floor. When she first entered the room, and took a glass of wine from a tray, she saw no one she knew, just Jackson, who was talking to two women she recognised as broadsheet journalists. Then, to her relief, she saw in the corner an acquaintance of hers and Hugh's from Oxford, and set off across the room to talk to him. But as she did so she heard Jackson call her name.

He shook her hand, smiling, congratulated her again on her good battle at Henlow, and introduced her. The journalists greeted her without warmth, having had their private confidences with the Home Secretary interrupted before they had succeeded in extracting a decent story out of him. As Jackson gave Nicola his attention each in turn drifted away, one with a pointedly ironic air. Nicola gulped down her glass of wine, too quickly, as always when she was nervous. He enquired about a human rights case shortly to be heard in Brussels at which she was to act as an expert witness, recommended she take some preliminary advice from X, a friend of his in the French judiciary, then spoke of a small private exhibition showing at a dealer's in the rue d'Orsay, next to the man's office. It was all pleasantly inconsequential, and after a few minutes there was a hand on his arm, and a whisper in his ear, and, with a rueful smile, he turned away from her and was being led towards a gaggle of trade union officials who had been waiting to speak to him.

There had been no fuss, no drama. Anyone watching them would have suspected nothing. But Nicola knew precisely what had happened. Henry Jackson, thirty and more years her senior, and a married man, had just told her that he was in love with her. She hoped she had told him that she was in love with him.

Jackson glanced across the room at her once more as he stood with the union men, and she met that glance, then turned to leave the party.

Henry had not parted from his wife, since for many years he hadn't really been with her. It was known amongst their friends, and indeed the press, that the two of them had led separate lives for so long that their marriage was like a phantom. That Alice Jackson was never seen with him in public caused little or no comment. She had for many years worked as a lecturer in Middle English studies at Edinburgh University; a long and sustained career, if erratic and spasmodic at times through illness. She was absorbed in her work still, although now approaching a postponed retirement. For nearly forty years her life had been confined within a tight circle of Scottish academics and professionals. She lived in a small, book-lined, untidy flat in Edinburgh's handsome New Town. She was there for eleven months of the year, away from it only in July when, in those years she was well enough, she travelled in Greece or Italy with a fellow member of the university, a friend from her schooldays.

Alice and Henry had met one summer at a Cambridge symposium on the island of Crete, when they were both barely in their middle twenties. In the days that followed they embarked upon an affair of coarse and consuming physical passion, and then they had married in rapturous haste in a registry office, with the British consul as the sole guest and witness. It had all been done so fast that they had had no time to decide where they would live, and the university term was shortly to begin. So Alice returned to Edinburgh, and Henry to his garret one-bedroom flat in an alley off Buckingham Gate, convenient for the House of Commons, where he was in his first Parliament as member for the North London constituency he had represented ever since.

After a year or so, with the relationship beginning to wane under the enforced separation, Alice made an attempt to find work in London. But although interviewed spasmodically for junior posts at various colleges within London University she was not successful. And then she became pregnant, with her first and only child. So she decided to stay where she was, in familiar surroundings, with a post in the university where she had taken her degree, read for her Ph.D, and secured her lectureship. Henry then tried to explore whether a Scottish constituency would be open to him, but apart from a marginal seat in a Glasgow suburb there seemed to be nothing available. A most ambitious young man, he was reluctant to lose the safe tenure he already held in London. There was a general election on the way, and Labour might win it. He had been a research assistant in the past to Harold Wilson. He had got on with him. Who knows? He might – just – squeeze into a junior post in Wilson's government.

So he stayed in London. In time their son was born, but over a period of some months it became apparent that Jamie was not entirely well. Fractious, destructive, screaming, he was virtually impossible to placate. Apparently uninterested in people, animals, traffic, when out in the pram he developed a fascination for shiny or twinkling objects, and would rock, and head-bang, and scratch at the pram's covers. He was fascinated too by particular sounds – a friction-driven toy, the sound of a sweet being unwrapped – whilst very loud noises that might have been expected to startle him, he ignored. Other sounds, though – a police siren, a barking dog – would cause him extreme distress.

Henry and Alice were initially baffled by his behaviour, and neither coped well; Henry, to his shame, became increasingly impatient and irritable, and Alice, under extreme pressure, grew ill natured as well. In time autism was diagnosed, and this helped, as the very fact that they had been able to establish a defined medical condition in their child brought some relief and focus. They could take action. They could do something. Jamie went daily to a specialist nursery. He had weekly therapy. But Alice was battling both post-natal depression and the intense fatigue caused by living so much of the time alone with the child.

Alice kept her job, thanks to the support of her friends in her faculty, but she was increasingly unable to cope. She was becoming defeated by her domestic environment. One day, without telling Henry, she went to see her doctor. It was 1964, and she was twenty-nine years old. Two benzodiazepines, Valium and Librium, had just been introduced to the market, and were considered in those early days to be miracle drugs in the treatment of anxiety and stress disorders – universally lauded as a safer alternative to barbiturates and meprobamate because they were thought not to be habit-forming. Forty years later, and Valium had proved with her to be not just habit-forming, but hopelessly addictive. Valium had taken its hold. She had made sporadic attempts to wean herself away, some more determined than others, but there had never been a real prospect of prolonged success. It had become not simply a physical dependence in her, but an emotional one too, blunting and dulling her nature.

The marriage too was now blunted and dulled. Henry recognized his failure within it, particularly his lack of patience with his sick wife. His life was increasingly spent in London, and Alice hardly ever now left Scotland. In consequence Henry saw his family less and less. He started to seek love affairs, sometimes brief and abrupt, sometimes longer term. Jackson was a highly sexual man, and he needed women, and he loved women. But the damage he had done to himself by his failure with Alice and Jamie was profound. Jamie had never really known him as a father. In the impatience of the bustle and drive of his political life Henry had not been prepared to allow the needs of their two lives to encumber him. He still didn't. He allowed himself no excuse. He knew he had let them down.

He hadn't seen Alice for three or four months at the time he met Nicola, and as the train drew into Edinburgh station he felt a familiar tug of anxiety. There was nothing particularly to dread in the visit: when he had spoken to Alice on the phone two nights before she had seemed stable enough, her voice quite clear and focused, and he had come for a pleasant reason. He had something to say to her that he was sure she would like. He had been quite looking forward to it. But still, the feeling tugged at him anew. There had been one particularly difficult visit to Edinburgh a few months before, when she had met him at the station, as always, but on that occasion he could see immediately that she was in a state of considerable distress. She had been drowsy, clumsy, sweating, confused, and his initial thought was that he should take her straight to hospital. But all she wanted was to go straight home, so he took her there. Once he had got her to rest on her bed he looked in her bathroom, and the story was soon told. Valium bottles were lying on the floor, tablets spilling. Henry had seen this before, several times over the years. She had been upping her dose, illicitly, trying to counteract the loss of the drug's efficacy because of the tolerance to it she had developed after such a long period of regular use.

But now the train had drawn to a halt, and he could see Alice waiting there on the platform, wrapped as she always seemed to be these days, in a great swathe of shawls and tweeds.

He smiled and nodded with his customary courtesy at one or two of his fellow passengers who had recognized him. Then he bundled up his papers and coat and went to greet her. They kissed, perfunctorily perhaps, but without coolness, and he glanced at Alice, making a quick assessment. He'd seen worse, much worse. But she was very pale, and he noticed around her mouth just a trace of white, a chalky remnant of the Valium in her saliva. At her best, she had sufficient pride to keep herself scrupulously clean and tidy. At her worst, and this was not it, she looked an unkempt wreck.

They took a taxi back to her flat, and sat in her kitchen with a pot of tea. He asked about Jamie, now a man in his thirties, who was housed in a gaunt Victorian institution out on the southern reaches of the city. She smiled, attempted an anecdote or other about the nursing staff there, then fell silent, and watched him. Henry reached out for her hand. She allowed contact for a few seconds, then quietly withdrew it.

'Alice, I've something to tell you, which I think you'll like, and I'm very glad to do for you. It's about money.'

'Money?' she said, without much interest or surprise.

'It's taken such a long time to clear up my father's estate, but it seems now that quite a large inheritance is due to me – after taxes, not far short of a million pounds. I had no idea he was worth so much; do you remember his air of heroic genteel poverty? I don't need anything like that amount of money. So I thought I'd use most of it to buy you an annuity, which will bring you an income of about £60,000 a year. I hope that will make you feel a little more secure, and comfortable.'

Alice remained silent, watching him, her hands around her tea cup. Then, tired, ill, without, he thought, any trace of the radiance and sharpness of her youth, she smiled, and shook her head. 'No, Henry. Thank you, but no.'

'No?'

She shook her head. 'No. I don't need money. I don't need anything much. I simply want to stay alive. I want to feel myself . . . useful, in however small a way. Useful. Connected to life.'

'I'd like you to have it.'

She shook her head again. 'No. No. It's good of you, but I want you to accept what I say. I really don't want it.'

She would explain no further. He was waiting for her to make then some comment, accusatory, bitter. She never did. She never had. They talked a little more, then he said goodbye to her at her door, and stepped out into the bleak chill of a grey Edinburgh evening in search of a taxi to take him to see Jamie. There was to be no easing of guilt for him. He was not going to be allowed to buy off his years of neglect by an easy gift.

'One reaps what one sows,' he muttered to himself. And at that a fleeting vision of Nicola floated through his mind.

Henry called Nicola at her chambers one afternoon and asked her to come around to his apartment that evening for a drink. Only five minutes before, Hugh had been on the line, and he and Nicola had agreed to go to an early movie and have dinner afterwards at a favourite little Italian restaurant of theirs very near to their house. Now, hating herself, she rang him back to say that the chambers clerk had just deposited another load of work on to her desk, so would he mind postponing the movie until the following evening? And, in a bright voice, 'I'm going to have to work late on this, so don't wait up or anything. It might be well past midnight before I'm home. I'm so sorry, I really am. Goodbye, darling. You too.'

She put the receiver down, then sat for several minutes with her head in her hands. She was shaking with self-loathing. She was by nature a good, loyal, responsible woman. She didn't lie, she didn't cheat, she was an honourable person, she believed in constancy, and here she was behaving like the worst sort of . . .

But she left the words unsaid. Essex tart, whore, trollop – any of those cartoon insults – there was no hurt in them. She was just as she had been all her life. She was not even particularly highly sexed, she suspected from her quiet observation of other people's lives. But she did know that she was not able or prepared to turn away from her feelings for Henry Jackson.

So she did what was to her inevitable, and in a curious way, right. She arrived at Jackson's apartment, shaking with nerves by now, at ten past six. They sat in his study, and talked, and pretended to sip their wine, and waited for the moment. Eventually, seeing that she had settled, he came over to her and held out his hands. They went to his bedroom and, to her relief, he drew the curtains. Then, confidently, firmly, robustly, he pulled her to him and began to make love to her.

Shortly before midnight she dressed, and caught a taxi home. As she turned the key and crept into their house, filled with the erotic excitement of what had happened to her, she experienced a sudden shot of physical disgust at what she had done to Hugh. She made herself go up to the bedroom, where he lay still, on his side, apparently asleep. She undressed, and slipped into bed beside him, so silently that she was sure she wouldn't have woken him.

But she needn't have bothered. Within minutes of her leaving for Henry's flat, Hugh had called her chambers, on the excuse of checking that she had her key. The clerk, who had picked up the telephone, expressed his ignorance of the batch of work that Hugh had teasingly accused him of dumping on her. His stomach void with fear, he found Jackson's address in *Who's Who* and, on the spur of the moment, drove there. He arrived just in time to see Nicola walk up the street, hesitate, press a security bell, and go in through the heavy double doors.

When Hugh woke the next morning, suddenly, after a miserable night of near complete insomnia, he had no idea what to do. He hated quarrels, and confrontation of any kind, to the point of being phobic; there was certainly a deep-seated fear which he sometimes thought of as cowardice. Now, watching Nicola as she slept, he told himself that perhaps there was nothing in it. She was a free woman, and maybe when she awoke she would tell him something happily convincing. Now dawn had come Hugh knew he would accept any story, and with relief. She looked perfectly serene, sleeping there. There was going to be some perfectly straightforward explanation.

So he got out of bed and set off for the bathroom, filled with resolve. Jealousy and suspicion were the worst things in the world. They poisoned the soul, and Hugh wanted none of that. The sun of a bright blue winter day was flooding through the window as he threw open the bathroom blinds, and Hugh always felt more cheerful at the sight of sun, and light, and space. He heard Nicola stir in the other room and called out a cheerful greeting.

'You were late, Nic,' he said. 'What time did you get in? I must have been asleep.'

'Midnight,' she replied, after a short pause. 'Maybe a bit after. I came home by cab. I'm glad I didn't disturb you.'

As he lathered on the shaving cream, humming so as to sound relaxed, his temptation was to let it go at that. But it wouldn't do. So he called out, 'What were you up to actually, Nic? I called your chambers a few moments after we spoke, and the clerk said you'd gone. And he didn't seem to know anything about a sudden load of work for you, so I wondered what had happened.'

There was silence for what seemed like several minutes, and then he could hear Nicola get out of bed. She arrived in the bathroom, and sat on the edge of the bath in her pyjamas.

'Sorry, that was a bit of a white lie,' she said, and when he glanced sideways at her he saw – and his heart sank –that she was blushing. He turned back to the mirror. 'It was silly of me, and I should have known better. Actually I went to a meeting at Henry Jackson's flat, a sort of future Labour leaders' group which he's experimenting with. I thought that you wouldn't like it, so I told you that silly little untruth.'

She shrugged, and her heavy breasts moved and swayed in her pyjama top as she did so, and Hugh wanted her. But instead he turned away, threw down his towel and climbed into the shower stall. He sang a Fred Astaire number and vigorously soaped himself, and Nicola went back into the bedroom. He knew, for certain, that she was lying, from the misery in her face. But why risk real disaster? Why risk anything at all?

So, much in character, Hugh did nothing. The incident was never mentioned again. But privately both began to realize that it was in that moment that the damage was done, and to an extent that would eventually prove irreparable. A straightforward confession of a single act of infidelity, and then a quarrel perhaps, and, after a day or so, reconciliation and an apology, and the healing acts of marital love-making, and there would have been little disturbance in their lives. Instead, it was the silence that did it. A silence of mutual conspiracy, for the more he thought about it as the days went by the more certain he was that he didn't believe her, and the more she thought about it the more filled with guilt she became. But by then she had been back in Henry's bed, and then again, and then once more, this time for a whole night on a totally fabricated alibi of an out-of-town parliamentary candidates' seminar.

It was too late now. Once the lie had been told, and accepted, it was cast in stone. Hugh knew that, and knew too that the fault was his as much as hers. Once the first act of deceit had passed over in silence, they were trapped. What now lay between them had grown too big for confession – for Nicola now, as much as Hugh, wanted their marriage to hold. Indeed, she saw little point in anything else. To her pain, intense pain at the time, Jackson had made that absolutely clear to her.

3

Ned and Katie Macaulay's older brother Giles lived alone in a
spacious house in South Kensington's Onslow Gardens,
surrounded by his texts and scholarly journals and books and
the painstaking, handwritten manuscripts on which, out of
the office, he was perpetually at work. He would have spent
his life in academia in one of the country's older universities,
had his father not made it clear that he was expected, after
Oxford, to take his place in the Macaulay Group. So this is
precisely what Giles did, becoming at the age of no more than
twenty-eight managing director to his father, Lord Kimpton,
as chairman.

He was dutiful and industrious, but had not within him
one jot of the creative or entrepreneurial impatience that might
have made his working life a satisfying experience. He immersed
himself in the minutiae of the safe, stalwart things in which
he felt comfortable: the company's pension scheme, the
employees' retirement home and benevolent fund, the in-house
property and legal departments. He represented the firm on
industry committees – the Newspaper Owners' Guild, the Press
Association, the Fleet Street League – and everywhere he went

he was considered a safe if silent pair of hands. He was busy enough, and popular enough, and caused not a jot of trouble to anyone, least of all to Lord Kimpton, who consulted him about nothing, and carried on as he had before, hiring and firing at whim, and interfering in the editorial policy of the Group's two great national newspapers, the *Daily Meteor* and the *Sunday Correspondent* – that and his new great joy – investing the Group's money in the acquisition of a wildly eclectic group of companies in the name of diversification and asset growth.

Giles was obliged to give his signature to these investments, which he did happily. They kept his father content, and out of his way. And Nicky Waring of Waring's, the determinedly Gentile, privately held, decades established, advisory bank, who acted as advisers to Lord Kimpton, certainly must know what they were doing. For form's sake, Giles asked Nicky Waring and James Emerson a perfunctory question or two, and accepted their elaborate response with simulated interest, then signed his name away. His ears rang with Waring's praise for his acumen and commercial boldness. Then, each night, at 6.35 precisely, Giles would set off home to Onslow Gardens, and his Siamese cat, and his books, and the manuscript of his current monograph. His cold supper and a bottle of burgundy would be laid out on a tray for him by his housekeeper, a starched napkin fresh each evening beside his plate, secured in a silver ring stamped with the Macaulay family crest.

That day Giles had left his house at his normal hour of twelve minutes past eight, after his solitary breakfast of a mug of tea and a slice of bread and butter. He went, as always, by bicycle. He had done so ever since he had joined the firm. Giles was quite untouched by the fact that his unaffected eccentricity had transmuted into a green, time-for-change, Cool Britannia, New Labour modishness. He didn't know it had. He had always simply liked riding bikes.

He set out with a light drizzle hanging in the air, but by the time he had reached Eaton Square this had turned to a hard, slanting rain. Giles didn't mind in the least. He buttoned his mackintosh right up against his chin, pulled down his hat, and pedalled on, humming a fragment of a Schubert quintet as he went.

Giles liked rain. It cheered him up. It reminded him of some of the most contented, solitary days of his childhood at the family's rambling old holiday house on the west coast of Scotland. There, with his pink knees and collared jersey, protected from the weather by nothing more than an old school raincoat and a sou'wester hat, he would spend every day on the beach. He took a daily picnic of a package of margarine and marmite sandwiches and a bottle of orange squash, and fished his landlines and collected his specimens from the acres of rock pools and rivulets that at low tide were exposed along the shore.

Those were days of the most pure, unstressful happiness. Best were those as a young teenager, his mother and father often hundreds if not thousands of miles away, and usually Ned and Katie away too, staying with their friends. He was never for one moment lonely. There was the ghillie, and the two gardeners, and the housekeeper and the cook and a pair of elderly kindly maids of all work. The food was porridge and fruit cake, grilled fish, homemade bread and over-cooked vegetables, and that suited Giles just fine. Each night a fire was lit for him in the library, and after his hot bath he would sit in front of that with his supper on a tray. And then, his meal cleared away, he would seat himself at the library's round table and study the marine biology texts from the house's vast collection of dusty, forgotten volumes. In this he was following in the traditions of his great uncle, professor of Marine Biology and Pathology at Edinburgh University, from whom the collection had been inherited.

It was that house, and that library, and those contented, solitary days on the blustery shore that in Giles's own opinion had shaped his life, both for good and for ill. He knew that he was too introverted. He detested his job, but felt it to be his familial duty. Outside of work he was too focused on his books and texts and laboratory. His holidays, for which he longed, were spent always alone at the family house in Scotland. He had no friends, apart from the limited acquaintance of academics with whom he corresponded and occasionally met at conferences. He knew he was lonely, but being emotionally and socially uneasy, it was outside his range to do anything about it. Given that, he took himself in the round, and accepted himself for who he was.

He arrived now at the entrance lobby of the firm's great Fleet Street offices, and wheeled his bicycle over the marble floor. He steered around the vast reception desk and the pair of moustached, uniformed commissionaires who guarded it. Then one of them leapt to his feet to aid him and, with a great show of obsequiousness, took the bicycle from him, and propped it against the wall.

'Inclement day, Mr Giles, sir,' came the man's predictable greeting. 'Good for the ducks.'

'Isn't it?' Giles replied and, as was the accepted procedure, handed him his sodden coat and hat.

'Shocking,' the commissionaire said, vigorously brushing at the coat to remove an imaginary blemish on its aged, wet, crumpled front. Then he turned, and seizing a cloth from a nearby bench, started drying the bicycle's handlebars.

'Oh, don't worry with that, Johnson, it's very good of you, but for heaven's sake don't,' Giles protested, but stood there helplessly as the rubbing and polishing was completed. Then Johnson straightened up, patted the saddle, and enquired whether a chauffeur should be summoned to check the air pressure in the tyres. Out of politeness Giles made a point of showing enthusiasm for this, then, in flushed embarrassment, he realized that it had been a joke. Chuckling, brushing away again at the coat and hat, Johnson disappeared off to hang them in some cupboard that Giles had never seen.

He went back into the lobby and pressed the button for the lift. As he stood there, the doors drew open of the chairman's private lift, which Giles was also in theory entitled to use, but never did. Lord Kimpton emerged, accompanied, as usual, by Miss Day, his secretary, now modishly restyled as his assistant, of some forty years standing. She was a woman of Lord Kimpton's own age, and her advancing years were somehow the more accentuated by her tightly coiffured head of blue-black dyed hair, and the angry crimson of her painted lips. Kimpton, in this instance uncharacteristically aware of changing social fashion, had recently suggested to her that she might from now on like to be known in the firm not by her surname but by her first name, Edith. She did not pretend enthusiasm. Miss Day she had remained.

'Good morning, Father. Good morning, Miss Day,' Giles said, smiling nervously. His own lift doors were sliding apart now, and he was wondering whether to step in and disappear, or let it go and stand there with his father to await his word. In the event he did both, first backing into the lift, then, changing his mind, coming out again and trapping the tail of his jacket in the closing doors. Extricating himself, he was left blushing in front of his unsmiling father and a glacial Miss Day. He could see out of the corner of his eye the two commissionaires chuckling as they observed the scene.

Lord Kimpton nodded at him. Miss Day didn't. Her bloodshot eyes bored into his, then lowered to gaze, contemptuously, at his damp trouser legs. He realized that he had forgotten to remove his bicycle clips, and bent down to do so. His father scowled. The Macaulay family went to and from their offices in chauffeur-driven Bentleys, not in bicycle clips.

'I'm just off to Waring's to see Nicky and James Emerson,' Kimpton told him. 'Acquisition opportunities and so forth. It was only arranged a few minutes ago. You could come, I suppose, Giles, but you're probably better off here. Don't you think, Miss Day?'

'Definitely,' she said, cold and emphatic. Giles accepted that she was in effect his father's number two at Macaulay. He didn't mind in the least.

'Mr Giles should stay here and represent the board at the staff council meeting,' she said, managing to imply that such a task was at the very peak of his competence. 'And there are the draft accounts for preliminary review this morning,' she said. 'Under Mr Rogers,' she added, with firm emphasis, lest Giles should form the impression that he was to be allowed to chair that meeting himself.

Giles thought about Miss Day a good deal. Once he'd seen

a cartoon doll of her appearance in a store at Heathrow Airport. He had brought it home to serve as an effigy into which each evening he might stick a pin.

Ned had made his appointment to see his father at ten o'clock the following day. It was now nearly 10.25 and his father still hadn't arrived at the office. Miss Day sat him down with the morning papers and a pot of coffee, but he was irritated, although he knew that it was absurd of him to feel belittled by his father's tardiness. Lord Kimpton had never been a punctual man. He must grow out of this tendency to regard his father's every action as a personal slight.

But then the door of the private lift drew open, and Ned rose to his feet.

'Ah, Ned,' said Kimpton, without any great show of enthusiasm. As was the habit of the Macaulay family, he shook his hand and then made some attempt at an embrace. But the gesture was awkwardly done, and Ned, himself a most effortlessly tactile man, felt the embarrassment of it.

'I'd forgotten you were coming, and your mother had one of her dinner parties last night – the Foreign Secretary, the new one. What's his name again?'

Ned told him, going with the conceit. The affectation of ignorance was typical of his father, serving to underline the point that the Macaulays owned two of the most powerful newspapers in the land, and it was with them, rather than here-today-gone-tomorrow politicians, that real power in the country lay.

'You wanted me, Ned?' Lord Kimpton asked, suspiciously, settling himself down at his desk.

'Yes, I did, Father, and thank you for making the time.'

Kimpton nodded, but said nothing, and Ned felt a familiar mixture of frustration and anger rise in him, although he was determined to show proper respect. He cleared his throat. 'As you know, Father, I set up my Banville Trust with a combination of Grandfather's legacy and my own trust fund, and I've used that to build up quite a substantial investment portfolio. Otherwise I'm involved in our family charities, but I'd like to play a much bigger role in the family's affairs. I'd like to get much closer to it all.'

'You want an *executive* role?' Kimpton asked, and Ned saw immediately, from his tone of amused incredulity, that the conversation would go nowhere. His father was wholly comfortable with the mild, gentle-mannered, unthreatening Giles. Kimpton was wholly uncomfortable, and always had been, with the sharply intelligent, restlessly ambitious, straight-talking Ned. More than uncomfortable; Kimpton, as Ned was privately aware, was actually afraid of him. He was never going to let him in. Ned, at the heart of things, knew that too.

'You want to *work* in the firm alongside Giles and me?'

Ned blushed, and immediately felt like a child. 'Yes. I care for the firm very much, and I'd like to play my part in it. This is no surprise to you, you've known for years this is what I want.'

'Ned, hold on. Of course we've skirted around this subject before. But I'm going to give you the same answer now as I gave you nine or ten years ago when you came down from Oxford. The company will be Giles's to run when the time comes. And that leads me to say this. I think it would be unhealthy to bring you in now to an executive role, not only for the staff, but the family. You'd never get along, you and Giles, and that would create such difficulty for everybody. Forgive me for being so blunt, but I don't want this subject raised again. And you do a very good job as a non-executive director! So stick to that, and your Banstead Trust, or whatever it's called, and all the other things you like to play with, and you'll do very well. Talk to your mother, why don't you? Maybe she can find something more for you to do. All those good causes of hers . . .'

Kimpton shrugged, got to his feet, and showed his son to the door, patting him on the shoulder as he went. Ned went down to the lobby in the public lift, nodding and smiling his greetings to various members of the staff. He was 'Mr Ned' to all of them, a style of address anachronistic these days in the wider world certainly, but natural to the order of this most traditional and hidebound of large family firms. The brothers had been 'Mr Giles' and 'Mr Ned' since they were small boys in shorts, Ned sitting on a high stool and banging away at a youthful Miss Day's vast old Remington electric typewriter, cutting-edge technology in the mid 1970s.

Now he was angry, and he was belittled. It had been his mistake initially, and he had regretted it for years. He had always assumed he would come into the firm when he had finished at university. His mother had encouraged him to think so. But he had backed away from the idea when no more than a second-year student, frivolously deciding that instead of joining the firm he was going to become a professional polo player in Argentina. He shuddered now at the memory of his crassness, made the more acute by the fact that he had then got, considering his intelligence, a very poor degree.

His mother, in an oddly irresponsible way, considering their closeness, seemed to find both the professional polo player ambitions and the third-class honours amusing. Lord Kimpton treated it as the opportunity he had evidently been looking for. Ned was disbarred from serving his career in the Macaulay Group. He had subsequently been given the consolation prize, on his mother's absolute insistence by that point, of a non-executive directorship. But that was all. Ned now knew, with absolute certainty, that for as long as his father was still around that was all it would ever be.

Ned sat in Hugh's office in shirtsleeves, his feet propped up on a cardboard packing case, his jacket thrown down on top of a pile of manuscripts in the corner. 'So how are we doing?' he said, without any great show of interest.

Hugh pointed at the management accounts beside him on the desk, which Joe had brought in only a few minutes earlier. 'Read them,' he said. 'Joe prepared them especially for you. Here – he's put a one-page summary at the front.'

Ned put on his rimless glasses, leafed through the accounts, then, starting again, went through them in proper detail, his head propped between his hands. He asked Hugh a question or two, then threw the papers over to sit on top of his coat, and folded his glasses into his breast pocket. 'Looks good,' he said vaguely, and folded his hands behind his head, staring at Hugh, clearly thinking about something else altogether.

'Do you want to have meetings on a regular basis, Ned, now that you're a shareholder?' Hugh asked. 'I can set that up if that's what you'd like. Joe can organize them for us in whatever way you want.'

Ned shook his head. 'Don't worry about that, for God's sake. Just keep me up to date, that's all. You run the place. I'm there if you need me.' He yawned, then looked at his watch. 'Let's have some lunch.'

Hugh had planned to miss lunch and spend the rest of the day at work, and in normal circumstances would have said so. But there was something about Ned's mood which made Hugh get to his feet and go with him. Twenty minutes later they were sitting in the preposterously grand surroundings of the Ritz Hotel, with a glass of champagne, and a waiter fussing over them. This was a side of Ned – indolently wealthy, trivially extravagant – that bored Hugh, and there had been times when he had said so. But his generosity and speed in rescuing Emerson Publishers was still very much at the front of Hugh's mind. This was not the time to criticize Ned for his wealth.

'Do you know something, Hugh? Being a member of a family like mine can be a pain in the neck,' Ned said suddenly, as if reading Hugh's thoughts. 'I'll tell you why. If I'd been born the son of a conventionally broke middle-class family, I'd have achieved something by now. As it is I've done fuck all, and am on the road to continuing in exactly the same direction. To achieve fuck all. Am I being too morbidly self-absorbed?'

Hugh had drunk his glass of champagne, with considerable pleasure, as he liked champagne of this excellence very much indeed, and so he ordered himself another. He'd have several while he was at it. If today he was at the Ritz for lunch, then so be it. The work could wait.

'Maybe a little morbidly self-absorbed,' he said. 'But what the hell, say whatever you want to say. But first let me say this: thank you again for what you did for me.'

Ned made a dismissive gesture, in any other hands and circumstances perhaps offensively, and muttered something which Hugh failed to catch. He really was in the foulest of moods. Hugh would try to make him open up and talk, but he knew of old how difficult that could be. And he was right about having had too much wealth and privilege. From the earliest days of their friendship, there had been too much money around Ned. It was his mother then that gave it to him, to an extent that had tended to isolate Ned from proper friendships with the other boys. There was too much splendour in the flashy new dropped-handle bicycle he arrived with at a time when he couldn't actually ride it. Too much of it in the sheeny grandness of the vast Daimler and chauffeur that later bore his mother down for exeat Sundays; and in the lavishness of her lobster and wild strawberries picnics at the Fathers' Cricket Match, to which most mothers brought their Vauxhalls and sandwiches and apples and bottles of squash.

'What is it, Ned?'

Ned shrugged, and drank his wine. In normal circumstances the most courteous of men to his social inferiors, he made, in Hugh's eyes, a petulant gesture at the waiter for him to replenish it. 'For heaven's sake, Hugh,' he said, shaking his head, 'have your lunch and talk about something amusing. The firm, the list. Tell me about what Anna Lavey says on sex for the over-eighties. Or that man of yours, or should I say now *ours*, who writes his novels backwards, and without punctuation. Anything at all, except me – or the fucking Macaulays.'

'Your father well?' Hugh asked immediately.

Ned rolled his eyes up to the ceiling and groaned. 'You're such a tit, Hugh,' he said.

Hugh laughed. 'Let me guess. You've made another attempt to be allowed properly into the firm, and they won't let you. Or rather your father won't let you.'

Ned was silent.

'I thought so. What about your mother? What does she think?'

'My mother? Are you mad? She's not the chairman. And she's not a Macaulay, if it comes to that. She's a fucking Henderson. Only Macaulays run the Macaulay Group.'

'Have you talked to Katie about this?'

'Yes. She seems to find it amusing. She keeps on bringing up that polo garbage, and laughing herself sick about it.' He shuddered. 'That wasn't the greatest moment in my life. But I was only a kid, with money to burn, given me by my mother. And, yes, I did behave stupidly for a time, I readily admit it. But now, nine or ten years later, I can do a lot for the firm, if they would allow me to. Giles is clever certainly, an honourable, good man, solid, reliable. But he's an academic, not a newspaper publisher. Father is, in a way, but he's disastrously out of tune with the times. And the pair of them are running the biggest privately owned newspaper publishing group in the country – the third or fourth in the world, actually. Think of that.'

Hugh recounted a story he had read in that morning's *New York Times*, predicting perilous changes in the way that newspapers would be forced to operate in the early twenty-first century, due to the advent of the internet.

'Yes – that's exactly the point,' Ned said. 'There's us, still the family firm, powerful enough in our own backyard, but contrast us with the Murdoch empire. We run our papers in the old traditional way. We have no eye to the future. We are afraid of the technological revolution that is developing all around us. We bury our heads in the sand. We're frittering our money away on so-called diversification, investing into areas of which we know nothing. We should stick to our last. Murdoch sticks to his last, but he embraces change within it. Whatever opportunities the new technology brings you can be sure that Murdoch will be there in the heat of the battle. And where will Macaulay and its 7,000 employees be then?'

Ned shuddered, and pushed his plate aside. Dabbing at his mouth with a snowy napkin, he gazed moodily around the room, nodded and waved with, Hugh thought, a barely acceptable show of enthusiasm at a woman in the corner, then looked back at Hugh, and tried to smile. 'Sorry, Hugh, I'm being a bore. I'm a very fortunate man, and I ought to be grateful for it. Let's talk about something else. You, Nicola, Emerson, next year's list. Anything you like.'

'Why did the day get off to a bad start? What happened?'

'Oh . . . Mother, since you ask. She can be very difficult, in case you didn't know. Difficult and quite unbelievingly demanding. She demands one's presence.'

'She wanted to see you?'

'She wanted – demanded – to see me. Today, for lunch, summoned as of ten o'clock this morning. I said I couldn't go, I had a meeting fixed with you, and if I hadn't I would have invented it.'

Hugh laughed. 'Who was the lunch for?'

'Henry Jackson, plus various other people, Hattersley, I think. A couple of others from the Wilson and Callaghan administrations. New Labour people too. Robin Cook. Derry Irvine. They're terribly grand, Mother's political luncheons. She's never quite grasped that this is 1997, and she's not Pamela Berry in the 1930s. Everyone is too poor, and too busy, and too meritocratic – though they do flock to these things of Mother's. So – probably I should have gone. Daisy said I was behaving like a child, and she was right, no doubt, but . . . Mother shows me off to Henry Jackson like a prize exhibit. Always has done.'

'Can't it be simply that she's proud of you?

'With Henry Jackson it somehow goes too far. It's not that I truly dislike him or anything, because I don't. But you're right, Daisy's right, everyone's right. I'm wrong.' He shrugged again and smiled in an attempt at happy warmth, and they spent a further ten or fifteen minutes talking about nothing very much. Ned paid the bill, went over to say something pleasant to the waiter he had been peremptory with, and they left the room.

4

Daisy's good for me, Ned thought, watching her as she breastfed the baby. God, she's good for me – and once again he remembered how it hadn't immediately seemed that way. Certainly not to Ned's mother. Rachel Kimpton was a clever and educated woman herself, despite all her brittle, sophisticate's chatter. She had taken one glance at Daisy when Ned had first produced her, put her down as a middle-class finishing school simpleton, and hoped that she would go away.

'Oh but she's sweet!' Rachel had cried, leaning back as if to study the divine object before her in better focus. 'Absolutely sweet – and so beautiful!' Then she turned away, making no effort to introduce her to an old friend who had appeared at that moment at her elbow. Ned had blanched, broken into a sweat, and led Daisy away. Daisy, mercifully unacquainted with Lady Kimpton's style, had not realized that she had just been insulted.

It was true of course. Daisy, only nineteen to Ned's immature twenty-five, had been far too young for marriage. But Ned, radiant with love and desire, had pushed for it with such energy and compulsion that she had been swept along in its wake. An engagement of barely four months was followed by a society wedding at St Paul's, Knightsbridge, at which Hugh, uneasy in this social milieu, was best man. Then, from the inexpert but joyful couplings of their Moroccan honeymoon had sprung the first of Daisy's almost biannual pregnancies, all of which she brought to calm fruition with the seamless competence that Ned had learnt in time to take for granted.

Perhaps at first, for all the sex and passion and babies, Ned, like Rachel, failed to take Daisy seriously. But a few years after their marriage he was brought up short, when he mentioned one evening, all too casually, that for the last few months he'd been infatuated with another woman, although nothing had come of it. He had expected that Daisy would accept this revelation as lightly and heedlessly as he was presenting it to her, finding it amusing perhaps, titillating even, but she had not. Instead, to his growing panic, she had taken the news with a calm, silent detachment. And then, two nights later, she had woken him at three o'clock in the morning and, sitting beside him on the edge of the bed in her dressing gown, had started to explain to him what he had done.

'You accuse me – but I've done nothing, Daisy!' he protested, struggling to wake. 'I never slept with her, thank God. It was just a silly, indulgent infatuation. I'm pretty nearly over it now. And nothing happened. Nothing happened at all. It was only in my mind.'

Daisy nodded and watched him, her hands in her lap. He pushed his hand across to hold hers, but without fuss, and with a little pat of reassurance, she disengaged herself. 'Everything to do with love is only in the mind. Infatuation, crushes –

those are just trivializing, self-deceiving words. What you did, Ned, in your heart, was to give someone else your sexual love, and you should be honest enough with yourself to face up to that. Unconsummated it may have been, I have no idea, and anyway it's largely immaterial. The truth is that you were unfaithful to me, and to your children too. I believe that marriage depends on the fact that whatever happens, whatever mistakes are made, whatever human failings assail us, I love you, and only you, and you love me, and only me. In the mind. And because we cannot be seen in the mind, and caught out there in a breach of trust, we thus extend to each other the biggest gift of all. Loving each other, and loving each other alone. In the secret place the other cannot enter.'

Ned was dumbstruck. For the first time, and in awe, he realized whom he had married. And from that moment they *were* married; not just a pair of immature, over-sexed, over-privileged, wealthy youngsters, but two adults with real, meaningful lives. Daisy, the expensively but trivially schooled daughter of a kindly but philistine Surrey stockbroker, had taught the highly educated Ned – clever, beautiful, lazy, rich Ned – the lesson of his life.

Looking at her now, breastfeeding her new baby, his new baby, calm, resolute, honourable, he thought his love for her was almost too much to bear. For all Ned's ease with love, and occasional failures of fidelity within love too, he had never forgotten what his wife had said to him that night, and never wanted to. He never pretended to himself that the treachery of deception and trust, in his mind as much and more than in the action, was anything other than what it was: a straight-forward, selfish, self-absorbed loss of honour, a treachery against the relationship that, accidentally almost, irresponsible in its juvenile, sexy inception, had proved in the end to be the making of his life.

Caroline, up in London again to see her widowed mother, had arrived to stay the night at Gilston Road before taking the train back to her small Exmoor farm the following day. Ned sat opposite her at the kitchen table, his dressing-gowned, five-year-old daughter on his knee, sucking her thumb, curling her body up against his chest. Daisy, baby on her lap, was talking with Katie who had just come into the house.

Caroline, their first cousin, was a favourite of them both. She was newly married, but judging by a recent telephone conversation she'd had with Katie, not at all successfully. Ned and Katie had decided not to bring the subject up while she was there unless Caroline did so herself.

With an arm around his daughter to hold her secure, Ned reached out with his spare hand for one of several bottles of wine that littered the table, and poured himself a glass. He asked Caroline to pass him the figs, purple and plump and ripe, and settled back into his chair.

'How's the firm doing?' Caroline asked. 'I've got the shares, of course, but I don't seem to hear what's going on. Shouldn't the dividend have increased a little as the years go on, or is that naive of me? And shouldn't we be sent a commentary with the annual accounts? Not that I'm complaining, but our side of the family never had much, and Exmoor farming is hardly the road to riches. There's the two newspapers, and I'm so proud of them, we all are, but there seems to be so much more these days? And tell me why we're not a public company after all these years, so that we could see some market value in the shares?'

Ned grimaced, and both Caroline and Katie saw Daisy look up from her baby and shoot him a warning look. Ned saw it too, and coloured. He hesitated before replying. 'You're right . . . going public is something that I am sure should at least be looked at, when market conditions are favourable. Though . . .' he glanced at Daisy, but she was looking down at the baby, 'well, I'm not sure taking Macaulay public is on Father's agenda really. He believes we should keep it all in the family, so it won't happen. Not while he's in the chair.'

'What's Giles's view?' Caroline went on. 'Isn't he managing director?'

'Yes, of course he is,' Katie said, cutting in before Ned could say anything aggressive. Caroline was family, but she didn't want the rift to become generally known. 'He's managing director, and one day he will become chairman, just as one day, as elder son, he'll succeed to the Kimpton title. And, as Ned will confirm, Giles and Father are very close, which creates stability.'

'And your role, Ned?'

'Oh – I'm just a non-executive director. I don't have a role. My views are largely immaterial, one way or another.'

'Well, do you agree with them?' There was quite a long pause.

'Not all the time, frankly. Too much diversification is going on.' He shrugged, smiled, poured himself some more wine, and turned to Katie with some remark or other designed to change the subject.

But Caroline persisted. 'Why are you only a non-executive?

Why aren't you part of the management team? You've always been so proud of the papers, and so interested in them.'

'Because I haven't been invited to. No doubt Father feels that one son in the business is enough, and that I should do something else in my life. Perhaps he's right, I don't know. I do have other interests, increasingly so, but . . .'

'But I remember you saying when you were a boy that all you wanted to do was . . .'

Ned didn't let her finish. 'Those visits to the Fleet Street office in the school holidays, watching the newspapers being put together, writing copy as if I was a reporter – it was all suggestive of my birthright, somehow. I was never discouraged from believing that I was going into the firm. But I pissed around at school rather, and again at Oxford, and no doubt that put Father off. Now I have the ability and desire to work, but I'm not allowed to.' He looked up at Daisy as she returned to the kitchen from laying the baby back in her nursery cot. She'd caught his last remarks, and he saw the sudden flush to her face.

'Oh, for God's sake, Ned,' Daisy said and grimaced. 'You're intelligent, you're charming, you're fortunate enough to be independently wealthy, you've got a wife, children. Let's stop all this ridiculous younger son bitterness and jealousy and – Christ! – obsession. Forget it. Get out into the world and get on with your life.'

She threw her arms wide, as if in appeal to the others, then stood there, gazing at him. There was silence. Ned stared down at his daughter curled up on his lap, and smoothed her hair. Daisy turned away towards the refrigerator, flushed, and surreptitiously brushed a tear from her eye. Soon Caroline and Katie got up to go, and Ned saw them to the door.

Katie put a hand to Ned's cheek. 'She's right. Maybe you should even step down as a non-executive and let Father and Giles get on with it. Let the firm go, because it's never going to be yours. It's bad for you, and bad for your marriage, and it's bad for the family – all of us, Mother included, and despite appearances to the contrary, I want the best for her too. I care about the family – a lot.' She raised her hand, and set off down the street.

On an impulse, he reflected later, in a sudden specious instinct to be cruel, Ned called out after her. 'Do you know anything about Mother and Henry Jackson, Katie? Were they lovers? Did Father know?'

She stopped dead, then turned, and retraced her steps so that she stood immediately in front of him, so close that he could smell the soap and water fragrance of her that he had known since she was a little girl. 'Stop this balls, Ned,' she said, coldly and quietly. 'Stop it once and for all. I know exactly what you're saying, and I don't admire you for it. All that vicious tittle-tattle. Leave Father alone. Mother can look after herself, but Father can't. He's out of your class, though I don't like saying that. But he is what he is, and I love him. I'm his daughter, and I want him left alone.'

Part Two

Three Years Later
– 2000

5

Rachel Kimpton sat at her desk, a great mound of letters and papers piled up in front of her. She was scribbling notes, banging on her computer keyboard, signing cheques, taking calls and making them. Her hair was tied back, and she was wearing glasses, a plain shirt and trousers and the minimum of make-up.

Ned sat in the corner, watching as the morning light illuminated her. She has a lovely face, he thought, always has done, and he remembered then the shot of happiness of a single childhood memory as she had bent over his cot one night, in evening dress, and kissed him.

Sometimes he loved her, sometimes he despised her. He loved her simplicities; he hated her pretensions. In his kindly moods he hoped that she had not become a joke. When unkindly, he rather hoped she had. 'What is it with you and Henry Jackson, Mother?' he heard himself saying suddenly.

At first she showed no reaction to his question beyond shaking her head to indicate her preoccupation with a report she was reading from a national charity of which she was chairman. She wrote some notes on the final page, then turned to him. 'Henry Jackson? What of him?' She shrugged, and turned back to her correspondence. 'We're extremely old friends, as you know. What else am I supposed to say?'

'He's always at your luncheons. Always has been, for as long as I can remember.'

She glanced at him once more, stagey bemusement on her face, then reached into her drawer for her telephone book. 'I've absolutely no idea what this conversation is about, Ned, to be frank,' she said, dialling a number. 'And I wonder if you have.'

But then, suddenly, without waiting for a reply, she put the receiver down again, and turned her chair to face him directly. 'Ned, darling – what is it? What did you come here for?'

Ned got up, and perched on the side of her desk. 'Is Henry Jackson my father? There's gossip, always has been. Is he?'

Ned had no clear idea why he had started this conversation. He'd decided to visit his mother to find out whether she might help him finally to get an executive role at Macaulay. But he'd started off on this other stupid tack, and now he was regretting it, particularly as Rachel was looking at him in horror, eyes wide. He said nothing more.

In time a touch of irony and defiance showed in her face. 'Yes, I've heard that story too, quite a number of times over the years, actually. I expect your father has as well. In fact I know he has.' She stopped for a moment, and gazed out of the window. 'A long, long time ago, Henry and I were in love. It meant so much to me that I thought it would break my heart. When it was over, after a year or so, I told your father about it. I'm not sure it was helpful, but I did. In some ways that was rather a dirty trick to play on him, rather like taking the problem off my plate, and landing it on his. And actually, despite what you say about Henry always being at my parties, it was four or five years before I dared to resume normal contact with him. We would bump into each other occasionally at other people's houses, but we made a point of never speaking intimately. But nothing's entirely private of course, and there were whispers and rumours and a certain amount of malice, and . . . there was a very great deal of pain, and for much longer than I had anticipated.'

Ned moved uneasily. 'Look, Mother, I'm really sorry, you don't have to . . .'

'You asked the question. I am giving you my answer. And now I must ask that you never, ever insult your father by questioning your paternity again. Never.'

Ned had raised the issue with her in a mood of bored petulance. He felt deeply ashamed. He didn't at all feel like Lord Kimpton's son, but then he hardly felt like Henry Jackson's either. She hadn't really answered his question on that issue one way or the other. That was odd. But, be that as it may, as he left the house he reflected that when he was in a certain mood his mother was too inviting a target for him. He saw in her an image of what he saw all too clearly in himself: a bit player, for all the apparent power and glamour of her, a dilettante, who, given her intelligence and her advantages, could have achieved a very great deal. But she had achieved very little. Instead, what she had was charm. What she had was wealth and position. What she lacked was courage. Rather like me, Ned thought. Just like me.

★

'So,' Giles said, smiling pleasantly enough, glancing at both his father and Ned, evidently resolved to try to keep the three of them within comfortable bounds. 'Ned – how's Daisy? And the girls? You must let me take you all out on a family expedition one Sunday. Where do you normally like to go? Kew Gardens for a picnic? Hampton Court? The Zoo? The Natural History Museum?' He nodded in an attempt to encourage him, and Ned managed to find some general, non-committal form of response to this kindly, well-meaning but most wholly unfamilial of men.

Now Lord Kimpton was arranging a wintry smile on his face too, muttering some compliment or other about his delightful granddaughters, whose names and ages he had quite clearly forgotten. But after the frigid first moments of his entry into his father's office Ned was grateful even for this, and smiled back at him.

'We're very pleased to see you, Ned, very pleased. But Father has to go down to the City in a moment, and I've got a pensions committee, so . . .'

Ned reached inside the big manila envelope he had brought with him and took out the papers that had been distributed for the board meeting later in the week, which he had carefully annotated all over the margins. Giles and his father gazed at them uneasily.

'We mustn't have the board meeting in advance of the real one,' Lord Kimpton said, in an attempt to be jocular. 'I see you've done a lot of work on the papers, which is splendid, but it's best to leave questions until we're all around the table, you know. My cousins, and Harrison and Rogers and so on. So let's leave it all until then – eh, Ned?'

'Well, that's rather the point. There's something I want to say that I thought it would be better if I first outlined privately to you and Giles. It's a major strategic issue which I thought you both might like to think about in advance. I do feel very strongly about it, and I didn't want to surprise you in front of all the others.'

Giles glanced across at his father, who shrugged, told Ned he was very short of time but if he could be very brief about it.

'Father − thank you − the issue I want to raise is this. I think the diversification programme which you and Giles are following is misguided. Misguided, and potentially a disaster.'

'Misguided?' Lord Kimpton's face darkened.

Ned pressed on. 'We are buying too wildly and too expensively into industries of which we have next to zero experience or knowledge. We know everything there is to know about publishing newspapers, but we have no experience of anything else. So why don't we stay with newspapers? Build up some really good regional titles, buy abroad perhaps. Start to think about what opportunities we might find for news distribution online, nationally, internationally, as the internet continues to settle and develop. Everyone else is exploring that area. We're very late off the mark. We should be extending the franchise of the two wonderful papers we own, moving them on into the future. Instead of . . .' − he held up a file with the Waring's name embossed across the front of it − 'a car distributorship and a consumer goods packaging company, which will come up at the board this week, to add to all the others we've bought through Waring's.'

He paused there, trying, as he had promised Daisy, to keep

anger and particularly sarcasm out of his voice. He was not sure he had entirely succeeded. He could see the rage beginning to show in his father's face.

Kimpton looked at his watch. 'I have to leave you now,' he said. 'But I must tell you that I don't agree with a word you're saying. We've bought some fine assets, and diversification is very much an accepted practice now for companies, like ours, that have had all their eggs in one basket. What does the future hold now for physical newspapers, print on paper? No one knows. Is the internet a threat, or an opportunity? No one knows. Are our competitors on a course that will make them money or lose it? No one knows. So what are *we* doing? We're investing in unrelated areas – safe, profitable, low-technology areas. Spreading the family's risk. Giles and I are protecting the family's wealth.'

He got up now, and paused at the door. Ned and Giles both got to their feet.

'You need to get on with your life, Ned. I've told you that so many times. Giles and I run the firm and, if I may say so, we are making a very good job of it. This is a time of change, and we know what we're doing. Frankly, Ned – mind your own business. Find your own business, your own niche, and . . . go for it.'

'Of course. Thank you for seeing me.' But as he spoke, Ned felt himself flush and his control slip away, just as Daisy had feared it would. 'Father – you don't understand what I'm saying. I'm trying to tell you that there are serious problems building up. You and Giles don't seem to understand that. We're making appalling investments – appalling – and we're going to severely damage the standing of the firm. Actually we've already done that, in my opinion.' He stopped then, and bit his lip.

'It's not on,' his father said, after a moment or two, and Ned sensed, and, despite himself, admired the effort of will it was taking him to control himself. 'Hear me, Ned, once and for all. Go and build your career somewhere else. I don't mean that unkindly. Be happy. You're a charming man, you have a delightful family. Be content.'

When Ned erupted into Hugh's office, Hugh failed to sympathize with him, and told him he was making too much of it all.

Ned grimaced. 'You're such a pompous ass, Hugh, you really are, pompous and . . . hyper-orthodox, somehow. You were like that even as a nine- or ten-year-old, with your pencil case, and your hair slicked down, and your ready stamped and addressed envelopes for your weekly letters home. Such a conventional little boy. Such a prick. As you are now. God knows what poor Nic makes of it all.'

And while Ned reverted back to his own problems, repeating himself, circling endlessly around the same ground, Hugh indeed wondered what Nicola made of it all. He wouldn't dare to ask her, for fear that the answer would devastate him.

'Are you listening, Hugh, for God's sake?'

'No, I'm not. I was, but I'm not now. There's nothing I can contribute. You've got to sort your own life out.'

'As everyone keeps telling me.'

There was silence for a few moments now. Ned gazed out of the window. 'I'd go for the coup, you know, if I thought I could pull it off. I think in the end it's the only way. One day I will. At the moment I haven't got enough shares to make it stick – just under 20 per cent. I'm the third biggest shareholder behind Father and Giles, but 19 per cent plus is not enough.'

'How much has your mother got? She'd support you, wouldn't she, if you're proved right and Macaulay gets itself into real trouble?'

'Five per cent. Her wedding present from Father, and there are no circumstances in which she'd help me against him. They hardly see each other these days, but she'd never do that. Out of loyalty, guilt, whatever it is, she never would. She doesn't regard those shares as her own, I'm sure of that. I believe she's quietly willed them back to Father if she predeceases him. She thinks they're Macaulay family property. She's right, actually, they are.'

'Well – she has her own position in life.'

'Yes, she does, in a way. And she has her own friends, some of whom I'm dubious about, but that's neither here nor there.'

'Who?'

'Oh, I don't know. Henry Jackson for one. Everyone admires him, and I can hardly fault his politics, and he's pleasant enough to talk with, but . . . oh, I don't know. I'm suspicious of him, to be honest with you. You know the story, of course? The gossip about . . .?'

'The gossip?'

Ned glanced at him, paused, then made a sharply dismissive gesture with his hand. 'Oh – him and Mother, years ago. To hell with it, it's such balls I can't even bring myself to tell the story. I'm off home. Thanks for the talk. I'm going to sit tight, stay on the board, do what I can to steer Macaulay away from too much disaster, and then, as soon as possible, make my run. Don't know how, don't know when.'

Whistling cheerfully now, saying something to Hugh's assistant as he passed which made her laugh, Ned was on his way.

But when safely out of sight, he muttered to himself in anger at his crassness. There was other gossip around Henry Jackson that Hugh and Ned had never discussed, for it was too seriously immediate and painful for Hugh for it to be trespassed upon. Ned had realized immediately, from the horror in Hugh's voice, that it was this gossip that Hugh had thought Ned was referring to so casually. Ned felt nauseous at his lack of tact.

The Macaulay Group had an audit committee, and Ned was on it, but it never met. Each year the accounts were prepared and brought straight to a board meeting for Lord Kimpton's signature. For this annual occasion the senior partner of the firm's auditors was present, an old school friend of Kimpton's. Nicky Waring, as the firm's principal adviser, also a friend of Kimpton's from his schooldays, would be there as well. The two of them stayed behind afterwards with the family directors for lunch in the panelled dining room, a ritual of sumptuous consumption.

Ned loathed the whole occasion. The amateur inconsequence of it, the extravagance, the mindless sybaritism, the dishonesty of it actually, for the signing off of the accounts was rushed and unquestioning and vapid – he hated it all. But he left Gilston Road that morning determined to play the day exactly right. He had prepared some questions to ask of the auditors, and he would do that courteously, and without aggressive tenacity, and – maturely: the responsible non-executive director, rather than the rebellious younger son. At lunch he would be conversational and pleasant, and although he would leave as soon it was conceivably polite, he would do so without making any great show of that. He had promised as much to Daisy, and she was right.

Which was almost what happened. The meeting had proceeded as it always did. Josh Compton, the auditors' senior partner, rattled through his presentation, complimented the directors on another excellent year, warned that his firm's rising overhead would oblige him to ask for an increase in fees, and suggested the chairman might now consider it appropriate to sign off the accounts.

But though still mindful of his promises to Daisy, Ned was waiting. 'Josh – hold on for a second – may I ask if you personally have examined the values at which we are carrying our investments in each of the companies we have acquired? And have you satisfied yourself as to the result? If so, would you be so good as to take us through each of them individually, to show us that our valuations represent a responsible and prudent view?'

Compton coloured and, looking for a lead, glanced up the table at the chairman. But Lord Kimpton was busy in whispered conversation with Harrison, the company secretary, who sat beside him, and he failed to catch his eye. So Compton cleared his throat and in his impossibly Edwardian accent said that whilst he personally was not entirely familiar with each and every investment, his audit staff of course were. And that Ned should be assured that the valuations had been most painstakingly analysed.

'Each one of them, Josh? Individually?'

Compton held his eye. 'Yes, each one of them.'

Ned nodded, and smiled unthreateningly enough, and Compton visibly relaxed. He waited for a moment with a cocked eyebrow, inviting Ned to continue, then turned back to the chairman. 'So if there are no more questions,' Compton began, 'might I suggest that you . . .'

'What about Rodin Additives?' Ned said.

Nicky Waring, sitting beside Compton as his fellow guest, assumed now his most silken, seraphic expression, and crossed his arms across his chest. Crisp cream shirt cuffs, secured by diamond and gold links, were displayed against the dark, sombre blue of his Savile Row suit and Brigade of Guards tie.

'Rodin Additives?' Compton repeated, idiotically, and Ned nodded, still in perfect politeness. 'I think I may have to refresh my memory by consulting my colleagues on that one, to be frank. Rodin Additives . . .' he mused, and Ned leant over the table and pointed out the name in the investment list.

'Ah, yes,' said Compton, and Nicky Waring beamed his pleasure. 'Of course. Rodin. We've held the investment at its original value, as you can see. We might have marked it up, of course, but we deemed it more prudent to . . .'

'You might have marked it up, and you might of course have marked it down,' Ned said, calmly. 'If you had thought that the investment was overvalued.'

Nicky Waring smiled with delight, and looking up the table brought Lord Kimpton into the joke. Puzzled, and by now slightly pink, Kimpton made an attempt at a chuckle.

'You calculated that it was prudently valued. So there we are,' Ned continued, his voice still calm.

Compton nodded, and everyone around him could sense the tension. Kimpton's cousin, up for the audit luncheon from Yorkshire, leant forward and cupped his hand to his ear, bending it forward at right angles. He had not the first idea what was going on. It looked worrying.

Compton licked his lips, and waited for the blow to fall. So did everyone else. It came, and brutally.

'I believe that Compton Auguste are Rodin Additive's auditors. Is that correct?'

Compton looked vague, as if trying to recall if out of the vast list of his firm's audit clients this might conceivably be one. Then he abandoned that, and nodded.

Ned smiled. 'I believe too that the Rodin board has asked you to find a new shareholder for them? And that this is not proving very easy, as their recent trading results are so poor that the price we paid for our shares last year is looking very high indeed?'

Compton tried to say something, but Ned held up his hand.

'And that you have managed to locate for Rodin just one possible new investor, after a long search? And that you have assured them that not only are we at Macaulay going to hold our investment at its original price, as we consider Rodin such an excellent prospect, but that we would almost certainly follow them with more money of our own? At the price we first paid? Despite, Josh, as you surely know, the fact that their sales are off at least 20 per cent, and they have lost key staff to a competitor.'

Total silence. Then Ned said, so quietly that all strained to hear him, 'Compton Auguste are contracted by Rodin for a fee of 5 per cent of the new equity you raise for them. I'm told the issue is aiming at £60 million – that's £3 million in fees for you. So you have in this . . . well, let's call it an inadvertent conflict of interest. And we can of course be sure that had you recalled that conflict of interest when you were presenting our accounts this morning, you would have brought it to our attention.'

Ned then turned to his father's deaf cousin, and raising his voice a little and accentuating his consonants, summarized for him what had been said. A sweet smile passed the old man's features. He had always thought young Ned would turn up trumps when he had grown up a bit. And personally he'd never cared for Josh Compton. He was delighted to be a witness to his discomfort. He'd been bullied by Compton's older brother at prep school.

But it was Nicky Waring who saved the worst of Compton's embarrassment, and the tension in the room was such that it was a relief to everyone when he did. Even to Ned, who'd had his triumph, and was uncertain how to move on. Waring laughed, patted Compton on the knee, whispered something in his ear, and laughed again, this time looking around the table with a great show of good nature and boyish glee.

'Dear, oh dear,' he said, wiping his eyes and shaking his head. 'Wonderful! Well done, Ned! What a sleuth! Old Josh here caught with his pants down! Absolutely priceless.'

He wiped his eyes again, gave Compton's knee a further pat, and turned to Lord Kimpton. 'Chairman, funny as this is, and I haven't enjoyed myself so much for years, it goes without saying of course that poor old Josh here had no idea of any of this himself. There'll be absolute hell to pay when he gets back to his office. Heads will roll, I can wager for that. Thanks to Ned here – and this is a most encouraging foretaste of what his contributions are going to be worth to this board in the future. But I suggest that you get Josh to go back and check every one of these investments himself, line by line, until he's absolutely comfortable. Then you can call another board meeting, sign them off, and everything's hunky-dory. Don't you agree?'

He smiled his way around the table. 'And now,' he said, 'we can get to the real purpose of the day, which is your marvellous audit luncheon. Am I right? The best lunch of the year, a wonderful occasion, I've been looking forward to it for weeks.' He spread his arms wide, beaming. Kimpton's two cousins glowered at him. They thought Nicky a cad, and always had.

So they went into lunch. But for all Nicky Waring's boisterous attempts at noisy bonhomie, the party this year was a miserable, guilty affair, and they broke up at barely half past two.

Giles nodded and smiled his morning greetings to the commissionaires, and stepped into the crowded lift. There were agonies of embarrassment for him, with his leg pressed up against a girl with the tea trolley, but they were now on the ninth and topmost floor, and he could escape. The board floor, it was called. Giles and his young Australian assistant, Sheila, shared this with his father, Miss Day, the boardroom, and his father's private dining room – as well as an open office housing several girls, always working furiously at their computers, which had been known as 'Miss Day's Secretariat' since the shorthand, notebook and typewriter days of the 1960s, and, nearly forty years later, still was.

Sheila – she had absolutely refused to follow Miss Day and be known by her surname – called out 'G'day, Mr Giles,' as he passed her desk, and continued to read her tabloid newspaper. She remained reading it when Miss Day passed.

'Mr Giles!' Miss Day called after him, and Giles turned, smiling inanely, to face her.

'Miss Day?'

'Mr Giles, I would ask that your office informs my office when you are about to leave each evening. If you recall, I have requested this before. Last night it was particularly important that you remained at your desk. There was a conference call coming in for Lord Kimpton from New York at 6.15. Unfortunately you missed it. Lord Kimpton was most displeased.'

Sheila looked up from her newspaper, cupped her chin in her hand and smiled sweetly. 'Yesterday was Mr Giles's birthday, Miss Day, as you well remember. Lord Kimpton was aware that Mr Giles had to leave the office at six o'clock exactly. I told him so myself. Mr Giles was joining Lady Kimpton at the Royal Opera House. For his birthday treat.'

Giles, uncertain as he often was with Sheila as to whether the use of 'birthday treat' was a bit of cheekiness or a charming example of Australian egalitarianism, was nevertheless delighted at her intervention. Sheila had been at Macaulay for a year, and had let it be known that she had decided to stay in the job for her remaining time in England. Somehow, that was that. Once, at the office Christmas party, she had come over with a sprig of mistletoe, sat on Giles's knee, and given him a gentle, fluttering little kiss on his forehead. She had leant back, studied him, then kissed him once more, softly, chastely, this time on his lips. Then, after another studied look, mistletoe aloft, once again. Giles had been absolutely entranced. It had been the first and only time in his life that a girl had kissed him. He now dreaded her move back to Australia. He couldn't even bring himself to think about it. Her presence in his life, after that one tiny encounter, had given him what he assumed was to be his only experience of existence as a passably conventional human being.

He went into his office and, as always, saw his mail laid out in a neat pile on his desk. This would have been read through previously by Miss Day, and copied as she deemed prudent for Lord Kimpton's inspection. Giles riffled through it, kept the absolutely easy letters for himself to handle, and redirected everything else to other members of staff. To the editors of the two newspapers went anything even remotely connected with their activities. To Harrison, the Company Secretary, went almost everything else. The balance was sent to the firm's press officer, a retired journalist from their *Daily Meteor*, who worked part-time, was paid full-time, and threw most of it into the bin.

Giles was just starting on his emails, which he would treat identically, when the telephone rang. The moment he picked up the receiver and heard Sheila laughing he guessed she'd been talking to Ned, who had probably been giving her his very good imitation of Miss Day. Before he could stop her, Sheila was putting him through.

'Mr Ned, Mr Giles,' she said, still laughing, and Giles grimaced in anticipation of what was to follow.

'Giles – good morning. I've got the board papers from Harrison. I asked for an item to be put on the agenda, and it hasn't been.'

'Item on the agenda?' Giles replied, feebly. Why couldn't he face up to his younger brother properly?

'Yes. I wanted a summary note on each of the two papers' planned editorial policy for the election year coming.'

'Their editorial policy?'

'With both the editors attending, then staying for lunch so that we can talk it through more informally. The suggestion's not in the draft minutes and there's nothing on the agenda. Why not?'

'You'll have to ask Father. He made the decision on that.'

'I tried to. Miss Day won't put me through.'

'Actually I don't think Father's here. In fact I know he's not. He's at a meeting at Waring's to discuss diversification strategy or something.'

'Christ, that's all we need. Then I'll try to reach him later in the day. But this is a formal request that my suggestion is actioned. I'm going to put it in writing now and send it round by messenger. And one other thing. I don't think that Father should be having meetings with Waring's on matters as important as to how we invest our money without you being there as well. Leaving Father alone with Nicky Waring is not in my opinion a good idea.'

There was silence for a moment. 'Ned – Father's not keen on that suggestion about the editors. It was Father who crossed out the text of what you asked for from Harrison's first draft of the minutes.'

'Why isn't he keen?'

'It's never been done before.'

Ned snorted with pretended laughter. 'Isn't that rather the point? And the minutes in any case should reflect what I said. They're legal documents. They are obliged to state a fair record of what is discussed. You know that perfectly well, so does Father. So does Harrison.'

'Well – talk to Father, Ned,' was Giles's eventual response.

'I will, but I'm talking to you too. I want what I said to be given the respect of being properly represented in the text of the minutes.'

'For the enlightenment of future generations of scholars?' Giles responded, in a rare attempt at wit that sounded merely sarcastic and petulant.

'Don't patronize me. Don't patronize me, and don't under-rate me.'

'For God's sake, don't be angry with me. Be more imaginative. Father won't last for ever, one day he'll want to retire, and then I see no reason whatsoever why you and I . . .' Ned started to interrupt, but – 'why you and I should not be friends,' Giles concluded lamely, having for a moment intended to say something very different indeed.

Ned knew that, and cursed himself for cutting Giles short when he was about to say something significant about their future together. But the damage was done, and after a further brief, uneasy exchange, Ned put the telephone down.

Daisy had come into the room while he was talking. 'You can be such a fool sometimes, Ned.'

'Don't patronize me, Daisy,' he said, his voice rising, and he was uncomfortably reminded that he had said exactly this to Giles only moments before. Daisy had no doubt heard him, and he knew that the repetition of it made him appear even more absurdly weak than he was. He tried to smile, but Daisy shook her head, and turned to leave the room.

Rachel Kimpton's dry martini arrived in the hands of a beaming waiter, and she gave him the sweetest of smiles, rolling her eyes in mock ecstasy as she took her first sip. Daisy looked at her tomato juice. It was prim and suburban, she thought. But she hated drinking at lunchtime. So why should she?

'The Connaught's martinis are the best in London, which is why I always come here,' Rachel said, and waved away both the menu and wine list, ordering Dover sole and spinach. Daisy toyed with the idea of ordering something different for herself, to stake out her independence, but then thought it an absurd, adolescent gesture, and followed suit.

Rachel asked some formulaic questions about her grand-children, then, that out of the way, came briskly to the point, as Daisy knew she would.

'It's sweet of you to allow me to take you to lunch, darling,' she said, and Daisy was taken aback by the endearment, wondering if it was accidental. Ned's mother had shown her some degree of increasing warmth as the years of her marriage to her son rolled out, but not much. Daisy didn't particularly blame her. She recognised that she'd gone into her marriage a sexy little child, party-going, chattering, inane. A caricature, it seemed to her now, of the middle-class Home Counties spoilt daughter that she had certainly been. Motherhood had played its part in her transformation, but it wasn't just that. It was the nature of her married state. She wanted to be not just a companion, but an example to Ned. She was good at familial love, and affection and warmth, just as he was. She could do that, but she wanted more. For both of them.

'Sweet of you to lunch with me because I know how busy you are, but I do have a reason.' As she leant forward to address Daisy now, concentrating, looking into her eyes, Daisy thought how much she preferred her mother-in-law when she put aside her sophisticate veneer, and simply talked, sensibly, without affectation.

'Ned's worrying me. Perhaps he's worrying you. All this obsession with the family firm. He has to understand that as long as Charlie wants to be active – and, frankly, I believe that will be until the day he dies – then Ned will have no place beyond his present role. Possibly, when Charlie does one day pass the firm on, Ned and Giles might be able to work together. But I absolutely don't intend to disturb matters now by talking to Charlie about it, or Giles, or – God forbid – Nicky Waring, or anyone else.'

Daisy nodded, and wondered why she had been summoned to hear all this. She knew it so well. But now it came.

'Daisy – I want you to steer Ned away from all this, and in a quite different direction. I can't do it, and Charlie certainly can't. You can. You strike me these days as a woman of quite surprising strength and tenacity. You clearly have a considerable hold over him and I admire you for it.'

She paused, and Daisy decided to delay her response until she had heard more.

'I have some ideas for Ned which you and I might mull over together. Politics is a possibility. A safe Labour seat might certainly be found. Another idea I had was the Foreign Office, and I'm sure you'd agree that he would make a most effective diplomat were he to put his mind to it. Actually, I have already had a word in the Permanent Secretary's ear about that, and he confirms that Ned would certainly be considered most favourably were he to . . .'

'No,' Daisy said now, and Lady Kimpton looked across at her in surprise, her sentence left unfinished. 'I'm afraid I can't. Or rather, I'm afraid I won't. Ned is his own man. I can't be an emissary for your ideas. I can only represent my own, when I think the time is right.'

6

James was asleep in the drawing room when Hugh arrived. He was sprawled fully dressed on the sofa in his investment banker's suit, his feet in their polished black shoes propped insolently on his late mother's finest damask cushions.

This tableau had no doubt been set up for Hugh, designed as a statement of James's contempt for his mother, dead or alive, and particularly for what he had always taken to be her suffocating, suburban gentility. He lay with his head thrown back, mouth open, plump cheeks wobbling on each exhalation of a hog-like snore. A glass of whisky, held loosely in one pink hand, had slopped on to his bulging shirt front.

They were physically so unlike each other, Hugh thought as he watched him. He had none of his brother's bulk, and he knew he was strikingly the better-looking of the two. Though James, as he remembered, had possessed his own brand of florid handsomeness as a very young man, before a certain coarseness had taken hold.

As Hugh tried now to take the glass from his brother's fingers, James suddenly awoke, sat up, brushed Hugh's hand away, finished the remains of the whisky in one gulp, and slammed the glass down on the rosewood table beside him.

'So – you're here,' he said, glancing at his watch. 'About fucking time. Didn't you get my message? I've got to get back to London. A board meeting first thing. What kept you, for Christ's sake? I'd have left hours ago, but Father needs one of us in the house with him at this time, I suppose, in addition to Foster. Though in his condition it hardly makes much difference one way or the other.'

Hugh ignored the original question. 'What happened to her, James?' he asked.

'I told you. She died. Passed on. Kicked the bucket. Expired.' James got to his feet, straightened his jacket, smoothed down his hair, and made for the door.

'James – I'm asking you – what happened to her?'

James stood there looking at him, perhaps momentarily struck by the thought that even for him he was being too strikingly obtuse. While looking around the room in search of something – his overcoat? his attaché case? – he explained, marginally more cooperatively. 'She had a stroke. Father's nurse called me at the bank. I told her to reach you instead but no one seemed to know where you were. So she got back to me again. It was extremely inconvenient, but I came down. She was in the local hospital by the time I got here. She was unconscious, kept alive by some machine or other. I told them to pull the plug on her. So that's what they did. In a couple of hours she was gone.' It was his attaché case he was looking for. It was behind a chair, and he set off for the door.

Hugh followed him. 'You told them to pull the *plug* on

her?' he repeated to James's retreating back. 'Shouldn't you have . . .?'

'Shouldn't I have bloody what? She'd had a massive stroke. She was brain-damaged, severely. She would probably have been without speech or movement. She was seventy-four. Her husband has dementia. She would have been a cabbage. I didn't hesitate for one moment. Of course I told them to pull the fucking plug. What would you have done?'

They crunched across the gravelled drive to James's car, a vast, sleek German model, and James began the tortuous process of levering himself into the driving seat.

'James.' Hugh waited for his attention, and his older brother looked up him, his hand poised to slam shut the door, the eyes so bloodshot that it occurred to Hugh that he should have attempted to persuade him to delay his departure until the morning.

'Yes?'

'I have to say that I would have liked to have been consulted before you made that decision about Mother. Why didn't you wait? Why didn't you speak to me first?'

'I told you – no one seemed to know where you were. In the end I got through to some adenoidal assistant of yours, who stuttered out some nonsense or other – I couldn't make head or tail of it. Anyway, it hardly mattered. I did what needed to be done. Decisively.' He nodded at Hugh, started up the engine and peered over his shoulder to reverse the car, flaunting his indifference as to whether or not Hugh's feet were in danger of the wheels.

'James!' Hugh called to him through the open driver's window. 'One more question. Was there any . . . any pain for her? Fear? Would she have known what was happening? Was she conscious at all?'

'How on earth would I know? She certainly wasn't conscious when she was found. Foster discovered her when he was locking up. He forced the door.' He looked up at Hugh and added, with an air of savage satisfaction, 'She was on the floor of the downstairs lavatory. With her knickers around her knees.'

He nodded at Hugh again and reversed away, calling out something to him about funeral arrangements which Hugh couldn't catch. And then he was gone, the great wash of beam from the big car illuminating the village cottages at the end of the drive so brutally that they looked as if they had been caught in wartime searchlights.

When Hugh awoke, he found himself in the spare room of his parents' house. He was lying in an unmade bed almost naked under an eiderdown, with his head rested on bare pillows. Foster, the general family servant, and a man of pronounced femininity, was putting a cup of tea down on the table beside him.

Foster had been with Hugh's parents since being demobbed in 1945, heavily decorated, after a war of spectacular and sustained courage as a rear gunner in Bomber Command, unlikely as that must have seemed to those who met him in civilian life. Hugh's earliest memory was of Foster hoeing and weeding in the walled garden, and really it had been Foster who had brought him up. His parents foreshortened the school holidays by sending him off to a religious or instructional camp, but when he was at home Foster was Hugh's only true guardian. James, six years older, had already drifted away from the family by the time Hugh was ten or eleven, spending his holidays in Norfolk with an aunt, his mother's sister. This woman so disliked Mrs Emerson that she had deliberately set about to acquire James for herself, as the most satisfyingly destructive way she could find of showing her spite. She had succeeded entirely, and James was almost never at home. So Hugh was alone, and without Foster his would have been a very solitary childhood indeed.

Hugh watched Foster now as he bustled around the room, tidying Hugh's clothes, brushing down his coat, singing a 1930s dance tune in a peculiar, high falsetto. Foster was always singing a dance tune, and always in this voice, like a caricature of a suburban housewife. Hugh's mother used to complain constantly about it. Hugh's father, even in his days of perfect health, had never seemed to notice.

'You might have caught your death, Hugh,' Foster scolded, putting a hand on his arm, as if he was still a small boy. Then, in his inimical, flaunting walk, he went across to open the curtains. Hugh had recognized Foster's effeminacy early in his life, but he only came to grips with the public notoriety of it when he was thirteen or fourteen. Then, sitting miserably at lunch at a friend's house in the village, he was subjected to a flouncing mimicry of Foster by the friend's father, all limp wrist and mincing gait. Hugh, a shy boy and anxious to please, had pretended to join the joke, laughing just as uproariously as the others.

But he had felt deep and immediate shame for his treachery. He had known, miserably, how well that shame was merited, for Foster was Hugh's confessor, confidant, teacher, laundryman, playmate and friend. And never in all the years of

Hugh's childhood had he betrayed him or his parents by one single instance of inappropriate physical intimacy. Occasionally the hand, as then, laid on the arm. Each night at bedtime, at Hugh's insistence, never Foster's, a robust, laughing hug. Never more than this, ever.

Hugh, who in later recollections had not once kissed his mother, let alone his father, and had hardly known his brother, had loved Foster with all the heart of an affectionate child deprived of any vestige of normal familial warmth. Watching him now in his eternal black slacks and a steward's white jacket, an old man, looking with his harshly dyed black hair every one of his seventy-seven years, Hugh loved him still. If Hugh's father needed – one day, maybe not too far into the future – to be slipped into an institution somewhere, and the house was then closed, what would become of Foster?

'We really cannot do that, Mike,' Hugh said later that afternoon, and half smiling, half wearily determined, held the Waterwell's buying director firmly in his gaze. 'I'm sorry, but you are asking for too much. I cannot possibly agree. We already give you the best terms of anyone. And with these promotional allowances you are asking for on top for Anna Lavey's new book – huge allowances – any increase in your annual buying discount is impossible for me. We love Waterwell's dearly, of course we do, but you ask for the impossible. I can't help. I'd like to, but . . .'

Hugh shrugged. He's a nasty little man, he thought, watching him. Struts around, asking for the earth, knows nothing about books, positively proud of the fact that he never reads. Little prick. I hope he has never seen one of our invoices to Amazon though. Our terms to them are several points better than Waterwell's.

The Waterwell's man gazed back at Hugh. What a jerk, he thought. Outside Anna Lavey they had nothing on their list, nothing, that Waterwell's should bother with, in his opinion. It was never like this in the music business. Professionals there, every man jack of us. The book trade? Pseudo-intellectuals to a man, jerks. He'd take another 1 per cent a year off Emerson just because of it, even 2. And so he did – 2 per cent. Plus a rich promotional deal on the new Anna Lavey. And he hadn't needed to show the Amazon invoice, which was folded in his coat pocket. He'd kept that one dry for next time.

Anna Lavey blew her nose several times, loudly, and after much wiping and snuffling she threw the paper tissue, sodden and crumpled, into the bin beside Hugh's desk. She was in a position at that moment to bully him, and this deliberately crass display was all part of it. She was going to make him wait before she responded to his request. He knew that, remained silent, and smiled.

'Well?' she asked at last. 'Is that it?'

Hugh nodded. 'Yes – that's it.'

'No apologies, no other explanations, no excuses?'

Hugh ignored her question. Any sign of weakness, and she'd be on him. He remained silent, leaving her to try again. Anna was incapable of dealing with silence. He'd discovered that over the years.

'I must say, I think it's pretty rich,' she said eventually, throwing the file back across his desk. 'Pretty rich and pretty damned insulting too. The payment is already two weeks late, and I want it. Why shouldn't I want it? It's mine.'

'I know, Anna. But I'm not asking you to forego it. I'm asking you to accept deferred payment of the royalties, for six months, with interest rolled up at base rate plus 3 per cent, and then a bullet payment at that point aggregated up into X plus the advance of £300,000 on your next book. That's all it is. The firm is temporarily short of liquidity; we are having to agree improved terms for the big chains, and I don't want to have any problem with the banks. It might actually be to your tax advantage to restructure the payment in this way. But anyway, if you do this it would be marvellous. If you don't, then fine. I'll find cash from another source, and we'll carry on as normal.'

'It won't be carrying on as normal,' Anna said, and the sulkiness in her voice told him that she would agree, but first must be wooed. He might possibly have to make one further small concession to close it, but that's all. He'd hold that for now.

'It's absolutely not fucking carrying on as normal. Normal is that the author, that's fucking me, gets her royalties on the day they're due – from the publisher. That's fucking you. That's normal. What you're suggesting is that I act as a money-lender to you. That's not fucking normal. That's fucking pathetic.'

Hugh put a smile into his eyes, but said nothing.

She looked at him, sniffed, wiped her nose with the back of her hand, and stared at her shoes. 'Wanker,' she said eventually. 'Total wanker, that's you. If you ran a half decent publishing company this would never have happened. Nor should it have happened three years ago, or whenever it was, when you had to get Ned Macaulay to bail you out. Though why Ned should have wanted to buy into a fucking awful outfit like this is beyond me.'

She glanced across at him to see if the barrage of insults had affected him, but it seemed not. He still said nothing. 'So why don't you get Ned to bail you out again, now that I think of it?' she asked, marginally less aggressively, sounding as if she was beginning to wonder if this suggestion might prove lucrative for her. 'Or not so much bail you out, but capitalize the firm to an extent that it might actually be able to do a decent job for its authors? I might even do a double deal on this. Ned capitalizes the company properly, then I invest an equity stake in it, on the back of his. After you've paid me this lot of royalties. Or even with this lot of royalties, provided I know that Ned is coming in. I wouldn't mind 20 per cent or so actually, now that I come to think about it. If I was on your board we might avoid these appalling cock-ups you steer us into, five minutes after we've got over the last one.'

She studied him again. 'Alternatively, of course, I could just sue for my money straight away, and go off and take my books to a proper publisher. Which is what I should have done years ago, had I not been such an idiotically soft touch.'

Hugh laughed. 'So that's settled then,' he said cheerfully. 'Interest at 3 per cent over base, and one bullet payment in six months, aggregated up with the contracted advance on the next book. Fine, let's go and have lunch.'

She gave up. She blew a raspberry at him, looked around for her coat and prepared to go with him, stopping only to scribble her signature beside his on the agreement he had ready and waiting for her on his desk. She grumbled a little more as they walked to the restaurant but without much malice in it. And actually he was grateful to her for signing up as he had asked, rather than spin the whole business out with her agent, and her lawyers, and her accountants, and all the rest of the professional entourage that followed her around these days, as her success and fortune grew.

She brought up again the prospect of investing into the share capital of Emerson, but Hugh put his hand on her elbow, and steered her into the restaurant. 'I don't think so, Anna, I really don't. It wouldn't work. Emerson's best left with me. And Ned Macaulay when he comes to a board meeting, which isn't very often.'

They sat down, he ordered them their drinks, and he smiled at her as warmly as he could, so as to take the edge off any rudeness in what he was saying. 'You need your independence from us, and we need our independence from you. And I don't want to risk spoiling our personal relationship.'

'Personal relationship! Christ!' she muttered sarcastically, rekindling the quarrel, but she lost interest, shrugged, finished her Bloody Mary in three gulps, then called for another. 'Suit yourself,' she said. 'Suit yourself. But never ask me to help you again. Ever.'

Hugh stared at her in total disbelief. 'Say that again, Nic, slowly.' He knew he had heard her correctly the first time, but he needed a second or two to gather himself. He was so shocked that he felt faint. He wanted to ensure that he was calm enough to respond appropriately.

She shrugged, smiled and reached out to take his hand. 'Here it is then – again, slowly. I'm going to have a baby.

Finally, after all these years, we're going to have a child. I'm pregnant.'

It occurred to Hugh that convention dictated that he should at this point shout with joy and seize Nicola in his arms. But he was truly thunderstruck. He was also instantly, terribly afraid. Maybe the child wasn't his. How could he know that the child was his?

But little by little, second by second, he fought to eliminate the fear from his mind. Perhaps they had been given another chance at a proper marriage – creating a real home and household, with school satchels in the hall, and kitchen tea, and homework, and summer holidays, and all the small effects of conventional, joyful family life. Maybe this would finally give her the excuse, if that was what was needed, to come home to him, to forget Henry Jackson, forget the fantasies and the compartmentalism, and the overblown romanticism, and the duplicity of the way she lived her life and . . . be with him.

'Nic, I'm . . . I'm delighted. Overwhelmed.'

But there was a hesitancy in him, and she saw in his eyes what he feared. And she knew too that he would be unable to articulate that fear. She wasn't going to do that for him. They'd leave it unsaid.

She threw open her arms. 'Come on, Hugh. We've waited so long. I'm pregnant, and it's just what I need – and it's just what we need. Fuck it, Hugh – no doubts, no reservations, this is wonderful news.'

She watched him, and for a few moments both were silent. 'And it's our news, Hugh,' she said, 'our news, yours and mine.' Maybe that statement, oblique as it was, would suffice. In truth she was not wholly sure who the father was. She hoped the baby was Hugh's. She thought it was. But the niggle of doubt had made her hesitate a day or so after doing the test before she told him.

She walked up to him, and pressed herself against him, her arms around his back, and as he held her he reflected that this was the first time for many months that she had hugged him. Their sexual life had continued, partly because without it they could not have pretended that nothing had changed, but what had been lost was the trivial but vitally important gestures of affection, as this was.

She looked up at him and smiled and, with her arms still around him, kissed him softly and tenderly on the mouth.

He smiled too, and kissed her in return, with all of the same gentleness. Maybe this was all that they needed. Maybe now she really would come home. And, once and for all, let Jackson go.

7

'It's the only way for us,' Giles said. 'Please accept what I say, Ned, and don't always look for an ulterior motive or duplicity, or something hidden from you and the other directors. Waring's think it's the only thing we can do. We don't have the money in the family to do this, and the banks won't put up any more debt without more equity going in beside it. In fact there's any amount of difficulty at the moment in hanging on to what we've got from them already. The situation really is very severe.'

Ned gazed at him, icy cold. At least now it was being admitted. He realized what an effort of will it must have been for Giles to have arranged this lunch to break the news – so out of character for him. He admired him for it. What was emerging was what Ned had always known. The Macaulay diversification programme was a fiasco of terminally wasted money.

'A bond issue? A good, old-fashioned bearer bond issue, with coupons attached?' Ned suggested, pushing away his plate, but the question was for form's sake. As a private company, in the current market they would never be able to sell their bonds to the institutions.

Giles shook his head. 'It won't work, unfortunately,' he said. 'Waring's looked at it, but interest rates are too unstable, as you know, and there's too much inflation in the air. And the reasons for asking for it are unlikely to please people, which would result in too much spotlight on us, in a way we've never been used to before. A bond issue was the first thing that came to my mind too. But it's not on. So we're down to the only possible alternative: to bring in a new shareholder.'

'From outside the family? For the first time ever? This will completely break the mould,' Ned responded.

Giles paused, then shrugged. 'Yes. The shareholder has to be from outside the family, because the family, even in aggregate, can't put together what we need so quickly. Nowhere near it.'

Ned nodded. 'A hundred million, you say?'

'A hundred million at least.'

'Christ. And this into a company that – five years ago? six? – was throwing off so much money from the two newspapers that we hardly knew what to do with it. Aren't I right?'

Giles looked mournfully around the restaurant, partly, Ned suspected, so that he could avoid his gaze, but partly no doubt because he feared they might be overheard. 'The two papers are still enormously successful, but by their old standards it has to be admitted that they're not achieving quite what they used to. Roughly 50 per cent of the cash they used to generate in the days when . . . Well, perhaps not half, less than that. Actually quite a lot less than that.'

Ned was so taken aback that the look of incredulous horror on his face was quite genuine. Normally he mocked his brother with shows of stagey irony, but this was real. He had been taken totally by surprise. He was appalled. 'Surely that's not right? You can't be saying that the two papers have lost most of their cash generation? You must be muddling something up in your recall of the numbers. I'm not asking you whether Macaulay overall is satisfactorily cash-generative because it's clear we aren't. I'd assumed that that was a function of these bloody awful diversification adventures of ours. But the two papers . . . Giles, you can't be right. When I first came on to the board seven or eight years ago they were generating £70 million surplus between them? Maybe £80 million? Their circulation figures are down, both of them, we all know that, but nothing in any way commensurate with dropping off £70 or 80 million of cash!'

His voice had now risen to a level where some of the other diners in the packed little restaurant were beginning to glance across at them, and Ned saw this. He paused, smiled at his brother to reassure and divert anyone hearing their conversation who shouldn't have been, and lowered his voice.

'Giles – what on earth is happening? Why don't the board papers give us a proper view of things? Why can't the accounts be prepared division by division, so we can all see exactly what's going on? All the numbers are so aggregated up into one box that no one can get a true understanding of the rhythm of it all in any way. And when I do try to ask a question and get to the bottom of anything, all that happens is . . .'

Ned paused, gazed at his brother, and said no more. Giles was the last man who needed to be bullied, so why do it? He'd told Ned all that he needed to know. Assets had been written up in the accounts, and down again, and up again, and every avenue of obfuscation and self-deception had been tried. But the truth was now there on the wall for anyone to see, and it was inescapable. And Ned was glad that it was. Macaulay was out of cash. Macaulay was penniless. Macaulay was utterly, totally broke. If an investor didn't close a deal with them soon – and soon meant well-nigh immediately – Macaulay would be bankrupt. One by one – his father, Giles, his mother, Katie – all of the family would have to come to terms with that.

Without one shadow of doubt, an era had come now to an end. But its passing would provide Ned with his opportunity. As he and his brother parted, Ned wondered if Giles realized that. It occurred to Ned that for the first time ever Giles had probably faced the truth. Their father should not be running the company. And if that meant that Ned had a chance now to strike, so too did Giles.

He wondered if Giles had thought of that too.

Nicky Waring called Lord Kimpton once again to underline that Macaulay must now look to a substantial outside equity investor if the situation was to be saved – and urgently. Knowing the Macaulay Group as they did, and fond of it as they were, Waring's thought it very important that, despite the urgency of the requirement, the right face was found to fit the bill. The wrong man – and further trouble would follow. The right man – and all would be well.

He was, however, delighted to say that they had found the answer. He and James Emerson would be debating it again over the weekend, but they really thought they had. It shouldn't be an English investor – didn't Charlie agree? – for that would be too close to home. Nor an American, for Americans were not at all of the Macaulay family's style. Nor were Canadians

107

of course. The Irish were out of the question. As for the Japanese, that went without saying. The French were a possibility perhaps, and he and James would see if they could come up with a name or two over the weekend. Italians absolutely not. Germans conceivably . . . Well, they'd go on thinking, but the best candidate of all, Nicky felt, and he was rarely wrong in his instinct for these things – put it down to a nose for it, put it down to years of experience, put it down to what you will – the best candidate of all was a certain Australian investor, whom Waring's knew well.

All right, Waring's must declare an interest in this, he was a client of theirs, of course he was, but putting that aside there was no question about it in Nicky's mind that the man for this was Rod Tadlock, the Sydney entrepreneur and media man. Had Charlie not met Rod? A little rough cut maybe, a little coarse perhaps some might say, tough when he had to be, a bit of an individualist – but what a charmer! An absolute charmer. And – have we settled on what we're looking for here, say £100 million for a 20 per cent stake, something on those lines? – with the sort of pocket that would make this an important investment for him, but not one of his biggest.

The last thing we want on the Macaulay share register is a potential troublemaker. What we want is a man who is proud to be concerned with such a prestigious English firm, as well he might; who respects and understands what Macaulay does; who can afford, and then some, to take his place at the board table. Who is then there when we need him, but the rest of the time keeps his mouth shut, and his opinions to himself. Wasn't that right? Were Waring's not on the right track?

★

'It's so good of you to spare the time to see us, Ned, it really is. How kind you are. Delighted to get your call. Couldn't meet with you quickly enough. Sweet of you. Wonderful. Perfect. Now then, James you know of course, but Jason?'

Ned nodded at James Emerson, then shook hands with a young man, perhaps in his mid twenties, who he realized was one of Nicky Waring's sons from his second marriage and, according to the press, the adored protégé of his father.

Ned glanced at James as he went to his seat. James beamed his plump, dangerous smile at him, and Ned thought to himself that young Jason Waring should watch his back. If he was under the impression that the bank was his on his father's retirement, he'd have a battle on his hands with James Emerson, and that's for sure. Then he had another look at Jason, and decided that he might be misreading him: Jason looked like his father – silkily tough.

'Fabulous. Wonderful, terrific,' Ned said, finding himself adopting the argot, and reached up to accept a glass of champagne from the Waring's butler, who then melted away. Ten years and more since the Thatcher-induced City deregulation, and Waring's still lived and talked as if nothing had ever happened. Perhaps, in their corner of the market, nothing much had.

'Such a privilege to have you here,' Nicky continued, gesturing to Ned to help himself to a canapé of foie gras from a silver tray. 'Believe me, such a joy. Macaulay we adore, of course. Adore the lot of you. Our favourite clients – yes, Jason? James? Charlie I've known for my entire life, and I love the guy. You know that. Love the guy. Would die for him, happily. My oldest friend in the world. You're family to us, that's what

109

you are – Charlie, Giles, your mum too, the lot of you. Our only sadness, Ned, is that we at Waring's feel we know you less well than the others. We speak about it a lot. We've always wondered, haven't we, James, how we could put that right?'

'Absolutely,' James said, with a rueful, questing shake of the head, and a wistful smile at Ned.

'So, Ned!' Nicky said now, opening his hands. 'What can we do for you? How can we help? Just say the word.'

'Well, I was hoping you might brief me,' Ned answered. 'Giles has told me what we're facing. We're out of cash, the banks won't put up any more, and we can't raise a bond issue. We need at least a hundred million in cash, and quickly. That seems to leave three options. We could sell some assets – but how quickly? And at proper value? We could put more equity in ourselves – but is that possible? Do we as a family have that sort of cash available? Or, thirdly, we find an outsider, a new shareholder. Is that where we are? Do you agree with that?'

James replied, having glanced first at Nicky. 'Yes. That's exactly right. We looked at a bond issue, but it won't work. As far as the family subscribing is concerned we don't think the family can raise the money, at least not in time. More bank debt can't be done – in fact the banks want their present debt paid down. So that leaves us with two alternatives: sell assets, or bring in a new shareholder.'

Nicky nodded to Jason, inviting him to break in. James's expression clenched with irritation, which he rapidly disguised.

'The trouble with selling assets,' Jason said, 'is that it's only the crown jewels – the two newspapers – that would sell quickly enough to bring you the money you need, by the time you need it. Even then, with both titles beginning to decline, we might find it hard to get a full valuation for them.'

He had made a mistake. James tried not to look delighted, and Nicky broke in hastily. 'Beginning to decline?' he laughed. 'The papers? I hardly think that, Jason. They're jewels, as you said. One or two little short-term problems perhaps, one or two things to fix, but if we were to sell them, goodness me, I think we could find some very interesting buyers indeed. Quite an auction. Gosh, very high valuations.'

And commensurately high fees for you, Nicky, Ned thought. 'Selling the papers is out of the question,' Ned said. 'Absolutely out of the question. But the other investments? The diversification assets we've acquired? We've done that once after all. We sold the commercial property portfolio we bought from that client of yours – and then resold back to him twelve months later. At a loss.'

Nicky chuckled in a kindly way, and went to collect the Krug bottle, to replenish Ned's glass. 'A cyclical thing in that case, I'm afraid, nothing more to it than that. You were most unfortunate in your timing. The other assets? Wonderful investments of course, the crème de la crème, but Jason is right, it would all take too long. Which leaves us, I'm afraid, with the third option. We need a new investor. And – putting it baldly – fast. Well, fortunately we feel we have the perfect man for you, the ideal solution.'

'In Rod Tadlock,' Ned broke in.

Nicky paused, uncertain of Ned's tone. 'Yes, in Rod Tadlock. You will be considering his proposal at your forthcoming board meeting.'

'Yes, we will. But I wanted to hear you say that all this has been left so late that we have no option but to bring in someone like Tadlock now, despite the fact that we've never had a shareholder from outside the family in the hundred years or so of the firm's life. And in my opinion shouldn't do so now.'

Nicky nodded sympathetically. 'It's hard to disagree with that. But we feel there's no other way. If you believe the contrary, then tell us. If you yourself, Ned, were able to put your hands on the sort of money that Macaulay needs, what a wonderful thing that would be! But I don't think you can. And there's this – we at Waring's know Rod Tadlock. We've worked with him. We trust him. He sees the chance of investing in Macaulay, and thereby taking his place on the board of one of the most prestigious and distinguished private companies in the world. That would be a great boost to his prestige and standing. He'll behave himself, you can trust to that. He's insecure, Ned, socially insecure. There's no way he's going to step out of line at Macaulay. He's too much in awe of you all.'

Ned, suddenly, was bored. 'He sounds a complete prick,' he said, pleasantly, putting down his glass and pushing himself to his feet. He nodded his farewells to James and Jason, as they too rose to their feet.

Nicky laughed, and slipped his hand under Ned's arm as he walked him to the door. 'Yes, he is a bit, to be honest with you. A prick, you're right. But he does have £100 million in folding money for you at this moment, and that's rather timely. Wouldn't you agree?' He bellowed out his laughter now, delighted with his folding money joke.

Ned smiled, nodded, and turned away. He had no idea what Waring's were up to, but he knew now what he would do. He would manipulate this situation to his own ends. Tadlock was the sort of man who liked to do deals. Once Ned had had a full look at him, he'd find one to suit.

It was the following afternoon. Nicky drank his cup of Earl Grey tea, served by the butler in Waring's exquisite bone china, and gazed mournfully across the desk at James Emerson.

'My dear chap,' he said, and reached across to pat him on the arm. 'It always comes hard, it always comes hard. Even when they've done their three score years and ten, and they've had their innings, and one should be ready and prepared for it. But one never is, of course. Seventy-four, you say? That's nothing these days, is it? I'm so sorry, old chap. Everything left in your lap, I suppose, the arrangements for the funeral and what have you? Tidying up the estate? Dealing with the lawyers, and all that nonsense? All down to you? Your father's not up to it?'

James shook his head, and Nicky noticed the wobble of his cheeks. The fellow would have to be careful of his weight. Getting fat. High blood pressure. Drank too much, of course.

'Father's gaga,' James said, 'has been for years. Yes – everything will have to be done by me. Everything. Not that I have the time.'

'God, no. That you haven't. What about that publisher brother of yours? Can't he do it?'

James grimaced, and shrugged. 'Hugh? Never there when you need him. Never has been. Hopelessly unreliable. Heaven knows what he gets up to. But speaking of Hugh, you do know that he's a minority shareholder in Ned Macaulay's investment company – the only one actually?'

He pointed at the name of Banville Trust amongst the list

of the Macaulay Group shareholders that were on the desk in front of Nicky Waring.

'Is he indeed?' Waring mused. 'How very interesting. Does that help, hinder, balls things up, what does it do? Does he have any rights? Anything in the Banville Trust articles? Their shareholders' agreement? Vetoes? Special rights? Anything we could use on him?'

James thought for a moment, tapping his teeth with a pencil. 'Anything we could use on him? It's the reverse of that which gives me concern. Hugh, as I said, is totally unreliable. Ned, I assume, we can bring into line.'

Waring nodded. 'Absolutely we can bring Ned into line. He's an indolent little tit – even after all these years. That ghastly audit lunch of theirs three or four months ago is seared on my memory. You remember me telling you how he caught old Josh with his pants around his ankles over that Rodin Additives company which went belly-up immediately afterwards? He shook us all rigid, and then lost interest again. All flash and rhetoric is young Ned. No tenacity at all, no guts. A spoilt young man, quite frankly. Rachel's fault, of course.' He gave a short bellow of laughter, and swallowed one of the cucumber sandwiches that Waring's butler had brought with the tea.

'Such a tit,' James agreed, and fell silent once more.

'You are sure, though, that we can bring Ned into line?' he asked again anxiously, after a while.

'Of course. Charlie can sort him out. He always has in the past. We're not dealing with Giles here, you know. Giles is a little more . . . complicated these days, in a strange way. More formidable, less easy to read. More of his own man. Take this briefing he has given Ned; that would have been unthinkable in the past. But he's done it. Maybe he's realized that his father isn't up to it. Maybe – finally – that's sunk home. About bloody time of course, but there we are.'

'That's right. In his own way, Giles is formidable,' agreed James, and once more silence fell as the two men stared down at the shareholder list.

'Ned's got about 20 per cent hasn't he, including Banville Trust? He bought a few loose shares last year, didn't he, when someone or other died and Charlie shared them round? Brought him up to 20 per cent?' James enquired.

'Nineteen point seven per cent. Add it up.'

James did so. 'Twenty per cent, nineteen point seven – what's the difference?'

'Potentially rather a lot. The Articles demand 80.1 per cent clear for a deal like this to go through. Ned would need 19.9 per cent plus one share to block it. He hasn't got that. He's got 19.7 per cent. And he won't get any more.'

'So we're all right then,' said James, though he sounded unconvinced.

'So we're all right,' said Waring. 'As long as he doesn't obtain any more.'

'And he can't?'

'He can't. I don't think so.'

'What do you mean – you don't think so? Where could he get them from?'

Waring gestured at the share register list once more, and they both resumed staring at it.

'Any other weak links?' James asked. 'You'd know, wouldn't you, having dealt with Charlie Kimpton for so long? No other

Macaulay relations lurking around the place who could rock the boat and do a deal with Ned?'

Waring shrugged. 'I don't believe so. In my view, Charlie should never have allowed Ned to pick up those loose shares last year anyway. I suppose he thought that if he let Giles have a few he had better do the same for Ned, or Rachel would be at his throat. Better to have Ned with fewer shares than more, in my opinion. He's a loose cannon. He's by no means sound.'

'Sound?'

'Sound. Loyal to Charlie and Giles. He's the reverse of that. He clearly thinks they've made a balls of it. Which they have of course, totally, but there we are – or rather Charlie has. But Giles should have stopped him.'

'Bought too many companies, did Charlie.'

'Bought too many companies. That's right. But what could we do? That's the way he wanted to go, determined to do it, get away from dependence on the newspapers, perfectly correct strategy in its way, couldn't fault it. We then got to work, found Macaulay some beauties, they then ballsed them up.'

'Hardly our fault.'

'Indeed.' Waring took one last look at the list, sighed, and folded it away into his inside pocket. 'The trouble is . . .' he started, then went silent, gazing out of the window at the crowds now pushing their way into Moorgate underground station on their early Friday night exit from the City.

'The trouble is what?'

'The trouble is I don't like the look of it.'

There was a long silence.

'You're right. Actually Ned's not such a tit,' James said thoughtfully.

'Ned's absolutely not such a tit. Giles is a tit. Ned's formidable.'

'That's it. That's the problem,' James agreed.

'So what can go wrong?' asked Waring, but then immediately answered his own question. 'Any number of bloody things can go wrong, if Ned puts his mind to it. With a 19.7 per cent vote he can't block Rod Tadlock's investment but he can make a point of upsetting the other family shareholders. Then what happens? All these tit-like cousins with a tit-like half of half a per cent of the company each, who've never had a proper dividend out of it in their lives and never will, and who've never even been allowed to see a set of proper accounts – they'll come tumbling out of the woodwork, shouting blue murder and wanting to know what's going on. Their big tit-like moment. Charlie has one of his apoplexies, Giles retreats to his stinks experiments in the garden shed, Rod buggers off back to Australia, and the deal's off.'

'And we don't get our fees,' said James.

Again, a long silence.

'And the company?'

Waring made a dismissive gesture of impatience. 'The company does what it should have done in the first place. Or rather in the second place. In the first place it shouldn't have bought all these fucking companies. But now it shows some intelligence. It realizes its power as a publisher of two major national newspapers. It goes to the banks, asks for time to work on a new liquidity plan, but meanwhile it pulls strings. Fingers the banks' chairmen, bribes the government with promises of editorial favours – all that sort of thing. So everyone's then agreed: fine old English family publishing company unluckily in difficulty, a national jewel, the two newspapers at the very heart of our precious freedoms of speech and expression, mortal danger the Frogs might take the chance to move in. Charlie, honourable gentleman of the old school, offers to step down. No one will hear of it. The banks cough up. Danger averted. Knighthoods all round.'

James nodded. 'And we don't get our fees.'

'That's right. We don't get our fees.'

'So we carry on with Plan A. We carry on with Tadlock.'

'Of course we bloody carry on with Tadlock. We've just got to watch young Ned, that's all. We'll have to think how that's best done.'

Rod Tadlock clicked his fingers for the waiter and told him to fetch the man with the carving trolley. He requested a second and larger helping of the rare roast beef, held his plate out for more potatoes and gravy, and belched.

''Scuse us,' he said. He pointed at his champagne glass with the prong of his fork. 'Gives me gas.'

Nicky Waring glanced quickly around the Savoy Grill to make sure they were not being watched, and laughed. 'How's your suite, Rod?' he asked, beginning to run out of small talk. 'Comfortable?'

Tadlock wiped at his mouth with a bundled combination of his tie and his napkin. He pushed aside his plate and, ignoring the question, said, 'So we're on – right? They want £100 million for 20 per cent, what they get is £90 million for 23, cash up-front, nice simple deal, I go straight on to the board, free hand to the management, my privilege not theirs, everyone's happy. Right?'

'Right,' confirmed Waring, glancing around the room once more, then making a little smiling shushing gesture, forefinger pressed up against his lips. 'Right. They're a little disappointed that it's £90 million rather than £100 million, but I explained that it would be a mistake to allow you too much investment – dilution, you know. Charming man as you are, couldn't be more suitable, but we must ensure that we keep the maximum percentage of the Macaulay Group ownership in the family. That sort of thing.'

'And we've got our little provision safely in the shareholders' agreement? Allowing me sole subscription rights at par in the case of a need for a further equity round? No one else can come in?'

'Not yet – but we will have. If not in the shareholders' agreement, then somewhere equally watertight and binding. We're working on that.'

'That's it. You'd better be. Otherwise the deal's off.'

Waring smiled. 'Of course. That provision is the whole point of the deal. If the Macaulay Group runs out of cash a second time, then you alone have the right to invest into the company. At par.'

'Which means that at that point I'll get control.'

'Which means that the moment that clause is triggered, then you'll own a majority of Macaulay. You'll have control.'

Tadlock nodded. 'And no one can stop me?'

'No one can stop you.'

'OK. Good. That's it. Perfect.' He gazed at Waring silently, and Nicky had the uncomfortable sensation that he was being evaluated on suspicion of probable treachery. 'Why should they agree to it?' Tadlock suddenly asked.

'Oh – because Lord Kimpton will be convinced that your subscription will get the company straight once again and that no more money will ever be needed.'

Tadlock nodded again, still staring at Waring. 'And?'

Waring smiled again, but could feel the sweat beginning to break out on his forehead. 'Well, no more than that really. The creditors are pressing, and the Macaulay family have never been in such an undignified position before. At the last minute you demand one more clause. They won't like that – I'll tell them that *I* don't like that. Hardly cricket. Not good form. But the cash is in your hand. And what you're asking them for covers a situation that will never happen. And I'm going to tell them to at least insist that the provision is time curtailed, so if the company doesn't need more cash within three years then you lose these sole subscription rights.'

'Why are you going to say that?'

'I think it's wiser if I appear to be entirely on their side. You can understand why.'

'I hope I can bloody understand why.'

'Look, Rod, I can absolutely guarantee to you that Macaulay will run out of cash again, and well within the three years. Charlie Kimpton will get through your £90 million like a dose of salts. Leave that to us. Well before the three years is up Macaulay will be yours. We're not talking years. We're talking months.'

'Just remember that I have no interest whatsoever in the garbage companies you've been selling them. What I want is the two newspapers. Them only. As a fit with mine.'

'I understand that, of course. I'm delivering the two news-papers to you, and we'll sell everything else off. And you're then delivering something to me: Waring's will take the sole advisory role in a complete restructuring of all the media inter-ests of your Antipodean & Global Group. One big restruc-turing, maybe simultaneously on Wall Street and London – the papers, the magazines, the television stations, the real estate, the lot. Waring's the sole advisers – with all the fees. 100 per cent.'

A long pause, while Tadlock picked at his teeth, and gazed at Nicky, transparently without enthusiasm.

'Yes,' he said eventually. 'OK. Correct. But first, pull it off. Get me Macaulay. And don't fuck around, Nicky, you hear me? Don't fuck around with me.'

He got up to go, leaving Nicky with the bill.

Over his breakfast at the Savoy that morning Rod Tadlock had read that he was now ranked the fourth richest Australian citizen, and a distance ahead of the fifth. This had amused him, since he had received in the previous hour two telephone calls from Sydney. One was from his personal bankers, concerned at his mounting personal borrowings, and requesting the deposit of further securities. The second was from Antipodean & Global's finance director, who wanted Tadlock's permission to start immediate talks with their advisers as to the prospect of getting away a substantial bond issue, so tight was the company's liquidity at this time.

After his lunch with Nicky Waring, walking along the Strand on his way to his favourite St James's barbers, Tadlock passed a beggar squatting on his heels in a doorway, a cap laid down on the pavement in which lay a collection of small change. The man glanced up in surprise as the expensively dressed man looked at it, burst into laughter, pretended to scoop it up, then proceeded happily on his way. Tadlock had suddenly been struck by the thought that in terms of ready cash the man was actually better off than he was. The houses, the mountain of shares in A&G, the plane, the boat, the Impressionist pictures, the polo ponies – the aggregate value of every asset he owned was vast. But huge as it may have been, it was exceeded by his borrowings, which were now on an heroic scale.

Rod's personal life had been a long journey: too many divorces, too many paternity settlements, too many parties, too many trips to the *chemin de fer* tables – too many of all sorts of things that Tadlock could no longer recall, though he had enjoyed every moment of it. Strolling along, still smiling, he reckoned that he must currently possess the largest negative net worth of anyone in the world and he felt rather proud of that. For he knew, with certainty, that within a few months he'd win the whole lot back. Three deals in recent months that he'd thought would complete, didn't. Any one of those would have put him right. All he needed now was to find three more. Fuck the bank, he thought happily. He might start a bear run on them, sell their shares short. Massively. That would concentrate their minds.

He was reminded of Nicky Waring. Halfway through lunch with Nicky he had suddenly had a very good idea, one of his best. It had come to him like a bolt of lightning and it had the advantage of not only delivering substantial funds in his direction, but at the same time ensuring that Waring's would not benefit, they'd get not a cent. Perfect. Just as it should be.

Rod had a great aversion to Pom poofs, and particularly those who spent their whole time trying to get fees off him. The fact that Nicky Waring, in his middle sixties, was married with five children to a robust young woman many years his junior did not for one instant divert Rod from his presumption as to Nicky's sexuality.

8

They had wondered whether to take Mr Emerson to the funeral, or leave him at home in the bedroom. Foster was in favour of that, worrying that the old man would be confused and frightened, but Hugh had decided that he should go.

So Mr Emerson went, dressed by Foster in his grey tweed suit and his regimental tie, his shoes burnished to a high sheen. Foster had trimmed and brushed his hair, manicured his hands, shaved him, tidied him, and sprinkled a little lavender water around the cuffs and the collar of his shirt, in the way the old man had done for himself in his dignified, almost dandified years. Walking with his stick, discreetly supported by Foster in such a way that his carriage appeared proud and upright, he was escorted to his pew at the very front of the nave, and sat there motionless, gazing straight ahead of him, silent.

Foster made room beside Mr Emerson for Hugh, then steered James into the place on his father's other side, in such a way that James was trapped. Foster, with Nicola crammed in beside him, then retired to the pew behind, immediately at the back of Mr Emerson, in case he needed support. James, who had gone straight to the church, shot Hugh a look of venomous disapproval at his father's presence, before sitting and bowing his head for a moment, hand on forehead, in a perfunctory imitation of a man at prayer.

There was no knowing whether Mr Emerson had understood what the service was about or not. His silence was broken only once, when Hugh, standing to sing the final hymn, glanced down at him and realized that he was murmuring something or another. Hugh hoped that the age-old familiarity of the tune and lines might have served to bring to his father some recognition, some awareness, even some sense of participation.

Let sense be dumb, let flesh retire;
Speak through the earthquake, wind, and fire,
O still small voice of calm.
O still small voice of calm.

Perhaps it had. He had stopped murmuring now and sat as silently as before, as the organ rumbled to its close, and the vicar said the final prayers, and Hugh, whose church-going waxed and waned, and at that time was most distinctly in the latter phase, felt a pang akin to homesickness for the self-assured, practised beauties of formal Anglican worship.

Foster took Mr Emerson by the arm once more, and smiled his way out of the church as the old man tapped his way down the aisle beside him. He put him into the back seat of the elderly family Jaguar, like his shoes polished for the occasion to a high sheen, and placed a plaid blanket around his knees. He sat as upright and unsmiling as a general in an army car. Foster climbed into the driver's seat, and set off to take Mr Emerson to the safe haven of his home and his bedroom. He would let him settle there for a few minutes, then, despite the need to watch over the little wake party that Hugh had insisted on, would bring him tea and his beloved anchovy toast, dress him as comfortably as could be in his corduroys and his dressing gown, and later, after he had brought him a little light supper on a tray, slip him one or two of Dr Winter's knockout pills, and get him to bed. He might well do the same for himself.

Hugh watched the Jaguar set off up the hill, turned to talk to some Rotherhurst neighbours, thanked the vicar and, smiling around at the stragglers, got them all organized into their cars and back to the house.

He saw James bearing down on him just as he and Nicola were climbing into his own car. 'You're coming back, James, I hope?'

James remembered to smile and nod at Nicola, then glanced at his watch. 'No. Yes, for the briefest of seconds. I have to get back to London. But I have to say I'm simply amazed – appalled – that you had the insensitivity to drag poor Father down here to the church, an act of quite staggering cruelty, in my opinion. I'm past disbelief that you didn't have the good manners to consult me over it first.'

Or me when you pulled the plug, as you called it, on Mother, Hugh thought, but left it unsaid. He looked at his brother now with a rare, perhaps inaugural sense of positive dislike. James was these days not simply an overweight, over-bearing ass; he had grown into something worse – a bully, and a venomous one at that. If James attacked Foster about this when he got to the house, then Hugh promised himself there would be a quarrel between them to end all quarrels.

But he replied now as calmly as he could. 'A matter of

opinion,' he said, then held up his hand to stop James from continuing in the same vein as before. Pausing, he pulled himself together. 'Come on, James,' he said. 'Now's not the moment. Let me give you a lift up to the house and we can talk about something else.'

James shrugged, gestured to his driver to follow them and, Nicola in the back, climbed in beside Hugh. 'Actually there is something else I wanted to mention to you, Hugh.'

There was a sudden and untypical conciliatory note in his voice, and Hugh wondered what was to follow.

'It's a small thing, but it suddenly came into my mind on the drive down, and I thought I'd sound you out on it. You probably have not the slightest idea what's going on, and there's no reason why you should, but have you heard that the Macaulay Group have got themselves into some difficulty, and that the family have decided to do the sensible thing in the circumstances and bring in another shareholder? You know that Waring's are their advisers, I'm sure. I only mention it because I know that you and Ned Macaulay are still as thick as thieves. Aren't you a minority shareholder in his Banville Trust, or whatever it's called?'

Hugh nodded. 'Yes, but a very minor stake. I don't know, 5 per cent or something. It's just me and Ned. Why do you ask?'

'No real reason. Banville hold a significant portion of Ned's shareholding in Macaulay, so it's a factor in all this, bound to be.'

'In all this?'

'In this business of bringing a new shareholder on to the board. Rod Tadlock. You may have come across him. Splendid chap, Australian. He'll be the new investor, subject to board approval, and he couldn't be a more happy choice in my opinion. I just wondered if you'd heard anything from Ned at all? I imagine he's delighted. He'd be a fool not to be.'

Hugh wondered what James was up to. Why this absurdly prolix approach? He knew of Rod Tadlock, and had once met him briefly. One of the A&G subsidiaries, a book and magazine publisher, acted as Emerson Publishers' agent in that part of the world. But what was all this about? Was James nervous of something?

'No,' Hugh said. 'Nothing. Should I have done?' He turned the car up through the gates, James's very grand German sedan following close behind, the capped and uniformed Waring's chauffeur at the wheel. 'Do you want a message passed to Ned, or anything like that?'

'Not at all. I just wondered if he'd briefed you on what was happening, that's all. Nothing more.'

'Why should he brief me? As I said, I have 5 per cent of Banville at the very most. Banville is Ned's. Whatever he wants is fine by me.'

'Of course, of course,' James said, manoeuvring himself out of his seat to greet the vicar's wife, all charm now and fluency, of a florid style that, Hugh mused, watching him, was somehow particular to overweight Englishmen of a certain age and class.

Hugh had just lied twice to his brother, at least by omission, and he was rather pleased with himself. First, Ned had of course talked to him about Rod Tadlock, and Hugh had passed on some mild gossip about him. And second, when Hugh had first become a shareholder in Banville, Ned had insisted that a provision should be included in the company's statutes that Hugh must be a co-signatory beside Ned in any future transaction. So Hugh was certainly briefed by Ned in Macaulay's affairs, and he would be again, in formal detail, when the time came for Ned to cast Banville's vote on letting in this outside shareholder.

James is up to something, Hugh thought. How ironic! For the first time ever he and James were crossing professional paths. From the look of it, Hugh's tiny shareholding in Ned's company might prove to be of influence. It was up to Ned of course. But there was something in James's manner that was very peculiar indeed.

James and Nicky Waring glanced at each other. Nicky spoke first. 'Giles – I have to tell you that James and I do have an agenda in bringing you here tonight with us on your own.'

Giles nodded cooperatively. Of course they had. They always did.

James gestured to the wine waiter for cognac for them all, then took over from Waring, leaning forward on the table, all concentration and resolve. 'Nicky and I feel that this is the moment to take you into our confidence, Giles. And we feel bad in many ways in taking the route we are now going to map out for you, because both of us – all of us at Waring's – but particularly Nicky and I, have known and worked with your father for so long.'

'For *so* long,' echoed Nicky, pulling deeply on his cigar.

'Well, we just love Charlie, to tell the truth,' James continued, 'we just love him, and there we are.'

'Love the guy,' agreed Nicky, shaking his head at the depth

of his devotion whilst nosing his cognac glass and tapping his cigar ash onto the Rules's carpet.

'So you must understand that everything we're going to say now has this in the background. Our very sincere respect and admiration for your father's achievements,' James went on. 'Love the guy,' Nicky said once more, nodding at Giles, and James repressed a flicker of irritation from crossing his face. There were moments when Nicky rather lost the plot. Time he was put out to grass probably. In his middle sixties now, he'd gone on too long. Sad, but that's how it goes. Time for James to take over the top job, and in doing so airbrush out that little tit Jason. Mustn't hang around, though. Maybe now was the time to see quietly how much support there might be among their colleagues for a change of . . .

Giles was gazing at him expectantly.

'Look, Giles,' he continued, pulling himself together, 'given the delicacy of this situation we have to ask you to allow us to speak in absolute confidence, with total certainty that what we are going to say to you stays with the three of us, and goes no further. Not to your father, not to Ned, not to anybody.'

'Ned?' Giles asked. 'Why mention Ned?'

'We do particularly ask you not to speak to Ned,' James said gravely, 'and if you bear with us for a few moments you'll understand why. Giles – I hardly know how to say this – it's a very delicate and sensitive matter, and there are loyalties here that are too painful to trespass on.' James glanced at Nicky, then hurried on before he had a chance to reprise his 'Love the guy' speech. 'But this is what we feel we have to put to you. Your father has done a marvellous job . . .'

'Quite wonderful,' murmured Nicky.

'But frankly the years roll by, and time goes on, and once you reach a certain age none of us, and I mean none of us, are as sharp and as acute as we once were. And when that happens it's the duty of one's colleagues and – yes – one's dearest friends, sometimes by request, sometimes by persuasion, sometimes, frankly, by coercion, to do the deed and clear out the dying wood, and get the ship moving again.' Out of the corner of his eye James could saw Waring glance sharply up at him. He ignored him, and continued.

'Well – I say this with the greatest respect for all Macaulay's wonderful achievements over the years. I really mean that, Giles. But, for all that, you directors, custodians of your family's heritage, and that of your staff and your pensioners, let's not forget them, are, for the first time in your history looking at a situation of very great peril.'

Waring nodded gravely, and muttered something about the absolute sanctity of the staff and pensioners' interests, and the need to never, ever forget that.

'Nicky and I wonder if that's really sunk home. We do wonder if you've really taken the whole force of that on board . . . Not you, Giles, you yourself are as sharp as a barrel-load of monkeys, but . . . some of you,' James finished lamely, put off his stride by an uneasy feeling that he had rather mixed his metaphors.

Waring took the opportunity to take over. 'What James is saying to you, Giles, is this. Number one – we have a deeply troubled Macaulay Group. Number two – we at Waring's came up with a solution, and I'm pretty damned pleased with this, given that the problem was presented to us so late in the day.

We came up with Rod Tadlock. Now we can go ahead with Rod's subscription. It's your family company, and if that's what you want, then so be it. Neither James nor I would dream of dissuading you.'

'Of course not,' James interposed. 'Never. We brought Tadlock to you, after all.'

'Absolutely,' Waring agreed. 'Tadlock is in one sense a good solution. But only if it really *is* the case that the best alternative is not possible. That is the family putting in the money themselves.'

'Oh, I assure you that it's beyond us,' Giles said. 'None of us has access to anything approaching £90 million in cash at short notice. Houses could be sold, I suppose, some securities, pictures, my father has a couple of racehorses, but no – really – even in aggregate, all of us in it together, £50 million in immediate cash is well beyond the family, let alone £90 million. And even if the family could manage to raise cash to that amount, would we simply be looking at another call on us a year or so down the line? Then what would happen?'

James and Waring looked at each other. James shook his head, and turned back to Giles. 'God, you're bright, Giles, you really are,' he said, shaking his head in admiration. 'So perceptive. And that's the point. That's why we at Waring's believe . . .'

He paused and glanced across at Nicky. The dramatic tension rose. There was a long pause. James leant forward. 'We believe that your father should stand down. We believe that you, Giles, should take his place. It's you who should take the helm of your great company. The time is ripe for change. Macaulay's future lies not in your father's hands, but in yours. It has to happen. Marvellous as Charlie has been.' James clenched his buttocks in anticipation.

'Love the guy,' Nicky said.

James fixed Giles with an intense stare. 'And, Giles, it's more than that. We believe, Nicky and I believe, Waring's believes, that not only should you take over sole leadership of Macaulay, but that it should be you personally, Giles, who puts in the £90 million.'

Giles grimaced. 'James, I really thought that I'd explained that that's absolutely impossible. Not only that, but . . .'

'You must hear us out,' Waring interrupted. 'You'll see we've done a lot of work on this. We've prepared a deal that's not only good for you personally, but good for Macaulay. And Macaulay, let me say it again, is a client we at Waring's are so deeply proud to represent. Deeply proud.'

'And honoured,' James added.

'That's right. Most deeply honoured,' Waring agreed. 'Now, James and I have a story to tell you. A most disgraceful, dishonourable story. But we have to tell it.'

He paused, and shot a glance at James. James, sombre-faced, gestured to him to continue.

'We introduced Rod Tadlock to you with the best motives in the world. You know we'd die for Macaulay, if we had to. We had to provide a solution, and quickly. We dropped everything, James and I, we flew to Sydney, we talked to Tadlock, we reassured him, we persuaded him, we brought him to London, we introduced you, it all seemed to go well. Until today.' He stopped, shaking his head, too shocked to continue.

James, reflecting that he hadn't been to Australia in five or more years, and nor had Nicky Waring, picked up the thread.

'Today Mr Tadlock asked us to do the most astonishing thing. He asked us to slip into the agreement – at the very last moment, mind – he wanted us to slip into the contract a little clause. A harmless little clause you might have felt, Giles – but Waring's is cut from a rather different piece of cloth than the Rod Tadlocks of this world. Waring's plays its cricket straight, and down the middle. No secrets, no tricks, no taking unfair advantage of the other side's position. We're an old-fashioned firm, with old-fashioned values. The City of London is not what it was, but Waring's is unchanged. What you see is what you get. Our word is our bond.'

'Absolutely,' agreed Nicky. 'Honest, transparent, incorruptible, that's our creed. Our clients come first. Our own interests we never even consider. Never give them a thought. You'll not find many like us these days.'

'You won't find an advisory bank like us *anywhere* now,' James insisted. 'You won't find . . .'

Giles felt he had grasped the point. 'So today Tadlock asked you to introduce a clause?' he interrupted. 'Saying what exactly?'

James nodded. 'Yes. Today he asked us to slip in – and not "introduce", Giles, as you put it – slip in a clause that gives him sole subscription rights over the next three years. Do you understand? He alone amongst the shareholders will be allowed to acquire more shares. You can imagine what we thought about that!'

Giles affected horror. 'Sole subscription rights! I see!' Actually that sounded to him like rather a good idea. Tadlock clearly had more money than sense. None of the rest of them had any sufficient ready money. It sounded like a very good scheme to empty that ghastly Australian's wallet as often as possible. Why not? 'Right!' He added, hoping that would pass as an appropriate tone of shocked comprehension.

'And we know exactly where that will lead, don't we?' said Waring. 'You've got it in one, I can see. Control for Tadlock, complete control, of one of Britain's finest private companies.'

'The cuckoo in the nest, that's the game he's playing,' James murmured. 'The bastard.'

'But . . .' How could Giles ask this without appearing totally naive? 'Well, to be honest with you I'm not exactly clear how that clause would lead to him acquiring control. First, we may not need more money over the next three years, though I admit I did earlier suggest we might. And secondly, if we did need any more money, surely then we might be able to attract more debt again, and use that instead?'

'Two things there,' James replied, 'but they make up into one. Tadlock is a very determined man. As a director he would be in a strong position to pretend a public concern over the strength of the firm's balance sheet. Hadn't realized the full horror of Macaulay's exposures at the time he put his £90 million in; a black hole in the accounts; hints of impropriety and concealment on the old family board – all that sort of nonsense. The Macaulay newspapers keep mum, as well they might, but the rest of the press will love it and run Tadlock's views as a front-page lead. The lending banks don't like the look of that, independent accountants put in to report, lots of whispering, questions in the House, all very nasty indeed. Heads might roll.'

Waring pushed aside his coffee cup, and leaned forward. 'I wasn't going to tell you this, Giles, but I feel now I need to. Tadlock tried to drag us into this today as well. He had the gall to suggest that we took a certain series of actions that would cause Macaulay's liquidity to come under threat once more, so that he could use that clause.' He looked very solemn. 'I ask you to forget you ever heard this, Giles. The very fact that we were approached in this way demeans the Waring's name, lessens us in the eyes of our peers. Please forget I ever told you what happened.'

There was a dignified silence as the three of them, staring at the table, considered the horrors of what Tadlock had tried to do.

'So we should keep him out,' Giles said, 'I can see that. But we'll have to find someone else and I do realize that won't be easy. Time is so against us.'

'Indeed,' Waring said. 'How right you are. But James and I are agreed on this. It's more straightforward than you realize.' He looked at James, then turned back. 'The solution is right here before us, Giles. It's you.' He paused. 'You're it, Giles,' he said. 'You're the solution. You're the future for Macaulay. And you know what? Your family are lucky to have you, very lucky indeed!'

'Absolutely,' James agreed. 'God, they are.'

'We accept of course that funding to this level is not possible for you. We've dealt with it. We have the £90 million available for you – immediately. All you have to do, Giles, is to give the word.'

Giles nodded. He hadn't the first idea what Waring was talking about. They were expecting him to say something. He licked his lips. 'Give the word?'

'Give the word,' James said. 'But first you must understand what Waring's have worked to arrange for you. It is no small thing, as you will see. We'd never in a thousand years do this for anyone else. We're devoted to Macaulay, for our sins, and that's the end of it.'

'And to you personally, Giles,' Waring added.

'Absolutely,' James agreed. 'That goes without saying. That's why we're here. And this is what we've done.'

And they told him. As the deal rolled out before him, his attitude moved from polite scepticism, to quickening interest, to intense excitement. He was going to be rich. Not just paper-rich, as he had been all his life, now he was going to be cash-rich. Very cash rich, and with that cash he was going to achieve his lifetime ambition: the development of the finest private marine biology laboratory in the world. The Giles Macaulay Centre for Marine Biological Research. This was the only true ambition Giles held. Increasingly so, the more incompetent he became in the normal interplays of conventional life.

He hated their world, but what clever people Nicky and James were. They were worth every penny of the £8 million in fees that they explained was to be the price of their completing this transaction on his and Macaulay's behalf. He'd been only too happy to countersign the letter to that effect James found he'd happened to bring with him, tucked away in his wallet. It was an inexplicably ludicrous sum, but they had come up with a masterstroke. Waring's had done it again.

Rod Tadlock looked across the desk at the tiny, shrunken figure of Nathan Epstein, and wondered how best to handle him.

Tadlock was not at his best with people like Nathan. Give him one of his fellow Australian entrepreneurs, and he would eat them for breakfast – puce-faced, loud-mouthed simple-tons, the lot of them. But Epstein – New York publisher, media mogul, Hollywood player, newspaper owner and real estate king – was one of a different league.

Epstein had heard much about this Tadlock. He had rather liked the sound of him. He was a gunslinger of the old school, that was clear, and Epstein had a soft spot for gunslingers. And, as Epstein watched him through his drooping, tired eyelids, he could see that he was taut and nervous in his presence. He would ensure that he remained that way. To that end Nathan allowed an expression of distaste to show itself clearly, if fleetingly, in his face, as Rod allowed a drop of coffee to fall from his raised cup and on to his shirt front.

'Mr Tadlock, I have enjoyed your description of events at the Macaulay Group very much. You have a colourful sense of narrative. Nothing of what you say surprises me, aside from, if I may say so, your several embroideries. I know Lord Kimpton moderately well, and have met not the older son, the heir, but the younger, reputedly brighter one, Edward. Ned. Kimpton and his son Giles have made the most unutterable nonsense of their affairs, of course, and you are certainly quite right in that. But, my dear Mr Tadlock . . .'

Epstein spread his hands wide in a gesture of bewilderment, and smiled coldly with his mouth alone. He left the sentence unfinished, and decided to submit this not wholly unappealing man to his favourite technique, silence. Make him take up the running, and see where that might lead, to Epstein's advantage. Over the next hour, at the very most. Then he had an afternoon appointment that he had been looking forward to all morning. A tryst, repeated every twenty-one days exactly, when Epstein was in New York, with a certain adorably plump and carnal pair of sisters tucked away in a discreet little apartment on the Upper West Side. Mrs Epstein, Dolly, was an excellent wife and an admirably devoted mother and grandmother, but not, for some years, a demanding woman in the physical side of marriage. Mercifully, Epstein thought, as a momentary vision of her person flitted across his mind.

He gazed at Tadlock, not unkindly, and said not a word, but by a flicker of his eyebrows he somehow managed to convey that he was prepared to hear more, but without any great enthusiasm for it.

Rod wondered whether to protest at the accusation of embroideries to the tale, but decided, wisely, to ignore it. Epstein was an ace poker player, a class act.

'So that's where we are,' Tadlock was saying. 'That's what will happen. I invest £90 million to get them out of their hole. They think that's enough. I know it isn't. I'm making sure it isn't. They'll have to take in more equity, and under the contract that equity can only come from me. By the terms of the clause, it's me and not them that decides the quantum of cash the company needs. I will take the view it needs plenty. Enough to give me control, investing at par. Then – bingo! – Macaulay is mine. The newspapers, their other investments, the lot.'

Epstein moved not a muscle. He was totally silent.

Tadlock could hear the infantile braggadocio of his own voice, but blundered on. 'But it's better than that. There's another deal sitting in this situation, and that's why I'm here today. A better deal – one for both of us.'

Was that the very faintest flicker of amusement that passed over Epstein's features? Whatever it was, the man still said nothing. Tadlock hurried on. 'You tell me you know the Macaulay family. Fine people and all that – but boy! So I see a tremendous opportunity for myself here. But the opportunity is actually much bigger than it appears. Because I'd love to own Macaulay – but there's something I want more than that, great as those two Macaulay national newspapers are.'

He paused. Epstein's silence was forcing him to play his cards too quickly. But he was where he was, and now he must get to his point. 'Mr Epstein – here's the deal.'

He paused again. Still no reaction from Nathan. He remained totally inert, watching Tadlock, expressionless. 'You and I go in as partners, signed and sealed before we get there. I front it up for us. I invest £90 million into Macaulay. A little later, I invest more. Then I have control. When I get control you and I move to stage two. Now we're on to something huge. Listen to this. Your TransAmerican Communications gets the two Macaulay newspapers – both of them. That's not all. With them you get my Australian papers as well. Did you hear that? All my Australian papers – the *Antipodean*, the *Globe*, the regionals, the lot. With those plus the Macaulay papers and your US titles what have you got? The most powerful newspaper grouping in the entire English-speaking world.'

Again he paused. Nothing from Epstein. He ploughed on. 'That's what you get, and it's as big as that. This is what I get. It's less, but I accept that, because it's what I want. I get TransAmerican's television stations here in America. I get TransAmerican's shareholding in the Hollywood studio. And on top of that I get cash, $300 million, US. So that's the deal. You get the newspapers. I take the television and movie interests. Plus the cash.'

Now Epstein did react. He laughed, and so uproariously and for so long that Tadlock thought he was going to choke

– preferably to death, the little bastard. Then he wiped his eyes and reached for his carafe of iced water.

'Tell me, Mr Tadlock, Rod. May I call you Rod? Tell me this. Where, my dear Rod, are you going to find the £90 million in the first place, let alone whatever you then need to obtain control? Let alone, if you'll forgive me for asking, the price of your taxi fare back to your hotel? From me?'

He reached into a drawer, took out a file and, still chuckling, pushed it across the desk to Tadlock. 'There we are,' he said. 'I was embarrassed for you to read it. You have here my . . . let's say my colleague's report on the state of your personal finances, and those separately of Antipodean & Global. Keep them – I have no further interest in them. You're broke, my dear Rod. Dead, flat, broke. So is your company. Now what do you have to say to that?'

Rod Tadlock bore the ups and downs of life with cheerful impunity – indifference really, as he considered his entire life, business and the rest of it, to be one great extended game of poker, and it was a fool who spent his time cursing his cards or the fluctuations of his luck.

Broke or rich, holding aces or not, the trick was to look a winner. And you only look like a winner if you feel like a winner. There was no difficulty in that for Rod. He had never for one second doubted the certainty of his victory in life since his days as a schoolboy urchin in one of the poorest areas of Parramatta. Officially, he had earned his money at the pensioners' home, cleaning toilets, sweeping floors and polishing shoes. Unofficially, and more profitably, he was a bookies' runner. The old men put their shoes out each morning for cleaning, placing their bets in the toes. That evening their shoes would be returned, with their winnings tucked inside, less 5 per cent for Rod. He got another 5 per cent from the bookies on all bets made. Then he had the entire proceeds of his Saturday afternoon collection box, which bore the legend: 'The Heroes of Gallipoli Families Support Fund'.

By fourteen he had left school; by fifteen he was a clerk in an insurance office. By eighteen he was selling, on the side, discounted car insurance policies from a rival firm. He was caught, and fired. But by now he had a Rolls-Royce. He was unable to drive it, but he was on his way. He bought and sold a crayfish cannery. His first foray into newspaper ownership was by means of a Brisbane paper in financial distress. For this he paid one dollar for the equity and the assumption of all the debt. He discharged the debt by paying ten cents on the dollar. He found another distressed newspaper in Adelaide, and did exactly the same. The Antipodean & Global Group was born. Further newspapers were added, followed by radio stations in Queensland; a book publisher, which acquired a second, and then a third; a Melbourne television station; real estate on the Sydney shore; three adjacent vineyards in the Hunter Valley. The Group just grew and grew, fuelled by debt which the banks couldn't lend to him fast enough. More real estate. More radio stations. Mines in Western Australia. Hotels in Adelaide. Office buildings in Perth. Luxury resorts on the Gold Coast.

Rod met the Queen. Rod met Don Bradman. He had the Midas touch. Antipodean & Global's stock soared in a bull market, then corrected, then soared once more. This was the great Australian company. This was the model for the future, commentators said, so safely spread in its range and the diversity of its interests. The mines weren't doing so well – but the vineyards flourished. Advertising revenues were down – but real estate boomed. There was balance. All seemed triumphant. All seemed an All Australian Poor Boy Makes Good morality tale.

But Rod never believed a word of it.

He dallied with the idea of moving his personal cash – during a brief moment when he actually had some – to the safe haven of Liechtenstein or the Cayman Islands, but he never got around to it. He continued exactly as before, and why not? He borrowed more and more money. He made more and more acquisitions. He went international. A golf course in Surrey. A hotel in Bali. A shopping mall in Copenhagen. And for himself a new plane, a new wife, and a new duplex, in Monte Carlo.

Then came the calls: one from his bank manager, and the second from the panic-stricken finance director. Rod found both hilarious. What was this, for heaven's sake? A little local difficulty. A poker play. Time for holding one's nerve and some lateral thinking and manipulation. In other words, life. Rod loved life. Rod was bored when things were easy. Rod liked danger. Danger was the time when winners won.

So if Nathan Epstein thought he had humiliated Rod, he was wrong. It was just the tonic that Rod needed to fire him up again. Now he understood the man. The card that Epstein had played on him was a familiar one. Research the guy a little, find out the bad news (and everyone has a pocket of personal bad news somewhere or other if you look hard enough), allow him to get into an exposed position by pitching too far and too wildly, allow him to brag and bluster. Let him go on with that until he's like an overripe plum on the tree, then hit him with what you've got. Screw him.

Rod strolled along Lexington Avenue in truly excellent humour. With the hot pretzel stands on every block, New York smelt the way it should. It looked the way it should too, with the cloudless blue skies of early fall, and bright sunlight beating down on to the sheeting aluminium and reflective glass of the Citicorp building. One day maybe he'd move here himself. Get this little liquidity problem behind him, and away he'd go. Most of all he'd like a Hollywood studio, and that was why he had made his offer to Epstein; some US newspapers, just to show Epstein what he'd missed; real estate in Florida; television stations; hotels. Just like Australia – but bigger, much bigger than Australia of course. Maybe he'd grown out of Australia, just a little. Perhaps he'd even become an American citizen – who knows?

Meanwhile – the Macaulay Group. What a wonderful way through he had now thought of! One of his best. He'd need to play his cards very carefully, and it was a little difficult as he'd hardly met the fellow, but that was the way to go now, there was no doubt about that. He'd get back to London on the morning plane, and start things moving.

9

Dolly Epstein awoke with a start, and found the young man was still sprawled across her bed on his stomach, snoring gently. Poor lamb, he looked exhausted, and now that she looked at him properly, rather underfed. She turned on to her other side and searched on the carpet for her watch. She liked nakedness when she was doing it, total nakedness, and even a watch or a bracelet subtracted from that.

She found the watch, and in her long-sightedness, holding it outstretched, saw that it was already nearly five o'clock. She must hurry. Not only was there this young man to dress and get out of the building before Nathan came home, but she had an appointment across town for drinks at six, and Dolly liked to be punctual.

She eased herself off the bed in search of her dressing gown – to be naked and wobbly and uninhibited in flagrante was one thing, but she didn't want to make a fool of herself post the event. Particularly with someone as absurdly good-looking as this adorable boy.

When securely wrapped and modest, and with her face touched up a trifle, she kissed him on the cheek to wake him.

When he was dressed she kissed him chastely once more, wrote him a nice little cheque, and smuggled him out down the back elevator. What a sweetie. She'd have him around again. Quite soon.

She glanced again at her watch, and had one final search around the apartment for any morsel of incriminatory evidence. There was none. She put on a pretty cocktail dress and her full make-up, and was out in the street and hailing a taxi safely before Nathan, himself as punctual as a clock, was scheduled to appear home. Actually, now that she thought about it, she remembered that he'd said that today he wouldn't be home until late.

This James Emerson fellow was staying at the Shrewsbury. The hotel was grotesquely overpriced, but the English were all the same. Put the poor impoverished loves on an airplane and pick up their expenses and they spent like they'd never seen money before. He sounded charming on the phone, and he'd reminded her that his brother Hugh was the London publisher for dear Saul. However, she was uncertain why he wanted to meet. He had said something about her charitable appeal, but in her deafness she wasn't quite sure what. But she knew of Waring's of course, plus he had the dearest accent, so here she was.

James came down from his suite to greet her, then took her up again, all smiles and English manners, and one of those silly over-styled suits and striped shirts that those people wore like a goddamn uniform. He sat her down and poured her a glass of champagne. Who in their right minds would pay for Krug, for God's sake, at the Shrewsbury of all places? Then they had chattered away inconsequentially and charmingly for a quarter of an hour or so before he came to any sort of point. Even then his initial approach was prolix, to say the least. But suddenly, abruptly, so much so that she almost choked on her canapé, she realized what this overweight James Emerson was up to and where he was coming from – and she blushed crimson.

James had explained it. Waring's wanted Nathan to sell three of his East Coast newspapers to Macaulay, in a deal to be financed by Waring's, with appropriate fees. It was to be delayed until there had been a change of management and control at Macaulay, the details of which James kept unspecified. They had approached Nathan already, and he had refused. Not only had he refused but he had threatened to report Waring's to the regulatory authorities. Waring's had been forced to take certain protective measures against this contingency, as Dolly would understand was the norm in these circumstances.

'There are those who might criticize us for such measures, Dolly, of course. Those who might feel that we overreacted a little, misunderstood Nathan in some way. But, be that as it may, we sensed that Nathan seemed to see us as the enemy. We felt we needed to protect ourselves therefore, and to do that we needed to learn a little more about Nathan than was in the public domain, let's put it that way. A touch of the private man behind the public face.' He paused. 'So that's what we did. And we found some surprising things. Most I wouldn't dream of burdening you with. But this I will. We don't think you're aware of this fact, and now that I'm about to tell you I recoil from doing so. But I must. Dolly – Nathan is unfaithful to you, continually.'

James went to his attaché case, took out two files, and

handed Dolly one of them. 'You'll find all the detail in there,' he said, 'and I can assure you that the research is of the very highest reliability.'

He paused while she quickly leafed through the file, closed it, and put it down on the glass table before her. She looked at him, wondering how on earth she was going to respond. But then he opened the other file, skimmed it through, shut it and handed that to her as well. 'And here's the other file, Dolly,' he said. 'Your file. It's much the same story, wouldn't you say?'

As she looked through that too, Dolly felt tired, exhausted even, the heavy weight of post middle-aged defeat upon her. She put the file down on top of the other, and wondered if her best line of defence might not be to insult him for his impertinence, gather the files to her and leave, saying that she was taking them straight to her lawyer. But she lost the moment by hesitating, and now he was speaking again.

'Dolly,' he said, holding up his hand. 'You mustn't misunderstand me. Waring's would never contemplate using that file against you. It exists because of a total misunderstanding between us and the . . . the research operatives, let's call them that.'

'Yes?' said Dolly, calm enough now to present sarcasm.

'Yes,' James replied. 'Absolutely! Look, the file is yours. Burn it, destroy it, forget all about it.'

'And the other file?'

James paused, and refreshed her glass, which Dolly allowed, wondering at her uncharacteristically weak compliance.

'We mean Nathan no harm. We think he's a great man, and all we want to do is to work with him. Now, with that in mind, here's what we think you might like to do. You say to Nathan that I've talked with you and that I've given you this very incriminating file about his personal behaviour. That you're very angry with me and Waring's for the way we've behaved, more angry with Waring's even than you are with him, though you think he's behaved appallingly. Remember, Dolly, that he has no knowledge of *your* file! And bad as Waring's behaviour has been, the three newspapers they're after are not amongst those that Nathan values most highly. So wouldn't it be easier to let Waring's have them? Otherwise, the next thing we know is that all this horrid and humiliating stuff about Nathan is going to be all over the press.'

He watched her benevolently. 'And you know what we can do for you in return?' He went to his attaché case, opened it, and showed her a cheque made out in favour of 'The Dolly Epstein Orphans of Israel Appeal', and there were enough noughts appended to it to make even Dolly stop for thought. He put the cheque back in the case, and returned to the table.

'I think we could help each other, Dolly, don't you? Remember it was Nathan and not us who cut up rough first. But that's his way, he's no patsy in these things, and we respect him for it. All we want is for our little deal to go through. And when it does – that's it! We intend no harm to Nathan after that whatsoever, I can assure you of that. None at all,' he repeated, showing her to the door. 'And none to you either, Dolly!'

He tapped the file that she held under her arm, the file on her own private life, and smiled most charmingly, reassuringly, as the elevator doors opened to return her to the hotel lobby.

★

James reached across the glass table, and pulled back towards him the file which Nathan had thrown down in disgust. Nathan was sitting in the same chair in James's suite as Dolly had been in barely an hour before.

'If you ever use that on Dolly I'll kill you,' Nathan said. 'You and Nicky Waring both. This is our business, Dolly's and mine, and no one else's. I won't have my wife humiliated by you or anyone else. Do you understand?'

'Nathan, Nathan.' James spread his arms, his face radiating friendship, concern, and bafflement at being cruelly misunderstood. 'I've admitted it – we made a little boob. A big boob. Our security people didn't understand their instructions. But anyone who deals with Waring's knows that we have an automatic check and search system on all our clients, and our clients' clients if it comes to that. Somehow Dolly got included in the system and the next thing we know is that this file on her appears on Nicky's desk. He's appalled, as you can imagine. So he puts me on the very next plane to New York to show you what's happened, and to apologize from the very bottom of our hearts. Dolly's file is yours to do anything you want with. And my apologies, Nicky's apologies, Waring's apologies, are brought to you with every drop, every last drop of sincerity we can muster.'

He shook his head in emphasis of the solemnity of his statement, and Epstein tried to stop a flicker of disgusted amusement, almost admiration, from crossing his face. Waring's were so appalling they defied belief. There was no one else like them.

'You can cut out that bullshit,' he said. 'I'll say this one last time, read my lips. If you or Nicky or anyone else at Waring's – by a silly accident or not, heartbreakingly sorry or

A summary of the agreement would be co-signed the next day by both of them, then delivered by them in person and together to a strong box at Lloyds Bank in Knightsbridge, and only the two of them would be key-holders. The key system would be of the double security kind: their two keys would be of separate specification and both would have to be employed simultaneously in order for the strong box to be opened. Thus they were ensuring that there would be no signed copies of the document floating around anywhere.

'That's it, I think,' Nicky said. We've been through it twice, but we should do so again if any points are unclear to you. Or have we clarity?'

It was confirmed that they had, and the two men shook hands without any attempt at cordiality, and departed their separate ways.

What I do for Waring's, Nicky thought, and smiled to himself. All this talk these days of money-laundering, but who's in a position to judge whom? Why shouldn't there be a little privacy and confidentiality in these things? What do people think the Swiss banks have been up to all these years? If them, why not us? What business is it of mine or anyone else's where the money came from? Or if its owners would now like it churned and rerouted a little?

But I tell you one thing, Nicky Waring, he said to himself, turning up the collar of his Burberry as the drizzle thickened into rain, you charge too little. Twelve and a half million pounds for a transaction of this sort is really not enough, given the risk of potential unpleasantness and the good name of Waring's.

Maybe that simpleton Giles should pay a larger slice. Where

were they at the moment? Eight million in fees from him. Twelve and a half million from these ghastly New Jersey people. Twenty million plus in total. That was as much as they would probably have made from a capital restructuring of Antipodean & Global, Tadlock being Tadlock. But it was too late to get more than twelve and a bit million with these vile people. Never too late to change the rules for Giles, though. He was as dim as Charlie. Dimmer. And that really was saying something.

And with the Eton memory in his mind of the fifteen-year-old Charlie Macaulay, acne-covered, terminally at the bottom of every class in every subject, Nicky Waring emerged from the gate into Battersea Park Road and, chuckling, climbed into his taxi.

Nathan Epstein had now travelled to London twice in the last three months, which for him was twice too often. He was a poor traveller: he felt exhausted, was disoriented by the time change and he missed Dolly. But as he went to the door of his hotel suite to admit Ned Macaulay he felt his energies return.

He offered him a drink, poured out a glass of Vichy for himself, and sat him down. He'd relax him for ten minutes with gossip, his alternative technique to deploying silence. He embarked upon a beguiling stream of stories, punctuated by name-dropping: improprieties in the Secretary of State's tax records, as yet unknown to the media; the precise interest rate cut coming from the Fed the following day; advice to short on the Florida & Tallahassee Bank, as he knew from the very mouth of the President of the Bank of Brazil that they were about to default on a major loan with them. Nathan in full flow tended to bewitch himself as much as his listener. In a moment he'd get to the point but meanwhile, telling a Jewish joke, which was actually quite a compliment to Ned as he normally reserved them only for fellow Jews, and those of long acquaintance, Nathan registered how intelligent Ned was. He'd heard rumours of Ned's indolence, it was true, but he'd done pretty well, Epstein imagined. And who was Nathan to judge Ned's life anyway? His own son, alcoholic and unhappy, living in sordid decline in a mountain shack in Nevada, the last that Nathan had heard of him, was a living witness to Nathan's own rank incompetence as a father of adult children, and how well he knew it.

'Now, to business, Ned,' he said, pointing a tiny hand at Ned's glass for a second drink, which Ned refused. 'I started to examine the Macaulay situation a couple of weeks ago, to see if there was anything I could take advantage of. At that time I thought that what was going to be on the table was a bona fide funding offer from Rod Tadlock. Shortly after that I verified for myself that Tadlock, and indeed Antipodean & Global, currently has no access to funds. I assume Waring's aren't aware of this. The only way that Tadlock could raise the £90 million is to be bankrolled for it by another party, which is why he came to see me. If he does raise the first tranche, then he will certainly be able to raise the second. For that's where the win is, of course: control of the whole group – and at a knockdown price.'

Ned nodded, and watched. He was still very much on his guard. He could understand Epstein's interest in the travails of his family firm, but why had Nathan approached him, and not

Giles or his father? Nathan couldn't know that as far as Ned was concerned the papers were going to stay in the family. He'd picked the wrong Macaulay. He realized that they had both been silent for a moment or two, and wondered how to respond.

But, as if he had direct access to Ned's thoughts, Epstein ploughed on. 'You must be wondering whether my agenda is to take the company from you and your family as cheaply and as quickly as possible. I would love to get possession of the *Daily Meteor* and the *Sunday Correspondent*, of course I would. I have no newspapers in Britain, and even today they are both marvellous properties. But you want to get control for yourself. Am I right?'

Ned nodded. He could see no point in lying to this oddly persuasive man.

'That's fine. That's as it should be. I can work within that. Perhaps in the future good things may flow to me from my helping you now. Maybe one day we will put TransAmerican and Macaulay together. But that's for another time and another deal and I have no intention whatsoever of trying to mix the two deals up. OK? Do you accept that? Meanwhile, what I'll gain is a very pleasant little profit from my participation in the public offering, when it comes. I'm looking forward to that.'

Ned shrugged and smiled, but somehow it sounded too easy. 'Of course I accept what you say,' he said, because he had to. 'But I do need to understand exactly what you have in mind. And why.'

Hugh had meant to return Ned's call earlier, but had been delayed in various meetings at the office. In the end it was evening before Hugh reached him, and Ned was already at home. Hugh could hear the cheerful noise of small children being bathed for bed, and Ned, having picked up the telephone, immediately dropped it to rush away and rescue somebody.

'Sorry about that. Look, something rather unexpected has turned up and we need to talk about it. I have to get back to these people tomorrow morning, and you and I need to be of one mind over it. Hell.'

Again the receiver was dropped, and Hugh could hear Ned call out to Daisy, then talk with her about something before he returned. 'Are you still at the office? Give me five minutes and I'll call you back. Meanwhile, could you dig out your Banville Trust file and have it in front of you?'

Hugh found the file – with some difficulty as he seldom looked at it. Leafing quickly through he saw its contents consisted of little more than the several sets of accounts filed since Hugh had become a shareholder, and the Articles of Association and the Shareholders' Agreement that Ned had drawn up at that time.

The telephone rang. 'Sorry to be troubling you with this, but I need to discuss this situation with you tonight, so I can deliver our joint view tomorrow morning.'

'Our joint view? To whom? On what?'

'Hold on, and I'll tell you. Have you met Nathan Epstein, or is he just a name to you?'

'Epstein? Oh, I've met him briefly in New York. We did a little deal together two or three years ago which proved very straightforward, and we found him pleasant enough to deal with.'

'OK. As you know, we were obliged to turn to Rod Tadlock of Antipodean & Global to bail us out, on Waring's introduction. Well, Tadlock's offer is on the table now, or about to be, and will be accepted, as at the moment it's the only one there is. With no alternative on the horizon I was going to vote my shares in favour – after a good look at the contract, which I haven't yet seen. And vote the Banville shares too, with your consent.'

'Which of course I'll give. As you know I would never block you in anything you might want to do with Banville. I've told you that before.'

'Not entirely what I want to hear, but thanks, Hugh. I'd like you to question me about things and stop me from doing anything stupid. Which is the point of this call now. Suddenly – astonishingly – we do have an alternative to Tadlock. Nathan Epstein has offered me funding of £90 million – effectively to take Tadlock's place in the deal. So I would offer the board exactly the same terms: £90 million for 23 per cent of the company. Aggregating together my personal stake and Banville's would bring me up to just under 43 per cent ownership.'

Hugh murmured something, and encouraged Ned to continue. He couldn't think where this was heading.

'But the point is this; Epstein tells me, from sources he won't divulge, that when we see the small print of Tadlock's contract we'll find an innocent-looking clause smuggled in, to the effect that when the company needs more cash, Tadlock has the sole right to subscribe it, at par. The initial tranche is not going to be nearly enough, which means that a little way down the line we will find Macaulay lost to Tadlock. Why?

Because by the terms of his contract Tadlock is the only place we can go for funding.'

Hugh whistled.

'How Epstein knows about this is beyond me, but it's rumoured that he has someone quietly on his payroll in every major investment bank in the world, just to give him the latest information on what everyone else is up to.'

There was silence as Hugh, doodling on a legal pad, was lost in concentration. 'So Epstein suggests you do exactly the same thing,' he said eventually.

'Correct. We do the same. We take over Tadlock's deal entirely. The £90 million, plus – this is the important bit – the secondary investment clause.'

Again a pause. 'Surely they're going to want to know where your £90 million is coming from? Then what do you say?'

'I don't know. Refuse to tell them. Tell them we've borrowed it.'

'We? Why not tell the truth? That you're getting it from Epstein?'

'Because that will lose me the deal. Epstein won't allow it. He's specifically told me so.'

'Why is that?'

'Because he doesn't want TransAmerican identified in that way with the deal. He was adamant. And anyway TransAmerican cannot, by its Articles, lend money to individuals.'

'Ned – I don't understand. If Epstein doesn't want TransAmerican to be identified and can't lend you the money personally, then how can you do this? Am I missing something?"

'Oh, that's easy. That's why I'm ringing. You are about to become one of the key players in this. TransAmerican are going to invest £90 million in preference shares and loan stock into Banville, if you will agree to that, and then whatever further sum is required to undertake the secondary subscription. They may not be able to lend money to an individual, but a subscription into a company they can do. Then Banville invests £90 million into Macaulay, and a little down the road Banville will gain control of the company. Then I retire Father, I get Giles to step down, and I get on with clearing up the mess.'

Hugh continued doodling on his pad. 'What's in it for Epstein?' he asked after a few moments. 'And how does TransAmerican get their money back?'

'What's in it for Epstein is that once Banville has control, we're going straight to the market for a public listing. At that point his loan stock and interest in Banville are repaid, and his preference shares are converted into equity, giving him a substantial minority position in Macaulay as a public corporation – about 11 per cent or so, when all the dust is settled. That will look to Wall Street like a very interesting strategic stake for Epstein, and done on the cheap, with all his loan stock converted back into cash.'

'And what about your great ambition, that the newspapers should never leave your family's control?'

'That's just it. On the secondary subscription Banville will invest not just enough to creep above 50 per cent, but to reach more like 60 per cent. We'll then be diluted by the public offering to 30 per cent or so, a minority holding of course, but the largest individual stake. Father will be left with around

15 per cent of Macaulay, Mother about 2, and Giles 10 per cent. This deal will make me the leader of the family, and the custodian of it. I'll still have the newspapers under my control – for the family.'

'Christ,' said Hugh, eventually.

'That's it,' Ned replied, pleasantly. 'I told you I had something to tell you. Can I go ahead, or can't I? I need your legal consent.'

The next morning it was not Nathan Epstein on the telephone at half past seven, when Ned was in the shower, but Rod Tadlock. Ned heard the ring and had run to pick up the receiver, towel around his waist, thinking that it would be Epstein. In his surprise, he had to ask the name of the caller twice, before the penny dropped.

Tadlock wanted to call on Ned at his office. Ned tried to put him off, particularly in the light of what Epstein had told him. He was persistent however, and pressed for a meeting.

'Can we cover whatever you want to say to me on the phone, Rod? Would you mind that?'

'How long have we got?'

Ned glanced at the alarm clock, remembered that he had promised to drop two of his daughters at their nursery school on the way to his office, and grimaced. He was dripping water on to the bedroom carpet, and he was running late. 'Could we do it in five minutes?'

'Well – I enjoyed talking with you, Ned, when I met you the other day with all the Macaulay board. I thought we'd get on well together. And if I am to proceed with this big investment into your company then I have to be comfortable that

I'll make a meaningful relationship or two amongst you.'

Ned, anxious to bring this to a halt, reflected that the only meaningful use Tadlock could have been to them was to have produced £90 million. But from what Epstein had told him he didn't have anything at all. And Epstein had now proposed to Ned this new route, which had excited him so much he had barely slept.

'Let me be frank with you. I'm not sure we have a deal. In fact I'm increasingly aware that there's no way in which we could possibly have a deal. That's what I'm going to tell my board. So – it was good to meet you, and I appreciate your call, but the more I think about it the more I . . .'

'Who says we don't have a deal? Of course we have a deal. Why else do you think I made the effort to fly all the way from Sydney at such short notice?'

Ned sighed. 'We, as you know, are desperate for cash. I know now your liquidity cycle is such that you don't have the money we need. Waring's will have to withdraw your name. I'll ensure that my father is . . .'

'Hold on for a moment. You're right – that deal is dead. Our cash flow cycle and your cash flow cycle are not running in synch at this time, so what we . . .'

'Rod, our cash flow cycle is not out of synch with anybody's. We don't have a cash flow cycle. It's expired. And I don't want to be impertinent, but my information is that at the moment you don't have one either.'

There was silence for a moment. Then Tadlock laughed. 'OK, you win. Let's tell each other how it is, which brings me back to the beginning again. That was going to be exactly the scene that I wanted to set with you, that was my point.'

'You didn't exactly seem to be presenting it that way.'

'No, I don't believe I was. I was a little taken aback by you, to be honest. Let's start again. Number one – you are where you are personally, and I know what you want, and I know how to help you achieve it. Number two – the Macaulay Group is dead on its feet, 100 per cent, unless one of you in the family can find a way to rescue it, and fast. Number three – none of you can do it on your own. You don't have the cash. Number four – I don't have the cash either, and nor does Antipodean & Global, as you rightly point out. But number five – I know who does, and so do you: Nathan Epstein. This is his market.'

Ned said nothing at all. He stood there picking his teeth with the index finger of his spare hand, staring out through the curtains at the pleasantly preserved Victorian terraced houses on the opposite side of the street. Where on earth was this conversation leading?

'I take your silence to mean that Nathan Epstein is actually the person you're talking to in secret at this time – you personally, unknown to your board. Am I right? And it was Nathan who told you of my liquidity difficulties, right?'

Ned still remained silent, listening to what was to follow.

'I thought so. Of course it was. But that doesn't matter. We have these people over a barrel. I said we – you, me and Nathan Epstein. We can all help each other. We all need each other if you'll give me the time to explain why. Give us a week, and all three of us can have from this situation exactly what we each want. We're sitting on the edge of quite a deal. But to achieve it, all three of us have to work together. You two need me, and I need both of you.'

Ned glanced at the clock once more. It was nearly ten to eight. He'd just be in time, if he abandoned his breakfast. 'Call me this afternoon, Rod, if you would. Call me this afternoon.'

10

The *Post* would have been aghast to have been labelled a salacious paper, though in its prim, repressive way, salaciousness was its driving flavour. There was amongst its suburban, curtain-twitching, Middle England readership an undying interest in the marital and extramarital adventures of others. Particularly those of at least minimal celebrity status.

The moment the cutting landed on the Editor's desk, he knew that this was a story that the *Post* should run. The piece was from the middle pages of that day's *Kent and Sussex Herald*, and was headed by a large photograph of Foster, trying to cover his head with a raincoat as he emerged from the doors of Ashford Magistrates' Court. He had been prosecuted on a gross indecency charge, rare in England since the law had been liberalized three or four decades before, and that alone would have meant that the *Post* would have shown interest in it. But this one was a cracker. Foster was a family servant of Hugh Emerson's, and Hugh was a sufficiently well-known man for an eye-catching headline to be written around the story.

'*Top Publisher's Chauffeur in Sex Shame*,' screamed page three. '*Magistrate Slams Filthy Act in Public Lav*' ran the subhead, and over three columns the *Post*'s public were regaled with the evidence of the Rotherhurst vicar, who had accidentally witnessed the event, together with the predictably vicious prejudices of the Emersons' neighbours, beneficiaries all, over the years, of Foster's famous tea parties in the walled garden for everyone in the village.

Two days later the *Post* was at it again, this time in their gossip column. Hugh found it on his desk amongst the morning's press cuttings when he arrived at the office.

Poor Hugh Emerson, the publisher that every literary luvvie loves to love, with the possible exception of the sultry, pouting novelist Margie Street, dropped last month from the great man's list as not quite the thing, has had a bad run of luck recently. First the family chauffeur is caught by the vicar with his pants around his ankles. Then his barrister wife Nicola wraps the family car around a lamp-post right outside Walton Street police station. As tired and emotional driving goes, that shows more than a little class. But all will be well. Nicola has most powerful friends.

Hugh, initially struck dumb with horror at reading those last few words, managed to reassure himself that they might not have meant what he had first assumed they had. Four days later, in the same column, he found:

Glittering literary luminary Hugh Emerson can be too charming for his own good. Friends report growing warmth and ease between him and Bishop's daughter Evelyn Lucas, who joined as his assistant from the Foreign Office a year or so back, and clearly thrives in the great man's company. But the unfortunate man has enough on his plate at this time, what with randy chauffeurs and tired and emotional wives. Ms Lucas, who readers will recall was named in a divorce case that precipitated her abandonment of a promising diplomatic career, is herself a novelist, of the ripped bodice, heaving bosom, all passions spent mode. Poor Hugh. This is not what he needs.

Actionable possibly, but at least the reference to Nicola's 'powerful friends' had not been repeated. Hugh threw the cutting straight into the wastepaper basket. He drew a deep breath and called for Evelyn Lucas to come in. He could see that she had been crying, and was now struggling, sturdy girl that she was, to pull herself together before other members of the office saw her.

Hugh pointed to the chair on the other side of the desk and shrugged. 'I'm so sorry, Evelyn,' he began, and wondered what to say next. This was hardly the occasion of a bereavement, or a matter of life and death. Could he risk turning it into a joke? 'Look, don't worry about it. Do what I am going to do. Chuck the thing in the bin and put it completely out of your mind. It's all garbage, it always is, and there's no point in spending one moment even thinking about it. Or worrying what others here will think, believe me. OK?'

'Nasty, vicious prattle,' she said. 'Actually my concern is not what people here might think. My concern is my parents.' She spoke very solemnly now. 'the *Post* is their morning paper.'

Hugh, despite himself, started laughing, tried to hide it, then gave up, and laughed so much that she too joined in. 'I'm sorry, Evelyn,' he said again, wiping his eyes. 'There was something in the way you said that. Oh dear. Ring them, do it before they read it. Sound light-hearted and self-confident, whatever you do. Honestly. Ring.'

She left to telephone, and when she was safely out of the room Hugh bent down to the wastepaper basket, scrabbled through it and read the piece once more. It wasn't so bad. It was spiteful stuff, but not much more than that. But there was a pattern here that was difficult to ignore. Someone was trying to rattle him with leaks to these journalists, and there was probably more to come. Was this a form of blackmail? If so, what did they want? Who were they?

Ned and his cousin Caroline sat in the corner of the country pub with pints of beer and bread and cheese, their wet Barbours thrown down on to the neighbouring bench. She and Ned, born within days of each other, had spent many school holidays in each other's company at their mutual grandmother's house on the Norfolk Broads, and had felt particularly close to each other ever since. She had written to tell him of her separation, and he felt guilty that he had not immediately gone to see her. Since her husband had left her, Caroline was farming the Exmoor smallholding herself, and times were hard. The two small children had been taken away from their local private schools and now went together to the little primary school in the village. When Ned had dropped into the farmhouse on his way back from Exeter, having dropped his three older children at their grandmother's retirement cottage, he was struck by how cold and uncomfortable it had become since he had last called there, in happier times for Caroline, eighteen months or so before.

'How often do you come down to the West Country, Ned? I wish we saw more of you.'

'Twice a year or so, to see Daisy's mother. Let's make a proper trip of it next time and spend some time with you too. All of us, if you could face it.'

They sat there for a couple of hours or more, talking of their children, drying out in front of the huge log fire, reminiscing, gossiping about family, discussing her circumstances now, good friends too little in each other's company. It was not why he had been to see her at all, but as he hugged her and drove away back to London he reflected how good fortune often stems from an attempt to engage with those one loves.

For the simple act of meeting up with Caroline to wish her well, and to see if she was managing to cope, had led, quite unexpectedly, to a major breakthrough in Ned's life.

Ned drew the car up outside his house in Gilston Road, and glanced up at the children's bedrooms on the second floor. He would miss them while they were away. One of the great private pleasures of his life was to arrive home in the evening and hear them call out their greeting to him as they heard the front door slam. No other relationship he had was as intimate. He still marvelled at it. His four daughters were now aged nine, seven, four and three, and he had not the slightest idea how he was going to cope when in due course they left home. He even resented the time lost to him when he took them away to stay in the country for a few days.

As he began to turn the key in the lock the front door suddenly opened in front of him, and there was Daisy, her hat jammed down over her ears against the rain, rushing out to wherever she was going, quite certainly, as always, late.

'Well done, darling,' she called over her shoulder as she pushed past him and ran out to her tiny car, parked, as usual, several feet from the pavement. 'Bless you, I've spoken to the girls, thanks so much for doing it, wonderful of you, how was Caroline . . . I'm desperately behindhand, see you later . . . Katie's in the kitchen, give her a drink.'

She tore the parking ticket off her windscreen, threw it in the back and, with a great lurch, swerved out into the road right in front of a garbage lorry. The driver stood on his brakes, and shouted curses at Daisy's disappearing rear. Ned shut the door behind him, hastily, and went to find his sister.

Katie was indeed in the kitchen, and he embraced her fondly. He had become uneasy about her in recent months. There had always seemed to be men in her life, but she had never settled with any of them. Now thirty-one, she was single and childless, and there was a growing aura of tiredness about her, a sense of defeat. He was glad her little studio house in Park Walk was so close that he could keep an eye on her. She made some sort of living from her expressionist paintings, most of which, had she known it, were bought by Ned. He used a gallery owner in Cork Street as a front for the purchases, and by now had two dozen or more stored away in his attic under drapes. He was nervous she might find them. Perhaps he should give some to Caroline.

They kissed in the perfunctory style they always adopted with each other, and Katie, without enquiring, made herself a large ham and pickle sandwich from what she found in the refrigerator. 'Mother thinks you're plotting,' she said, with her mouth full. 'Are you? Actually don't answer, because I know you must be. Mother's always right, she hears everything.'

'Is that why you've come round?' Ned asked mildly, trying to find the corkscrew.

'No, I came to borrow £30 off Daisy. But now that I'm here I would like to talk about it. Mother's worried, and she's frightened of saying anything to you directly.'

Ned laughed. 'I can't think why. Mother has always taken me for a complete simpleton. She's never been frightened of saying anything to me – and with extreme directness.'

'Well, let me say it for her,' Katie replied. 'It's this. Ned, sweetheart, be careful. Please be careful.'

Ned heard the seriousness in her voice. 'Careful of what?' he asked, his back to her, still pretending to rummage in the drawer.

'Careful of . . . making things worse. I know Father's made a mess of everything, and in a way Giles has too. Mother knows all that better than anyone, and she accepts that something is going to have to be done. But she doesn't want Father hurt – particularly by you.'

'What on earth does that mean?' Ned asked, turning now to face her. 'What do you mean – particularly by me?'

Katie sighed. 'Father and Giles between them have made a bad mess of our affairs, there's no doubt about that. But don't use this as a chance of revenge. Work with me, work with Mother. We'll get really good advice – absolutely not from those ghastly Waring's people incidentally – and we'll decide between the three of us what should be done. Please, Ned.'

Ned looked at Katie and, very unexpectedly, thought he was going to burst into tears. He loved his sister, and he'd been protecting her all his life. He knew how clever it was of his mother to use her as an emissary. But it was too late now, and anyway he was in the right. If there was an element of revenge in what he was doing, then so be it. He was doing the right thing for everyone in the family, and any delay or indecisiveness now, and it would be too late.

He shrugged. 'I'm sorry, Katie.'

She nodded, resignedly. 'I don't want blood all over the place, all over the family, please don't do that. Please, Ned . . . show . . . show respect.'

Respect, Ned thought. What an unexpected word for her to choose. But she was right. The issue at the bottom of things was that he had no respect for his father whatsoever. Love perhaps, but no respect. And that was something he hardly liked to admit to himself, let alone anyone else. Particularly to Daisy, now he came to think about it.

'So where are we, James?' Nicky Waring asked. 'How do things look?'

It was the end of the day, and they were sitting in Nicky's office, a nearly empty bottle of extremely good claret open on the desk. James was in his shirtsleeves and his scarlet braces, and Nicky in an aged yellow cardigan which he kept in the drawer of his desk, so worn that one elbow had a large hole in it.

'Well, let's count it all up. We've got the funds from the New Jersey people to finance Giles's bid. The money's sitting there in escrow as of this morning, and as soon as Giles makes his move we get our fees up front out of that. Twelve and a half million pounds. Giles is on the hook and panting to go. He's signed the contract for our eight. So we're on course for the £20 million plus overall. Good going.'

Nicky, wine glass in hand, put his feet up on the desk, and massaged his scalp. 'If Giles makes his move,' he said.

'Well of course Giles will make his move. We left him absolutely dribbling at the prospect of it.'

Nicky leant forward for the claret bottle, and poured himself more wine. He put his feet back on the desk and resumed massaging his scalp. 'That's true, of course,' he said after a moment or two. 'He was like a cat on heat. Telling him that as soon as he got control we'd then work to break the group up and sell it off bit by bit, to his quite immense financial benefit, did the trick. He knows he needn't worry about actually having to run the things, and the two papers in particular. So, with all that done – what can go wrong?'

'Nothing can go wrong. Charlie will agree to it when we flatter him about how wise it was of him to have seen Giles's promise so early, and to have groomed him for succession. How marvellous that Waring's, in our loyalty and affection for Macaulay, have managed now to come up with a solution that keeps continuing ownership in the family, instead of allowing that parvenu of an Australian to get his hands on the family silver. Charlie must understand that it's very hush-hush, but very old money – old Ivy League, Wall Street money. From fine old families. Very fine. Very old. But Charlie must realize that we've had to throw a lot of extra resource at this, so we'll have to adjust our fees just a little, we're embarrassed to say, perhaps by another couple of million. Oh come on, Nicky, there'll be no problem with Charlie if we handle him right.'

Nicky sighed. 'I suppose not,' he said. 'Probably you're right. But why do I have this feeling that we've missed something? That we've forgotten something that could stop this from working?'

'Well – let's go through all the components of it. The money? Sitting there and ready to go. Charlie? We've discussed. Tadlock? Nothing was signed, everything was on a handshake, more fool him, and he can now piss off back to Sydney. Ned? What can he do about it? He hasn't got enough shares to block it, much as I'm sure he'll want to. The other directors? Milksops, the lot of them. They'll do what they're told. So there we are. It's all cut and dried.'

Nicky nodded, but without conviction, and he remained pensive. 'Nathan Epstein?' he murmured after a moment.

James frowned. 'What about Nathan Epstein? He's got nothing to do with this. All Epstein's going to do is sell us those three East Coast papers we want for Macaulay, once we've got all this business tidied up. Sell them, or have his private life all over the front pages of the New York tabloids. His wife's too. But that's all for a later date. Epstein's got nothing to do with this part of the deal.'

'Nathan Epstein has had something to do with every single part of every single deal in this fucking sector since he was a kid in short pants,' Nicky said. 'And will continue to do so, believe me. Mixing things with Nathan Epstein in the way you've just done in New York didn't strike me as being exactly the brightest . . .'

'Hello,' he barked down the telephone. 'Who is it? Why, Charlie, we were just speaking of you, James and I, hoping that you were coping. Wanting to assure you of our total personal support and loyalty in these difficult times – all of us here. Absolutely. You're very kind. We don't deserve it. Bless you.'

Nicky looked across and winked at James, but then suddenly the amusement drained from his face, and he was sitting bolt upright in his chair and reaching around for a pencil and a legal pad, listening intently. 'What was that? How many shares? From whom? What do you mean it's too late? How do you know that, Charlie?'

He was quiet then, listening to what he was being told, writing down on his pad the occasional word and number. 'And you've checked the legal issues with Fairmeadows, you say? Give me that bit once more.' More listening and doodling, his expression now growing more and more concerned. 'Well, if that's the situation then we must adjust accordingly. And you know what? I see some advantages already. Truly. Yes, I do. Let me have a little chat with James here, and I'll call you back at home later tonight. Yes, I will. And Charlie, we're right behind you, you know that? Always have been, always will be. You can count on us. Personally.'

He replaced the receiver, and gazed at James. 'Fuck,' he said. 'Fuck.'

'What's happened? What is it?'

'What's happened? That little sod Ned has found some impoverished country cousin with a few hundred shares and a nasty overdraft. Caroline somebody or other. Ned's given her the money she needs in return for taking a lease on the bene-ficial interest in her shares. So the cousin keeps title to them but Ned can vote them as his own holding. It sounds daft, but remember this is an entirely family-held company, and their rules have evolved over the years to suit themselves. A conven-tional transfer of those shares to Ned the board could have blocked – but not this. Charlie's checked it with Fairmeadows.'

175

'And – don't tell me – Ned now has the 19.9 per cent plus one share he needs to block any deal he doesn't like the look of?'

Nicky pointed to some scribbled numbers on his pad. 'That's it. He now has a block.'

'Which he'll use against Tadlock, if we go back to where we were before, and run with him.'

'Which he might use against Tadlock, I don't know. But which he will certainly use against Giles, when that one is put before him.'

James hitched at his groin, picked his nose and stared out of the window, deep in thought. 'We've just said goodbye to £20 million in fees,' he said eventually.

'That's it. Twenty million.'

Neither said anything for a few minutes. Then James glanced across at Nicky. 'So we drop Tadlock, drop Giles and cuddle up with Ned,' he said. 'Reposition. Think laterally. Find a new angle.'

'That's it,' agreed Nicky. 'You're there. We drop Tadlock, we drop Giles, and we drop Charlie. Then we go with Ned.'

James nodded. 'How do we do that, Nicky, actually, in your view? What's our play?'

'How do I know what our bloody play is? We'll have to think, won't we? That's what we do for a living. We'll have to bloody think.'

11

Hugh glanced at his watch, saw that he was going to be late, and cursed. Normally the most dreamily passive of drivers, he took a chance and swung his way at right angles across Hampstead High Street and into Gayton Road, narrowly avoiding a bus that tried to accelerate into him. The driver leant on his horn but could produce from it no more than a cross little bleep, and Hugh could not resist a vaguely insulting wave of his hand as he drove away.

Passing Waterwell's bookshop in the middle of the block, he could see that the queue for Anna Lavey's signing session stretched all the way up the hill towards the underground station. There must be five hundred people waiting for her there, he thought, perhaps more. Anna's vast popularity with her Middle England public had now reached a pitch that bewildered Hugh, but he wasn't complaining. People read what they wanted to read, and Anna gave it to them.

He saw a parking space, recognized it as very tight for the Audi, but reversed into it, too fast, in case he lost it to a quickly closing rival. He felt the jolt as he hit the bumper of the car parked behind him. A woman was sitting in the driver seat, and she, like the bus driver, promptly pressed her horn and shouted her rage at him. This was becoming a most un-Hugh-like Saturday afternoon. Late for Anna's signing, cursed by other drivers, it was all proving a most untidily stressful experience. Hugh avoided the petty stresses of life as best he could, given the major stresses that were there in his life whatever he did. He thought of this as he walked at an uncomfortably brisk pace up the hill. Then he turned into the bookshop, and saw to his relief that Anna, her back towards him, had clearly only just arrived herself. She was being shown to the signing table by the manager, and Hugh observed her on her professional best behaviour – charming the young man with some little anecdote or other as, dimpled, she smiled and nodded her way through the crowd, her hand on the young man's arm.

It came to Hugh that in her early middle age, and her success, Anna had grown much more physically appealing than she'd been in her gaunt, aggressive twenties. She was plump now, flatteringly so, and presented herself just as a Jewish agony aunt and journalist of a certain age and with a huge popular following should: her dark hair drawn back from her forehead, her unfussy, longish skirt and quite simple shoes, a layer or two of soft cashmere jersey over a silk blouse, strings of costume pearls, her face, with its immaculate foundation sheen, dramatized by a great slash of scarlet lipstick.

She saw Hugh, gave a cry of delight, as if they hadn't met each other in years, and held her arms out to him. As she kissed the air some distance from either side of his cheeks the crowd, copies of her book held to them, stood smiling at Anna's lovely affection and warmth for this dark, comfortably dressed man. Then, charmingly, coquettishly, she made a great business of introducing Hugh to the young manager, whom he was perfectly well acquainted with, and had been for some years.

'Look at all these lovely people, Hugh darling!' she cried, and Hugh, playing his part, stood there nodding and smiling at them all. Then, taking over from the manager, who was pink with pleasure at Anna's attentions – she had greeted him by his first name, loudly, and, in front of all the staff, kissed him! – Hugh showed her to the table.

She put her great carpet handbag down on to the floor beside her, this bag a familiar prop of hers, in her practical, no nonsense, fame-doesn't-turn-her-head mode. Then she sat, took a pen in her hand and, the gracious celebrity with her fans, she turned her face up to smile radiantly at whomever was first in the line. And, for the briefest of moments, she froze.

Hugh saw it. He looked at the woman standing before her, and wondered who she could be. But the moment was over; Anna, quite recovered, was shaking her hand, calling her by her name, complimenting her on her appearance, then signing, in a great flourish, the six copies of the book that the woman held clutched to her stomach, and with a charming little smile and word now sending her on her way.

And so she continued for the next two hours and more, smiling, laughing, chattering with Hugh as he sat beside her, signing with a great show of good heart all the special messages and dedications that were asked of her. She autographed not only her books, but loose pieces of paper, the palm of a child's hand, a copy or two of her latest newspaper column. It was a generous, virtuoso performance, and it came to its finale in a spontaneous round of applause from the bookshop staff, and the presentation to her of a little bouquet, which she pretended to smell, and held to her as if she was the Queen Mother herself, all simple but regal gratitude and kindliness.

'What a turn you gave them, Anna,' Hugh said, as the two of them sat alone in a little spare office at the top of the shop, having a cup of tea and munching on a plate of cucumber sandwiches, cut wafer-thin by the bookshop manager in deference to Anna's gentility. 'What a trouper!'

'Well, you should complain, darling,' she replied, all stagey sarcasm, and scratched at her crotch. 'How many copies signed and sold for you today? Seven hundred? Eight? Christ, think of the money you'll make on that. You work me to death, of course, way beyond my contract, you're so unkind about that, but there we are.'

Hugh ignored the complaint. 'Anna, who was that woman at the head of the line when you first sat down? She seemed to give you rather a fright.'

Anna grimaced, helped herself to the last sandwich and, her open mouth still full of bread and sliced cucumber, reached for her cup and gulped down the rest of her tea. Hugh had seen Anna off duty, eating alone with her on many occasions over the years, and in this mood. He had always recoiled from the physical indelicacy of it. Anna was aware of this, he knew, and played the game the more.

'She's a cunt, that's who she is,' Anna said. 'I can never shake her off. A fan, you might call her, if you were in generous mood. She first wrote to me at the *Chronicle*, when I had that daily readers' problem page there nine or ten years ago. Some balls-aching whinge about something or other in her life to which I published a bog-standard Girl Guide's response. Then a second letter arrived, much on the same subject, so we ignored it. Then another. And another. And finally, one morning as I was coming through reception the security man stopped me quietly when I reached the lift and pointed her out to me. She was sitting bolt upright on a chair on her own with . . .' – Anna was an instinctive and highly accomplished light actress; she now made a pudding face, circled her scalp, and opened her legs wide – 'you know, a face like a pig's backside, a bloody great purple hat plonked askew on her head, lisle stockings and missionary's knickers. There she sat, trying to catch my eye. I went over to say hello, not knowing of course who in the hell she was. Now she follows me every place I go. I'm surprised you've never noticed her before – in the crowd at every book signing, always in the front row of the audience when I'm doing a live talk. I've even found her in my fucking garden in Dorset. And she writes to me endlessly – personal, impertinent, intrusive letters. All the time writing to me. Cards, Christmas presents. Never, ever leaving me alone.'

She opened the lid of the pot to see if there was any more tea.

'Poor you,' Hugh said feebly, and wondered if he could now send Anna on her way back to her husband Bobbie, so that he too could get away.

'Bloody right, poor me. I've thought of the police, but her behaviour probably stops short of harassment, in the legal sense, and the *Meteor* won't allow that anyway. Their lawyer man advises against it, and the editor, that prick Paul Hopper, doesn't think the publicity would be good. You know what it is – I'm supposed to be Matron. The Lady With the Lamp. Always on duty, always there with the enema pump and the bed pan, available night or day to the the *Meteor*'s fucking readers and their fucking problems.'

Hugh laughed, because he was expected to laugh, and got to his feet, suddenly yearning to return to Nicola and Danny, their new-born son. He was bored now with Anna. He often was. Her coarseness offended him. Hugh thought of Bobbie, and pitied him.

Miss Anstruther arrived home in Pimlico, put on the kettle, and made herself a pot of tea. She gave the cat a hug and sat down in her armchair before the gas fire, with her feet up on an ottoman. She sipped at her cup, and glanced across at her six copies of Anna Lavey's new book. Then she got up from her chair to get one, carrying the cat with her. Easing herself back into the cushions she leafed through the book, then gazed at the glossy front cover and its picture of a gentle Anna in soft pink cashmere, chin resting on her hands, smiling reassuringly and caringly into the camera's lens.

Miss Anstruther kissed the photograph, then reached up to take another down from the mantelpiece. This was in a wreathed silver frame, and was her favourite, a publicity shot of Anna kneeling by a Christmas tree, placing on its boughs little silver and gilt glass balls, the back-shot a collage of out-of-focus cards and logs and presents and paper chains.

She loved the whole idea of Christmas. It spoilt it not at all that she had for some years spent it alone in Pimlico with the cat, the television, a bottle of sherry, and a Marks & Spencer turkey dinner for one with chestnut and cranberry sauce. She looked at the photograph and wondered if it really had been taken at Anna's home in Dorset. She did hope so. It looked so lovely, with the log fire blazing and the pretty Christmas tree, and the presents, and Anna in that nice cashmere sweater that suited her so well.

She'd had this photograph now for two years, and last year she'd sent Anna for her present an angora jersey very like the one here, only in a lovely soft cream colour and a slightly different collar. She'd hoped for a personal reply, but she knew how busy Anna was, poor lamb, and she was pleased anyway to get the printed card of acknowledgement from her secretary at the *Daily Meteor*.

One day perhaps she'd see Anna in the jersey, perhaps even on her now weekly television programme, *Letters to Anna Lavey*. She was so lovely on that, so kind and helpful. She knew just the right thing to say to people, to cheer them up, and help them help themselves. She was firm when she had to be, mind, but that was a good thing, and often the kindest thing. Sometimes people needed to pull themselves together and buck up, rather than spend their time trying to put right what couldn't be put right and sit there moping. Miss Anstruther didn't believe in moping. She'd learnt that from her father, the Major, and her splendid younger brother Jeremy, killed as a handsome nineteen-year-old soldier in Northern Ireland in 1979. What's past is past, old girl. Buck up and get on with it.

She kissed the photographs again, then replaced the silver frame on the mantelpiece. She put the book into the book-case, alongside a copy of every other title that Anna Lavey had ever written, including her own favourite, a single romantic novel, published a few years back. Her books, particularly the later ones, were so lovely, so helpful to people like Miss Anstruther, living alone, perhaps the tiniest bit lonely some-

183

times, but it doesn't do to be sorry for oneself. Ask Anna anything, and she'd know what to say. It was women she really understood best, of course, not men, and you could see that in what she wrote.

Despite herself, Miss Anstruther wished so much that Anna hadn't married, and she tried to put the fact of it out of her mind most of the time. She'd seen her husband actually, years before, just at the time when Anna's initial column had appeared and Miss Anstruther, having seen her picture, first developed an attachment for her. She'd been waiting inside a telephone box, hiding there to catch a glimpse of Anna one Saturday morning as she came out to shop. Eventually she had emerged from her house with this man whom she realized straight away must be the man she had married, Bobbie Turner, and had a baby by. Sweet little Andrew, he must be sixteen or seventeen now, of course, how time does fly, but for many years she had always remembered him on his birthday with a card and a little present, and although she didn't send things now she often thought about him and said a little prayer.

She'd never put her real name on the card, she wouldn't want to be that intrusive, just 'Love from Donald Duck' or later 'Batman' or something like that, always something different. Anna would have guessed of course, the sweetheart, and that made it all the nicer. Andrew was so adorable when he was tiny, and she'd watched, hidden in the crowds at Hamleys and Harrods as Anna took him each year on his Christmas shopping treats.

But no, she hadn't liked the look of the husband, and she didn't imagine poor Anna did much either. She knew as much actually, from reading between the lines of some of Anna's interviews. He was nowhere near good enough for her. A weak face, she'd thought when she had glimpsed him that day, and a bit of a beer belly on him.

She went over to the table, spread the other five books out into a fan, and wondered to whom she would send them. They'd make lovely Christmas presents. She decided on who would get them, changed her mind, then put them back in a pile and went to store them in her bedroom cupboard. In there was a box file containing copies of all the letters she had sent to Anna over the years, and the occasional typed but personally signed replies. She took that out now, and looked through it. Then she remembered that odd image that had come into her mind a day or so before: she had trapped a moth in an empty jam jar, and watching it, not unkindly, thought how nice it would be to trap Anna too, not in a nasty way, but to keep her so that she was there for her all the time, every day, every waking moment.

She counted on her fingers. Seven weeks until Christmas – and only six weeks until the day of days. This year she was going to do something she'd never in her life dared to do before. This year she was going to give Anna a surprise. She was going to call at her house, the weekend before Christmas, and put her present right into her hands.

She sat back on her bed and imagined the scene. The surprise on Anna's face when she came to the door and saw who it was – just like that lovely look she had given her only a few hours before in the bookshop. The others in the queue must have been so surprised, and so envious, when they heard Anna call her by name! Anna would give her that same lovely look, and then she'd take her present, and she'd see how nice it was. And

Anna would lean forward and kiss her on both cheeks, and give her a little hug – perhaps even ask her in for a Christmas drink by the fire. And they'd talk away together, and then when she got up to go – she wouldn't stay long, she wouldn't outstay her welcome – Anna would kiss her again, and ask if she might call her Elizabeth after all these years, and she'd say, yes, of course you can, and Elizabeth, she'd say, come again and see me very soon, you know where to find me, and thank you again for all the lovely things you've given me over the years, and for all your friendship and devotion to me, and she'd wave her off at the door.

Miss Anstruther sighed, got up from the bed and went to her cupboard to decide, once again, what she would wear when that day came. As she looked through the jerseys the picture came to her mind of the soft cream angora sweater she had sent Anna last year. Perhaps Anna would be wearing that when she came to the door. Anna would remember right away that it had been Miss Anstruther who had given it to her, and they'd have such a laugh together about that. Just like they had had in the bookshop.

She loved a laugh, did Anna. Anna was so lovely. Anna was Miss Anstruther's life.

It was half past six and Anna had been drinking for most of the afternoon. Bobbie had stormed out in a rage, she hadn't seen Andrew for days – she didn't know where he was – and Christmas was less than a week away.

The thought of it appalled her. She hated Christmas. She hated the things she had to do for the *Daily Meteor*. Reading lessons at carol service after bloody carol service, this year on

186

television for some charity, exuding good will, pressing the flesh and – she had just remembered – *Thought for the Day* on Radio 4 next week, drivelling away about the common values of the true spirit of Christmas and the true spirit of Jewishness. Anna the rabbi.

She poured herself another gin, and gazed out at the rain. Fuck Bobbie. She should never have had him back the last time of course, and that was only a year ago. But she'd missed him – she'd known him all her adult life, and she couldn't live without him. Particularly if for the rest of her days she had to live with the vision of him with that trollop she knew he was seeing.

Bobbie was her man, but fuck him. Storming off like that a few minutes ago – it was her that should be doing the storming off, the way he treated her. She swallowed her gin, poured another, tripped over the carpet, cursed, and heard the door bell ring. Bobbie no doubt, gone without his key, thought better of it, come back to apologize.

'Coming!' she shouted as the bell rang once more, clutching on to the banisters, must hold on, she'd fall if she didn't, the last time she was this pissed she'd thought she'd broken her back, she'd come down in such a clatter. Glass in hand, she kicked some junk mail out of the way, and pulled the door open, ready to blast Bobbie before allowing him in again.

But it wasn't Bobbie. It took her a second or two, so surprised was she, but it wasn't him at all. It was that Miss Anstruther woman, grinning like an old monkey, pushing a bunch of flowers at her with one hand, and a package, all Christmas wrapping and ribbon, with the other.

She ignored them both, and looked at her with total,

undisguised loathing. 'Why don't you fuck off,' she said, her voice rising. 'Why don't you fuck off. And take this garbage with you. If I ever see you snivelling around me again ever, I'll get you locked up. Do you hear what I say? Fuck off. And never, ever let me see your revolting face again. Here or anywhere else. Ever again. Now – fuck off!'

She slammed the door, and cursed her way up the stairs again. But the violence of what she had said and done had shocked her back to some level of sobriety. She knew she had gone too far. She knew she had made a mistake. She knew that this action would come back to haunt her, and she knew she deserved it. In her deepest soul she was not an unkind woman. She'd been through too much for that, and seen too much, and felt too much. As she'd shouted her cruelty at the woman, she had seen her receive it, eyes widening in panic, flinching at each word, each blow.

Anna sat on her bed, and buried her head in her hands. That was a dreadful thing she had done. A dreadful thing. She'd killed that woman with what she'd just said to her.

12

Hugh had known Adrian Wate since their schooldays together, though not well. But his patience finally snapped on reading a further piece in the *Post*'s diary column the following day, hinting at a rumour that Emerson's financial state was once more precarious, and he picked up the telephone to speak to him, and was put straight through.

He attempted some introductory small talk, having not seen Wate for several years, but found himself too angry to sustain it. 'I'm not a complainer normally, but what on earth are you people up to, Adrian? What does the *Post* think they are doing with me? That's four stupid, vindictive, sniping little diary pieces in rapid succession, and I don't understand why.'

There was silence for a moment.

'Yes, I've seen them. They have been a little rich, I agree with you. But you know how we run things at Consolidated Press, Hugh. Each of the papers is a law unto itself and has its own market niche and style. We have almost no central input into editorial policy, except in major matters of strategic direction. I may be Managing Director of the Group, but I'm pretty impotent in these sorts of areas, and that's the way the board wants it. I don't blame you for complaining though. I'd do the same. But to be honest with you, Hugh, there's very little I can do.'

But Hugh persevered. 'Much of this stuff is actionable, you know that. I'm not a litigious man, but the way I'm feeling at the moment I'm going to go for Consolidated if this stuff doesn't stop. That's four stories, and no doubt there's more to follow.'

Hugh sensed Wate hesitating, and weakening.

'I can't tell them to drop you as a diary target, Hugh, I just can't do that. The *Post*'s readers love this sort of gossip about people with a public profile, as you well know. You and I might deplore it personally, but people like us are not the readership. I could tell them to be careful, I suppose, but that would probably do more harm than good.'

'I find that difficult to accept, Adrian, I really do. Put yourself in my shoes.'

'I am putting myself in your shoes and, as I've explained, there's nothing I can do.'

'I'm sorry to be persistent, but I'm not prepared to let this continue.'

There was a silence, and Hugh deliberately left it unbroken. Then, reluctantly, Wate said, 'Well, there's one thing I could do, I suppose, if I handled it very carefully. I might just about risk that, for old times' sake. But, I don't know, even that might be too ... You know, Hugh, your famous friendship with Ned Macaulay makes things a little more difficult for me, if you don't mind me saying so. Rival newspapers, all's fair in love and war, you know how it goes. But I suppose I might just about risk asking ...'

He drifted away, clearly thinking it out.

'Asking what, Adrian?'

'Well, I suppose I might be able to find out who's feeding them the material, in a roundabout sort of way. Somebody is, somewhere, for whatever reason. I might be able to find that out at least, but that's absolutely as far as I could take it, and I can't promise they'll tell me. But they might, if I handle the question tactfully, and a bit obliquely. It's possible they might. Do you want me to have a go at that?'

When Adrian Wate did call back, the following afternoon, it was with information that left Hugh totally bemused, then extremely angry. The source of the stories was Nicky Waring.

Hugh's acquaintance with Nicky Waring was very slight, but they had met socially on the odd occasion over the years, and had once served together on a fundraising committee for the restoration of a bomb-damaged Wren church in the middle of the City. Beyond that, nothing, and with the world of literary publishing a million years away from the realm of advisory investment bankers on the make, they might well have never met again. But he was on the telephone now to Waring's within moments of Adrian Wate's call, still literally shaking with rage.

First there were the three private secretaries to clear, singly, and up against mounting levels of corporate hauteur.

'I'd like to speak to him now, please,' he found himself saying to the last and grandest of them, trying to keep calm, but knowing he was failing. 'I couldn't give a damn what he's doing. I want to speak to him right now.'

'I'm afraid Mr Waring is not available to take your call,' she repeated, slowly, pedantically, as if to a backward child.

191

'He is in a meeting. I am not able to disturb him. I will take your message. Please give me your number.'

'How do I make this clear?' Hugh replied, hissing his anger at her. 'Either you get Mr Waring out of his imaginary meeting right now, and bring him to the telephone, or I am going to get into a taxi, and come straight around to your office, and personally, with the greatest of enthusiasm, take him by the . . .'

'One moment please,' she said, and he could hear her speak to someone, her hand partly covering the receiver. There was then a banging noise, as it was knocked on a hard surface, and Nicky who came on the line.

'Hugh! What a surprise! How lovely. James one minute, you the next!' The voice went suddenly sombre. 'And this gives me the opportunity, Hugh, of saying how deeply distressed I was to hear of your mother's death. I am so terribly sorry. As I've said to James, if there's one thing I can do to be of assistance to you both in your sad loss, however big, however small, then you have only to ask. You have my most heartfelt, heartfelt sympathy. I can only say that when my own dear mother passed . . .'

Hugh, despite himself, felt the acutest edge of his anger begin to ease under this avalanche of insincerity, but he interrupted. 'Nicky, I want to know one thing. Why, in the name of God, did you do what you've done?'

'Sorry?'

'Why have you been feeding this disgraceful, vicious material to the *Post*? And think before you answer. I want a clear statement of truth. Recognize the word? Truth.'

'My dear Hugh,' he laughed. 'My dear old thing. What on earth are you . . .'

'Nicky, hear me. I want a clear, unequivocal explanation of this. Now.'

There was a pause. 'Why don't you come round to the office, Hugh? Why don't you come around tonight, and we'll have a chat and a quiet drink. I'm sure that whatever misunderstanding there is we'll clear up in no time. Why don't you do that? Then we could all have dinner together – you, me and James. Gosh – I'd like that. I'll get Fiona to book us into Le Caprice. No, Sheekeys. More fun. Good idea?'

'I don't want to come to your office, and I don't want to have dinner with you. I just want to understand why you've done what you've done. We can do that on the telephone. Just explain to me what all this is about.'

Nicky sighed. 'Well, there we are,' he said, the disappointment in his voice indicating sadness at failing to persuade dear old Hugh out of this absurd tantrum. 'Let's talk on the telephone then. Hold on for a moment and I'll transfer this on to my private line.'

The line went dead, and then there was Nicky once more. 'Gotcher,' he said. 'I'm back in my office and the door's closed. Hugh, old dear, what is this?'

'Nicky, you're a complete shit. And it will save a lot of time if I tell you that I've been to the Managing Director of Consolidated Press to ask for his help. We were at school together. I'm fed up to the back teeth with these stories that have been appearing in the *Post*. Particularly the piece this morning, which may have done Emerson's untold harm with the literary agents. I asked Consolidated to tell the *Post* to stop it. They couldn't do that, but what I did get was the name of the person feeding them this stuff – you. And let me say this . . .' – he hurried on to cut out any immediate response – 'I really would be grateful if we could do without the denials and all the rest of it, and come to the point. I'm absolutely mystified as to why you should do this.'

Dead silence, then a clearing of Nicky's throat. 'Deep waters, Hugh. Deep waters.'

'Keep it absolutely simple. Just tell me why you did it.'

Again, a long pause. Then Nicky surprised Hugh by being oddly direct. 'Well, let's explore this. Banville Trust is going to be a key player in the Macaulay Group excursions that are about to begin. You may have a minority position, but you can wield considerable power. You can block Ned Macaulay if he wants to vote Banville's Macaulay shares in a way you might not wish. It follows therefore that a third party, whoever that might be, may want to persuade you to block Ned's vote. That in turn could be the catalyst for control of Macaulay falling into the hands of whoever that third party was supporting in the battle for control of the company. It may be that the third party has not yet decided whom to support. But the third party would wish in any circumstances to have your personal position under their influence.'

'Delightful. So Waring's are attempting to coerce me by demonstrating that they can damage me and my family and my company through the press. And my own brother is one your closest colleagues.'

'Now I never commented on that wild rumour of yours, and I'm not going to now. I'm simply pointing out to you that a third party, circling around this situation at Macaulay, would no doubt consider having you on their side to be a considerable bonus. So if I was you I would turn my mind to what there might be in this for myself. You have something to sell, wouldn't you say? Something of great value which others want, and would no doubt compensate you for very handsomely indeed. That's a very strong position to be in.'

Hugh wondered for a moment whether to protest at that specifically, but had lost the energy for it. 'So what is this third party of yours going to feed to the *Post* next? Can you tell me that?'

'How on earth would I know? All I would advise you is that if you are able to identify this third party, then you make contact and confirm that you will work with them over the Macaulay situation to your mutual advantage. And I should spell out to them exactly what you want, financially or otherwise, for doing so. And then, if that's a reasonable proposition do you know what I think would happen? I would guess the *Post*, starved of any more material, will then decide to move on and leave you alone. And leave your wife alone. For she is a little vulnerable, poor Nicola, isn't she? A little bit open to gossip?'

There was dead silence.

'You're a shit, Nicky. A total shit.'

'I recall you saying that.'

'And how would you know anything about anything?'

'Exactly. Just what I was going to say. It's just a hypothesis. How would I know?'

The Banville Trust offices were on the top floor of a particularly dingy Edwardian block in the shadow of St Paul's

Cathedral. They had been chosen by Ned with relish. The obvious cheapness of its rent and the mournful gloominess of its aspect were in pointed contrast to those of the Macaulay Group itself, just down the street, housed in an extravagant and grandiloquent landmark building.

That morning four of them sat around what was politely referred to as the boardroom table. This was a coffee-ringed and scratched, flaking object that Ned had taken over for free from the office's previous tenants. They had also left behind the matching chrome and plastic chairs on which he, Hugh, Rod Tadlock and Nathan Epstein now sat.

'So that's what we do,' Ned was saying. 'At the meeting tomorrow morning I will produce for them this letter here from Rod, addressed to the board, confirming that he has withdrawn his offer to subscribe into the company. When they've absorbed that, I will produce this second letter, from me, stating my willingness to invest myself, through Banville, the same amount of money as Rod, and on almost the same terms. We invest £90 million pounds now, for 23 per cent of the common stock, and then have the sole right to subscribe further funds in the future, at par, and at my sole discretion as to how much, and when.'

'And you have already formally made your offer now, Rod, haven't you?' Hugh asked. 'Subject to contract obviously, but a formal offer for £90 million for 23 per cent now, and then the further subscription rights?'

Tadlock nodded, 'Yes, by registered delivery to Charlie Kimpton a few hours ago, with copies simultaneously to Fairmeadows and Waring's. As Nathan suggested.'

'And both Fairmeadows and Waring's will definitely be at

the meeting in attendance?' Epstein asked. 'You've arranged that, Ned?'

'Yes. I called my father to request that, without giving my reasons of course, and he agreed.'

Epstein nodded. 'And Hugh's consent to Ned casting the Banville vote in Ned's favour? We've got that?'

Ned held it up. 'Signed and sealed. We got Macleish's to draft it last night.'

'And Banville's subsequent agreement with Antipodean & Global?'

Tadlock passed a file across to him, which Epstein looked through, then pushed back to him.

'In there as you can see are the heads of agreement, which the board in Sydney have accepted subject to contract, in the confirmatory letter they got over to us by courier last night,' Tadlock said.

'No changes? Just as we left it?'

Tadlock took an envelope from his case, and passed it to Epstein. 'Read it. No changes. On Banville Trust's acquisition of a majority interest in the Macaulay Group, the Antipodean & Global board agree to recommend to shareholders a takeover of Antipodean by Macaulay on the terms specified in the heads of agreement, this immediately to be followed by a public listing of Macaulay, now including Antipodean, on the London Stock Exchange.'

Epstein studied the letter, replaced it in its envelope and returned it to Tadlock. He gazed at him for a moment or two, then smiled. 'That will make you a rich man, Rod, an exceedingly rich man. All those embarrassing temporary liquidity troubles over and done with. Antipodean & Global gone to

197

Ned here, but you personally back in the money, safe and sound. Am I right?'

'Right,' Tadlock said. 'Back in the money. Back in play.'

Lord Kimpton disliked board meetings intensely and, if he could have had his way, would never have held them.

He rapped the table, a huge, highly polished mahogany affair, and gazed around him. Giles sat on his right, under the portrait of his uncle, the Brigadier. On Kimpton's left, under the picture of the first Lord Kimpton, was the Company Secretary, Harrison. Beside Harrison was the Director of Finance, Rogers. Then there was Ned, looking well groomed and competent, and opposite him the two other family directors, Kimpton's first cousins. The deaf cousin was permanently anxious that he was missing the debate. The other made a point of never reading a board paper and never saying a word. At the end of the table sat the advisers, attending the meeting at Ned's behest. Nicky Waring and James Emerson were there for Waring's, and the saturnine, elegant Jeremy Eastham for Fairmeadows, the Macaulay lawyers.

'Let's begin,' Kimpton said crossly, looking at his watch and wondering how long this damn fool nonsense would take, and when he could be safely at the bar at White's. 'Harrison?'

'No apologies for absence, my Lord,' he said, as quiet as a mouse. He patted the pocket containing the filthy smelling briar pipe which would be lit and sucked the moment he was released and back safely in his office.

'The minutes of the last meeting?' Harrison prompted, breathing the words deferentially in the direction of the Chairman's ear.

'Minutes of the last meeting,' Kimpton growled. 'Taken as fair record,' he stated firmly, brooking no dissent, and signed them with the gold pen which Harrison held out for him, then retrieved with a show of humble gratitude.

'Matters arising are covered by the agenda,' Harrison whispered.

'Matters arising are all covered by the agenda,' Kimpton instructed the meeting.

'Item one,' came the whisper. 'Mr Tadlock's subscription. Papers are before us.'

'Item one. Proposed subscription by Mr Tadlock. Papers are before us.'

Ned, who had been sitting up to that point absolutely still and silent, now reached into the inside pocket of his jacket, took out an envelope and passed it up to his father. 'Chairman, this envelope contains a letter to the board from Mr Tadlock, a copy of which I have already seen,' he said, and glanced around the table. 'I think you should read it immediately, and inform the meeting of its contents. As you will see, the letter supersedes the board paper.'

Lord Kimpton tore angrily at the envelope flap, out of the corner of his eye seeing Nicky scribble a note to James Emerson beside him. He didn't know which irritated him more in the presence of his friends from Waring's – being called 'Chairman' by his younger son in that irritatingly ironic manner of his, or 'Father'. Either sounded insolent. And Harrison was the only person from whom he would take guidance as to what he was going to inform the board about. He read the note quickly, and passed the letter to him. Harrison read it, and raised one eyebrow.

199

'Tell them what it is about, Harrison,' Kimpton complained, as if he had made that perfectly clear in the first place.

Harrison cleared his throat. 'Gentlemen, the letter tells us that Mr Tadlock has decided now to withdraw his offer to subscribe into the company.' He looked around the table, surreptitiously patting his pipe, and gathered his features into an appropriately ambiguous form, lest he got out of kilter with how they were to react to this news.

There was silence. 'What was that?' asked the deaf cousin anxiously, but everyone ignored him.

'Why?' barked Kimpton, as if Harrison himself was to blame.

Harrison shrugged sadly, and shook his head. 'I'm afraid I don't know, my Lord. He doesn't say.'

Eastham whispered something to Nicky Waring and then looked up at Kimpton, looking for permission to speak. But before he could do so, Ned, reaching into his other inside pocket, took out another envelope. This time, without a word, he passed it straight to Harrison.

Harrison opened the envelope, read the contents and glanced up at Kimpton's livid features. 'With your permission, Chairman?'

'Go on, man, get on with it.'

'Mr Ned has put to the board in this letter an offer in replacement to the one withdrawn by Mr Tadlock – on, it appears at first reading, the same terms.' He looked it through once more, then passed it to Lord Kimpton, who glanced at it, then pushed it down the table towards Eastham and the Waring's party.

Eastham picked it up, read it, then handed it to Nicky and

James. 'May I, Chairman?' Eastham asked, and carried straight on. 'I believe the board must remind itself that the company at this moment is on the brink of insolvency, unless the banks will change their minds and allow the repayment extensions and additional debt that they set their minds against last week.' He turned to the Director of Finance. 'I believe you would agree with me, Mr Rogers? That there are insolvency issues here that must be addressed?'

Rogers nodded miserably, eyes down.

'And your latest contact with the banks was when?'

Rogers now looked in desperation at Lord Kimpton, who glowered back at him, furious. Rogers gulped. 'Yesterday. Last night.'

'And their position was what?'

'Unchanged.'

'No more debt?'

'No.'

'No extension to the repayment terms?'

'No.'

'No increase to the working capital facility?'

'None.' Rogers licked his lips, ashen-faced. He glanced in terror around the table, trying to find an ally. Everyone avoided his eye, except Ned, who nodded, and watched him in calm good humour.

'In these circumstances I must remind the board of each director's individual and collective responsibility to ensure that the company does not trade illegally,' Eastham continued. 'Now my understanding was that Mr Tadlock was in a position to complete his investment of £90 million very quickly indeed. That, we are informed, is no longer available to us. We are therefore in an extremely serious position.' He paused, and waited for a response.

Lord Kimpton looked like he was about to explode. Giles was trying to catch Nicky Waring's eye. Ned was staring out of the window. Harrison was patting his pipe.

'Given that, I believe the board will wish to do two things. First, to explore whether there is any alternative now to accepting Ned Macaulay's proposal, subject to contract; and, if not, whether Ned is actually in a position to complete the transaction under a very tight timetable. We will need formal assurance of that, in a form that we can depend on in law. We have days, in my view, and not weeks. It's as serious as that.'

'What was that?' came the plaintive appeal from Kimpton's cousin, leaning forward now, cupping the flap of both his ears out a full ninety degrees. No one took any notice of him.

'Days, not weeks,' Eastham repeated, courteously but with emphasis, looking directly into Kimpton's eyes, and sat back in his chair.

Lord Kimpton looked to Harrison, who nodded gently, and slipped to him a note that he had been quietly writing whilst Eastham was speaking. Kimpton looked at it, then put it in his pocket. 'My view exactly, Eastham. Thank you,' he said firmly. He turned in the direction of his deaf cousin. 'We have days. We don't have weeks. It's as serious as that,' he bellowed, accusingly, then looked down the table to Nicky Waring, telegraphing his need for assistance.

'May I, Chairman?' Nicky said. He looked around the table, his face etched in sincerity and gravitas. 'Let me say this. These are dangerous days, gentlemen, difficult days, worrying days. Your very future — the future of this magnificent family company – is in grave peril. We at Waring's, privileged to serve you, have been burning the midnight oil in our anxiety to find a solution for you. We suggested Mr Tadlock to you, and Mr Tadlock, for reasons best known to himself, has now let us down. But we are not defeated. Ned, magnificently, mindful of his family's need, has now stepped into the breach. It is the view of Waring's, gentlemen, advisers to the Macaulay Group for well nigh four decades now, that you should embrace Ned's offer with open hearts and gratitude and relief, and consider yourselves very proud that he has extended it.'

James, beside him, nodded emphatically in support, redoubling the vigour of this when he succeeded momentarily in catching Ned's eye.

'And may I add this one comment, Chairman?' Nicky continued. 'It's this. It was always Waring's view that Ned was the man for the job, the only man for the job, were it only possible to persuade him to pick up the burden. Well, we learn now that he had no need of persuasion. Cometh the hour, cometh the man. That's valour, gentlemen, that's leadership. Ned is our champion, and my only pride is that we at Waring's knew that all along, and have strived to find a way whereby our dearest wishes for Macaulay could be realized. Ned is your future. Can I say, in all humility, that it will be Waring's honour and privilege to work with you, Ned, in the years ahead – another link in that great, strong, unbreakable chain that binds Macaulay and Waring's together, and has done for so many wonderful years.'

There was complete silence. Then Giles, until that point invisible, looked up. 'Then why did you offer to finance me to do this, Nicky, and not Ned?' he asked mildly. 'Why did you suggest, not ten days ago, that I took the £90 million off someone or other to make the bid that Ned has just made, and then fire him off the board, and fire Father as chairman, and lead Macaulay myself?'

A delighted smile spread across Ned's face. Harrison retired behind an enormous handkerchief. The deaf cousin craned anxiously forward. Kimpton looked puzzled.

Nicky and James smiled up the table at Giles, wholly unabashed, amused at the misunderstanding. 'My dear Giles,' said Nicky, laughing. 'My dear Giles, dear oh dear.' He turned to James, and the two of them enjoyed the joke together. Then he turned back to Giles, and said, with kindly concern, 'We may have mentioned to you in passing perhaps – as an afterthought maybe, that if Ned couldn't or wouldn't for any reason step into the breach then an alternative might conceivably be yourself, but – really! Fire Ned from the board? Fire the Chairman? Too preposterous!' He laughed again, and James joined him.

Eastham smiled coldly as Nicky and James continued their merriment, nodding up the table to Lord Kimpton. Giles went crimson, then fell silent once more, staring down at his papers.

Eastham coughed. 'I'm sure you want to press on, Chairman,' he said.

'We should press on,' Kimpton informed the meeting sternly, and Harrison breathed something into his ear.

Kimpton looked crossly down the table once more. 'Eastham, would you care to assist us to move matters forward at this point?'

'Certainly, Chairman,' Eastham replied. 'First, I take it that the directors are not aware of any alternative sources of funding at this point. May we be sure of that?'

Harrison whispered, and Kimpton told Eastham that that was the case.

'In that case, may I suggest that there are two issues that the board would wish to clarify with Ned. We note from his letter that the subscription is to be made by the Banville Trust rather than by him personally, so we will need to see a Resolution from the Banville board empowering Ned to make his offer, reinforced in this instance by signed confirmation from Banville's minority shareholder. Secondly, we need formal confirmation that Banville have the funds in place, the £90 million, to complete this transaction.'

Ned nodded, reached down into his briefcase and took from it a leather-bound file. He looked into this, took out copies of several documents, and pushed them across to Eastham. 'Here they are,' he said. 'Macleish's will be acting for me and for Banville Trust, as you can see. You have there the Banville Board Resolution, you have Hugh Emerson's signed and witnessed consent, and you have a certificate from Banville's bank confirming that they are holding on escrow against the completion of this subscription the sum of £90 million. Finally, you also have Macleish's draft of the subscription agreement,' he paused, 'the terms of which I have to make clear are non-negotiable.'

Eastham scanned the documents through, and looked up at Kimpton. 'May I, Chairman?' he asked, but proceeded straight on anyway. 'All seems in order, but I must point out to the directors that there is one difference between this agreement and the abortive one we had with Mr Tadlock. Ned's agreement allows him to make a second subscription, at par, at any time of his own choosing and to whatever quantum he at his own discretion decides. Mr Tadlock's agreement in this respect was a trifle more curtailed. This means, as you all must realize, that if Ned personally, or the Banville Trust, or the pair in aggregate, have the funds, then Ned will take control of the Macaulay Group at the moment of his choosing. It's my responsibility to be certain the board understands this, and is aware of the consequences.'

Harrison leant towards Lord Kimpton and spoke to him openly and at length.

Kimpton, frowning, nodding, suddenly flushed bright crimson, slapped his hand on the table and, ignoring Harrison's attempts to calm him, turned back to Eastham. 'I regard this as an outrage!' he said, his voice trembling. 'An outrage. I will not allow it. If my son has funds available to him – and I would like to know where they came from incidentally – then he should make those funds available to the firm in a different manner altogether. I run this firm and I will continue to do so for as long as I choose, at which point Giles will take over. That is absolutely my final, irrevocable word.' He slapped the table once more and stared defiantly down at the others.

Eastham nodded, shrugged, smiled his thin smile, and looked across at Ned.

Ned pushed himself up in his chair, smoothed back his dark hair, and turned a calm face towards his father. 'Chairman,' he began, and Kimpton winced his annoyance. 'I have made it clear that the terms of Banville's subscription are non-negotiable. I also want to make it clear that I do indeed intend to invest further in due course and to take control. When I have control I will take over the chairmanship from you, and you will retire, and Giles also will be required to step down at that time. I intend then to drive the Macaulay Group on to become one of the great news and media companies of the world – to the very great benefit not only of whatever new shareholders we may have acquired by that point, but also of our own family shareholders, who for many years have been treated rather worse than dirt.'

'I will not accept it,' Kimpton said.

'You will accept it,' Ned replied. 'If you don't, the firm will go into receivership. The family's shares, including yours, will be worthless. Additionally there will be legal proceedings taken against you, personally – by me. I will sue you. By refusing a genuine, properly formulated offer of equity funding at this critical juncture you would not only be disgracing your care of the shareholders – your family – but severely damaging the interests of the creditors, including the banks. The consequences of that are too painful to contemplate.'

There was absolute silence. Ned had insulted his father, and contemptuously.

Then Eastham said quietly, 'I have to advise you, Lord Kimpton, that what has been said is true. Your company is on the brink of receivership. We have before us a bona fide offer of equity funding to an adequate scale to protect the creditors 100 per cent. In the circumstances in which you find yourselves there is no question in my mind but that the board should accept it. Must accept it, actually. There is no choice.'

Kimpton's colour had moved in the last few moments from an enraged crimson to a deathly, haggard pale. 'Very well, then,' he said eventually, glancing for a moment at Harrison, sitting miserably beside him. 'Very well, we will accept my son's offer. But I of course resign – immediately.'

As he was gathering up his papers Giles stirred in his chair. 'Me too,' he said. 'I resign with Father.' He got to his feet, and set off for the door, ahead of his father, leaving his papers abandoned on the table. Then he stopped, and turned to Nicky Waring, and to Ned's horror he saw that tears were running down his brother's face. 'You're amoral people,' he said. 'You have the standards of the gutter. You first set me up, and then you refuse to take my calls, and then you abandon me. I wanted to make an alternative suggestion to you that I believe would have worked for Father, and worked for the family, and worked for the company, but I couldn't get through. You set me up, and then you cast me adrift. You're shits.'

As Nicky and James started once more to produce their amused, baffled, kindly chuckles it was Ned who responded to his brother. 'I know, Giles. You're perfectly correct. Waring's made their offer to you, funding you with £90 million. But when I got control of Caroline's shares, which gave me a block, they dropped you. And do you know where they were getting their money from to fund you? From New Jersey sources that were wholly disreputable. Drug traffickers? Arms dealers? Who knows? It was illegal money, and Waring's were laundering it. You fell into very unfortunate hands.'

He looked across at Nicky and James and grinned. 'Waring's,' he said, 'old money, old establishment, shitty old Waring's. You're well rid of them, Giles. You really are.'

'You are correct as to where Waring's got Giles's £90 million from, Nathan? I sincerely hope so. In the heat of the moment I couldn't resist saying it. But it was worth it. The look on

Nicky Waring's face I shall remember and treasure for the rest of my days.'

Epstein smiled. 'Absolutely correct, I can assure you of that, though they'll protect themselves now, and cover their trail with obfuscation and bluster and nothing will come of it.'

'They must be wondering where on earth I got the information from.'

'They must certainly have done at the time you said it,' Nathan said, 'but not now. They were told this afternoon. And they'll know why. Waring's and I had some unfinished business.'

'Who told them?'

'That's the fun part: the bank themselves. I had a certain line of pressure I could apply against the Ethical Bank of New Jersey. I know them of old. They shouldn't have accepted those funds for transiting. I talked to them. They did what I asked them to do. They told Waring's it was me.'

Ned laughed. 'God, Nicky and James, what idiots they are!'

'Yes, they are. But I tell you how it all adds up. You won. Rod Tadlock won, or will do in a month or two. I did too. Your father lost, but actually he deserved to. Giles lost, I suppose, but we all know that he was never happy in the firm. He'll go off to his laboratories now, and his scientific journals, and when you take Antipodean & Global and then go for the big public listing he's going to be a very wealthy man for the rest of his life, given the shareholding he's got, and he'll put that to very worthwhile use indeed.'

Ned thought about his brother, and winced as he remembered his tears. Such a good man. But at least now he was free.

'And you know something, Ned? Nicky Waring and Hugh's brother didn't really lose either, if truth were told. The money-laundering thing will never stick on them, and I've had my fun with that, and I shan't pursue it any further. They've failed to collect some very large fees, and they've lost Macaulay as a client, but give them a couple of days and they will have forgotten the whole thing. Being Nicky Waring is an unusual way of life, to put it mildly. He is a totally, terminally, incorrigible man. He thinks of nothing, nothing, but the accumulation of fees.'

Ned smiled at this, but he knew Epstein too was driven by nothing else much but money – no doubt in this transaction as much as any of his other's. He had made the deal for Ned, there was no doubt about that, but it wasn't philanthropy that governed Epstein's actions. Ned was by no means sure he knew what would prove to be Epstein's eventual goal in this. He would never entirely trust him. But, for now, sufficient unto the day . . .

Ned got to his feet, stuck his hands in his pockets, walked over to the window, and gazed down towards the Macaulay Group offices, just the other side of Ludgate Circus. 'Victory,' he said, but his voice was leaden. 'It's a funny thing. I've wanted to run Macaulay since I was a small kid. And now that I'm about to – for all the excitement ahead – just at this moment I feel flat, to be honest with you.'

All three were silent for a moment or two, Ned still staring down the street, Epstein and Hugh watching him, waiting for him to speak.

'You know something?' Ned said at last. 'A generation back, two generations back, we did such marvellous things. Founded and built these two great newspapers, created charities for the needy, said brave things, did brave things. Now I've snatched the company away from my father, and it's up to me. I have to pick the firm up, and give it back its confidence and its position in the world. It's my responsibility to the Macaulays now, past and present.' He turned and laughed, suddenly in good heart again, and came back to the table to retrieve his papers. 'It's a matter of family honour, pompous as that may sound, a matter of our family's honour.'

Giles sat on his mother's bed, and, for the first time in many years, reached out to hold her hand. She had retired early that night, tired and unhappy. She was on the edge of sleep, her Angus Wilson novel dropped to the floor, when she heard Giles's voice and the knock on her door, and called for him to come in.

He told her then what had happened and, unusually for her, she had made a point of allowing him to tell the whole story without interruption. She had heard it all already, for Ned had called her earlier in the day, and after that her husband. She had lain in bed expecting Charlie to come up and see her when he got home. In what condition she hardly dared to guess. Certainly he would have been to White's, which might have either encouraged him to drunkenness, or just possibly, in the company of his oldest friends, he might have been calmed and comforted.

Either way he had taken the most mortal of blows. Drunk, Charlie was not an entirely pleasing man to deal with, and she had so dreaded his arrival home that she had even considered locking her bedroom door. But that would have been an act of vulgarity, the gesture of a second-rate wife, and a second-rate woman. What Charlie needed was help and reassurance. Whatever sort of wife she had been to him over the years it was her duty now to give him that, and in a way that she knew no one else could. She accepted the burden gladly, and with something approaching pride, for she was certainly not proud of herself for the conduct of her marriage, and particularly for the conduct of her erotic life. There had not been in recent years many opportunities for her to repay Charlie for the love he had borne her, nor to recompense him for her own dishonesty – for she knew it had been that in the way that she had half pretended, half assumed love for him in return.

But it was Giles who had come to her now, and as he took her hand she made a point of squeezing and caressing his in what she hoped was a pleasing, convincing portrayal of maternal love. How strange it was that she had never really taken to Giles. How unattractive a feature of her personality that was; additionally so, given her untidy, secretly unattached relationship with Katie too. She was sure that had served to injure her daughter deeply. The truth was that all her maternal affection and focus had been concentrated on Ned. To the profound mutual harm, she was certain, of both of them.

Giles had finished now, and she sat up in her bed, and put her arms around his neck. It was a gesture that surprised her, and pleased her, as much as she could see it pleased him. Awkwardly, he put his arm around her too, and they stayed together in that way for a moment or two, before she kissed him on the cheek, and then, gently holding his face, on the forehead. She lay back again on her pillows, her dressing gown tucked around her, and, holding one of his hands in both of hers, smiled.

'My darling,' she said, and gently massaged his forearm in a manner that she suddenly remembered had lulled him when he was a very small boy. 'Hold on, my darling. This is not the end of anything for you, please realize that. It's a timely, wonderful rescue from a life you hated, but performed out of a sense of duty. You're going now to have a very distinguished life. I'll help you to do that. Together, we'll build something wonderful.'

And to her astonishment, and to her pride, she meant it. Giles, staring at her, open-mouthed, saw that too. In a single physical gesture of maternal love, she had made him whole. How simple it was. How wicked of her never to have done this before. How stupid of her not to have seen that all she had needed to do for Giles was to show him love. She'd ruined his life – singlehandedly, coldly, she had destroyed him. Now, maybe, she could make that good.

Part Three

Four Years Later
− 2004

13

It was Ned who read the letter first. When he called Hugh the following day he found that Hugh too had just received a copy of it. He had it in front of him when Ned telephoned, and continued reading it as they talked.

Dear Mr Macaulay

I have been a devoted reader of the Daily Meteor *for many years, and I was so interested to hear you on the radio yesterday afternoon talking about its centenary this year, and all the ups and downs the paper has been through over that time.*

You were so interesting, not to say moving, about the editorial standards for the Meteor *and the* Sunday Correspondent *that your family have always held most dear, and how careful you and your family have been over the decades to play straight and to play honourably and to tell the truth, however painful at times the truth might be.*

I so admire you for that, and it made me all the more certain that the standards you aspire to are all that we should be looking for in the national press, which at its best is an example to the rest of the world of the very aspiration and good morality of the British people themselves.

Given that, I thought you would be interested in reading this cutting from the Broadwich Echo, *some twenty-six years ago. I wonder if the young lady we read of there has quite the personal claim to good morality that she should have, given her position these days as your best-known columnist, counsellor and 'agony aunt' to those of your readers who, in their pain and their vulnerability, turn to her for advice and help.*

I think not.

Yours ever,

Elizabeth Anstruther (Miss)

'What on earth do you make of this, Hugh?' Ned asked. 'I'd drop it in the bin, and I probably will anyway, but I thought I'd call you first, given the fact that you and I share Anna Lavey, in a manner of speaking.'

'Hold on a moment, I still haven't read the cutting she sent with it. Here it is. '*Teenager leaves baby on police station doorstep,*' he read out aloud, then fell silent as he read the supporting copy.

A teenage girl from Hackney in East London, whom we cannot name for legal reasons, was understood to have been questioned last night over the identity of a baby girl, only a few hours old, who was discovered over the weekend abandoned on the rear steps of the police station in Mafeking Street. The baby survived, but a spokesman at Jubilee Hospital described her condition as extremely weak and poorly on admittance, when she was put immediately into intensive care.

Nurses named the baby Margaret, in honour of Princess Margaret, who opened the new maternity ward earlier this year, and the hospital spokesman told the Echo *that it is hoped that in a day or two she will be making good progress towards a complete recovery.*

'Well, I don't know what to make of it,' Hugh said. 'If this Elizabeth Anstruther woman has any evidence that the teenager was Anna Lavey, then of course there's a story in it, given Anna's public profile. But I've known Anna for years, and I've never had any hint of this before. Maybe it was her. Maybe this Miss Anstruther woman is a crackpot. God knows. So what do we do about it?'

There was silence as Ned considered the options, and Hugh let him. 'Actually I don't think I can just drop it in the bin, much as I'd like to. Anna Lavey is news, there's no two ways about that. And if a quarter of a century ago she abandoned an illegitimate child, a baby only a few hours old, for Christ's sake, on the steps of a police station in the middle of a freezing winter night, and then . . .'

'Summer.'

'What do you mean – summer?'

'It was a summer night. Look at the date on the cutting.'

There was a pause. 'All right, summer. For God's sake, Hugh, there is a very big story here indeed, and if we don't run it then Miss Moneypenny or whatever her name is will feed it to one of our rivals. And they will love it – assuming that it is Anna, or was Anna. The only way we're going to find that out is to ask her. Do you agree?'

'I suppose so. Yes, I agree.'

'So will you?'

'Why me? You're the newspaper people.'

'Because I don't know her, not really, not with any intimacy. And because this sort of thing is what Hugh Emerson is famously good at. You know that. Smiley, reassuring Hugh, everyone's confidant, everyone's cuddle – just your ball of wax.' He laughed, but Hugh, irritated by the caricature, which he'd heard too often from Ned in the past, didn't join in.

'OK, I'll do it, if that's what you want. I'll go around to see her, rather than do it on the telephone. But I think we should agree on something. If she denies it, seriously denies it, then we should support her – which would mean, as far as you are concerned, ignoring the story, whether or not the *Herald* or the *Comet* or any other paper runs with it.'

Ned hesitated. 'I'd have to think about that. I don't see how we could avoid giving the story coverage if one of the others does. No one would run it without being sure they had the facts right, otherwise Anna would sue them to kingdom come. So if one of the others went public . . . I don't know. But look at it this way, Hugh. If this story is true, and Anna decides in time to come out and tell the whole story, just think of the book you're going to get from her!'

Hugh asked Anna to lunch, but took the precaution of ensuring that they were given a table hidden away in the corner by the bar, where they would be able to talk without the risk of being overheard.

He found her in cheerful form, amusing, flirtatious with the waiters – all charm with a woman who slipped up to the table to ask her for her autograph. Sipping water, Anna Lavey, with her public around her, was behaving at her best.

Hugh asked what she had in mind for her next book, with the implication that this was the reason he had invited her.

'Yes,' she said, 'my next book. I'll tell you, and you must be as brutal with me as you wish, because you have an instinct for these things, if you think it's not going to work. I want to get away from yet another retread of my columns, you know what I mean, and instead of telling people about how to live their lives, I want to tell them something about mine.'

'You want to write a memoir?' Hugh asked in surprise. She had always refused to consider it.

'Yes. At least I want to write about how it all started – my childhood in the East End; a homage to my family, as much as anything else, because they deserve it.' Anna paused, for dramatic effect, and Hugh sensed she was delivering carefully rehearsed lines.

'I'm not sure I ever really told you this, Hugh, but we were terribly poor. I'm talking dirt poor. There was nothing. We lived a caricature of a certain sort of Jewish life, in the East End, at that particular time. Father was a tailor, and not a very good one, judging from the amount of work he got. My mother arrived in London from Poland in the 1950s when she was little more than a child. She never learnt much English, but she made what money she could by taking in washing and ironing and simple sewing and mending. We lived in the sort of poverty that you would find it difficult to credit. You wouldn't believe that such deprivation could have existed in London, and in your time. But we survived, my family and I. I had nothing as a little girl, and yet I had everything. I had my mother's lap to rest in, and my father's knee to climb on, and my own little arms to wrap around them both.' Anna stopped, and smiled, self-deprecatingly.

'God, I'm going to burst into tears if I come over all schmaltzy like this. Sorry to embarrass you, sweetheart. It's those physical things that I remember most of those earliest days. Later, more general things – my mother and father's teaching, and their patience, and their wisdom and their goodness. And you have to understand the background: there was not much food, and the house was tiny and filthy; dark and damp and cold. It was quite awful. But there was love and laughter, and fighting and reconciliation and security and Jewishness and . . . well, joy, in a word. I have not one jot of religion in me these days, as you know, but they were jewels of God, my Mum and Dad.' She pulled a little face, as if to apologize for her emotional candour.

Hugh, listening to her, watching her, came to the conclusion that for all her sentimental exaggerations of her childhood, and in this telling they verged on the grotesque, this was where the strength and assurance of the woman came from, and from that her achievements. She had given him a very good opening, if he could find a way to use it. Any fool could see that this Miss whoever it was with the Pimlico address, with the prim writing style of a spinster of a certain age, was danger writ large. If the Macaulay papers did not give her what she wanted, then she'd be off to the others, and nothing would give them more pleasure, if they were sure of the facts, than destroying the reputation of the *Meteor*'s star columnist.

'I can't tell you how excited I am about what you're telling me, Anna,' he said. 'I've always wanted to persuade you to write your memoirs, and now you're there before me. And without being vulgarly commercial about it, that whole field of Jewish family life, and the warmth and humour of it – particularly perhaps London East End warmth and humour – think of Arnold Wesker amongst others – is so strong. The book could be very big indeed. I'll make sure it is.'

Anna laughed, and put her hand on the waiter's arm as he brushed down the tablecloth, whispering something to him that made him smile in delight.

'I'm sure you will, darling,' she said now as, in a performance which Hugh always hated, she frowned into a tiny mirror, pouted her lips and applied scarlet paint to them, then pressed them together to bed it down. 'That's what you're there for. That's what you do.' She bustled her lipstick away in her carpet bag, smiled at him, and laid a finger on his cheek.

Hugh struggled to restrain himself from recoiling. He was not good at unexpected physical contact.

'And you're a sweetie, darling, everyone says so. I don't know why I'm so beastly to you sometimes, but I simply can't resist it, I've known you so long. But you do really think that I might risk this book? You think I could make it work?'

'I love it, Anna, I really do,' he said. 'It will be marvellous. Tell me – are your parents still alive? Brothers? Sisters?'

'Oh darling, my mother and father both died centuries ago. No sisters, no brothers, no uncles, no cousins. Just me now. I'm all that's left.'

Hugh nodded and let his expression show his sympathy for her. She'd had a tough life, there was no doubt about that, but she was such a solid personality – though so erratic too. One day – at least privately in front of him – a foul-mouthed, ill-mannered harridan, the next a woman of gentility and charm, if a rather strident version of that. She was always acting. What role did she play for her husband, or was she no more consistent with him?

'Tell me one thing, Anna, so that I can go away and start shaping this book in my mind and think how we might go about publishing it. You've mentioned your childhood years. But the later teens – sixteen, seventeen? Were you still at home then? Still at school? Were those years particularly formative for you?'

She gathered up her carpet bag, glanced at her watch, and began the process of getting on her way. She shook her head. 'Nothing more or less formative then than there had been before, I would say. I left school at the normal age, and went straight into student nursing, but we'll make a book out of that another day.'

There was something in the way she said this that made Hugh pause. He sensed deception. But he risked a jocular, throwaway question as they both got to their feet, smiling broadly as he asked it. 'Boyfriends, Anna? Babies?'

Anna gave a shriek of laughter, slapped his hand and acted indignant. 'Lots of boyfriends, darling, a Jewish princess like me, but babies!? Darling! What sort of girl do you take me for?' She blew a raspberry at him, made a fuss of the waiters, and smiled and waved and charmed her passage out of the restaurant and into a waiting taxi.

Hugh stood at the pavement and closed the door behind her. As he raised his hand into a wave, she leant towards the window. 'I almost forgot! You'll never guess who I'm off to interview now. For my Great Contemporaries series in the *New Statesman* – next week's issue. Henry Jackson, darling, that's who. Isn't it a small world!'

Hugh shrugged, smiled and waved her on her way, but his insides felt as if they had turned to water. He had no idea that she knew. He liked to think actually that nobody knew, though there had been occasions in the past when he had realized that he was fooling himself in that. But Anna! Anna was capable of doing much damage with this, if she was in a mind to. And he suspected that she probably was, were Hugh to cross her. That was a warning shot he had just received, and he should make no mistake about that.

A week later Hugh bought a copy of the *New Statesman* from the newsstand in Sloane Square, and read the article as soon as he got back in the car. The article was a long piece, and showed Jackson in a particularly good light. Retired from active politics eighteen months or so before, after his resignation from the Cabinet in a row over the tightening of immigration laws, it was becoming fashionable to mourn him as a big hitter lost too early from the liberal wing of affairs, and one of the great Prime Ministers that should have been. His private life, however, remained a closed book, and no journalist had ever been allowed to speculate as to the circumstances of his long marriage, and his life alone in that quiet, gaunt apartment building in Whitehall, facing down on to the river. Anna had clearly got not much further than anyone else, though Hugh could see that she had tried, and he thought he knew why.

He turned his great head towards me, and I thought for a moment that he was going to treat my question with absolute disdain. This was the man who once, famously, walked out of a live BBC television studio when he decided that the interviewer's line of questioning was impertinently tenacious about his personal life. But it was not disdain he showed me then, but rather a sense of brooding conjecture – should he answer, or shouldn't he?

I had been so cautious in my approach to him, so tactful, and actually so well prepared (we journalists all know the horror stories of his impatience, bordering on contempt, for those who come to interview him without doing their homework) that for a man as naturally courteous to women as Henry Jackson he would have found it difficult to snub me now. So he didn't. That quite wonderful, full, sexually vital smile came to his face, and that was all I got, and we moved on. We talked of his Mastership, just announced, of Jesus College Cambridge, and from that those most radical recent statements of his regarding the scope and funding of higher education, which have appeared to enrage the Secretary of State and the Opposition in equal measure. We discussed the reviews, uniformly good, of his new biography of Lloyd George. We went over the reasons, once again, as to why he had refused the Prime Minister's request that he should go to the House of Lords to lead the party's benches there. Pleasantly, easily, he brought the interview to a close, and showed me to the door. Like every journalist before me, I was no nearer than before in understanding what Jackson's emotional life might hold – and an emotional life is there, you can be sure of that, and in spades, for the man exudes roman-ticism like a panther exudes grace.

It is in the public record that their only child, a son now in his thirties, is profoundly autistic, but neither Jackson nor his wife, Alice, an Edinburgh academic, have ever commented about their marriage, and one knows that they never will. Jackson is

*without a shadow of a doubt one of our Great Contemporaries,
and even now, at seventy years old, the Labour Party must rue
the day they allowed him to pass out of active political life with
his intellectual energy and drive so clearly maintained. He's a
very good, perhaps nearly great historian, if we accept the judge-
ment of his peers. I would say too that he's a very good, perhaps
genuinely great man. But nature abhors a vacuum. And as
long as he lives, the private, romantic life of Henry Jackson will
continue to absorb the speculation of all us hacks. Or should I
say us women hacks. Frankly, seventy or not, he's as damned
sexy as that.*

A traffic warden rapped on the window to move Hugh on,
and he nodded to him and fired the engine. He drove up Sloane
Street, then got stuck in the inevitable traffic jam at the junc-
tion with Basil Street, and reminded himself, as always, never
to go this route again. He tapped his fingers on the wheel,
turned the radio on, turned it off, and, as the traffic eased,
inched the car forward.

What Anna was not going to be allowed to do was to harm
his family, Hugh thought. He would stop that at all costs.
Their mutual inability to face the fact of Nicola's relationship
with Jackson was both a help and a hindrance in the preser-
vation of their marriage. But, as always, he came now to the
same conclusion. To open the subject up, after all these years,
would achieve nothing. It was more likely to break their
marriage than stabilize it. They were close, he and Nicola,
even given her secret life, often very close, and Danny, a clearly
perceptive child, could see that they were, and draw his
reassurance from that. It was a bizarre way of life, it really was

– but unorthodox as it was, it worked up to a point. And working up to a point was, in his mind, as good as Hugh and Nicola could hope for, given where they had been.

Miss Anstruther was no fool. She took her *Guardian* every day with the *Daily Meteor*, and on Sundays both the *Sunday Correspondent* and the *Observer*. She had read more than enough about morbid obsession and the behavioural pattern of those afflicted by it. But she had meant no harm, and she told herself she had done no harm. She should have stopped it of course, but she had loved Anna Lavey. She knew she was an extremely lonely, near friendless woman, and her behaviour had reflected that. This had been her indulgence. Yes – she had loved her. She recognized that she had possessed no other emotional outlet. Take that away, and there would be very little left of her indeed.

But four years ago it had indeed all been taken away. She could recall to this day every detail of returning home from that dreadful encounter. There she had been at her front door, fumbling in her bag for her key. She had wandered in, clutching at the walls of her narrow little hall, muttering to herself, trying to cry. Crying would help. She had poured a glass of gin and the warm, flat tonic water that remained in the bottle at the back of a cupboard, but it had tasted cloyingly sweet and medicinal, and she had spat it out into the kitchen sink. She had thought of making a cup of tea, but had found that she couldn't be bothered to fill the kettle. So she had laid on her bed, fully dressed, arm across her eyes, sobbing sometimes, calling out for help to the God that she addressed nightly in the same childish, sentimental terms as she had since a little girl. It was only at that level that she had any ability to deal with God at all.

Tossing and turning, trying to find some relief from her despair, in the bleakest hours of pre-dawn she had gone to the kitchen to lie with her head in her decades' old gas oven, the gas taps full on. She might well have gone through with it, she thought, had it not been for the cat, who had wandered in after her to check what she was doing. Seeing that she was on the floor he had pushed and nuzzled his head up against her forearm with such persistence that she withdrew her head from the oven, rubbed his ears, picked him up in her arms, turned off the gas taps, and went back to bed.

All the next day she had stayed there. The telephone rang, but she left it unanswered. There was a rapping on her front door shortly after, but she ignored that too. But at last, as dusk was falling, Miss Anstruther had suddenly felt strong. She got up, made tea and toast, fed the cat, pulled her morning paper out from her letter box to glance at the headlines, and gone to run a bath. And as she lay there, her mug of tea beside her on the window ledge, her toes pushed comfortably up by the taps, murder was in her heart.

Counting back, it had been more than twelve years that Miss Anstruther had been in love with Anna Lavey. She had made herself repeat that, because it was a phrase that she had never quite allowed herself to use before. She'd been in love. She said the words again – in love, passionately, romantically, in love. Not all of that was quite true, but she was in the mood for bitter, exaggerated self-recrimination. She'd wasted her life on it, frittered all those years away on this stupid neurosis. But what she felt in herself now was unmistakable: the raw, physical aggression of Anna's attack had turned her obsessive love into the polar opposite – pure, cold hatred.

Miss Anstruther knew that she had made an utter fool of herself. It had happened, and history could not be rewritten. She shuddered with disgust at the image of herself on Anna Lavey's doorstep, that inane grin on her face, thrusting out her dampened, schoolgirl-crush presents. That bloody bunch of flowers and that over-wrapped, over-ribboned package, in which lay folded neatly in its tissue paper the bloody silk shirt she had spent weeks choosing and had clutched to her breast like the swooning virgin that she was.

She had run some more hot water with her toe, and told herself that she was no longer hurt. She was no longer remotely in love. What Anna Lavey had done to her had been cruel to the point of viciousness, and she would embark on a path of revenge. The more remorseless it was, and the more calculated, the better it would be.

She had climbed out of the bath, towelled herself down, gazed with perfect satisfaction in her late mother's big gilt mirror at her mottled, naked body, and begun to make plans. She hadn't felt so purposeful for years. Still naked, she sat on the bed, cut her toenails and considered what she would do next. All this time she had been dabbling around on the fringes of Anna's personal history, in her adoration of her, in her desire to know all there was to know about her. The object of it all, the delicious fantasy, had been that she would be ready to enter her life one day – as her assistant perhaps, her housekeeper, or best of all Anna's nurse and companion as her health slipped away in some terminal but prettily unravaging illness. What Miss Anstruther had gleaned from her mild little searches over the years was that there were constant surprises to be found in Anna Lavey's past. In her old incarnation Miss Anstruther sought only lovely snippets of Anna's history; the bijou cottage in Norfolk in which she had lived with little Andrew, in the golden days of Bobbie's exile; the primary school in the East End at which poor Anna had spent her early childhood; the nurse's hostel in Smithfield where she had been domiciled during her initial student training. Now, however, Miss Anstruther set busily to work, and it was anything but the sentimental trinkets of life that she was looking for.

The apparently minor falsehoods of Anna's accounts of her family history had aroused her interest. From the entry in the Hackney register of births, for example, Miss Anstruther knew not only Anna's true date of birth, but also her true name – Anna Levine. The primary school records, found in the basement archives at the town hall, told a similar story. The hospital's entry records showed that she went into nursing training at the age of twenty rather than seventeen as she always claimed, and, instead of qualifying, had dropped out after barely six months. There were discrepancies in the pattern of her whereabouts for a couple of years or so after that. All in all it was . . . well, spotty, as her friend Gilly Lane put it, trying to appear interested as Elizabeth, for the umpteenth time in their little meals and walks together, described what she had found and what she couldn't find. It was good to see Elizabeth so animated, though Gilly remained only partially aware of its causes. Elizabeth had given her a sanitized account of a confrontation with Anna Lavey which seemed to have quite turned her against the woman, but not much more than that. Whatever the cause, Elizabeth's campaign was applauded by

Gilly Lane, who had little time for that Anna Lavey woman, who encouraged people to moon around whining about what might have been.

'And I tell you what, my dear – I can show you all manner of ways of finding things in public records that most people don't even realize exist,' she said to Elizabeth as they walked in Richmond Park that wet and blustery Saturday afternoon. 'A librarian's training like mine is just what you need for that sort of thing. And now we have the internet to help us too! When we get home you must lay out for me what you're looking for, and I'll tell you how to go about it. It'll be fun.'

And so it had been that Miss Anstruther made her way down to Broadwich, and caught the bus to Jack Lynch's house. She was there on a Friday morning, taken as part of her annual holiday allowance of twenty-five working days. Never before had she taken an odd day off like this, but a couple of weeks earlier, in a moment of stunning revelation, she had unearthed a lead so unexpected that, even in her most fevered imaginings, she could never have thought it possible.

The teenager could have been another Anna Levine, it was true. Miss Anstruther's searches in the Hackney archives had shown up at least six other Levine families living in or closely adjacent to the borough at that time. It was a Jewish neighbourhood. It was also possible that the name Anna was a family nickname, and had been used in error for the girl's real name, both in the police records and in the consequent newspaper report. But the connection between Hackney and Broadwich, a county and an awkward journey apart, seemed such an unlikely prospect for two people of the same age and same name: another

Anna Levine, about to give birth, also of her approximate age, also from Hackney, also in Broadwich at that time?

And now Miss Anstruther knew for certain why Anna Lavey, née Levine, was there. She'd gone to seek help from her sister, help which had clearly been refused: Anna's sister, the one who lived in Broadwich – the sister Anna said she didn't have.

Miss Anstruther stepped off the bus and shivered at the cold, salty wind blowing in off the sea. She looked around her. She had never seen such bleak desolation in her life. What a place to live. What a place for a child to grow up.

Nicola arrived outside Henry's apartment building almost half an hour earlier than they had arranged, and it was only the good fortune of glancing across at the entrance before getting out of the taxi that saved her from walking straight into the path of Anna Lavey. Henry had come down to the street to see her off, and Nicola sat there for two or three minutes more to ensure that Anna had really gone, and Henry was safely back in his flat, before paying her fare and going into the building herself.

Nicola had read the *New Statesman* piece of course and was bewildered by its tone. Henry Jackson was a politician, a statesman, a historian. He was, or had been in his prime, one of the best-known people in the country. Were Britain to become a republic, as she had read a few months before in a *Spectator* article, then his name would probably be one of a half dozen or so public figures that the nation might have elected as the first President. Anna Lavey was no fool, but the article she had written had seemed so wholly . . . well, inappropriate somehow, and for one normally so careful of her journalistic voice, it was an odd miscalculation for her to have made. Yes, he was a romantic man, in private. Yes, there was a very strong aura of sexuality about him, there was no doubt about it. But there was no show of these things in him. The cartoonists had long ago abandoned the image of him tossing his leonine locks in vanity, as it had never captured the essence of the man. Intellectual vanity perhaps, though those who knew him well would have called it more a sublime intellectual self-confidence. He was a private man because he was a private man. He would never allow a jot of intrusion into his life of this kind. Surely Anna Lavey knew that. So why had she been back to see him today?

The door of Henry's flat opened. She hugged him as she always did and immediately felt strong. They went together into his vast, book-strewn study and she sat on the cushioned window ledge as he finished a telephone conversation he had interrupted to open the door for her. He smiled across at her now as he talked, grimaced his impatience with the caller, and finally was free.

'What on earth was Anna Lavey doing here with you today, Henry?' she asked immediately. 'I saw her as she left. She's not wanting to do another piece on you, is she?'

'She was asking if I would do an interview on her radio programme – have you heard it? That series in which she acts as a sort of amateur therapist or analyst or whatever it is, I never know the difference, and her stooges lie on her metaphorical couch and talk, with, I imagine, quite horrifying candour about their private lives. Absolute drivel, I should think. Can you conceive of me wanting to do it? Or being able to do it, to be less grand about it. I'd be perfectly hopeless. The Prime Minister would adore it, of course. Why didn't I think of that? I should have suggested it to her. Better still – I'll suggest it to him. And he'll take me seriously too. He's never entirely recovered from what he perceives as his theatrical triumphs over the death of Diana.'

Nicola smiled, and touched his arm, then withdrew her hand. 'Why is she so interested in you at the moment anyway? I don't remember that she's written on you before, has she?'

Henry shrugged. 'No, I don't think so. I was the second in a series of six in that *New Statesman* series. I imagine the remaining four will now run for the hills. I would if I was them. I thought her piece on me was entirely without merit or interest. Trivial to the point of absurdity. Don't you agree?'

'Yes and no. She didn't capture you at all, or have any insight into anything very startling, that's true. But . . .' Suddenly, she shook her head and threw up her arms. 'Oh, Henry, I'm sorry. I don't want to talk about Anna Lavey. I don't want to have a proper grown-up conversation with you at all. I just want to say something that I know I myself made the rule should not be said. But . . . I . . . love you, that's all.'

They stood there, looking at each other. Nothing more would develop from this now, and she had known that for a long time. The affair had gone as far as it was going to go, and was now quietly retreating. Not for her at all – the reverse of that – but she suspected, she knew it was for him. There would be no divorces. There never was going to be. They would never live together. Henry had never even seen Danny. She had no real understanding as to whether Henry still loved her or not – really fond of her, no doubt of that, caring of her certainly, but in love with her still? What was true was that because of Henry her professional life in the last few months had been markedly on the rise. It was Henry, she was all but sure, though they had never talked of it, who had arranged behind the scenes for a certain human rights brief to be sent to her chambers – a case that was so absolutely within her personal orbit and expertise that it could have been written for her. There were other things too: a call, within the last few hours, from the chairman of the Labour Party asking if she would allow her name to be given special activation on the parliamentary candidates' list, as there was a certain safe suburban London seat becoming vacant that could suit her well, and the Party would like her to take it; a request from Oxford University Press, where she knew that Henry's friend and cousin was the Secretary to the Delegates, enquiring as to whether she would be interested in editing their new *Guide to International Law of Human Rights*. Henry had helped her, and was continuing to do so. What she dreaded, but tried to cast away to the back of her mind, was the suspicion, in her bleakest moments her certainty, that he was doing all this in preparation for an end to their relationship.

'I love you, Henry,' she said once more, as the fear closed in on her. He stood there looking at her, and she knew that she saw, as she had before in recent times, an unmistakable glimpse of unease in his eyes. She was right.

'There's something else about Anna Lavey that I do need to tell you about,' he said, and there was a shot of alarm in her now at the tone of his voice. She sensed what was coming. 'I'm pretty sure she was fishing. She is on our trail and will make trouble. You do need to be ready for that. We both do. She's quite a dangerous woman.'

14

Rachel Kimpton knocked on the door, then walked into her husband's bedroom. He was sitting in his pyjamas and dressing gown in an old leather armchair, a breakfast tray of toast and marmalade and coffee laid out on a low table before him. He looked up from his newspaper as she came in, and made a half-hearted and clumsy attempt to get to his feet. But she leant down to kiss him on the cheek, and handed him an extravagantly profuse hand-tied bouquet of his favourite lilac, damp and glistening, cut early that morning from the garden. She went across to sit on his bed, watching him as he took her little note from the envelope and read it. She smiled, and reached out her hand to him.

'Happy birthday, darling Charlie,' she said. 'Happy birthday.'

He grinned at her in his sudden, wolfish way, great ivory teeth showing, put the note back in its envelope, and blew her a kiss. 'Bless you, sweetheart,' he said, and Rachel thought yet again, with a twinge of guilt, that too much of their lives had been spent in isolation from one another. They had been married for well over forty years, but truly intimate for no more than a few dozen months, and those a very long time ago. She had always told herself that he was best suited to male companionship. He certainly appeared to thrive within the conventional male habitats of his class and station: his club, the House of Lords, the boardrooms of the City of London, his own Fleet Street office in the days when the Macaulay Group was his personal fiefdom. But with his loss of Macaulay to Ned, his self-confidence, so apparently unassailable before, had seemed to seep away. He was alone at home, either in Mayfair or in the country, more than she had thought that he would be. She felt concerned when her mind turned to the subject, which she knew was not as often as it should have done. She probably loved him, but the point was not so much love as that he belonged to her. He was hers. What she would have abhorred above all else would have been a public awareness that their relationship had declined to the extent that it had. The history of her emotional and sexual life was one thing. Her responsibilities of public, and indeed private fidelity and loyalty were quite another.

'You've not forgotten that I'm taking you to Covent Garden tonight, have you, Charlie?'

He shook his head, and gave his great grin at her again. He really did seem in very good heart this morning. She could see that he had already been through his morning mail, and she glanced over at the pile of opened envelopes and letters on his table to see what was there. She saw with relief that the children had remembered him. She recognized Giles's handwriting on one envelope, and Katie's on another, and then what looked to be a vast homemade birthday card from Ned's children, organized no doubt by Daisy. Nothing specifically from Ned, it would seem, but that was not surprising. Perhaps the honest, true course for the pair of them would be to keep out of each other's way for the rest of Charlie's days. He was seventy-one that morning and looked, she thought, a good deal older. She wondered how many years he had left in him. She would do all that she could to make them as comfortable for him as possible, though the nature of their marriage was such that her scope was limited. She doubted that he felt the need for her physical presence more than he had it already. But she would keep stress and unpleasantness out of his life. And – vitally for her self-respect – she would shower him with conjugal affection and loyalty.

He pushed himself to his feet now, and picking up his grandchildren's card, carried it across to her to look at. 'Sweet children Ned's got,' he said. 'How kind of them. I'm hopeless at grandfathering, but I'm extremely fond of them. I really am.'

She held the card, and looked at it. Daisy had certainly done her best with it. Through Daisy – who knows? – perhaps a reconciliation might be possible. One day. Before Charlie went.

Giles pushed himself back in his chair, put his legs on the desk, and, luxuriantly, stared out at the rain sheeting down on to the vast old plane trees of Onslow Gardens.

Solitary, friendless, abandoned by corporate life, paying for the losses, increasingly heavy, of his newly launched *Journal of Marine Science*, Giles had never in his life been so happy, not even in his teenage days on the wind-blasted, empty beaches of western Scotland, fishing with his beach nets, munching on his sodden Marmite sandwiches. Never had he known such stress-free contentment. He wanted this to go on forever, and why shouldn't it? He had no debt of any description, his living costs were less than modest, he was housed, fed, clothed, furnished and complete. No one bothered him. Everyone left him alone. Well – almost everyone left him alone, and that one person did not was a wonder to him.

Even with the *Journal* to pay for, on top of the costs he had absorbed in establishing his triumphant Giles Macaulay Centre of Marine Biological Research, his investment income comfortably exceeded his outgoings. He was rich and he was happy. He was a lucky man. If he had even more money there'd be more research funding, more discreet little bursaries for needy scholars, and more co-funded marine biology projects between him and Imperial College, not half a mile from his door, where he was becoming a regular benefactor, and a shy, frequent diner at their high table. One day, through his large personal shareholding in Macaulay – accelerating in value now as a public company under Ned's direction – he'd have yet more funds at his disposal to spend on his pet projects. But all in good time. Life, for the first time ever, was a fulfilled, peaceful affair for him. Thank God he'd been released from a lifetime of displacement in the enforced service of his family firm.

He glanced over at the mantelpiece, and saw that it was past nine o'clock. He'd been sitting there, editing away, the house absolutely quiet and empty, since shortly after two. The telephone had rung twice, and he had ignored it. If it was anything important they would email. Giles preferred communication by email. These days he seldom answered the telephone at all.

He stretched his arms out above his head, yawned, and tickled the ears of his Siamese cat, who had at that moment wandered into the room and jumped up on his lap. He dropped her gently on to the carpet, and went off to the dining room to see what supper had been left out for him on his tray. Standing, he peered under the starched lace cloth with which his housekeeper Marjorie had covered it. He picked up a slice of smoked salmon in his fingers and ate it, then another, and then, sitting at the table and smoothing the starched napkin across his knees, he took up his knife and fork and finished the rest. There was a joint of Bradenham ham on a large oval serving plate beside the tray, this too covered in a cloth. Giles carved three or four generous slices of that, dumped some of her homemade pickle on top of it, helped himself to some potato salad, and poured a glass of burgundy. Munching, he gazed around the room, perhaps his favourite in the house. It was cased all round in dark mahogany bookshelves, the books packed tight, meticulously ordered by author and subject, as was Giles's entire library, the housing of which occupied every single room of the house, including the bathrooms and lavatories.

He pushed his plate aside, poured himself the second of what would be four glasses of wine, picked at his teeth, and gazed out of the window once more at the rain. Tomorrow, Saturday, he'd give himself a morning in the bookshops, then he'd set off on one of his favourite walks, which would be made not in the least less enjoyable if it was still raining. He would tramp up the hills to Highgate, swing a great detour west around the farthest reaches of the Heath, then make his way home through Hampstead, Parliament Fields, Primrose

Hill and Regent's Park. Twelve or thirteen miles, the way he had invented the route, then a hot bath, and either eggs in the kitchen, or supper on his own with a book in the little Italian restaurant he liked on the corner of Old Brompton Road and Cranley Place.

He carried his tray through to the kitchen for Marjorie to clear up when she arrived in the morning. And there, as he put it down on the dresser, he saw the envelope. It was on the top of a pile of letters that had obviously arrived in the delayed morning post and been sorted by Marjorie. He knew the handwriting so well, and now he hesitated for a moment, his heart thumping, before he could bring himself to open it.

It would be, as usual, a message of love. She had written at least three or four times a week for the past twelve months and although he had written replies on each occasion, he had never sent them. He had feared breaking the spell, desperate to avoid the rejection he was sure would follow if he responded. Giles read the letter through once, twice, and then, after a long pause, once again. He sank to the floor, leant his back against the dresser, folded his forearm across his eyes, and alone and secure as he was, allowed himself to cry.

It had all been done for him – the decision had been made. Sheila loved him. Sheila would not take no for an answer. Sheila was unfazed by his lack of response. She had no intention of letting him go. She was going to come to the house tomorrow, Saturday morning, and take him with her. She had bought the air tickets, and the car would take them on to Heathrow at noon. They'd be at her parents' house in Brisbane on Monday. She was marrying him on the Wednesday. They were then to honeymoon on the Gold Coast, and the hotel

243

suite she had booked for them, jutting out over the reef, had a glass floor. So he could watch the tropical fish.

Ned telephoned Hugh at home, and apologized for the lateness of the call.

'Don't worry about it. I'm sitting here in the kitchen with Danny on my knee trying to persuade him to go back to bed. What's the problem?'

'I'm not sure if it is a problem, but I thought I would tell you about it straight away. I've had another letter from that Miss Anstruther woman, asking for a response to the one she wrote earlier. Can I just read my reply, to make sure you're happy with it? The usual stuff in introduction, then "*I have to say that we see no connection between Anna Lavey, to whom we assume you are referring, and this unnamed teenager who apparently abandoned her baby on the Broadwich police station steps. However, if you wish to write to Ms Lavey, I suggest you send it to me personally here at my private office, and I will then forward it on to her. All further correspondence, if any, should be between you and Ms Lavey direct, if that is what Ms Lavey wishes. Yours etc.*" How about that? Too abrupt? Too unhelpful? What do you think?'

There was a pause. Then, before Hugh could say anything, Ned spoke again. 'I know you told me that you had not asked Anna point-blank about this baby business, but you did so indirectly and she was quite clear in her response?'

'Yes — I skirted around the point, but in a light-hearted way. I was too jokey. I should have told her exactly what had happened. As it was, she made a joke of it as well, and that was it. And . . . well, it's her business, after all.'

'Actually I don't agree,' Ned replied. 'She's a big property for the *Meteor*, and she negotiated a very valuable contract with us when she joined, so if there's trouble brewing then I want us to be ready in our response. You know what the *Daily Monitor* is like, the *Comet* too. If they can run a personal destruction piece they certainly will do so. And they *can* run one, if Miss Anstruther is watertight on her facts. For all I know she's already been in contact with them. She probably has.'

'Have you talked with the *Meteor*'s editor about this? What's his name again?'

'Paul Hopper. Yes, to be quite honest with you, I have. In total confidence of course, but I thought he should be forewarned. Just in case. And I wanted his view.'

'And his view was?'

'That he very much hoped the story was true, because then we could get Anna to come out publicly in a big splash story, banner headlines, front page, nice and lachrymose and desperate, and the *Meteor* could trumpet off in search of Anna's lost daughter. The *Meteor* finds her, she's living in poverty, no – wait a minute, better than that – Paul wanted the daughter to be terminally ill. How does it go?'

Ned laughed, and Hugh joined in, without much enthusiasm. Anna had fired him a warning shot, and the thought of what she might do next greatly concerned him.

'Yes,' Ned continued, 'there's a painful reconciliation scene and she dies in the sobbing Anna's arms. Not a dry eye in the house. Pure Verdi. Sorry, Hugh, I've never claimed that the *Meteor* is *The Times*. The *Sunday Correspondent* is, and we wouldn't dream of covering the story in that. But the *Meteor* does what it does, and Paul Hopper is that sort of editor. Look at the circulation figures. All the ground we lost four, five, six years back is well on the way to being recovered. Middle England loves us, and deservedly. Maybe not deservedly. They love us typically – that might be the better way of putting it.'

'Let's get back to your letter to Miss Anstruther. Yes – send it like that. Meanwhile . . .'

'Meanwhile you'll have another conversation with Anna? Great. That's what I hoped you'd say. And this time . . .'

'This time I'll get her to tell me what, if anything, happened. I'll put it to her quite straightforwardly and directly and see what she says,' Hugh said, trying to sound confident.

'That's it. This time get her to tell you the truth.'

'It's so kind of you to see me again, Mr Lynch,' Miss Anstruther said as she made her way through the cramped little front passage, so narrow that she had to turn sideways on to avoid the bicycle leaning against the wall. 'I don't mean to intrude, but, as I explained to you last time I was here, I'm your insurance company area manager, and we think you've got a small rebate due. I've just got to have one more look around.'

'Jack's the name. And you're not intruding. I never see anybody and I'm only too glad of the company, Miss . . ?'

'Anstruther – but call me Elizabeth. You must call me by my first name. Everyone else does,' she smiled, lying, wishing very much it was true. Now that both her parents were dead, only Gilly Lane called her anything other than Miss Anstruther. She'd worked at the dusty little law firm of Marr & Marr for over ten years now, and although these days the partners attempted spasmodically to remember to call her by her first name, she'd been Miss Anstruther there since the day she had joined, and would remain so until the day she left. But it was a nice little lie to tell. And she felt surprisingly the more self-confident the moment she had told it.

'Elizabeth. That's nice,' he said, as they sat down to their pot of tea. Picking up his cup and saucer he gazed mournfully out at the rain lashing against the windows of the little cement-rendered house, the last in a row that petered out into the desultory, sodden fields on the outskirts of the small, ugly town.

'That's nice,' he said again, and she realized that he was still speaking of her name, and not the insurance rebate, which didn't seem to interest him at all. In the circumstances, Miss Anstruther reflected, that was just as well. He sounded, bizarrely, as if he had really considered the name, finally confirming that he liked it. 'Elizabeth,' he muttered again.

It didn't take much to please him, poor man, she thought. Jack Lynch appeared to lead a life even more solitary than her own.

'Do you get out much?' she asked brightly.

'Darts every other Tuesday. The Conservative Club on the monthly whist nights. Bowls on Saturday afternoons in the summer. The corner shop every morning for the paper and the milk. No, I don't get out much. Hardly at all. Should I?'

'Yes, you *should*, Jack!' she cried, bright as a button, relishing this wholly spurious role of the jolly extrovert. But she wondered at the slight hint of a challenge and sarcasm in the way that he had spoken.

'Of course you should! You need to get out of yourself, Jack! Get out of the house and meet some new people and do some new things! Darts every other Tuesday . . .' she laughed, and poured him another cup of tea. She replaced the pink tea cosy, quilted and stained, and noticed that it was almost identical to her own, which she had to remember not to use when Gilly Lane came around, as she clearly thought it common.

'We used to go out,' Jack said, dipping his digestive biscuit into his cup, then slowly masticating it, his drooping moustache holding the crumbs. 'Yes. In the old days, when Ruthie was alive. We used to go all over the place — Margate, Canterbury, on the coach, Dover once, to see the steamers. Ruthie liked to get out and about. I don't, much.'

'Well, there we are. I'm sorry about your wife, Jack. You've been alone a good few years now, haven't you? Four, was it? As long as that?'

'Five,' he replied. 'Nearly six. I've been bloody miserable, to tell the truth. Pardon my French, but so I have. Ruthie was only just forty. She should still be with me. I'm bloody miserable, and bloody lonely.'

'But you had your daughter!' Miss Anstruther risked, pointing at a photograph of a small girl, bustling around in the pretence of finding Jack's sugar bowl.

Jack sipped his tea. 'She's not my daughter,' he said. 'I told you that last time. She was our foster child. Ruthie suddenly decided one day — over our breakfast table, as bold and decisive as that, she was like that, was Ruthie — that as we had no children of our own we'd foster one. She was only twenty-two or so herself, you know, but she went straight down and got this one from the council. Only a baby, just a few weeks old. Sweet little thing, she was. Sarah, we called her, though Margaret was her real name, we were told. Nice name, Sarah. Jewish, you know. I'm not, but Ruthie was — Jewish.'

'And what's happened to her then? Does she live nearby?'

'I haven't a clue. I haven't seen her nor heard from her for years. She walked out on Ruthie and me when she was sixteen, and that was it. Eight years or so, give or take. The police looked for her for a bit, or told us they did, but there was never any trace of her. She just disappeared.'

Miss Anstruther shook her head in sympathy, and went over to the windowsill to look at the photograph of the little girl in her school frock, clutching a tennis racquet, laughing delightedly at whomever it was taking the picture.

'She was a little cracker, she was. She felt like my daughter. The same for Ruthie too. Even more so for Ruthie, I think, looking back on it. And then Sarah upped and left. Terrible how much you can love someone, and the next thing you know they've gone, and gone forever. As if they had never been with you in the first place, that's the pain of it. But there we are – I was brought up by foster parents myself, dozens of them actually, one every five minutes. And the real people of my life – the only people of my life – have gone. Sarah first. Then Ruthie.'

He fell silent again, gazing at the rain, and Miss Anstruther had one final careful look at the photograph, but it could have been any pigtailed, well-cared-for child from any happy family.

She went to clear the tea things back into the kitchen. 'What did you say your wife's name was, Jack?' she called over her shoulder. 'Her family name before she married you?'

'I didn't,' Jack said. 'But it was Levine. She gave that name to Sarah too, so that Sarah should have a proper surname. Levine. Ruth Levine. Jewish name. She was a Jewish girl, as I said. From Hackney.'

'There's no point in being angry with me, Anna,' Hugh said.

'Ned Macaulay got a letter from this woman, enclosing a cutting from some local newspaper, from 1980 I think it was, telling of some unfortunate teenager who had left her newborn baby on the steps of Broadwich police station. The woman stated in so many words that the teenage girl was you. Ned told her in return, in no uncertain terms, that it was nothing to do with him or the Macaulay Group, and that if she wanted to write to anybody about it she should write to you. That's it. End of story.'

Anna blew her nose, and studied him, without apparent warmth. Then she gave a hint of a smile, pointed to the bottle, and when he shook his head, helped herself to another large glass of whisky. 'That's it. End of story,' she aped, savagely, to the standard, as always, of a professional stage mimic. He didn't enjoy it. She exactly caught the tone of over-earnestness, over-intensity, he knew he tended to carry.

'You're such a prick, Hugh,' she said, mildly contemptuous. 'Nice-looking and friendly and clever and the rest of it, but you're such a prick when you put your mind to it, you really are. You're too much of a coward to come to the point. You come around here to my house on some inane pretext, and then you don't even have the guts to come out with what you actually want to say, or rather with what Ned Macaulay told you to say. You're a prick.'

She waved him aside as he tried to interrupt. 'I'll tell you what you really want to say, since you're not going to yourself. What you really want to say is that if it's true that I'm this Dickensian girl with the love child abandoned in the snow then you and Ned Macaulay and that other prick Paul Hopper want to know about it. And now, if not sooner. Am I right?'

She studied him, waiting for his response. He shrugged and nodded.

'Well, I've never been to fucking Broadwich, or whatever it's called, as far as I remember. And I've never been so insulted in my life as by your poisonous, disgusting question, had you the guts to ask it. And my only child is Andrew, temporarily late of this address. And not only is he my only child, but – would you believe this? – I've only had one lover in my life, old-fashioned girl that I am, and that's Bobbie, whom you've fucking met, also unfortunately late of this address. Tell that to Ned Macaulay, and tell it to that prick Paul Hopper, and tell it to anyone else who wants to know, and hop it. Off you go, Hugh, piss off. You're beginning to make me seriously, seriously angry.'

She leaned closer, and her voice dropped to a whisper. 'And I'll tell you something else. Sort your own life out before you start mucking around with mine – your marital life. You know exactly what I mean. Get your own life in order, my friend. Or don't you have the guts for that either?'

Miss Anstruther was a very bad driver indeed, but occasionally she used Gilly Lane's twenty-year-old Vauxhall, still with barely 60,000 miles on its clock, which she kept in a garage behind the pub at the end of Winchester Street. It was used so seldom that each time it was taken out the tyres were soft.

Three weeks after her visit to Jack Lynch, Miss Anstruther decided, waking up one crisp spring Saturday morning, that she would call on him again and take him for a drive. She wondered if he had been as much as a dozen miles outside Broadwich since his wife's death, unless bowls' matches dragged him a little further afield. He needed to get out – perhaps they would reprise one of the trips he had made with the intrepid traveller Ruthie – and that would be her excuse for inviting him. But the real reason for going down to Broadwich that morning was that there were a lot more questions that she wanted to ask him, now that Anna's life was beginning to reveal so much more than she could ever have expected.

Gilly grumbled a little when Miss Anstruther called her. It was such a lovely day, why didn't they make that trip together to Blenheim Palace that they had been talking about? Or leave Broadwich for another weekend and go to the British Museum? But by half past nine Miss Anstruther had, at the fourth attempt, managed to back the car out into the street, with only the smallest of little scrapes on the wing. And within two hours of that she was banging the knocker on Jack Lynch's front door, gazing around as she waited at the dingy windblown street and surrounding muddy fields, bounded by collapsing fences of broken, rusted barbed wire. Anna's abandoned daughter had spent her childhood here. And maybe not without good fortune, she thought, considering what might have been her fate. Whatever Jack may or may not have been, she liked the sound of Ruthie Lynch. She had clearly been an exemplary surrogate mother.

Now Jack was opening the door. Although he had responded to Miss Anstruther's suggestion of a trip with obvious reluctance when her early call had dragged him from his bed, she saw that he had taken the trouble to dress with great care. His hair was spread neatly across his scalp, his forehead shone, and if the sleeves of his blue blazer were ludicrously long, the brass buttons and the regimental badge on its breast pocket were clearly of great pride to him. But with his white shirt, his bowls' club tie, grey flannel trousers and brightly polished brown shoes he looked painfully stiff, and his expression was one of total misery.

'I thought we'd go to Dover, Jack!' she cried. 'Why not? Like you did with Ruthie. To see the steamers, and have a pub lunch or something like that.'

Jack sighed, tried to look enthusiastic, and climbed into the front seat beside her. 'Come on, Jack, live dangerously!' she joked, back in her jolly Girl Guide role. She liked it very much. 'Off we go! An hour from here at the most.'

But the drive wasn't a success, for all Miss Anstruther's chatter. Jack hardly said a word, and gazing straight ahead of him as she drove, appeared to show not the slightest interest in the countryside they were passing, nor the chilly, azure beauty of the day. Nor indeed why it was that Miss Anstruther, the insurance company area manager, whom he had met only twice, and who never seemed to talk about insurance, should have wanted to drive all the way down from London in this rackety old car to take him out. He asked no questions, gave the most perfunctory of replies to her bright conversation, and appeared to Miss Anstruther, glancing sideways once or twice, as the very picture of abject and compliant melancholy.

She'd never get anything out of him at this rate, she thought. Perhaps he'd like a beer or something. Maybe that's what he and Ruthie used to do when off on one of her little outings.

So she pulled into a desultory looking pub forecourt. With Jack following behind she strode into the saloon bar of an ivy clad Rose & Crown, which lay off the main road, but close enough to it to catch the constant whine and growl of traffic.

Jack agreed to a pint of bitter and a plate of ham and pickle, and Miss Anstruther, struggling to think of something, ordered a pork pie and a glass of cider, which she hadn't drunk since her childhood when she was given it on special occasions by her father, the Major. As the drinks were poured she noticed that the glasses were filthy, and she had to steel herself to drink from hers.

But the beer seemed to do the trick. Jack took a deep draught of it, sighed, took another, and wiped his moustaches. 'Good drop that,' he said, and although it wasn't much, they were the first words spoken unprompted since she had arrived at his door. She led him to a corner table, sat him down with another pint, and went for it.

'Tell me, Jack,' she said, 'I don't want to be nosey, but there's something I wanted to ask you after we spoke last time. Are you absolutely certain that Sarah never made contact? With your wife, I mean? No messages, or a post-card perhaps? Do you think it might be possible that your wife, perhaps on Sarah's wishes, was not . . . well, not open about it with you?'

Jack shook his head, finished his sandwich, and wiped his mouth with his handkerchief. He had almost finished his second pint now, and Miss Anstruther got up to buy him a third.

He shook his head once more when she returned. 'No. Why would Ruthie want to keep it from me, and why would Sarah want it that way anyway? We were a very close family. She felt like our daughter, and I think we felt to her like parents. I'm sure we did.'

Miss Anstruther went to sip at her cider to be companionable, then remembered the smeared filth of the glass. She smiled at him, as gently as she could. 'Then why did she run away, do you think?'

'Why did she go?' Jack repeated, smoothing his moustaches and staring out of the little leaded window at the traffic thundering down to the channel ports. Miss Anstruther watched him, and waited.

In time he turned back to her, and looked at her. 'Why do you ask?' he said. 'Why are you so interested in all this anyway?' He blushed. 'I don't want to be rude of course, it's very nice of you to take me out for a drive. I'm afraid I said that too quick.'

Miss Anstruther decided to keep her advantage, and not waste the moment by attempting an explanation that she knew would be unconvincing. So she pressed straight on. 'Why do you think Sarah went?' she asked again, and smiled once more.

She had a pretty smile, a sweet smile as several people had told her over the years. It was by far her best feature. But only very rarely indeed had she been manipulative enough, or self-confident enough, to use it to her advantage. She smiled again, and made sure that warmth and reassurance flowed from it.

'Do you know what I think one reason might be?' she said. 'Maybe there's more than one, I don't know. But let's try this. I think your wife might have told Sarah who her mother was.'

Jack looked at her with sudden attention, and surprise. 'Told her who her mother was? Ruthie didn't know who her mother was.'

'How do you know she didn't?'

'Because she would have bloody told me, that's why. She would have told me if she'd known.'

'Why?' she asked, as quietly and unthreateningly as she could, and Jack, staring at her, made no answer.

There was a long, long silence.

'You know what happened, don't you,' he said eventually, his voice hoarse. 'You know everything, don't you? You know the lot.'

She waited for a moment, and nodded. In fact Jack was right, but not wholly right. She did know some of what had happened, but not, as she was beginning to realize, as much of it as she had believed earlier. Jack had been in trouble many miles away and many years before Ruth or Sarah had come into his life, with a sexual indecency conviction as a very young man, for which he had received a suspended sentence. The Broadwich social services people had never been aware of it. Perhaps he had harmed Sarah, perhaps not. It would all come out in the wash. Paul Hopper was on that trail, and he'd discover what had happened, Miss Anstruther was sure of it. Looking at Jack's haggard face, she found herself wishing that there was a possibility he wouldn't.

Perhaps it was a combination of the two that had driven Sarah away – finding out who her mother was, and years of unpleasant difficulties with Jack. Perhaps it was neither. But, whatever it might be, Paul Hopper would find out in time where the girl was, and would get in contact with her, and he'd get the answers. That's what the *Daily Meteor* did. Gazing at Jack now, understanding his loneliness, recognizing that he and she, in their mutual inadequacy, were kindred souls, at that very moment she wished she'd never gone anywhere near

Paul Hopper at all. But she had. She'd done it. it was too late now.

Hugh delivered Danny to his first day at school, in the reception class for four and five year olds. Danny had been excited for weeks, particularly over his new uniform and satchel and cap, but now that the day had come he was taut with nerves. As Hugh helped him out of the car, Danny clung tight to his hand, staring at the other children, then looking up to Hugh for reassurance. Hugh jollied him along, chatting to him, willing him to hold his nerve until he could hand him over to a member of staff, and leave as fast as possible.

As they entered the building Hugh saw the reception class teacher, and he led Danny over to her. Beside her, files in hand, asking something or other, was another young teacher. She smiled at Danny as he was handed over, made a great show of admiring his new satchel, beamed a smile at Hugh, then turned to walk away to her own classroom. Hugh, despite himself, stood and watched her go. He thought her enchanting. Beyond enchanting – totally lovely.

He turned back, and, as if in mild curiosity, asked Danny's teacher, now about to lead Danny away, who she was.

'Oh, that's Sarah Levine,' she said. 'She teaches the seven- and eight-year-olds. Danny will love her when he gets to her class.'

Paul Hopper cursed when he saw Miss Anstruther's name in his diary, and called through to his assistant to blame her for it.

'I don't care what she said to you. We've got what we needed from that woman and I don't want to be bothered by her again. So get rid of her. What did you say? She's where? This note of yours says 10.30. All right, it is 10.30. Send her in then, for God's sake. But get her out of here again in fifteen minutes, do you hear? Ten minutes, five. Invent something. An urgent phone call, an anthrax attack. And Tina? No coffee, do you hear? Give the woman coffee and she'll be here all morning.'

'Miss Anstruther!' Hopper beamed a few seconds later, as he went to meet her at the door of his office. 'A great pleasure. You haven't caught me on the easiest of days, I'm afraid, but come and sit down, you couldn't be more welcome. You can tell me what you've been up to. Coffee? A pot of coffee, please, Tina,' he called, and came back to the sofa.

Miss Anstruther sat on the chair opposite him, pressed her knees together and regretted she had come. Paul Hopper's office, all gleaming rubber plants and chrome and glass, was the sort of room in which she felt entirely ill at ease. And Hopper himself, flush-faced, loud-voiced, fast-talking, was the sort of man who frightened Miss Anstruther into a state of stuttering inarticulacy. But she must hold her nerve.

'Still on the trail, eh?' Hopper said, ignoring his assistant as she banged the coffee tray down on to the low glass table that lay between them. 'That's good, that's good,' he went on, without waiting for a reply, and pushed an overfilled, slopping cup across to her. 'Very good indeed. Excellent. Never know what you might find, a nice lady like you, asking all the right questions and looking unthreatening and sticking to it. Much better than us newshounds, eh? They see us coming a mile off, not like you, nice and quiet. Miss Marple, eh? Our very own Miss Marple.'

He gave a great bellow of laughter, drank greedily at his coffee, and took a large bite out of a croissant. 'Breakfast?' he enquired, and waved his hand in invitation at the tray, but Miss Anstruther shook her head, and to her horror found that she was blushing too.

'I wanted to see you, Mr Hopper,' she said, 'because there were some things we discussed last time which have been worrying me a little in recent days.'

'Things?' Hopper asked, helping himself to a pain au chocolat.

'Yes. Well, it's this. Because I didn't hear back from Mr Macaulay as quickly as I thought I would, perhaps I got a little over-excited about everything, and perhaps put things a little too . . . extravagantly when I burst in on you that evening. A little too dramatically.'

'Extravagantly? Dramatically? My dear Miss Anscombe, Anson, sorry – Anstruther, you did just the right thing in coming to see me. This is going to be a big, big story when we are ready to run it. And we have you to thank for it. Actually, you're part of the story. You told me what Anna Lavey did to you, and the *Meteor* does not approve of celebrities treating ordinary folk in such a manner. Good folk, the man or woman on the bus, ordinary, simple people, people like you. You fans made Anna what she is, after all. Without you she's nothing. She should have remembered that. She will now!' he laughed. 'My God, she will.'

'It's not me I'm worried about,' Miss Anstruther said. 'It's other people. Like Mr Lynch.'

'Mr Lynch?'

'Jack Lynch, Anna's sister's husband. The one who raised Anna's daughter.'

'Oh – that Jack Lynch. The flasher. Why on earth are you worried about him? He's going to be one of the best bits of the story.' He traced a headline in the air. '*Anna Lavey Abandoned Love Child To Sex Fiend's Care*. They'll love it.'

Miss Anstruther winced. 'Can you tell me something, Mr Hopper?'

'Paul, Paul,' he smiled, generously.

At that moment Tina put her head around the door, and looked meaningfully at her watch. 'There's an urgent call for you, Mr Hopper. Mr Thurlestone from Human Resources. He's holding.'

'Tell him to piss off,' he said. 'I'm in a meeting.' He nodded encouragement at Miss Anstruther for her to continue.

'Well, it's this,' she said. 'I know I brought you the story in the first place, but that's why I feel so responsible for it all.'

She gazed at him. It had certainly been quite a journey. She had got so caught up in it she had lost awareness of the consequences of what she was doing. First of all tracing the Levine family through the old Hackney housing register, once she realized which one it was, and finding they had three children living with them there: David and Ruth, the twins, then, five or six years younger, Anna herself. The picture in the Hackney paper of David, gone to Australia, winning some big prize there for something or other, with his sister Ruth, now recently married, it had said, and living in Broadwich. The following of the trail down to Broadwich, and through the help of Gilly Lane getting the assistance of the librarians there in checking back the press cuttings of that time, and suddenly coming across this story of the teenage mother, from Hackney, abandoning her baby at the police station. The help of the librarian who had worked in Broadwich all her life, and knew everybody and everything, and her husband, a policeman, who remembered the case, and put her on to some old records of it. It had been so many years after the event he thought it all right to tell her the girl's name – Levine – though he shouldn't have done. And he told her how the police had established the mother's identity when having abandoned the baby she started haemorrhaging, and been forced to seek help at the little cottage hospital. The council, when Miss Anstruther had gone to them, confidently, with the name the policeman had given her, proved only too happy to tell her who had fostered the poor baby: Mrs Lynch, one of the most well-liked people in the town. Fostering's one thing of course, and adoption quite another – they'd never have told her in a thousand years if it had been adoption. As a fostered child, Sarah always remained under the council's charge.

'It's Sarah I'm most worried about,' she said.

'Margaret, as I remember it,' Hopper interrupted. 'Not Sarah. Margaret, after Princess Margaret – and that's another nice little twist to the story of course. Gives it a nice period feel. We can work something around that,' he mused, again tracing a headline in the air with his thumb and forefinger. '*Anna's Little Love Princess*, that sort of thing. The *Meteor* loves the royals.'

'Well, Ruth and Jack called her Sarah, which brings me to Jack Lynch. It was you who rang me to say that you'd checked him out and found that he had this conviction against him in the past. How did you know that?'

'Ah. Miss Anstruther, an old hack's instinct. A poor little baby girl abandoned, left out on a doorstep, depths of winter, blue with cold, strangers take her in, you have a nose for these things when you've been in newspapers as long as I have. First the couple who took her in are saints, both of them, simple, loving people, hearts of gold. Then we move the story on. The woman's a saint, but the man's a rogue, poor baby X in peril, what can we do? Or you can run it the other way around, but the *Meteor* prefers it the old-fashioned way. The *Meteor* likes mums. It didn't take us long. Years before, in Lancashire, Yorkshire, somewhere, John Douglas Michael Lynch, or whatever his name is, up to no good, exposing himself to young girls, the dirty sod, found guilty, suspended sentence, all there in the public record. Just what we were looking for.'

Miss Anstruther gazed at him. 'Does Mr Macaulay know about all this?' she asked suddenly.

'Ned? Why do you ask? He owns the paper – but I'm the editor.' He shrugged. 'Look, Miss Anstruther, you wrote to him originally, so of course he knows about it. He then asked my view on the story, and I gave it. Then you came to see me, and I heard it from the horse's mouth. So to speak . . .' he laughed, but Miss Anstruther could not be bothered to register that there had been a joke. Her fear and shyness had gone.

She looked up at him. 'I really don't want Jack Lynch hurt, Mr Hopper.'

'Paul,' he said, in automatic response, but she ignored that, as she had the first time.

'He is a quiet, pleasant man, and I don't believe it's right or proper or ethical for him to be blackened by your paper for something of which he might be completely innocent.'

'Completely innocent? Hardly. It's all there in the public record.'

'I don't mean that, though his sentence was suspended, so I doubt it was anything too dreadful. I mean the inference that he interfered with Sarah when she was with him. I don't think you should suggest that without a certainty on your part that he was indeed guilty of harming her. You can't possibly know that, unless you have spoken with Sarah.'

Hopper nodded. 'Unless we have spoken with Sarah,' he repeated, and grinned.

Miss Anstruther looked at him, and suddenly caught his meaning. 'So you do know where Sarah is.'

Hopper shrugged, 'Margaret. Maybe, maybe not.' He paused, then continued, not unkindly. 'I'm not sure you're quite suited to the life of the news sleuth, Miss Anstruther. But it was you who came to us. We're only following your lead, just as you asked us to, remember?'

He got to his feet, made clear the meeting was over, thanked her, found her coat, showed her to the door, held her arm as she got into the lift, and behaved in every way as the courteous youngster showing respect and good manners to an old lady. This struck Miss Anstruther as somewhat self-deluding, as there was probably no more than four or five years between them.

'Christ!' he said in mock despair to Tina as he passed her desk on the way back to his office. 'What I do for the *Meteor*.' Then he carried on with the day's work in high good humour.

As she found her way to her bus stop Miss Anstruther wondered, for the first time since her dreadful confrontation with Anna Lavey, what she had set in motion. More than that, she wished now, profoundly, that she had never started this business at all. She didn't want Jack Lynch hurt and she didn't want Sarah hurt. She also realized, with a sickening, absolute clarity, that she no longer wanted Anna hurt either.

What was the point of it? Why all this hatred and revenge when it was she herself who was at fault? She'd wasted years of her life in an obsession with Anna Lavey. She should have had the good sense and the strength to have pulled herself together and stopped it – to have recognized that she was behaving like a parody of a lonely, forlorn spinster. But she hadn't, and she'd made a fool of herself, and though Anna had most horribly insulted her, in truth she had deserved exactly what she had got. She had behaved like an idiot.

But now it was too late and Paul Hopper was unstoppable. And in a way he was quite right – it wasn't that he had come to her. She'd been to him, pink with excitement and lusting for revenge, and fed him the story and set him on his way. For the first time in her life Miss Anstruther had committed an act of premeditated, vicious harm to another human being. God only knew how many more would be hurt before this thing came to its conclusion. 'Miss Anstruther's Revenge!' she muttered to herself. What terrible damage one can do to people, what terminal, terrible damage, if one puts one's mind to it.

15

Sarah Levine sat on the edge of her bed and pulled on her tights. Yawning, she reached out for the mug of tea which she had made for herself twenty minutes earlier, and allowed to go cold, and gazed out at the rain.

She remembered she had left her umbrella at school, and cursed. Five past seven already, and she'd set the alarm clock for half past six. She should have got out of bed right then, as she had meant to. There were thirty minutes precisely now to finish her washing and dressing, make some vague attempt at doing something about her face, have a second cup of tea, which in her mild hangover that morning she most certainly needed, and to correct twenty-three essays on 'What I Most Like About My Family'.

She found the paracetamol bottle and took two tablets, then one more, swallowed them with the remains of her tepid tea, and shuddered as she remembered what had happened the previous evening. She had planned to go to a movie on her own, an early showing so that she could get back to the flat in time to have a fried egg on toast, mark the essays, finish work on the half-term reports, which were already a couple of days behind schedule, and before she went to bed start to allocate parts for the Easter play, which had fallen into her lap once again this year.

Instead she had gone from the cinema into a café, and a thirty-something man with the most startling blue eyes she had ever seen had taken the stool next to her. He'd seen the film too, and loved it, though she hadn't, so they talked about that, and the other movies they'd seen recently. He'd said he was just going back to his flat around the corner for a Tesco lasagne and she was welcome to share it. So she did, and two bottles of supermarket Chianti, and then she was on his bed, and her clothes were off, and so were his . . .

Why did she do these things? She never enjoyed it much with strangers anyway, it was so awkward and tense.

And the next thing she knew it was past midnight, and she left him a nice little note – anonymous – but she'd had to walk home because she couldn't find a taxi, and now she'd have to give that cinema a miss, for months, which was a pain because it was the most convenient for her to get to. Oh God. Also it wasn't payday for another ten days and she was not at all sure that she had any balance left on her credit card and she had wanted to buy a pair of shoes that weekend and go to the hairdressers. For the first time in almost three months.

The essays were sitting in a shopping bag in the kitchen. She sat at the table, glancing up at the clock, as she went through them one by one, ringing the spelling mistakes, drawing little smiley faces on as many of them as she could, plus a word or two of admiration if it was at least remotely credible to do so. Her rule was to try to get through every term without one single comment, oral or written, to one single child that he or she might later recall as discouraging. And if one couldn't succeed in achieving that, with a class of seven- and eight-year-olds, for God's sake, in Sarah's view one shouldn't have become a teacher in the first place.

A quarter to eight. Five minutes late, but if she ran to the tube station she should just be all right. She stuffed the essay books back into the shopping bag, and swallowed the rest of the tea and the two stale chocolate biscuits she saw sitting beside the empty bread bin. She threw on her raincoat, half tripped over her cat, who had just arrived inside from a night on the tiles, and set off down the street.

Half-term in two weeks, thank God, she thought, panting now and renewing her resolution to actually attend the gym she had become a member of nearly a year before. She'd go every day for proper two-hour workouts: she needed to lose at least ten pounds. Last night she'd seen Jed or whatever he was called have a good look at the size of her thighs and she could hardly blame him.

Then she remembered again about her credit card, but before she had time to curse herself for that she suddenly remembered too the *Meteor* thing. She'd had a letter from them the day before saying that her name had been put forward anonymously, by one of her school parents she assumed, for a 'Teacher of the Week' competition on their woman's page, and all she had to do to collect £500 was to go to their office and be interviewed by one of the staff, perhaps even the editor, they'd said, and have her picture taken. She'd arrange that for Monday, and she'd get them to give her the cheque straight away, and get it into her bank. £500! What a stroke of luck! That would keep her going until payday very neatly indeed. How nice of whoever it was to put her up for it.

The train came into the platform, and she struggled her way towards a vacant seat and flopped down into it, neatly taking possession ahead of a businessman approaching it from the other direction. 'Oh – sorry!' she said, as if in surprise, settling down, pretending that she had only that moment noticed him. She mopped her brow. God, she was unfit. But this time, she really would go to the gym, trim the thighs, lose ten pounds – no, twelve – eat less and cut out the wine. Well, perhaps not cut out the wine entirely. Two glasses, never more. Three at the outside. That's what she'd do, and stick to it.

Her train drew into Hammersmith Broadway station, and with her duffel bag thrown over her shoulders and the plastic shopping bag in her hand she shuffled in the queue to the escalator. How lucky the *Meteor* award thing was. She could do with £500. It wasn't easy sometimes, having absolutely zilch family to fall back on, borrow £50 from when you needed it, inherit a few sticks of furniture from, that sort of thing. But then lots of people were for one reason or another in much the same position as she was. Most people had far less than one thought. She had just as much as the majority of people did, maybe more.

And Sarah reflected, in a moment almost of wonder, that what she had above all was a very precious thing indeed. She had the gift of happiness – she was always happy and that was a rare thing, she was sure of it. That really was a blessing. Fuck the rest of it.

★

Paul Hopper had been looking forward all weekend to his interview with Sarah Levine. Everything was in place. Tina had arranged the photographer, and she'd organized the bouquet – enormous, he'd told her it should be – which would provide the picture he wanted. Anna Lavey's lost baby, found at last by the *Meteor*, the daughter clutching her flowers to her poor little slender frame, Paul's caring arms around her, smiling tearfully at the camera. Perfect. But wait a minute – even better than that, miles better than that, why not get Anna there as well? Trick Anna into coming into the office by some ruse or another. Then two bouquets, mother and daughter, both of them in tears. Paul's arms around them, '*Love's Return*' the headline, no, wait, '*Lost and Found – Anna's Secret Heartbreak Over*'.

No, he thought, not yet. Anna might smell a rat. He and she were such enemies that he'd never find a credible excuse to get her into his office at such short notice. And anyway, great as that picture would be, it would probably be safer to wait until he had all the pieces of the jigsaw in place. There was Ned Macaulay to consider as well. Ned was fretting a little, best not to rub his nose in it too much, although he'd never make a true newspaper man and that was for sure. No – have the daughter in, and get the picture of them together. That was the important thing. Then make friends, get her confidence, extract her story and see what they'd got. Whatever it was, they had a great story to run. Later, when he was absolutely ready, they would find a way of arranging a meeting between mother and daughter, get that picture too, and splash the lot.

Tina rang through to say that the girl was coming up in

the lift. Hopper surrounded himself with correspondence and a file or two, and arranged himself on the sofa in a suitable posture for a famous Fleet Street editor at work, but never too busy to spare a few minutes from his hectic day to talk to one of their competition prize-winners.

'Hello!' he cried, as Tina brought her in. 'Sarah Levine? Our prize-winning teacher? Marvellous, Sarah. Wonderful. I've been looking forward to meeting you. A pot of coffee, Tina please, for our teacher of the week!'

The photographer was shown in to join them, and Sarah smiled on cue, and sat where she was put, and wondered just how long this was going to take. But the editor must be such a busy man he'd want to rush through it, get the photograph and be done with it, and that would suit her just fine. She wondered how she was going to handle the business of the cheque. She could hardly ask him for it. Perhaps she should do it through his assistant. But she did need to take it with her, that was for sure.

'Hey, what am I doing? First things first!' Hopper said, and reaching across the table picked up an expensive-looking envelope, which he handed to her. Inside, she found, was the cheque, which, being as usual without a handbag, she stuffed into her pocket. She wondered then if she had been supposed to sit there with it in her hands, looking grateful, as the photographer took his picture. But now the editor, Mr Hopper or whatever his name was, was handing her the most enormous bouquet she had ever seen. And the photographer was firing away at both of them, standing very close, on his instructions both of them smiling into the camera with a more enforced appearance of rapture than Sarah thought could possibly be justified by a rotten little weekly prize like this.

At last the man was finished, after several rolls of film, and with him out of the way she and Hopper settled back into their seats for what Sarah hoped would be the briefest of conversations.

'Now there's something I have to tell you, Sarah, and you'd hardly credit it,' Hopper said, smiling broadly, shaking his head at the queer surprises that life brings. 'It really is the most extraordinary thing, but you and I have met before!'

He paused, nodding his head. 'The moment I saw your name it rang a bell, and I couldn't for the life of me think why. Then suddenly it came to me. Now here's the most incredible thing. I'm a working-class lad from the North, as I am sure you can tell.' He paused suddenly to sneeze, and Sarah guessed she was supposed to assume an expression of wonder and disbelief at the statement, so she did. He had absolutely no trace of a northern accent, more East End of London than anything else, but it was difficult to tell.

Hopper blew his nose several times on a vast blue handkerchief, shaking his head and smiling. 'Yes, a working-class boy from the North. And you won't guess who my best friend in the street was when we were kids? Well, I'll tell you. Jack Lynch!'

He looked at her in triumph. She looked back at him in horror, which she did all she could to disguise, but knew that for a second or so she had shown it all too clearly.

'Gosh,' she managed in the end, and attempted a bright little smile.

'And when you were a toddler of eighteen months or so,

I happened to be in the Broadwich area so I called in on old Jack, who I hadn't seen in years. And there you were, sitting on his knee, proud as Punch!'

'Gosh,' she said again, and began to feel the physical numbness of shock. She had no idea what to say, and wanted only to flee. There was a horror looming ahead of things exposed and opened up. And here was this florid, loud-voiced man, all braces and mouth and vulgarity, gazing at her now with what looked like a bullying resolve to pursue the story.

She smiled at him in desperation. With every second that passed she wanted more and more to get up and flee, but she didn't know how to do that.

'Yes – proud as Punch! And I assumed you were his daughter, but he told me you were a foster child that his wife had taken on, but that you were so sweet he had rather taken to you. He certainly looked as though he had! So that was when you and I met before, Sarah! Oh – and saying that reminds me of something else. Jack said your real name was Margaret, after Princess Margaret. I remember that for some reason. Does that ring a bell with you?'

She shook her head, the fear in her increasing as he continued. There was a merciless quality to it. She felt that in some way she had become the prey, and she had no idea what he was doing or why.

'Margaret?' she replied. 'I don't think so. My name is Sarah, and always has been as far as I know. My parents always called me Sarah, so . . .'

'Your parents?'

'Well – I mean my foster parents, obviously.'

'Jack and Ruth Lynch.'

'Yes. Of course.'

'And what name is shown on your birth certificate?'

'My birth certificate? I don't think I've ever seen my birth certificate.'

'Of course you've seen your birth certificate. Everyone's seen their birth certificate. You know perfectly well the name on your birth certificate. The name your mother gave you. Your real mother. Margaret's your name. Margaret Levine.'

There was a pause. Sarah stared at Hopper. Why had she slipped, in her fear and surprise, into telling him that pointless, inconsequential lie? She was now on the defensive, and in the wrong. So she corrected what she had said.

'No,' she said, 'not my mother. The nurses, they called me Margaret. And Ruth later arranged for me to have as my surname her maiden name, Levine. So you're right. Margaret Levine is the name on my birth certificate.'

Hopper nodded, and smiled at Sarah wolfishly. 'That's it,' he said. 'You've got it. The nurses gave you a name because your mother, whoever she was, didn't appear to have called you anything. Clever girl, now we're getting there. Margaret's the name on your birth certificate. We both agree on that. So why didn't you say so in the first place?'

Again a silence, as the two of them gazed at each other, Hopper, mocking, aware that he had the upper hand. But the strength and focus was beginning to flood back into Sarah as the initial shock subsided. 'What is this, Mr Hopper? What on earth is going on? Thank you for the prize and everything else, but I'm afraid I'm already late for . . .' And then she noticed the tape recorder, hidden under a large envelope on the seat beside Hopper, quite clearly turned on and recording their conversation.

As she stared at it he took it from its hiding place and laid it on the table between them. 'A tape recorder,' he said, quite unabashed, and made no attempt at an explanation. 'We'll come back to the question of who your mother might be in a moment, but meanwhile let's sketch things out. There you were, sitting on Jack Lynch's knee, as pleased as Punch, and Ruth, or Ruthie, or whatever her bloody name was, in the kitchen baking ginger-bread men. One nice loving family. Right? Except it wasn't really a family because you were just a foster child – right? – and the odd thing is that although you were all as snug as a bug in a rug, Jack and Ruth never made it more than that. They never took the next logical, loving step and adopted you. Should have done, some might say, given the circumstances of it all.'

'The circumstances of it all?'

'Yes, that's what I said. That's another thing we'll come back to in a moment, but first let's just cover the question as to whether this family was as idyllic as you say. Was it?'

'I didn't say it was idyllic.'

'Ah, so it wasn't?'

'Look, I didn't say that either. Idyllic, not idyllic, these are just words. Nothing is idyllic all the time, that would be an impossibility. You know that as well as I do. Everyone knows that.'

'So your family life was like that, was it? Not idyllic all the time, but idyllic for some of it. Is that right? And which were those idyllic moments, those glimpses of eternity?' He gave his huge, wet-mouthed grin, which she found intensely disagreeable. She shrugged, blushed, reached to pick up her duffel bag, and made to go.

'I'll tell you when they weren't idyllic, or anything approaching it,' he called after her as she reached the door. 'The bad times were when Jack was . . . well . . . let's say when he was . . . bothering you . . . leave the rest of it unsaid – am I right?'

She froze, and turned back to him. 'Leave what unsaid?' she said, incredulously. 'What on earth do you mean by that?'

He nodded, and smiled at her. 'It's all right, dear. I know, you know. There's nothing to be frightened about – or ashamed about, if it comes to that. I'm sure he couldn't help it. Some people are just made that way. But it would be good if you could tell old Uncle Paul about it. And if you did, I'm sure I could help you in some way. You're our Teacher of the Week after all.'

She shook her head. 'You've never met Jack Lynch, have you, let alone me? You'd never heard of him before, had you? I really have not the slightest, vaguest idea what you're talking about,' she said. 'Not a clue. Have you?'

'Yes, dear, actually I have. Though you're certainly right I've never met Jack Lynch, thank God.'

She shook her head again, in a gesture of total, angry incomprehension, and once more turned to leave.

'Why did you leave this sometimes-if-not-always-idyllic home at sixteen?' he called out now. 'Why did you do that to two people who had been so kind to you? That wasn't very nice, was it? Not very grateful?'

She turned and spoke very softly. 'Because . . . because . . .'

Hopper patted the sofa beside him. 'Come on, Sarah. We're

all friends here. Tell me everything. Tell me about Jack Lynch, Tell me about his wife. And tell me who your real mother was, the one that left you on the police station doorstep. That one. Your mum. Who was she?'

'I don't know who she was. I've no idea.'

'No? Well, I have, my dear. So come and sit down and let's have a good chat about everything.'

It was parents' evening at Danny's school. Hugh had gone on his own, as Nicola was away in Germany, working on a prospective brief that her chambers had been told was coming to them. Hugh did the same as all the other reception-class parents: he admired the exhibition of wildly unpromising first attempts at art, looked in the exercise books, and nodding and smiling at the others, sipped at a glass of warm white wine.

He delayed his departure from the classroom, wandering around, pretending to be absorbed by the various items laid out for the parents. He hadn't been able to shake the image of Sarah Levine from his mind since Danny's first day at school. He was hoping beyond hope to see her. And then, miraculously, there she was, walking in, talking with another teacher, laughing, greeting parents she knew.

Hugh watched, willing her to see him. And then, suddenly, she did, glancing his way, and then away, and then, clearly recognizing him, walking across the room to greet him.

She introduced herself. He introduced himself. She asked if he was the publisher. He said he was. They talked easily and pleasantly for five minutes or so about not very much – she in formulaic enquiry as to the state of the publishing world, he of her teaching career. But Hugh felt growing within him that certain breathlessness, that inimical frisson of excitement and engagement that he hadn't known for many years. What was it about her? Her warmth? Her fluency? Her face, with its trivial, lovable imperfections and flaws? All of those things perhaps – or none of them. But something was there.

She smiled, put out her hand to shake his, turned away, and it was all over. Hugh went to his car and sat there, keys in his hand, gazing out along the street, lost in thought. He realized the significance of what had happened. He was capable – still – of falling in love. There could be another life for him. Perhaps this girl could fall in love with him. Perhaps another marriage, a different marriage, a marriage of true, lasting, mutual fidelity was within his grasp. Perhaps that would be for the best for all of them.

16

Henry looked across at Rachel Kimpton, and stared at her for several moments. 'I didn't realize you knew about it,' he said. 'I'm rather appalled to know that you do. Somehow I thought . . . oh, you know how it is, one always believes one's private life is just that – private. But it's good that you've told me now. It was Ned who talked with you about it, I assume? If so, I wish I'd had the sense to . . .'

'No, it wasn't Ned. You know how friendly he has always been with Hugh Emerson, from the time they were small boys together. He protected him as a child, and I'm sure he protects him now. Whatever Ned's faults, he is a very loyal man, and he would never gossip about Hugh – or, by extension, Nicola. To me or to anyone else.'

'Loyal?' Henry smiled. 'Charlie might not agree with that. But I know what you mean.'

'I'm not so sure about Charlie, you know. He seems with time to have found his peace. Ned's done such a good job with the firm, and Charlie acknowledges that privately, as far as I can tell. We've never discussed it, except very obliquely. But there was a certain sort of loyalty as well as bravery in Ned's actions at that time. Better to strike, and save the family firm, than to stand back and let it go. And his public comments thereafter about his father and his brother healed a very great deal of the hurt. The family has always meant a great deal to him. And Hugh Emerson, to him, is family. He made Hugh deputy chairman of the Macaulay Group, you know – non-executive of course, but it was a good appointment for Hugh, and I think a good move for Ned as well.'

Henry watched her. She got up from her perch on the windowsill, and went to sit in the armchair in the corner, facing Henry at his desk.

'Frankly, I've heard about your affair with Nicola Haile from several people. Tittle-tattle of course, just that, some probably well informed, some clearly not. I'm frightened for you, Henry, to tell the truth. You're safe up to a point – you're a public man, but you've never led an ostentatiously conventional private life. No one can mock you for false piety. I think the country warms to you just because of that. But the tabloids will have a field day when the story breaks. Which it certainly will, given all this gossip, and pretty soon, I'd guess. The circumstances of your wife . . . your son . . . and this particular affair. It seems surprising, somehow, out of character. Or is that unfair of me?'

Rachel sometimes thought that it was with Henry Jackson alone that she was wholly fluent, and straightforward. With him there was no guilt, no affectation, no responsibility, no seeking of gain. She wanted nothing from him, and knew he wanted nothing from her – except, for each of them, not so much friendship as a pleasant awareness of mutual under-standing and knowledge. They had known each other for so many years. Their physical passion – about which Rachel had not been candid with Ned when, so suddenly and shockingly, he had asked whether he was Henry's son – had long dwindled into comfortable affection. But that affection was there, and indelibly so, and there was frankness between them, an ease.

He said nothing, but stared out of the window at the sullen greyness of the sky. She watched him, and remained silent for a few minutes. Why was she telling him this? There had been so many women in Henry's life, not untypical perhaps in a man of his sort, and she had never resented them. But she did mind about Nicola Haile. Why? She'd been fond of Hugh when he was a schoolboy companion of Ned's, very fond, and protective too, once she had realized the bleak inadequacy of Hugh's own family life, but she didn't want to feel responsible for him now. Nor was it a jealousy. It was a sense that Henry was in the wrong, and he was making a fool of himself, and that in time it would all blow up in his face. She could see the tabloid delight in it now. And perhaps, horrifyingly, their story might not stop at titillating trivia over Nicola Haile. What if they delved around and came up with more? About Henry and her? And, God forbid, the full truth, the whole story about the two of them?

Henry turned his head, and stared at her. She watched him. His political career was finished of course, for all intents and purposes, but he was a great man, as that truly appalling article by that woman Anna Lavey had said. She'd got that right, if nothing else. And Rachel didn't want to see the autumn of his life spoilt by the prurient cruelties of a gaudy tabloid scandal.

'Why?' he said at last. 'I'm not sure I know why. She's

very intelligent. She plays me very well. She has a complexity about her mind and her bearing that I find endlessly beguiling. What can I say? One begins to pile cliché on cliché, but in truth it's not so complicated. I love her, but I don't want to break up her marriage. I don't want to break up my own, and you know full well the reasons for that. But this has been a very big thing for me. It still is. For a period at least, it has consumed my life. I'm aware that it must end, and it will have to be me that does it. I've got to find the strength – before the story breaks. And, like you, I suspect we have very little time.'

Nicola was surprised to receive Ned's call, but made herself sound as welcoming as possible when he asked if he might come around. Hugh was away in New York on business, but when Nicola mentioned this Ned said it was her he wanted to talk to. Then he laughed, as if anxious not to sound threatening, which only aroused her suspicions the more.

He arrived, as Ned often did, at least half an hour later than they had arranged, and their first fifteen minutes or so was spent on a rather edgy anecdote about some junior minister who was trying to squash a story about his marital infidelities. She followed Ned's performance as closely as it was necessary for her to do, smiling at the appropriate moments, but her mind was calculating what was to follow, for she was now in dread of that. She had hardly allowed herself to think that it might be about Henry, but when the moment came she knew instantly, despite Ned's convoluted opening, that was indeed what it was. She went absolutely cold. For months, years, she had been waiting for Ned to do exactly this – speak to her about Henry, and in doing so to take Hugh's side against her.

He asked her who she was still in touch with from their Oxford days. He reminisced a little, uneasily, and by Ned's standards, unamusingly. He was too tense for that. And then it came.

'Philip Hudd, Nic? Do you remember him? He was in our year, and read English I think, or History. New College. Tall, glasses, surprising smile, easy manner, really nice man.'

'And now the editor of the *Monitor*,' she smiled, encouraging him to do his worst, whatever it might be. He knew as well as she did that Philip Hudd had been in those days one of Hugh's friends. They still saw each other occasionally, she believed. The problem was that Philip had never liked her. They had exchanged some quite bitter words at a party in their student years; she had asked him why he was so unfriendly with her, and then regretted her directness, because he told her. And in terms which she believed Ned would have endorsed. Philip had said that he found her too self-absorbed, and too prone to self-pity. He had then, covering his mouth in mock dismay, pretended to throw his arms around her and beg her forgiveness, but the damage was done.

Philip had meant what he said, and they both knew it. Ned had been in earshot, and turned to watch them. No doubt both of them now, as her life with Hugh had turned out, were more than ever of the same opinion. Hugh was important to them. She wasn't. Ned saw her regularly, but only in Hugh's company.

'That's right. Editor of the *Monitor*.' He paused, and to Nicola's alarm, blushed. She had never seen him do that before. Then, also entirely uncharacteristically, he sighed, turned to face her head on, and remained silent, staring at her, as both of them waited for what was to follow.

Finally, he cleared his throat. 'Nic,' he said at last, as a statement rather than as an introduction to anything, and it occurred to Nicola at that moment that Ned was the only other person in the world who used Hugh's diminutive nickname for her, which was a mark, she knew, of nothing whatsoever about an intimacy with her, but only of his fondness for him. 'Nic. There's something I have to say.'

'About Philip Hudd.'

'Partly about Philip Hudd. Mostly about you – and Hugh. And in some small way, about me too.' Ned sighed again, and gazed at her, and she saw the faint pinking of anger begin to flush now to his cheeks.

'What I have to say is about you, and Hugh, and my friendship for him, and the entire fucking nightmare.' He stopped, and gazed unhappily at her. 'It's a balls up. I don't myself think it is any more important than that. I know about love – believe me. I know how one can screw up God knows how many lives with a single, selfish act of deception. I've done it myself. The problem in your case is that you've got a complete simpleton for a husband. Hugh is unworldly, and he's forgiving, but mostly he hides away from something he doesn't understand. He can't envisage life without you. So – he buries his head in the sand.'

Nicola folded her arms across her chest. She wanted to cry, but bit her lip to prevent it, and gazed at Ned as directly as she could.

'Perhaps you think you're doing no harm – I don't know what you think. What I do know is that you are destroying

Hugh. And because Hugh is the anally retentive, buttoned-up tit that he is he's never going to say anything to you. I'm sure he's hoping that one day it will all be over, and you'll be home with him forever, and everyone can pretend nothing ever happened. You could call that the most heroic example of self-abnegation and unselfishness. I think it's more a case of him being a coward.' He paused, 'And you being a self-indulgent, self-obsessed . . .'

He stopped himself just in time, stared at her, then put his head in his hands. 'I'm sorry, Nic,' he said. 'I'm sorry I said that last bit. I had planned to say this stuff to you more gently than that.'

They watched each other. Nicola's first instinct had been to pretend she didn't know what he was talking about. But by being silent she had let him continue past that point. 'You're talking about Henry Jackson,' she said, in a flat, resigned voice.

'Yes. I'm talking about Henry Jackson.'

'You said you wanted to talk about yourself,' she said, playing for time, thinking fast, wondering how best to position herself.

'I am talking about me. Hugh's my friend, I want to help him. No – more than that. I want to rescue him.'

'Rescue him from what?'

Ned shook his head, angry again. 'For Christ's sake, Nic,' he said, 'I'm trying to be frank. Mostly I'm concerned about Hugh. After that I'm concerned about you.'

Nicola looked at him. 'Look, I do know what you're talking about, of course I do. But this is something that concerns Hugh and me. The two of us, and no one else.'

Ned shrugged and, turning his face away, muttered something which Nicola failed to catch.

'Ned – please. Why should we quarrel? Most marriages are pretty inexplicable, looking from the outside. It's like that with Hugh and me. You can have no more idea than any other outsider about what really happens between us. Any more than I have any real idea of the intimacy and . . . the balance of your life with Daisy. Hugh has made his judgements as to how he copes with the . . . let's say the compartmentalization of my life, and how our marriage can survive, and I respect him for it and I . . .'

'Oh, bullshit. Balls!' he interrupted, his voice rising, and Nicola drew back from him in quite genuine physical fear. She had no idea that he was capable of such anger. 'You can't hide behind Hugh's failure to address this thing. Hugh is wrong to hold all this stuff back. The fact that he does so feeds the situation. You take advantage of that. Compartmentalization – Christ! I've said it already. You're self-absorbed. But it's more than that – you're totally, monumentally selfish.'

'As Philip Hudd said to me that day at Oxford,' she said, flushing. 'In your hearing. All those years ago.'

'Yes, as Philip Hudd said to you at Oxford. I've never forgotten it. I thought he was absolutely right.'

'And you never wanted me to marry Hugh.'

Ned was about to speak, but for a moment put his head again in his cupped hands. There was a long pause. 'We're going too far. This is not what I wanted to happen.'

'It's OK, Ned,' Nicola said quietly. 'Finish it. Say what you feel you have to say. We can't stop there.'

She waited, but Ned would not respond. 'You think that

in my self-absorption, as you call it, and self-regard, I'm allowing myself to . . .'

He looked up, and interrupted her. 'I think you have lost your moral compass. Maybe you never really had one. I told you earlier that I know about love, and I know about deception, and I know what is good and what is bad. I'm an expert on it. I know everything, and I know it from my own experience, and I don't admire much of what I know about myself. So this is what I believe. I believe you're hiding from yourself. I believe that what you do with Henry Jackson is not as dignified, and forgivable, as a cry for help or even a love affair. I'll tell you what I think it is: good old, common old adultery.'

He paused, and there was total silence as they stared at each other. His words had stirred Nicola now into a sudden shock of defiance, and real unstoppable anger. Why should she take this? Why was she sitting there, passively, listening to this stuff?

She found herself shouting now, flushed, for a moment wholly out of control. 'You don't like me. That's fine. I don't like you. You talk about marriage in this sanctimonious way. You lecture me about adultery, then hint about having done it yourself. How dare you! Leave me alone – and leave Hugh alone.' She stopped, shaking, the tears ready to come. They sat there gazing at each other. Then, in time, Ned said quietly, 'Well – this is what I've come to tell you. It's not good news. Philip Hudd has the story. His paper may well decide to run it. And whereas I think you deserve that exposure, I don't think Jackson does entirely, odd as that may sound. I think he was trapped.' He shrugged, got to his feet, and prepared to go. But then he turned back to her once more. 'Nic – you're a considerable girl, everyone knows that. You're an absolute winner. But you're also a killer. You've used Hugh, and you've humiliated him, and he's not the man to do that to. He's too good for it.'

He walked to the door. 'And that, in so many words, was what I came here tonight to say.'

Anna Lavey went grumbling down the stairs to answer the doorbell, her dressing gown wrapped haphazardly around her body. The bell rang again, and she called out to whoever it was to wait, for Christ's sake, while she fumbled in the drawer of the hall table for the key. Eventually she found it, opened the door, and there was Bobbie.

'Christ!' she said, truly taken aback. 'I know you, don't I? Haven't we met? Somewhere on the rocky path of life?'

'Hello, Anna,' he said.

'Hello, Bobbie,' she replied, and they stood gazing at each other. 'You'd better come in, it's your bloody house,' she said, and pressed herself back against the wall to let him pass. She bent down to pick up the letters from the doormat, and he slapped her lightly on the bottom as she did so.

'Piss off,' she said, but he could hear her good humour, and she followed him down to the kitchen to make them both a pot of tea.

'Shouldn't I be angry with you, I can't remember? Didn't you go off with some tart, or was that someone else?'

He stared at her, rubbed his eyes, yawned, and gave a small smile. 'Piss off, Anna,' he said.

'You too, ducks,' she replied, and they sat silent for a few minutes, looking out into the small garden at the back of the house, their hands cupped around their mugs.

'Have you come home, or what?' she asked eventually, without any great show of interest one way or the other, but both of them could hear the tightly suppressed pleading in her voice.

'Yes,' he said, after what seemed minutes, and continued gazing out into the garden, sipping occasionally at his tea.

'Look – this isn't some bloody Pinter play,' she said. 'This is life, darling. In real life, in moments of high passion, people don't communicate in long silences and bloody monosyllables. They shout. They scream. They weep. They get pissed. And they bloody fall on to their bloody knees in front of their bloody wives and they bloody ask for forgiveness. That's what they bloody do. In real, bloody life. They say sorry for their bloody adultery.'

He looked at her. 'Sorry for my bloody adultery, Anna,' he said.

'That's all right, sweetheart,' she said. 'More tea?'

'Sorry I was rude to you when you came round to the house that day, sweetie,' Anna said. 'I'm so sorry, I really am, I behaved like a complete cow. I feel quite dreadful about it.' She pushed her plate away, sipped some mineral water and blew Hugh a kiss. 'No booze for one whole week, and I feel the better for it. I usually go on the wagon in October or November, but I nearly didn't this year. And then Bobbie came home, and so I did.'

'Bobbie's back? Excellent. All friends again?'

'Yes. We always are actually, but then I get pissed and

abusive and throw things at him, he meets a nice bit of skirt and off he goes again. And I miss him like no one has ever missed anybody. Then one day, out of the blue, he's back. It's been going on for years. Perhaps this is the last time. I hope so.'

'How old were you when you married, Anna?'

'Twenty – both of us. And twenty-one when we first broke up, at the time Andrew was born. Back together at twenty-four, then another departure, then together again at twenty-six or seven, then more or less together ever since. Apart from the temporaries, like the one that's just happened. He's my best mate, though, and I'm proud to say it. I can't live without him, I'm so fucking unstable.'

Hugh nodded. 'Yes,' he said eventually, 'you are – unstable as hell. But your readers would never guess that. You give them really good advice, full of good honest common sense and practicality. It works because you don't talk down to people. You don't patronize them. It's a class act, Anna, it really is.'

'Thanks, sweetheart,' she said, digging in her carpet bag for her lipstick. 'I think I followed all that. You like what I do.'

Unusually for him, he felt a wave of genuine affection for her. She was what she was. And in moods such as this she was the most pleasant company.

'Actually, you know, what I try to get people to understand is that much of life is just accepting the past and not worrying about the future. Shutting the door on the dreadful things, kicking them out of sight, and getting on with life.'

'Out of mind too?'

'Sometimes that's possible, mostly it isn't. But still – get on with life.'

'You speak with such acceptance that it's hard to believe you're not religious.'

'I've seen religion and what it can do, and I didn't like it. But would I put anyone else off it? No, I wouldn't, I never have. Maybe for other people, I don't know . . .'

'Where did you meet it, Anna? Religion?'

She stared at him, as if suddenly suspicious of what he was doing. 'I met it with my family, bless them, and they were kind and lovely people, but it didn't help me. So there we are.'

'But you said that you've seen what religion can do, and that you didn't like it.'

'Yes, I did. And now, sweet Hugh, I'm off and on my way. Thank you for my lovely lunch. And don't forget that you owe me a royalty statement. An honest and accurate one this time, if you don't mind. One with a cheque attached to it, not an IOU.' She stood, gathering up her belongings.

Hugh stood too. 'Will you ever tell me the things in your life that are too terminal to look in the eye, Anna? Please do. I think it would help.'

'Help who?' she laughed. 'You think there'd be a bestseller in it, that's what it is, you greedy bugger.' She pretended to rap him on the head with her napkin, and then, as always, gathered and confident in her public mode, doing everything to ensure that her departure was observed by as many people as possible, she charmed and smiled her way out of the restaurant.

'A great woman, that Anna Lavey,' Hugh heard some elderly man say to his woman companion, as he passed their table.

And, with reservations, it occurred to Hugh, and it surprised him, that in many ways he agreed. But she was as manipulative a person as he had met – and as dangerous, when she put her mind to it, when she perceived herself to be in danger.

Jack Lynch stirred his coffee round and round until Miss Anstruther was about to ask him, teasingly, to stop. But then he did so anyway, carefully tapping the spoon on the cup's rim so that the drops on it fell straight into the cup. Holding the saucer carefully under his chin, he raised the cup to his lips.

For his trip to London he was wearing precisely the same clothes as he had worn for their motor down to Dover. Miss Anstruther realized now that they were not only his Sunday best, but probably the only clothes he had outside the corduroys and flannel shirt he had been wearing both times she had called at his home. He had taken especial care this time though. The hair was not so much slicked down against his scalp as affixed to it. The shoes had been polished up to a quite astonishing sheen, as if they were of wet plastic. And his moustache looked as if it had been clipped, for beneath its overhang a newly exposed white stripe of skin showed.

He looked tidy and kempt, but patently uncomfortable. She wished now that instead of this Pimlico brasserie, all faux Brittany with its cascades of onions and tricolours and reproductions of ancient Michelin posters, she had taken him somewhere like the self-service restaurant at Peter Jones. He had sat there staring miserably at the French Provincial menu until Miss Anstruther, realizing what was happening, took over and briskly ordered a medium rare steak and chips for them both, and another pot of coffee.

'I was so pleased when you rang me at home,' she said. 'And what a surprise! But you still haven't told me why it was you wanted to meet.'

'It's just that you left me in rather a state, last time you came down,' he said. 'You left me wondering who exactly you were, and what you wanted. And I wondered even more when I rang the insurance company the next day, and they said they had never heard of you. They suggested that I should get straight in touch with the police.'

Miss Anstruther's face went bright scarlet, and her stomach lurched. Jack looked at her sadly, and returned to his coffee, his saucer once more held under his chin, in protection of the bowls club tie.

'I think I owe you an explanation, Jack,' she said, and he nodded his head in agreement. He didn't seem particularly angry about what she had done. Not so much angry as placidly baffled, as he appeared to be by most of the things that passed through his life.

Her mind racing, she tried to think up a fresh lie with which to compound the earlier ones, but quickly decided against it. She couldn't go through all that again. Miss Anstruther the newspaper sleuth had rather died for her after that last meeting with the ghastly Paul Hopper. So she would tell Jack now, in explanation of her conduct, something close to the truth.

'I'm sorry, Jack. Let me start again. This whole business has been so unlike me, I do promise you. The insurance company was right. I've nothing to do with them whatsoever.'

'I know,' Jack replied, and aimed a lugubrious stare at a particularly nubile waitress.

'But I don't mean you any harm, I can promise you that. Do I look like a woman who would want to harm you?'

He sighed, and turned his gaze to her. 'I don't know what a woman who wanted to harm me would look like,' he said. Miss Anstruther decided that he had made a joke, so laughed, to ease the tension of the moment. Jack smiled too, but only with his mouth, and Miss Anstruther wondered if she had ever seen any living creature with eyes as sad as his.

'Then if you're not an insurance lady, who are you, Miss Anstruther?' Jack asked mildly. 'And what is it you want?'

'I'm an assistant in a small firm of solicitors,' she said. 'That's all. Marr & Marr. Right across the street from here.'

'Solicitors? Jack frowned. 'Why solicitors? What do they want from me?'

As he said it she could hear the shot of fear, and the defensiveness, and the resignation in his voice. She knew in that second that the material that Paul Hopper had dug up about Jack's past was accurate. Jack Lynch had been up against lawyers and the law before, and it had been the death of him.

She shook her head. 'There's nothing to be worried about. My job has no relevance, I swear to you. I work there, that's all, and I'm not important, and this business has nothing to do with my work. This is all about . . .' she hesitated. How on earth could she describe to him what it actually was about? A witch hunt?

'All about what?' Jack prompted, and she pulled herself together.

'All about . . . well, all about a line of investigation I've got myself involved in.' And increasingly wish I hadn't, she thought.

'Investigation? Are you a detective then?' he asked, and this time his face showed a look of complete panic.

Oh my poor Jack, she thought. Let's hope there's nothing new. Please God let all that stuff be in the past. 'I'm not anything much at all. I'm just rather a foolish woman, of a certain degree of . . . of isolation, who started something off, and then lost control of it. For many years I had one of those silly emotional fixations on a woman very much in the public eye. If I did not exactly harass this woman, then it was a near thing. One day I arrived at her door with a Christmas present. I had no right to trespass on her privacy in that way, but I did. She insulted me very badly indeed when she found me there, and I was deeply upset. She had consumed my life, actually. And if she had realized that, she might perhaps have . . .'

Her voice trailed away, and she looked at Jack. In embarrassment probably, he was staring down at his plate. This was much too sophisticated for him, she thought. He was the wrong audience for this sort of stuff.

'Oh, Jack, I'm sorry you have to listen to all this. But I wanted to punish her, so I started to delve around, and I came across the story of the baby girl born in Broadwich all those years ago, and abandoned by her teenage mother on the police station steps. I came to the conclusion that the mother was this famous woman. I went to one of our national newspapers with what I had, and now I'm afraid they're pursuing investigations of their own. For the baby that you and Ruthie fostered was the baby abandoned on the police station steps.'

'By Anna Lavey,' Jack said calmly, and to Miss Anstruther's absolute astonishment. 'The baby's mother. Or rather Anna

Levine. Of course I knew that. What do you take me for? I knew it, and Ruthie knew it. Anna was Ruthie's younger sister. That's why she fostered Anna's baby. We told Sarah that since she didn't have a surname we'd given her Ruthie's maiden name. There was guilt there for us, if I'm quite frank with you, at least there certainly was in my eyes. Because when Anna came down to get help from us, nine months pregnant, sixteen years old, she and Ruthie had the most terrible row, and Ruthie threw her out of the house.'

Miss Anstruther watched him talk without meeting her eye, as though she weren't there before him.

'It seemed so out of character for Ruthie to do that to her sister, silly little girl though she was at that age, if I'm honest. But Ruthie threw her out, and a few hours later Anna gave birth to Sarah in a barn. You can see it from our house, right at the bottom of the fields, down by the railway line. And then she took Sarah down to the police station, and later she was found there on the steps.'

He paused, still looking away from her. 'Shocking story really, isn't it? She should have had her baby with us, at home, upstairs in our bed. But whatever the two of them said to each other was so bad that Ruthie threw her out that night to have the baby in a barn. In this day and age, on the straw, amongst the filth of animals, as if she was herself a wild beast and not a human being at all.'

He stared out into the street, and she watched him, herself silent. 'Ruthie told me that night that she never wanted to hear Anna's name again, or speak to her again, ever. And she didn't. Although it must have been as obvious to Ruthie as to me that Anna Lavey, when she started to become famous, and her picture was in the papers all the time, was Ruthie's sister. But we never spoke of it.'

Jack paused then, and shrugged, and appeared to want to talk no more. Miss Anstruther paid the bill, waited for an age while he went to the gents, then saw him out into the street. She offered to get him a taxi to get him back to the station, but he shook his head, and said that he would rather stretch his legs, and he was looking forward to a little stroll and explore, he had been to London so seldom.

'Goodbye, Jack,' she said. 'God bless you.' And to her own surprise, and clearly to his, as he backed away immediately after, Miss Anstruther leant forward and kissed him on the cheek.

'Goodbye, Miss Anstruther. Thank you,' he replied in his quiet, melancholy voice, and turned away. She watched him go, suddenly certain that she would never see him again. But after a few paces he turned again.

'You remember that just now I used the phrase "wild beast" about Anna? That's what Ruthie said to me at the time, when Anna had left the house that dreadful night. Ruthie said that her little sister was an animal. I've never forgotten it. It was such a strange – such a terrible thing to say. But that's what she said. She said Anna was like a wild beast.'

Ned had been distracted by the noise outside his office door. 'Sorry, Paul, I missed some of that. Run it by me again?'

'I was just saying that we've got such a big story here that I don't think we've got any choice but to run it. Like it or not, Anna Lavey is a big star. If we don't run it, skipper, someone else will, you can depend on it. The *Comet* for a start. If that woman Miss Anstruther doesn't get what she wants from us she'll be straight off there, I can tell you. She probably already has.' He nodded meaningfully.

'Do you think we should get her in again, Paul?' Ned said. 'Tea and biscuits and sympathy? See if there's anything more to talk with her about? It might discourage her from going elsewhere. What do you think?'

'We could do that,' Hopper replied. 'That's something we could think about, I suppose. But don't you think Miss Anstruther has pretty well served her purpose? I've seen her sort before. You get these old ducks, they've a bee in their bonnets, a couple of scores to pay off, a little bit of poison to lay about the place, and once they've started you can't stop them. All we need to do now is to keep her happy and quiet until we go with the story. You'd better leave that to me.'

'And what exactly is the story now, Paul? Still as I heard it a couple of days ago?'

'No, better. It was good before, but now it's sensational. Anna has the baby, leaves her on the doorstep, fostered by this couple, they bring her up, no contact from Anna whatsoever, she goes her own way, makes money, becomes famous, the daughter runs away from home. Why? Child abuse – just as I told you it would be. The man who fostered her has a sexual offences conviction in Darlington thirty or so years back. Suspended sentence it may have been, but that makes no difference. He was found guilty. It's all there in the public record.'

Ned nodded, but he didn't like it. He felt neither distaste nor disapproval but only a vague sense of pity for an elderly man living in the shadow of an ages-old suspended sentence for some gruesome little act of furtive sensuality in the grey, grim world of 1970s Darlington. He could think of nothing more dispiriting.

And there was also the question of Anna Lavey. He was not going to allow this story to be sprung on her by the very newspaper that carried her column. He was aware of a difficulty between Paul Hopper and her, without knowing the detail. Probably it boiled down to a situation where two people with greatly inflated egos jostled for personal space.

'I see, yes. So the story has moved on.'

'It certainly has. And we've researched it very strongly and safely, I can assure you of that. We have a meeting as soon as I'm through with you with the libel lawyers, to run through what we have.'

'And you'll talk to Anna in advance of course, you have assured me of that.'

'Absolutely.'

'So that she can have the opportunity of cooperating with you, correcting any obvious mistakes of fact, so that what you present is fair and true.'

'That's it.'

Ned gazed at him. He had absolutely no idea what was actually going on. This story of Anna's past was sensational, there was no question of that, and now that it had got this far the *Meteor* might as well have its scoop. Also the lawyers were good – they had kept the Macaulay Group papers out of trouble for years. It was just that . . . looking at Hopper, and listening to him, there was something in his response that was so transparently lacking in good faith.

'I'm sorry to be persistent, Paul, but I'm going to ask once more. You give me your word that you'll warn Anna in advance, and let her cooperate with you, if she so wishes, and that you'll give her time to do so?'

'Cross my heart,' Hopper replied, looking saintly, crossing himself, and Ned recoiled at the crassness of him.

'Can I see the final story, please, before you run it?'

Hopper shook his head. 'Now that's not a fair request, skipper, if you think about it. When I joined you from the *Comet* I had written into my contract an absolute guarantee of editorial independence. Specifically, you do not have the right to vet or to veto my copy. You know that.'

He was right, of course. Ned had never liked that clause, but at the time he had only just succeeded in wresting control of the Group from his father and brother, and to lure Hopper away from the *Comet* was a considerable coup. Hopper had been absolutely unyielding that the clause, as drafted, should be there in the contract before he would sign.

Ned shrugged, smiled, and got up to see Hopper to the door, congratulating him on a story the *Daily Meteor* had run the previous week on some skulduggery in the motor car industry. Then he went back to his office, still highly uneasy. In contrast, Hopper went on his way to the lawyers delighted with himself at what he would do to Ned. Thank God Ned had no approval of copy. How wise it had been to insist absolutely on that clause in his contract, the clause that the *Comet* would never allow, which was why he had moved.

This was going to be the big one. The Anna Lavey story was going to be a cracker, an absolute cracker. And that tit Ned Macaulay, a boy in a man's world, in Hopper's opinion, was not going to be given any opportunity of getting in the way of it.

★

Hugh called Anna immediately after Ned rang him at home that evening. It was only the day after their lunch together, and he was going to find it difficult to rehearse much the same things as he had said to her then. But there was no doubting the urgency of Ned's concern.

He plunged straight in. 'Anna – Ned has made it absolutely clear to me that there's trouble brewing, and immediately. The story of the baby girl abandoned in Broadwich all those years ago is not going away. It's about to break, and rightly or wrongly your name is attached to it, and we need to discuss what to do about that.'

There was a long silence. 'Can you come round?' she said eventually.

'No, I'm afraid I can't. Danny's asleep upstairs, the nanny's on holiday, and Nicola is . . . is unwell.'

Anna laughed. 'God, poor Hugh, she's as bad as me.'

Hugh grimaced in annoyance at his own clumsiness, but didn't respond. Nicola had certainly drunk far too much that evening, but Hugh was not going to admit that to anyone.

'You could come round here if you want,' he said, 'or we can cover it on the telephone.'

'Not the telephone. I'll come to you. I'll be there in ten minutes – fifteen. Make a pot of coffee, and lock the booze away. From all of us.'

Half an hour later he heard a taxi draw up outside the house, and went to let Anna in. It looked as if she had been on the way to bed when he had called her, for she was wearing no make-up, and she had clearly just thrown on a sweater and a pair of old trousers to make the trip. Hugh thought she looked rather endearing, older possibly than when in her professional kemptness, and for some reason more tinged with grey, but somehow all the more agreeable for that. And she was absolutely free of drink.

Having checked on Danny, and quietly pulled Nicola's bedroom door shut, Hugh ushered Anna down into the basement kitchen, and they sat with the coffee tray at the huge pine table.

Anna nodded at him. 'First, tell me what Ned Macaulay said.'

'He's in a very difficult position, as I understand it. He doesn't have anything resembling complete editorial control over Paul Hopper, and he told me that despite getting reassurances from him he's very uneasy about what he's going to run. But he's certain now that Hopper will run the story, and that he has the evidence he needs to do so.' He paused, and watched her. Thank God she was absolutely sober. The only way now was to tell her everything – quickly and brutally – and get it over with.

'This is the story Hopper has. When you were a teenager you had a baby daughter and, for whatever reason, left her at Broadwich police station, in Kent. The baby was only hours old, extremely fragile, nearly died, but thank God didn't, and was taken into care. She was fostered, but ran away from home when she was sixteen, and has not been in contact since. And there is some rumble of a story that the foster father had a past conviction for a sexual offence – with the obvious implications of that, as to why the girl eventually ran away.'

Anna sat completely silent, staring down at her coffee cup. After what seemed to Hugh to be several minutes she looked up. 'Is that it?' she asked. 'Is that all of it?'

301

'Yes.'

'Nothing else at all?'

'Nothing. Why?'

'Do you need to check with Ned Macaulay to make sure that's the case?'

'No. I was very careful to make sure I had exactly the right message to give you. So was Ned. We went over it several times.'

'Are you absolutely certain of that?'

'Yes, I am.'

'The story you've just given me is the one that the *Meteor* will be running, and only that?'

'Anna please, for God's sake, accept what I say. I've promised you that is the entire story.'

She nodded, wearily, now in acceptance of it. 'They do know it was me?'

And then, before Hugh could reply. 'Because it was. It was me.' She looked up now, and she looked old and tired and without spirit.

'I'm sorry, Hugh,' she said at last. 'I found it too difficult to tell you the truth before. And too . . . unnecessary, somehow.'

They both fell silent again.

'What a shit Paul Hopper is,' she murmured at last. 'What an enemy of mine he has proved to be.'

And as Hugh began to explain to her where the story had come from, and Miss Anstruther's role in it, and Ned's wish to protect her from too much harm, and the ways and means by which she might alleviate the potential damage to her, one thought began to dominate his mind. There was one aspect of Anna's reaction to this that was beginning to surprise him very much indeed. All her questions and anxieties revolved around herself. She never once, during the course of what proved to be a very long night together in Hugh's kitchen, expressed concern or interest or even curiosity about her daughter. It had been that part of the tale that Hugh had been most concerned about: the child's running away at sixteen, and the lack of knowledge as to her whereabouts or indeed safety. But Anna's entire focus was on herself, and what the breaking of this story might do to her.

Eventually she had finished and wanted to go home, and he telephoned for a cab. As he saw her into it, he reminded her that Ned had told Hopper that he must under all circumstances speak to her to check the facts of the story before he ran it.

'I don't want to see him, and I don't want to talk to him. What he has is true, at least the parts I know about, and you can tell him too that I won't deny it and cause a fuss. So let him get on with it.'

But as Hugh waved her off, her words echoed in his mind. 'What he has is true,' she had said. What exactly was she implying by that? He repeated the phrase to himself once more, as, shaking his head in puzzlement, he went back inside the house. God forbid, there was clearly going to be more to come. Why couldn't she tell the whole story now, right away, and get it all over and done with?

17

'I loved that piece that Anna Lavey did on you for the *New Statesman*,' Philip Hudd said. 'Such warmth. That's Anna's great strength, don't you think? Humanity. Call it what you will. Plain good journalism of its particular sort. I admire her work enormously – don't you?'

Jackson tried to find something appropriate to say, but there was an uncomfortable silence, and he let it continue.

'Are you still there, Henry?' Hudd asked eventually, and Jackson disliked the assumption that someone whom he had met less than half a dozen times in his life could adopt without permission first-name intimacy with him. Certainly, he was the editor of one of the country's national tabloids, but it jarred with him in his present mood.

'Mr Hudd?' he said in reply, but immediately he knew he had made a mistake, and it was too late to correct it. It was always wrong, and dangerous, to snub people in that way. Philip Hudd was not such a fool, and not such a philistine either. His paper was both – foolish and philistine – but that was by the way. And now he recalled something else. He was a friend of Hugh Emerson's.

'Look, I have to come clean with you,' Hudd was saying now, and Henry could hear the new coldness in his voice, and cursed himself once again for his pomposity. 'Whatever her strengths as a middle-brow journalist,' he was continuing, 'Anna does have a habit of gossiping rather, and she's just been gossiping to me. Now, I'm a newspaper editor, and listening to gossip is part and parcel of my professional life.'

He paused for a moment, and Henry stood with the receiver held to his ear, gazing out of his study window at the river. He realized, and it surprised him, that although he had known this was coming it still made him very badly frightened indeed.

'Mr Jackson,' and as he resumed addressing him by his surname Henry winced once more, 'this is difficult for me, but it's best that I talk frankly. There's trouble afoot, I'm afraid. It's common knowledge in Fleet Street that Paul Hopper at the *Daily Meteor* is about to break a big story on Anna Lavey. No one knows what it is, or no doubt we'd try to run a spoiler first. But Anna wants pressure put on Hopper to stop it – and she's found a way of potentially hurting Hugh Emerson so badly that she reckons that he will enlist a favour from Ned Macaulay to stop the story from happening. And the favour will be to call Paul Hopper off the scent, however difficult that might be for Ned.'

'Hurting Hugh Emerson?' Henry found himself repeating, pointlessly, but anxious now that this conversation should be pushed right on to its conclusion.

'Yes, hurting Hugh Emerson. Mr Jackson, would you like me to repeat to you what Anna Lavey told me, or would you rather I left it unsaid? And before you answer, remember, and I don't wish to be impertinent to you, that Hugh is my friend.'

There was complete silence for a full two or three minutes, and this time it was Philip Hudd who deliberately left it unbroken.

'Let's leave it unsaid, Mr Hudd, may we? I know what you're saying. I understand. I appreciate your call. Please leave me to do what has to be done.'

'What's the matter, Henry? Why did you call me with such urgency?' Nicola sat in the same winged chair in Henry's study as Anna Lavey had been ushered to when he had given her the interview. He pulled up a stool and sat in front of her, holding both her hands in his, and tried to smile. When he spoke, his voice was so quiet, so subdued, that she had to strain to hear him.

'Seventy-one years old next birthday, and fifty years almost in politics, and I still have no ability to face up to the most difficult and painful things of life as coherently and bravely as I would wish. And this is the most painful and difficult thing I have ever said to anyone – by an incomparable distance.'

He stopped, and gulped, and she saw, for the first time ever in her eight years of life with him, that there were tears beginning to well up in his eyes. He brushed them away, angrily almost, as if hating to show her a sign of weakness. 'What's happened is what I've dreaded, but had somehow managed to tuck away into some recess of my mind and ignore. And now that's no longer possible.'

'What isn't? What are you talking about?' she asked,

breaking her hands away from his now, putting them up to her face, guessing what was coming, dreading it.

'A newspaper has the story, the *Monitor*. The editor called me, Philip Hudd. I'm not sure if Hudd is going to run it, because I doubt he has any firm evidence, but maybe he will. I'm not sure if I mind the exposure for myself or not. But I do care about it for you. And for Hugh. And for your small son. And I know now what has to be done. We're going to do it together.'

Nicola shook her head, and closed her eyes as the sobbing began to rack her body.

Anna went back to her normal habits the following day, after a couple of weeks of abstinence. She had several glasses of white wine over her lunch with her agent, and a bottle and a half of burgundy over her dinner at home with Bobbie. They bickered, but amiably enough, made love immediately after their meal, and fell heavily and happily asleep. She'd had a good day, and a contented evening. And she knew now exactly what she had to face from Paul Hopper and the *Meteor*, provided Hugh actually knew what he was talking about. It had sounded to her as though he did.

She was beginning to see how she could convert the Hopper scoop to her own advantage. She'd spent some time that afternoon drafting a press statement that could then be converted straight into an article in the *Meteor* the following day, if Hopper would do it. Followed perhaps by a long interview with a sympathetic journalist in the Sundays. The statement spoke of her single moment of madness as a young love-struck girl with her handsome boyfriend, later tragically killed in Northern Ireland in service to his country. Her shame at the prospect of telling her devout and devoted parents about what had happened. Her concealment of her pregnancy even until the last moment of it. Her flight to Kent, the garden of England. The birth in the barn, like the Bethlehem stable almost in its calm simplicity. The laying of the baby, wrapped in its swaddling clothes, on the steps of the police station. Her concealment behind a pillar as she watched the stout, honest figure of the kindly police sergeant come out and take her up in his arms. Then, each year since, her pilgrimage there on the baby's birthday to lay a posy on those very steps. The heartbreak that had never healed. The thoughts and hopes for her lost baby that were with her every waking moment of her life.

She had thought of 'prayers', rather than 'hopes', but decided that that would not sit well with her readers' recollection that she herself had no religion (whilst always of course respecting it in others). So she left it at that.

It was very good, she knew that. So good in fact that she toyed with the idea that she might use it as the basis of an interview that very day with, for example, the *Prefect*, and thus ruin Hopper's scoop. But she thought better of it in the end. It would be prudent to see exactly what Hopper ran first, then tweak her material to fit. And also she felt at least marginally under Ned Macaulay's protection, and that might in the end prove very valuable to her. She would lose that if she was duplicitous with him. He had after all fed her the warning.

So Anna went to sleep content that she had the situation under control. She slept for eight hours, dreamlessly and peacefully, and awoke to hear the morning papers being pushed through their letterbox. She gave herself a few more minutes in bed, then eased Bobbie's leg off hers, pulled on her dressing gown, and went to make herself a cup of tea. She sat down at the kitchen table, laid down the papers and checked the headlines in the broadsheets. It would be the next day at the earliest before Hopper ran the story, so at least she had twenty-four hours grace before that, which gave her plenty of time to plan how she was going to break the news to Bobbie. She'd find a way; that was the least of her worries. Bobbie was not exactly a great sentimentalist.

But when she turned to the *Meteor* she found that almost the entire front page was given over to the story. And as Bobbie came down himself a few minutes later, he found Anna, white in the face, gazing at a large picture of a beaming Paul Hopper with his arms around a smiling, happy-looking girl in her mid-twenties, clutching the most enormous bouquet. And over that the headline:

ANNA LAVEY'S ABANDONED BABY –
WE FIND THE DAUGHTER ANNA DUMPED
IN SEX FIEND'S CARE

Sarah Levine was at that moment sitting at her own kitchen table not three miles away, staring in horror at the same picture and headline. The only reason she had the *Daily Meteor* was because the widow in the flat opposite, pink with excitement, had thrust the paper at her as she had reached sleepily out into the corridor to bring in her bottle of milk.

That odious Paul Hopper man had tried to say something

about this to her before she'd upped and fled – thank God with the cheque safely tucked away in her pocket. But she had been feeling by that point so nearly hysterical that she had pressed her hands over her ears, like a schoolgirl, before running helter-skelter down the staircase and making her flight to the park. And after crying there for half an hour or so with the abandon of a child, she had felt completely strong again, and thrust the whole thing back into the recesses of her mind.

Over the years Sarah had acquired the most fireproof capacity for self-protection and denial, and she knew why it was there and where it came from. It was like an act of self-hypnosis. Given what had happened to her in her life, she could not have carried on without it. It left her the stability to be what she knew she was, a quite exceptionally good teacher of young children.

And nothing, not even this, was going to change that. Sarah had one goal: she was determined that her own life – not her existence as subject to the maternal ownership of some revolting, coarsely behaved woman she had never met and never wanted to – her life would be one of achievement, calm and balance. A real life. Nice life. Clean life. Ordinary life. The life that real, nice, clean, ordinary people have, living real, nice, clean, ordinary lives.

Hugh was looking at the photograph too, the *Daily Meteor* spread across his office desk. It had taken him a moment or two, his brain racing, to realize who the girl with Paul Hopper was. He stared at her picture in absolute jaw-dropping aston-ishment. This woman, this wonderful woman, was actually

Anna's daughter. The daughter Anna had abandoned and denied. Sarah Levine, his Sarah Levine, was Anna Lavey's first child.

When Miss Anstruther got through to Ned Macaulay's office he was at first very reluctant to speak to her, and his assistant fobbed her off. But less than an hour later she tried again, so fraught that she felt she was on the point of breaking down. This time Ned took the call, and he could hear the tension in her voice, although she was struggling to remain calm.

'Yes, I have it in front of me right now,' she was saying. 'I really am so appalled at what I've done. It's completely sprung out of control, and I know I started it all, but I just want it to stop. And before you tell me that I ought to speak to Mr Hopper about it, I've rung his office every five minutes for the last three hours, and finally was told that he was not able to speak to me, and that I should leave his office alone, or he would take the appropriate measures to make me do so – whatever that might mean.'

Ned realized that she was starting to cry now and he grimaced, the telephone pressed to his ear.

'Please stop it. Please, please stop it,' she was repeating now, her voice dropping away almost to a whisper.

Ned passed a hand across his eyes. 'Miss Anstruther, try to calm down,' he said, as gently and as reassuringly as he could muster. 'There, that's better. Well done . . .' then he continued giving soft, familiar words of comfort, just sufficient for her to know that he was still there, and kindly, and concerned for her. In time both of them were silent. Ned's assistant looked around the door to point at her watch, for Ned was due at a meeting with the bank, but he waved her away, then immediately held up five fingers to show that he needed at least that long to finish the call.

He allowed the silence to continue. Eventually he could hear Miss Anstruther blow her nose, then sigh.

'What can I do?' she said at last. 'It was the photograph of the girl that absolutely broke my heart. She is so like Anna as a young woman. But there's no happy ending for her in this – you do know that, don't you? This will end in tragedy, not in happiness. She ought to be left alone in peace to get on with her life, away from Anna, away from everything about Anna.'

'Well – we've rather done it now, I'm afraid,' Ned said gently. 'I've spoken to Paul Hopper, who says that he had Anna's consent to run the story. It's up to Anna and her daughter what they both do now. They're two grown women.'

'Mr Macaulay, please believe me. There's going to be the most awful tragedy.'

'There's nothing I can do now, Miss Anstruther. It's not a question of believing you or not believing you. There's nothing I can do.'

Again Miss Anstruther fell silent, and again Ned waited for her to bring the conversation to a conclusion rather than do it himself. He dearly wished she would. She did. The line went silent. She was gone. Ned sat thinking for a moment or two, then sighed, got to his feet, and went off to his meeting. He didn't feel in the least good about what had happened, but they had newspapers to sell, and this was a classic story of its kind, and he had seen no option but to let it run its course.

★

'This is getting better and better,' Hopper said. 'Well done. How did you manage to dig this stuff up?'

'It fell into our lap, Paul. Dropped off a tree. We had a call straight away. This bloke recognized her immediately from her Soho days. Professional photographer, specializing in you know what. I know him of old. Bought stuff off him before. Expensive, mind, but worth it.'

Hopper was still chuckling, delightedly. How right he had been a few weeks back to bring Johnnie in from the *Comet*. He was perfect for a story like this.

'Oh – and you haven't seen these. Here's the best bit of all. He had these photos tucked away in his files and dropped them in this morning. What do you think? Too risqué for the *Meteor*? Or could we run them if we tidy them up a bit?'

Hopper took the photographs from him, and whistled. 'Christ!' he said, shaking his head, as he gazed at a dozen or so photographs of Sarah Levine in the nude, taken when she was perhaps just eighteen. They were soft pornography, conventional, languid bed poses.

'I think we could, just about, maybe with just a touch up here and there. As long as I don't tell Ned Macaulay first. We'd need to wrap some good copy around them of course – to maintain the *Meteor*'s moral high ground. You know the sort of thing. Very responsible. Very shocked. Very salacious. You know our readers.'

He thought for a moment. 'Something like "Anna Lavey's long lost daughter was forced to act as a nude model when she first ran away from her sex-fiend foster parents as a young teenager. The *Daily Meteor* shows these pictures for one reason and one reason only, to honour a loving, intelligent girl too

313

scared to say no. How poor Anna must wish now that she had been able to save Sarah from the attentions of London's evil sex barons. The *Meteor* says this must never happen again. Where were the social services when poor Sarah needed them? Where was help for Sarah, and all the other damaged teenagers out there on our streets? The *Meteor* demands to know. Miss Lavey was not available for comment last night."'

'That's it. Perfect.'

'That sort of stuff. Plus a good headline. I don't know, *"Anna's Love Child Was Naughty Nude."* Something like that. Short and snappy. Yes. Have a go. And don't forget to extend the story on to how Sarah, all alone, no mother, abused and ruined by the sex fiend foster father, is brave enough to put the evil of Soho behind her and gets herself to Teachers' Training College. *"The* Meteor *salutes Sarah's courage."'*

'And then?'

'And then, the day after, we'll have a picture of Anna, dark glasses, no make-up, looking terrible, refusing to comment, scurrying away from her house pursued by the paparazzi. Plus one of Sarah, looking demure, smiling nicely, nice figure, good legs, short skirt, every inch the school teacher, arriving at the school gates.'

Johnnie laughed, retrieved Sarah's pictures and went off whistling to his own office. This story was going to do him a bit of good personally, there was no doubt about that. Paul was right. It was an absolute cracker.

From her bedroom window Sarah watched the woman standing on the opposite side of the street, gazing up at her windows. She'd been there for at least an hour, and was clearly waiting for her, but hadn't come across to ring her bell. She looked harmless enough, a woman in her full middle years, in a coat and scarf and flat shoes. There didn't seem to be anyone with her.

Suddenly making up her mind, Sarah ran down the stairs to the front door and went out to speak to her, smiling directly into her eyes as she crossed the road so that she did not put her off, since she seemed so mild and inoffensive and frightened. 'I saw you looking up at my window. Don't stand there, you look frozen and it's beginning to rain. Why not come inside?'

'I'm so sorry,' Miss Anstruther said, and she knew she was blushing. 'I just wanted to get a glimpse of you really, and now I have, and – look – I'll just be on my way. Please don't think that I'm stalking you or anything!' She laughed, idiotically, nervously. She raised her hand in awkward farewell, and started to walk away down the street.

Sarah watched the arch of her back, and the hunch of her shoulders, and thought she looked irredeemably, hopelessly sad. She ran the few steps after her, laid a hand on her arm, and persuaded her to come up for a cup of coffee.

Miss Anstruther continued for some moments in much the same vein when she got there, still hopelessly overwrought, deliriously over-praising Sarah's humble furnishings in the tiny, narrow rooms, apologizing, spilling her coffee down her skirt, and then fussing around in fear that Sarah's already mottled carpet had been stained.

'Miss Anstruther,' Sarah said, then was immediately concerned that she might have misheard her name. She tried it again, almost sure that she was right, but pausing long enough for the woman to correct her if she wanted to. 'Miss Anstruther? Please don't worry about anything. I'm quite harmless.'

She tried to make it sound like a little gentle, self-deprecating joke, and mercifully it seemed to have its effect. Miss Anstruther looked noticeably calmer. Encouraged, Sarah said just a touch more briskly, 'But this is a rather unusual encounter, and you must tell me what it is you want.' Raising her eyebrows, she made it clear she was waiting for an answer.

Miss Anstruther blushed all over again, and Sarah wondered if the woman was actually unwell. 'I've seen the *Daily Meteor* this morning and I just wanted to say how sorry I am. More than sorry – I'm totally appalled by what has happened, and I couldn't live with myself without saying that to you. First the piece with you and the editor, and then those truly awful photographs of you . . .'

'I really don't understand. Why did you need to come here to say this to me? And how did you know where I lived?'

Miss Anstruther shrugged. 'The telephone book. I thought you probably would live in London, so I went through all the directories, and there you were.'

'But why did you want to come?'

Miss Anstruther sighed, and hesitated, but seemed to gather her strength. 'Because it's my fault that this has taken place. It's such a long story, but I made a nuisance of myself to your mother, and she then . . .'

Sarah held her hand up. 'Please, no. I don't have a mother. You mean Anna Lavey, but I don't want to go into that. I don't want to have this conversation.' She got up, and made it clear that she would like Miss Anstruther to follow suit. She did so, but, standing there, she then continued as if she had not been interrupted.

'I made a nuisance of myself to Anna Lavey, and I was then so badly insulted by her that I totally lost my head, and all I wanted was to get revenge on her. So this is what I did . . .' And she told the whole story to Sarah, at first in breathless outline, and then in detail, right from the beginning, right from the days of her first infatuation all those years before. She was there until almost midnight, in the end sharing a supper of scrambled eggs and toast with Sarah in the little kitchen. By the time she left, both of them had acquired from each other a much greater sense of the extraordinary texture of both Anna Lavey's life and Sarah's too.

For the first time, Sarah truly understood the immediate circumstances by which Jack and Ruthie had come into her life. And Miss Anstruther, whilst at least knowing now that Jack's behaviour to Sarah throughout her childhood had been as immaculate as she had always hoped it would have been, had now come to terms with a darkness in Anna's life so complete that it was beyond Miss Anstruther's comprehension how she could ever have borne it. Or Sarah too.

When Sarah awoke the following day she knew what she had to do. Term resumed that morning, and rather than wait for the headmistress to call for her, she would ask to see her. The *Meteor*'s stories had to be faced up to. She was sure the school would be supportive of her, but rather than get into the day with the children, dreading all the while the summons to come, she'd get it over with herself, preferably the very moment she got there, if Mrs Summers was free.

She was at the school at barely after eight o'clock. No sooner had she used her key to the back entrance and dumped her bags in the staffroom than she was surprised to hear her name called from the end of the corridor, and then to see Mrs Summers herself. They both smiled at each other, but Sarah could feel the nervousness in them both.

'Sarah, dear,' Mrs Summers said, and holding open her study door ushered her in and pointed to the armchair in the corner of the room, and sat herself opposite it on her sofa. 'You've been in the papers!' She smiled brightly, and not unkindly, but it was at that moment that Sarah knew she was not going to survive. She nodded, and frowned, to show at least that she realized that the publicity around her had mattered to the school.

'Well, all I can say is that I feel nothing but the greatest compassion for you, Sarah. We'd no idea of your personal circumstances when you first joined us. We regard you as the best young teacher we've ever had at the school. The children adore you, and you deserve every single bit of it. You've been quite magnificent. Thank you very much indeed.'

Sarah nodded, and smiled. She told herself that she must not cry before she was safely on her own. She could feel her chin and her lower face start to quiver and she dug her nails into the palms of her hands. And now the blow struck.

'But I'm afraid you will have to go, my dear. I spoke yesterday to the chairman of the governors and I can only say that he was absolutely adamant on the point.'

'What have I done wrong?' Sarah managed to say, but only just, her voice beginning to crack.

Mrs Summers sighed, then leant across and held one of

Sarah's hands in hers. 'I don't know that you've done anything wrong, my dear. It seems to me actually that you've done most things quite heroically right. But it's the photographs. We really can't have a teacher in our school whose naked body, posed in some degree of pornography, has been all over the national press. This is a private school, the parents pay their fees and they have the right to tell us what they will accept and what they won't. And they've told us they won't accept this. The chairman of the governors made that absolutely clear to me yesterday.'

She pressed Sarah's hand, then released it. 'I am so terribly sorry, Sarah. If I can help you in any way in the future I would be proud to do so – references and so on. Perhaps, in a year or so, when all this dust has settled, another school . . .'

Sarah suddenly felt strong enough to stand, and bring this to an end. She shook hands formally with Mrs Summers, told her that she would clear her possessions from her classroom immediately, whilst Assembly was still on, and made for the door.

'Tell me, Sarah, when you went to your college you were eighteen years old, barely that, still a child, with no support, no family, nothing whatsoever. What gave you the courage to do that, after all you had been through? And how did you find the money to get you there?'

Sarah turned around, and looked at her, anger in her eyes. 'You saw how I got the money. And you saw what gave me the determination to do what I did, and start something worthwhile in my life. You saw the photographs. Don't you understand? It was that.'

★

Sarah went first to the playground, and then walked out to the beech trees at the end wall, so that alone, and with a wintry wind in the bare branches, and the damp quiet of it all, she could allow the tears to come. Then, when she had managed to steady herself, she hurried back to her classroom to collect her belongings.

She went on through the door, passing her forearm across her eyes, then tucking her handkerchief back into the sleeve of her cardigan. She stopped dead. Sitting alone at her desk in the empty room was one of her pupils, who had evidently arrived too late to go to Assembly.

'Hello, Lucy!' Sarah cried, as brightly as she could manage.

'Hello, Miss Levine,' the child replied, and smiled up at her, gap-toothed and, in Sarah's enhanced emotional state, quite heartbreakingly appealing.

'Late again, Lucy Walker?' Sarah laughed, in mock approbation, whilst she emptied all the small possessions she could find into a plastic garbage bag.

'Sorry, Miss Levine,' the little girl said, and Sarah shut her locker door and smiled at her afresh, a victim, as she knew, of a recent and particularly unpleasant divorce.

She tied the neck of the sack, and gazing at the child, realized that she was about to burst into tears once more. She knew she shouldn't do it, but partly to hide her tears and face from her, though mostly in sheer overwhelming need for immediate human touch and warmth, she dropped the bag, stepped over and bent down to reach for the little girl, and hold her in her arms. 'Goodbye, Lucy,' she said, and was relieved that her voice proved reasonably steady.

'Goodbye, Miss Levine. My mum told me this morning

that she was sure you'd be leaving us. But why? We'll all miss you so much.'

'Because . . . because . . .' She shrugged, held the child away from her, and, as if she were her mother, smoothed the hair back across her forehead. 'You're one great kid, Lucy Walker. God bless you.'

'God bless you, Miss Levine.'

It was Bobbie who pointed her out to Anna. He had seen her there the previous evening as well, standing half-hidden under the tree, gazing across at the house. This time, as Bobbie parked the car, she stepped out and walked up to them. Anna gave her a wan smile, at first not seeing who she was, but accustomed to people recognizing her in the street. But then she did know who she was, and her face eased into a look of weariness, but not, as Miss Anstruther saw immediately, anger.

'Miss Anstruther, we meet again.' She spoke with what sounded like a mild attempt at sarcasm, but there was no sense of bite or threat to it, and Miss Anstruther was reassured by that.

'Yes, we do,' Miss Anstruther said, and glanced across at Bobbie, who was standing there impatiently at the car door, waiting to drive off again somewhere. 'I'm not here to waste your time, not on this occasion. I want to say a couple of things, but first I simply want to say I'm sorry. I truly am. I've wrecked your life.'

Bobbie grimaced and started to say something, but Anna held up her hand to stop him, and Bobbie climbed back into the car and drove away. Anna shrugged. 'Well . . .' she paused, and gazed at Miss Anstruther. 'In a way, perhaps, but in another way . . .' She paused again, and left the sentence unfinished. 'You want to speak to me,' she said. 'You'd better come in.'

She turned into the house, and Miss Anstruther followed her. Anna led her upstairs and sat her down in the big sitting room and, by a movement of her hand, invited her to speak. Miss Anstruther made a bad start, so nervous was she, and Anna so silent and uncommunicative. She could hear herself apologizing for their previous, disastrous encounter, and for bothering her now, and for trespassing into her home, and would no doubt have gone on to a whole catalogue of apologies for other intrusions and impertinencies had Anna not stopped her, with a not unkindly gesture. She took off her dark glasses, yawned, got off the arm of her chair to sit in it properly, and gave Miss Anstruther a short, weary smile. 'Come on, Miss Anstruther. What is it you want?'

Miss Anstruther drew a deep breath. 'Miss Lavey,' she began, but Anna interrupted her. 'I used to be Anna, I think. Let's return to that.'

Miss Anstruther blushed. 'There are two things. The first is this: I want you to know that it was me who first went to the *Daily Meteor* about what happened at Broadwich with your baby.'

'Yes, of course I know that,' Anna said in reply, but without much sign of interest or animosity, and Miss Anstruther continued.

'And the second thing is that I've been to see Sarah.' She stopped there, held her breath, and waited for a reaction.

'You've been with Sarah? You went to her flat?'

'Yes.'

'In Notting Hill?'

322

Miss Anstruther looked at her in considerable surprise. 'Yes. 32a Cheps . . .'

'Number 32a Chepstow Lane,' Anna finished for her. 'Before that she was at 156 Wandsworth Bridge Terrace. Before that at 143 Hammersmith Street. Above an all-night grocer's.'

Miss Anstruther gazed at her. 'So you've known all this time that she was in London?'

'Yes.'

'Have you seen her?'

'Yes.'

'Has she seen you?'

'No.'

'How often have you seen her?'

'At least twice a month, at least that, for about the last three years or more, when I first realized where she was.'

'How did you know?'

'On an impulse one day I picked up a London telephone book, and there was a Sarah Levine. So I got straight into the car and drove round and waited nearby. An hour or so later there she was, walking up the street clutching a whole lot of bags. Looking . . . absolutely unmistakable. A few days later I followed her by foot as she left the house one morning, and that's how I discovered she was a school teacher. It was her first term there, I found out later, she had only just left her training college.' She nodded. 'Yes, I've seen a very great deal of her indeed, in one way or another. The miracle is that she has never seen me, or at least I don't think she has. I cover my face, because I'm easily recognized these days. Though I've never been sure whether she knew that Anna Lavey was her mother. Maybe she didn't.'

Miss Anstruther had come to press Anna to meet with Sarah, but now she didn't know what to say. She was rescued by Anna getting to her feet, and gently shepherding her to the door. 'I've appreciated this, Miss Anstruther. Considering everything, it's been brave of you to have made contact. Thank you.'

And now they did no more than nod and half smile at each other as Miss Anstruther went out into the street, and bustled away in the drizzle in the direction of the underground station.

18

The young Englishman standing on his doorstep had a pleasant, smiling face. David Levine was late this morning, and he was anxious to get to the laboratory, but the lad had a nice way about him, and it seemed rude to turn him away too abruptly. If he gave him half an hour or so, at least the Melbourne rush-hour traffic would have eased.

Levine looked again at the expensively embossed card: 'William Kessell, Private Secretary to Ned Macaulay, Chairman and Chief Executive, The Macaulay Group.' He made a mock show of wonder, pocketed the card, showed him into the house and sat down with him on a veranda facing out on to the gardens.

'Remind me, William – can I call you that? – What papers do Macaulay control these days?'

William listed them all, British and Australian, with what Levine thought a charming enthusiasm.

'Yes, the *Daily Meteor*, I thought so. And that I assume is why you've come to see me?'

William was taken aback. He had planned a much more prolix route through to the subject than this. He started on

325

that anyway, but Levine held up his hand, and cut him short.

'It's OK, William. Don't worry with all that. I've been following the Anna Lavey story on the *Meteor*'s website, and that's why Ned Macaulay has sent you to see me, I'm sure. That's fine, I'm happy to talk. As you realize, Anna is my sister. She seems to have airbrushed my existence out of her life, but that's who I am.'

William nodded and reached into his jacket pocket for his preparatory notes, but Levine simply talked on.

'I've read lots of her stuff over the years, as you can imagine. She's a terrible liar, you know, she always was, a compulsive liar actually.'

'Why, Mr Levine? Why do you say that?'

'Dr Levine, if we're going to be formal. But we're not, so David is the name. Why does she lie?' He fell silent, gazing out into the garden, and William wondered how he could encourage him to open up. He wished he had remembered to give Levine his proper title. How crass of him. This was the first important task that Ned Macaulay had allowed him to undertake since he had joined him from Cambridge and he was desperate to be able to email back to London a story that would do him credit.

'Why does she lie, David?' he said softly.

Levine turned to him, and sighed. 'You want the story? OK, I'll give you the story. Little snippets have emerged in Anna's pieces over the years, a sort of Beverley Nichols story of a poor but happy home, East End Jewish, everyone hugging each other, a little too religious maybe, but that adds such a touch of authenticity to the tale, doesn't it? The real story is something completely different. We came from a family so unpleasant that they scarred all three of us for life – me, Ruth and Anna.' He fell silent again, and once more stared out over the garden.

William, gaining his confidence now, deliberately left him undisturbed. At last, he almost whispered: 'Was there violence?'

Levine sighed. 'Violence?' Again, there was a long, long silence. 'I don't know. I suppose I should try to understand it. It was so many years ago. They married very young and they had children very young. They were very, very poor. They barely spoke English. It was very hard for them – and yet the scale of it, the . . . foulness of it.'

'Was there violence?' William whispered again.

'Yes, there was violence.'

'To you, and to your sisters, or to your mother, or all of you?'

'To all of us. It was . . . very difficult.'

'I think it was worse than that,' William said gently, 'much worse than that.'

Again, the long, long silence.

'It was bad,' Levine said at last. 'There was no love at all. Not between my parents, and not between us children either. We bought favours from our parents, my mother as much as my father. We informed on each other. We set each other up. We did everything we could to be in our father's favour and escape the beatings. We were terrified. It was pure evil. It was a violent, disgusting experience.'

He turned to William. 'I'm not sure I can add to that. My life, Anna's life, we've both moved on. Ruth did too, in the limited time she had to do so. It was all many years ago. Best buried and forgotten.'

327

But William still had his card to play. 'Anna looked after herself, bought her favours with sex, David, am I right? That's the final piece of the jigsaw in Anna's story, isn't it? Her way of buying your father's favours?'

Levine turned again to face him, his hands folded behind his head. Eventually, he nodded. 'Yes. That's why Ruth threw her out of the house to have her baby. That's why Anna's daughter ran away when Ruth told her, in revulsion no doubt – panic, horror, all those things. It's the final piece of the jigsaw, and Anna may or may not be able to face up to it. It's quite a lot for her to face up to. She used to have sex with our father, because that way she was protected. It was never rape. It was regular and it was compliant, and it was ... triumphant somehow. Anna's victory over Ruth and me. Perhaps that's unfair. It probably is. But it's how I remember it.'

He got to his feet then, and William too, but Levine hadn't quite finished. 'Anna came to Ruth pregnant,' he repeated. 'Ruth threw her out. Anna's daughter, Sarah, is our father's child.'

William had his story now. Ned had sent him because he wanted to understand everything, so that he could make a decision as to how much rope to allow Paul Hopper. William knew that now there was nothing more to come – from anyone. They had it all. He'd tell Ned that.

Ned Macaulay handed the *Evening Flag* across to Hugh as he stepped into his office, and smiled. 'Defeat into victory,' he said. 'Have you seen this? Given the circumstances, Anna Lavey has had a stunning revenge on Paul Hopper, though I suppose I shouldn't be saying that with such glee. Read it.'

Hugh looked at the headline, '*World Exclusive: Anna Lavey Tells Her Tragic Tale*', then turned to the story, which ran over the entire centre spread, and showed pictures of Anna as a much younger woman. The byline was that of Valerie Wake, a romantic novelist who had built her successful journalistic career around reliably soft and fawning interviews with celebrities, and was thus much in demand by them and their agents. Anna must have done her piece with her only that morning.

There are times when I despair of the basic humanity of my chosen profession. Times when people in public life, and those tied to them in love, are subjected to intrusion into their innermost heartbreak to an extent that to my mind is unforgivable. I know I'm not alone in finding the Daily Meteor's *current exposé of Anna Lavey and her wonderful daughter to be one sickening example too many of this sort of journalism. And I found it a privilege therefore to talk on record today with Miss Lavey, laid low in grief as she is, and to hear exclusively what really happened in her tragic life, and what she hopes the future may hold.*

Wearing a cardigan, no make-up and an old, comfy silk shirt, Anna Lavey looked both gentler and slighter than I remembered her. She is in her bone structure and her bearing a truly beautiful woman, and her speech, carefully modulated, modest, well considered, has that lovely calm resonance of a woman at the peak of her years. She is an icon of course to many hundreds of thousands, probably millions of people, and deservedly so. Her columns, her books, her broadcasts all speak of a woman not only of generosity, worldly wisdom and good old common sense, but huge kindness as well. She is a very good woman, and as I heard her tale unfold I wondered at that. We learn now that life has treated Anna Lavey tragically, more tragically than any of us could possibly have guessed, and yet her courage and resilience remain.

I asked her first if Sarah Levine was indeed her daughter, which she immediately, eagerly confirmed, and did so with her face alive with love and pride. She remembered the photographs she had taken of Sarah secretly as she played in Anna's sister's garden; her devoted sister Ruth, who fostered little Sarah and brought her up. She recalled the bootees she had stolen one day from Ruth's washing line when she knew the house was empty, and smuggled away with her to have and to hold and clasp to her. The secret, hidden glimpses of her over the years. And – heartbreakingly this – the lock of hair, which Ruth had sent her quietly and tenderly on the child's seventh birthday.

So why did she let her daughter go? Anna Lavey cried when I asked her this, and I would have backed away, but she insisted on telling me the truth. She was too young of course, barely sixteen when Sarah was born, but one felt that the real reason lay in Anna Lavey's great self-awareness. She was, as she told me, an adolescent as ill-equipped to be a real mother as one could imagine. Emotionally crippled by the privations of a childhood in a near destitute East End Jewish family, she ran away as soon as she knew that her little daughter was safe in her sister's care. And the teenage years that remained for her were a devastating patchwork as she described them to me of fighting for a living in the meanest streets of the capital; of one nervous breakdown, and then a second; of an eating disorder of the most severe nature, and the near starvation that followed; of struggling with the memories of an earlier childhood in which

Anna hinted violence and sexual abuse were a constant, daily threat. Here she is at her most brave. She has no idea who Sarah's father was and told me that. And you know that what she really means by that is that the father could be one of so many who used her in her innocence and childish desire to please within a familial situation of raw, total deprivation. She challenges you to condemn her for that. I can't. Which of us could?

It's a desperate tale, and yet it is saved by love. She forgives her sister for, unbeknownst to Anna, exposing her daughter to her convicted sex offender of a husband, from whose ministrations poor Sarah fled as a sixteen-year-old child. She forgives everybody. She forgives the cruelties of her childhood. She forgives everything bad that has ever happened to her. And above all else she loves her daughter, and hopes that one day Sarah can find it in her heart to love her too. She will. Everyone does. Anna Lavey attracts love like the blossom the bee.

'Wow!' said Hugh, and handed it back to Ned. He smiled. 'I love the cardigan, no make-up and comfy old silk shirt bit. And you're right. She's killed the story stone-dead. The *Evening Flag* people must be laughing their heads off. Surely the *Meteor* will drop it now?'

'They'd be lynched if they didn't. There'd be blood in the streets. And particularly if they started anything nasty about who the father was. The way that was handled was very smart. Do you think that Valerie Wake was in on the secret?'

'No, I very much doubt it. She was carefully, meticulously set up by Anna to say just the right thing in exactly the right way, and she did it. Wouldn't you think?'

Ned shrugged. 'Probably. It feels like that, doesn't it?' He was at his desk now, rummaging through some papers. He shook his head, and came back to his seat. 'I can't find it,' he said. 'If I come across it again I'll send it on to you. It's a nasty little twist in the tail. The husband – Jack Lynch? – killed himself the day before yesterday, poor little sod. Strung himself up on an apple tree in his garden. I was sent a cutting this morning from the local paper.'

Hugh grimaced. 'Who sent it to you?'

'That Miss Anstruther woman. Remember her? There was a little note attached to it. She ended it with a quote "*Judge not, lest ye be judged*". She asked me to send it on to Paul Hopper, but I'm not going to, as you can imagine. Not quite his line.'

'No, I doubt it is. An odd business this has been all round, hasn't it? So much poison stirred up by the very Miss Anstruther who is now sending us homilies. But maybe she never anticipated the amount of damage she was going to wreak.'

Ned nodded, then smiled. 'A hell of a book in this, Hugh, wouldn't you say? The real story, I mean, not that Valerie Wake garbage. Anna Lavey finally tells all?'

Hugh yawned, and stretched, and started to get to his feet. It would of course make an enormous bestseller, but his mind was full of Sarah. She needed to be protected from any more exposure. 'Maybe. Personally, I don't think Anna should write it. It's a step too far. And if she does write it – will I publish it? God knows. Sufficient unto the day. Come on, Ned, we'll be late. Let's go.'

Ned looked at him, quizzically, surprised at his reaction, then he too got to his feet to leave.

★

Three days later Ned looked across at Paul Hopper, and felt no compassion for the man. But he did feel amusement, and also a shred of affection, for the first time since Hopper had joined the *Meteor*.

'Straight away, Paul, if you would – clear your desk and go. And as I say, if you behave yourself and keep to our agreement, then we'll go on paying you monthly in full until the end of your contract, in six months' time.'

'And I keep the Roller for that time too?'

'That's what I told you – you can keep the car.'

'I like the Roller,' Hopper mused, 'that's my little weakness, really – and the wife's. We spend most of the weekend in it.'

'I'm sure you'll get another one.'

'Who from?'

'The *Prefect*. The *Comet*. The *Globe*. The *Universe*. *Church Telegraph*. Wherever you go next. You're a Roller man, Paul, anyone can see that. And I don't imagine you're going to be out of an editor's chair for very long, do you?'

Hopper took a long pull at his cigar, and grinned. 'Who knows? Musical chairs really, isn't it? But I tell you something, Ned, I've enjoyed it at the *Meteor*. A fine paper, lovely traditions. Pity about the readers, but there we are.'

Ned shook his head. 'Don't blame them. The readers' petition was whipped up by the people at the *Flag*, as both of us know – and the jamming of our switchboard with callers' complaints. With that Valerie Wake piece on Anna Lavey they had you out to dry. But that's not why I'm firing you, Paul. I'm firing you because you're uncontrollable. You've shown that over the last couple of weeks. I can't work with that.'

'Fair enough, skipper,' Hopper said, and glanced at Ned to make sure that he had irritated him. He settled himself deeper into his chair, showing no signs of moving, and pulling again on his cigar, he tapped the ash insolently into Ned's crystal bowl of floating hyacinth heads. 'Fair enough, you're the boss. But I tell you what, you've got one nightmare of a liability on your hands with that Anna Lavey, I can assure you of that. I'll never let her go now. She's become my hobby, somehow. If I was you I'd drop her, before the cat's really out of the bag.'

'What cat?'

Hopper tapped the side of his nose, and smiled at Ned. 'That'd be saying, wouldn't it? But every day that passes I come to learn a little more. That woman's like a walking compendium of dark secrets, and one by one I'm going to unravel them for the delectation of the British public, from the pages of whatever fine newspaper I next decide to edit. I've got a one-track mind, and I'll get that cow, if I die in the effort.'

'Why do you hate her so much?' Ned asked.

'Because she's a bully and she's a fraud. And she's a coward: she's totally unable to tell the truth about anything. Always has been, always will be.'

Ned grimaced in his distaste and got to his feet, forcing Hopper to do the same. Ned took his arm, and led him to the door. 'Goodbye, Paul,' he said. 'Good luck.'

'Goodbye, skipper,' Hopper replied, and for a second Ned thought that he was about to tap his cigar ash off down the front of Ned's suit. But he held it poised in front of him and smiled, his face too close to Ned's for good manners. 'Let me tell you one more thing,' he said. 'I come from Hackney too. My life wasn't that great either. I didn't know the Levine family, but I doubt they lived in much more poverty than the rest of us did. But I don't make a meal of it the way she does. She's disloyal. She deserves – believe me – everything that she's going to get.'

When Anna came home that evening she found Bobbie sitting at the kitchen table with a bottle of beer, reading the interview with Valerie Wake in the *Evening Flag*. He looked up and nodded at her, and then continued reading. She went to stand against the dresser, watching him, waiting for him to finish. There was a half-finished bottle of red wine beside her, but she decided not to touch it, knowing that on her second or third glass she was more likely than not to explode with anger if he said something critical or quarrelsome, and tonight of all nights she couldn't risk that. He had disappeared from home the day of the first article in the *Meteor*, and come back only that morning. She had no idea where he had been and in the circumstances she had no intention of asking him.

He finished the article, turned the page, and with no comment whatsoever started to read the sports results. 'What's for supper?' he said eventually, without looking up, apparently engrossed in the football scores.

She swallowed. 'Can I make you a risotto?' she asked, but knew that her impersonation of the devoted suburban housewife was lamentably weak. She had it in mind to go on with a bright little enquiry as to whether he would like his risotto made with prawns or crayfish, as both were in the freezer, but suddenly she could not be bothered with it. Fuck him. He was a sod, and they needed to have this out. If it was the end of their marriage then so be it. She took the wine bottle by the neck, took a large glass from the cupboard, filled it, downed it, poured another, and joined him at the table.

'Well?' she said.

'Well the fuck what?' replied Bobbie, still without looking at her, as he now turned with much show of interest to the solutions to the previous day's crossword puzzle, which, as Anna knew, he had never attempted in his life.

'Don't do this. We have to talk about this business, now that it's out in the open.'

He yawned extravagantly and continued to gaze at the paper.

'For Christ's sake, Bobbie, if you don't need to talk about this, I do.'

He looked up now, and regarded her with the minimum of interest. He shrugged. 'I don't need to talk about anything. If you do, talk.'

She sighed. 'I'm not up to a row, I'm really not.'

'I don't want a row.'

She poured herself another glass of wine, went to the bread bin, made herself a piece of toast and cheese and came back to the table. She deliberately sat further away from him, and kept her eyes down. 'Ask me anything you want, Bobbie, just ask.'

He looked across at her. 'OK,' he said, 'I will. Here goes. Where is your daughter? And why did you never tell me about her? And if you've ever come across a worse example of deceit between wife and husband I can tell you I haven't.'

She pushed her plate away, and turned her face to him. 'She lives in Chepstow Lane. And the reason . . .'

'I don't mean literally, for God's sake. I can see from the paper that she lives in Chepstow Lane. I mean where is she?

Why aren't you looking after her? Why have you had nothing to do with her?'

'I'm not sure I know really. Because of guilt, because of what I did to her. Because of everything that happened.'

'What did happen?'

'You can see what happened.' She pointed at the paper. 'It's all there in the *Evening Flag*.'

'No, it's not. That'll all be balls. I'm asking you. What happened?'

'For Christ's sake, Bobbie. Don't make me have to go through the whole thing again.' She put her head in her hands. She felt suddenly, overwhelmingly, exhausted. She felt a great wave of self-pity wash over her, and then the tears came, great sobbing bursts of them. Bobbie watched her, apparently impassively, refusing to do what she was longing for him to do – to stretch out his hand for her to hold. Then, unexpectedly, that was exactly what he did, and she took it, and held it in both of hers.

'Do you mind if I start at the beginning?' she asked a few minutes later, when she had calmed herself.

'Not now,' he replied. 'You and I are going to have to spend the next few years over that. Let's just say that you had a terrible childhood. Your parents treated you like dirt. And your sister?'

'Yes, they treated her worse in some ways,' she said, and was immediately struck by the fact that she had told the truth, and without hesitation. She had become so used to falsehood. Ruth's beatings were as violent as could be imagined. Ruth had never allowed the compliant behaviour that was the alternative.

'What about your brother?'

She looked at him in surprise, and shock. How did he know about him? But she was spared from lying when Bobbie went on.

'He called here this afternoon from Australia – David. Obviously I had no idea he existed, but I've had so many surprises in the last few days one more didn't seem to make much difference. He was very polite and friendly. He talked a lot. He seemed genuinely concerned about you. He gave me his number and his email address and I said you'd get back to him.'

She shrugged. 'Well, now you know. I have a brother. It was the same for him. He and Ruth were twins. They tried to protect each other, I expect, when they could, but what I remember is the reverse of that. All three of us had to look after ourselves, and only ourselves, in order to survive at all. It's a rare thing for twins to have their mutual trust severed in that way, but that's what happened with us. And they never saw each other again, I imagine, once David had gone off to Australia. He lied about his age and got his passage as a steward on a merchant ship. He just packed up and went early one morning without a word to anyone, including Ruth. I remember that very well. And that night she left as well. I can't think why she was still there actually. She was eighteen. Maybe she wanted to protect him – or me – or maybe my mother. She got a job on a farm just outside Broadwich, and almost immediately she met Jack Lynch and married him. He wasn't exactly a great catch, but that's what she did, and who can blame her for it? Maybe she and David patched things up between them eventually. I don't know.'

Bobbie released her hands, and went to the refrigerator for another bottle of beer. He came back to the table, and this time sat immediately opposite her. 'Yes, Broadwich. You went down to have your baby. To be with your sister. But she wouldn't have you there. Why not?'

Anna gazed at him. She wanted to be rid of it all now, tell him everything, get it all out, release the secrets and the lies and the evasions, and be free of it. But much as she wanted that, it was still too difficult for her to do. There was nearly twenty-five years of concealment to overcome, and it had become part of her being. She took a deep breath, but she was unable to do it. 'I'm not sure,' she said, miserably, and put her head in her hands.

There was a long silence.

'I tell you what, Anna. You need to be able to say this to me, maybe in time to Andrew too, but certainly to me. At the moment you can't do it, so I'm going to say it for you. The reason that your sister threw you out was because she knew who the father of the baby was. The baby's father was your father. That's a pretty shocking thing. Can you blame her for that?'

Anna said nothing at all, and remained with her face concealed in her hands. He waited for her, but then continued. 'I know this because your brother has just told me. He told me everything. He said that he and Ruth made contact eventually, and began to talk a lot. Ruth had described to him what happened that night when you arrived at her house. It was cruel of her, you were after all just a kid of sixteen. She made up for it later, or tried to, by bringing your daughter up. Then Sarah fled from her at the age of sixteen, your brother said, because Ruth told her at that point who she was, and what

339

she was. Your child, fathered by your own father. And who can blame Sarah for her reaction? Who can be surprised that she ran away from it all? What she had been told was more than anybody anywhere should be asked to accept about themselves. Jesus Christ!'

Anna made herself look at him, but she was unable to find anything to say in response. He nodded, and made some attempt at a smile. 'That's OK, Anna. That's it, we've done it now. Everything's out and gone. And there's a silver lining in it all, there really is. From the moment that Sarah took control of her own life, everything began to look very different. In truth, what happened since is pretty marvellous. I've seen her photographs, like everyone else has. She's lovely, she looks a truly wonderful girl. Yes?'

'Yes, she is. I've seen her and she is.'

'Good, I'm glad you've seen her. That's what I was going to ask you next. Have you spoken to her?'

'No. No, I haven't.'

'Don't you think you should?'

'I don't know.'

'I'd like you to. I want you to.'

Anna turned away, then made herself face him again. 'I can't, Bobbie. I've thought about it so much, and I know that I can't. I don't know what there is that I could possibly say to her. I've no right to ask anything from her, nor expect anything from her. There's nothing I can do for her either. I've seen her, and watched her, and that was a wonderful thing. The kindest thing I can do, and certainly what she will want, is for me to stay out of her life. So that's what I'm going to do. Actually, that is what I *have* to do.'

'Are you sure?'

'Yes, I'm sure.'

'No change of mind?'

'No change of mind.'

Bobbie nodded, and shrugged. 'It's your choice, I suppose.'

'No. There is no choice. What Sarah needs, and what Sarah is going to have, is privacy from me for evermore. The story's out now, and it's gone, and she's safe. She's strong, and she's healthy and she's . . . heavens, I don't know. She's a real person. And out of the filth from which she came that strikes me as a miracle. If I wasn't an atheist I would say . . . what would I say?'

'You'd say what you've just said. That she's a miraculous girl. And so she is.'

'Yes, that's right. She is. She's an absolute bloody miracle.'

19

Hugh had known for days that something was coming. Nicola, when she was home, had been painfully courteous to him, and when he had tried to put his arms around her she had stiffened, before perfunctorily returning the gesture and freeing herself. In normal times, whatever her mood, she would have been careful to respond warmly. But in the last two or three weeks she had been coming home late from her chambers, leaving before breakfast the following morning and working weekends.

That evening she had arranged for Danny to spend the night in Hampstead with her aunt, and when she came into the house at a quarter to eight she went straight into the sitting room to join Hugh, who was working there with a drink, correcting some page proofs. Without removing her coat she sat down, hands thrust deep into her pockets and, sheet-white in the face, asked him to listen to her.

When she spoke the words tumbled out, sounding to both of them as if they had been rehearsed. 'Hugh – this is not going to be easy for either of us, and I feel terrible to have to tell you, and I hate myself for it, but I'm afraid . . .'

She paused, gulped, and looked at him in panic.

He watched her, and nodded, prompting her to say whatever she had to say, and get rid of it. He knew what it was and, waiting for it, he felt eerily calm. 'Go on, Nic.'

She sighed, and put her head in her hands. 'Go on,' he said again.

'I'm afraid I'm leaving you. Danny too. I'm going to leave home. I want to be with Henry.'

She still couldn't get her head out of her hands and look at him, but he didn't blame her for that. The incongruous thought struck him that this was the first time that he and Nicola had acknowledged between them that Henry Jackson was her lover. And by the use of his first name she was reflecting the fact that they both, for a matter of seven or more years, had known exactly what was happening.

Hugh found that he had nothing to say. But now she sat back and turned her eyes to him, and there was a sadness and yet an exhilaration that meant, he knew, that she was serious and determined.

'Seven years, Nic, it seems too long.'

'Too long?'

'Too long for so much pain, if that's what it was – and guilt.'

'Maybe. To be honest with you, there's not much pain at the moment, and not much guilt either. There was, and there probably should be now, but there isn't. I'm so sorry, Hugh. I did need him very much, and I still do. More than ever, probably. I never meant things to turn out this way.'

Hugh nodded. He felt nauseous and empty, and the only emotion he was able to identify in himself was overwhelming

343

disappointment. He was not harking back in bitter-sweet memory to the days of their happiness and intimacy together in the first years of their marriage – that he knew would follow – he was quite simply sick with disappointment that all those years did not bring with them what he had always anticipated: Henry Jackson gone, the marriage intact and constant, Nicola and Danny together in a conventional, loving, mother-and-child relationship.

'Love,' he said, and shrugged. It was all that he could find to say, so numbed was he now.

'It's not just a question of love, Hugh, it really isn't that. I love you, and have done ever since we were kids together at Oxford. Please believe that. And I love Danny, catastrophic mother as I've been. It's Henry. I want to be with him, I have to be with him.' She gestured in frustration. 'All the trite phrases – I feel I can't live without him. And I don't want to live without him. He's getting old. I want to be with him.'

Hugh got up and stood. 'You'd better go then, Nic. I'm not going to try to stop you. I'll get something fixed up for Danny during the day tomorrow, and that will give you the chance of having a clear run at the house so that you can take anything you want.'

She got to her feet as well, and they stood facing each other, her hands thrust once more deep into the pockets of her overcoat. 'I am so sorry, Hugh. One day I'll be able to find another way of saying that to you. But that's what it is. I just am so sorry.'

Hugh nodded, and tried to smile. 'Maybe it's not such a surprise. But it does hurt. It hurts like hell. It's been so long.'

He went to the door with her. He wanted for himself the familiar sight of her back, as she walked down the path and out to the pavement. He had always loved the hold of her back, and the carriage of her as she walked, and the set of her neck, and the bend of her arms, and the careless, unselfconscious fall of her hair across her shoulders. He was waiting for her to turn then, so that he could see her face once more, but she swung away out of sight and was gone.

'I love you, Nic,' he said, quietly, only for himself to hear, and he could feel the swelling of his throat, and hear the crack and break in his voice. After all this time, it was over. Finally. Over.

There had been very few times over the years when Nicola had spent a whole night in Henry Jackson's bed, and she wished with all her heart that he had been there with her now. He was in Paris for two days, lecturing at the Sorbonne, researching a possible book on Marshal Pétain, and a guest at a dinner at the British Embassy for the French President. He wasn't aware that she was there in his flat of course, and knowing that he was away she'd chosen this as the moment to make her break and come to him. She hadn't made contact with Henry since he'd told her they must end their affair, but she had kept hold of the key to his flat.

He would be home in London in less than thirty-six hours, and she told herself she was happier than she had ever been. Perhaps it was true. She no longer truly remembered what she had felt with Hugh in their earliest days together and she found it very difficult to think of him at all, mostly through guilt, partly through a determination to concentrate her mind on her future life with Henry. That was too wonderful a prospect to fully grasp.

There was nothing she wanted from home other than the holdall of clothes she had already removed, and as soon as the shops opened she went to buy the few additions she needed, and a bag of toiletries from the chemist. It was not her clothes and toiletries she was concerned with – it was Henry. Henry was going to come home and he was going to find his flat as he had never seen it before – full of warmth and comfort, and domesticity. She searched in the cupboards for vases and containers, and she thrust into them the great armfuls of flowers she had bought at the barrows in the street market off Warwick Road. She went out again, this time to Partridge's, off Chelsea's Kings Road, and bought a side of smoked wild salmon and some caviar and, imported from heaven knows where, wild strawberries, green mangoes, a magnum of Bollinger, a clutch of packets of his favourite charcoal biscuits. Then, parking her car on a yellow line in St Martin's Lane, she half ran, half walked her way up to the antiquarian booksellers in Cecil Court to see what she could find for him as her most special, her most intimate present to him ever, and came away half an hour later with Hogarth Press first editions of Virginia Woolf's complete works, each book containing within it one of Woolf's personal, signed letters.

Nicola knew that she was losing her balance and control, but she could not contain herself. She was so happy, so released, that she did not want to contain herself. This was the great, decisive moment of her life. She had made the decision. She was going to be with Henry Jackson for evermore.

But it was not to be. She heard the news on the car radio

as she pulled up in front of the apartment building. Henry had collapsed that morning on a Paris street with a massive heart attack, and had died where he lay. Messages from the great and the good the world over were pouring in. He was barely ten days short of his seventy-first birthday, and apparently still at the peak of his powers, and he was gone.

Nicola left the car with its door hanging open and the radio blaring, and ran down to the river. A policeman found her there an hour or so later, sitting on a bench, bent forward, sobbing, racked with pain. For precaution's sake he walked with her to the nearby police station, and settled her down in a waiting room, haggard with despair, clutching a mug of tea. A young policewoman sat silently in the corner, told to watch over her for as long as was needed, until she had quietened.

Ned rang the bell at least half a dozen times before Hugh came to the door. He was barefoot and unshaven, and his black schoolboy's hair fell carelessly down over his brow. Looking at him, Ned felt a wave of love and, reaching out, wrapped his arms around him in a great bear hug. Hugh put his arms around Ned too, and they stood there on the doorstep for several moments before Hugh disengaged himself and took Ned into the house. He led him into the sitting room, where books and manuscripts and pictures had been pulled down from the shelves and walls and left in stacks on the floor. Ned's immediate fear was that Hugh had spun completely out of control, but when he spoke he appeared quite calm and collected.

'Clearing up,' Hugh said. 'I can't stay here. For both our sakes, Danny's as much as mine, we need to move on. What we need is a completely fresh start. I've told the agents to find us a house a sufficient distance from here that we don't find ourselves gazing at every tree, every paving stone, every corner store and associating them with Nic. We need a new part of London. Near you perhaps, near Katie. Near anything and anybody that isn't part of our old lives with Nic.'

'The nearer you are to us the better as far as I'm concerned, but I am part of your life with Nic,' Ned protested. But he wished he hadn't said it, knowing it rang false.

'No, you're not,' Hugh said, sitting on the carpet and sorting his books into piles. 'You're part of *my* life, period. You distrusted Nic from our Oxford days, and by the end you actively disliked her. If there's been any block in our friendship, any difficulty between us, it's been that. You thought she had ruined my life, but you're wrong. I don't give a damn how unconventional the relationship looked from the outside. Maybe it didn't work for her, and I'm not even sure about that, but it worked for me, believe me.'

They were silent then, Hugh moving books around, Ned watching him.

'Will you and Nic have another go together in time?' Ned asked eventually.

'God, no. We'd do more harm than good.' They were silent again for a little while – Hugh sorting books, Ned unsure what to say. 'At this very moment all I want is to put those years behind me, and get on with my life. And Danny needs to get on with his own life too. We can't do that in this house. She's all over it. It's her overcoat that I find myself looking at, you know the stuff she always wore, comfortable, shaped to her somehow. I never met anyone so beautiful and yet so devoid of personal vanity. There's an empty wine glass of hers still sitting up in her study and even now I can't make myself clear it away, because she had drunk from it, she'd held it in her fingers, and her mouth had touched its rim.' He fell silent again for a minute or two, picking up books, putting them down again, clearly thinking of other things.

'I loved her a lot, Ned, but now it's over. And I've got to get out of here. Danny has gone already – he's in the country with Foster, and I'm going to collect him when I've got our housing sorted out. We need normality, both of us – work, school, life – as quickly, as immediately, as we can possibly achieve it. So there we are.'

He looked up now, pushing his hair back from his eyes, and making some attempt at a smile. 'Don't worry about me, Ned. Thanks for coming, I knew you would. Sorry I didn't reply to your notes, or to your emails and telephone messages and the rest of it. I'm all right now – or rather, I will be all right.'

Ned got to his feet, and smiled at him. 'I tell you what, Hugh, don't shave, don't change, don't pack, don't do anything, just come home with me now. Daisy's there. The kids are there. Katie too. Come home, stay the night, and we'll talk and we'll eat and . . . we'll wrap our arms around you, Hugh. We're good at that, all of us. Daisy, me, Katie – it's what we do.'

20

Sarah spent her first day away from school in a daze of unhappiness. Unable to sleep at all that night, and by four o'clock in the morning in a mood of such bleak despair she found herself thinking of suicide. She thought she would be better out of bed and in the kitchen, so she went there in her dressing gown and made a mug of tea. She tried to cry, and did so, then sighed and went to lie down on the sofa in her tiny sitting room where, fitfully, she dozed until after eight.

She had absolutely no idea what to do next. Instinctively she knew she should plan no more than an hour or so ahead, until the shock had worn off sufficiently for her to think more clearly. So she showered and dressed, pausing once, leaning over the basin, to cry once more, then set off for a walk. She'd call at a bookshop or two as she went.

All Sarah's knowledge and experience of literature was self-taught, starting from her hours browsing around the bookshops of Charing Cross Road as a lost seventeen-year-old in Soho. Once started, she read incessantly. Unable to afford to buy, she read standing up in bookshops, or sitting on their floors, she read in public libraries, and on park benches with her penny copies off dealers' barrows. She read everywhere she could, using for the framework of her self-education the dog-eared copies of the various Norton Anthologies of English and American Literature that she had found one evening thrown in a cardboard box outside Dillon's great bookshop in Bloomsbury's Gower Street.

Three or four hours later, by now right up in Hampstead, she bought a marked-down paperback copy of the collected poems of W. B. Yeats off an Oxfam rack, then sat at a coffee-shop table with a caffe latte and a croissant and browsed through it. It calmed her, as she knew it would. Yeats was a special, reliable favourite. She knew every poem there, and some by heart.

> *Had I the heavens' embroidered cloths,*
> *Enwrought with golden and silver light,*
> *The blue and the dim and the dark cloths*
> *Of night and light and the half-light,*
> *I would spread the cloths under your feet:*
> *But I, being poor, have only my dreams;*
> *I have spread my dreams under your feet;*
> *Tread softly because you tread on my dreams.*

She recited the lines inwardly, and the tears, quite unexpectedly, started to flow again. She tried to conceal them, sitting with her elbows on the table, the heels of her hands pressed tightly into her eyes. She realized why she was crying. It was beauty, no more and no less than that, just the beauty of Yeats's sublime, enriched imagery. It was white and clean and pure.

★

When finally she had arrived back at her flat late that night a hand-delivered letter was awaiting her on the floor of the hall. She tore it open.

Dear Sarah

I hope this note catches you safely. We've made several attempts to reach you by telephone today, but there was no reply.

Would it be possible for you to come to the school tomorrow morning? We would be so grateful if you would – I'll explain why when I see you. Perhaps we could say at nine o'clock promptly, so that I can catch you immediately after Assembly and before the first class?

With best wishes

Kate Summers

Sarah wondered whether to go. It would surely be better to leave it now that the break had been made. But she wanted to behave well. She fully understood that the school had been put into a hopeless position over the *Daily Meteor*'s handling of the story, and particularly those awful pictures. And then that truly dreadful slush in the *Evening Flag*, which she had seen people reading in the Tube. Perhaps Mrs Summers needed her to sign some statement or other, a letter of apology to the parents. Whatever. She'd do as she was asked. She'd loved the school and now that she was leaving it she wanted to do so in as dignified a way as possible, given the nightmare circumstances of it all.

So she went, having woken at seven after an altogether more healthy night's sleep. She arrived exactly as she had been asked to do – promptly at nine o'clock – and empty with nerves.

But the moment she had turned in through the school gates there was a smiling Mrs Summers walking towards her, hand outstretched, and two or three other teachers too. They walked her in, Mrs Summers saying something which Sarah could hardly catch about a specially convened governors' meeting, following an emergency parents' petition led by Hugh Emerson, and there had been a rethink, and a profound hope that Sarah would come back and be happy with them again, and how welcome she would be, and how loved she was. And then she was there, standing at the door of her classroom, and twenty-three beaming small children were on their feet and cheering her.

Sarah shrugged, and smiled, and turned back to Mrs Summers, but she and the other teachers were gone, and she was alone. 'Thank you, everyone,' she said, as steadily and brightly as she could manage, and turning her back to them busied herself at rubbing down the blackboard until the class had settled.

Postscript

One Year Later
– 2005

Nicola gazed out of the window as the plane touched down at Logan Airport, the runway fringed with light snow. It was grey, misty, bitterly cold. She liked that. She liked Boston. Her new life was about to begin, a different life, in a different world, and she knew she had made the right decision. The moment she was interviewed, she knew she was making the right choice. It had felt right for them too – and the contract had been offered to her the very next day. She was to have a double lectureship in both International Law and International Politics. The salary, by British academic standards, was vast. The caveat was that there was to be an initial trial period of twenty-four months. But to her that was meaningless: she was going to stay here for the rest of her life.

Harvard had arranged for a taxi to meet her. Secured on the dashboard in front of the driver was a framed photograph of a boy of five or six, gap-toothed, grinning, in Red Sox uniform, clutching a baseball bat.

Danny's age, Nicola thought, torturing herself deliberately, waiting now for that nauseous sensation of voidness to hit her. It came, and she flinched. She shook her head. She had to move on. She was strong enough to move on. She was a strong woman and there was a strong, purposeful life ahead of her.

'My dear.'

Hugh felt a hand on his shoulder and turned to see who it was, spilling wine from his glass as someone else jogged his elbow. The Penguin Books party, riotously noisy, was in full swing, and Hugh was beginning to find it fun. He liked his role as the owner of a house that published not only well regarded, hardly marketable but widely reviewed literary fiction, these days predominantly in translation, but also – wholly incongruously – the increasingly bestselling Anna Lavey. These days he was a figure of substance. He enjoyed that. It was in ironic contrast to Emerson's earliest years, when he'd had to endure endless badinage about how much longer he could stay in business.

He brushed at the wet patch on his jacket, then looked up to find Claus Huber holding his arm.

'Hugh, my dear,' Huber repeated. 'I'm very, very cross with you. What a partnership we could have made! What a team we could have been! But never mind. All water under the bridge. But I've gossip for you, my dear. You must watch Anna Lavey. All this publicity, all these column inches, one can't pick up a paper these days without her story there. But she's lunching, she's plotting, she's going to do the dirty on you, Hugh. I saw her this very day, at Le Caprice, with those awful HarperCollins people. They were pouring wine down her, my dear, in the most vulgar way. She'll leave you for them, Hugh, you can be sure of it. They'll pay her the earth.'

'Leave me?' Hugh laughed, and raised his hand to Sarah,

who had arrived at the party late and was crossing the room to join him. 'I don't think so, you know, Claus,' he said. 'I don't think so. Anna and I – well – we know too much about each other for that these days, quite frankly. We're too intertwined. We're peas in a pod, Claus, we two. Peas in a pod.'